ROYAL marriage MARKET

AN UNLIKELY LOVE STORY

ROYAL marriage MARKET

AN UNLIKELY LOVE STORY

Heather Lyons

Also by Heather Lyons

THE COLLECTORS' SOCIETY SERIES

THE COLLECTORS' SOCIETY (#1)
THE HIDDEN LIBRARY (#2)
THE FORGOTTEN MOUNTAIN (#3)
THE COLLECTORS' SOCIETY ENCYCLOPEDIA
THE FOURTH AND FINAL BOOK IS COMING SOON!

The Fate Series

A Matter of Fate (#1)
Beyond Fate—a novella (#1.5)
A Matter of Heart (#2)
A Matter of Truth (#3)
A Matter of Forever (#4)

The Deep End of the Sea

Royal Marriage Market
Copyright © 2015 by Heather Lyons
http://www.heatherlyons.net

Cerulean Books
ISBN-13: 978-0-9966934-1-7
First Edition

Cover design by DCP Designs

Without limiting the rights under copyright reserved above, no part of this publication may be reproduced, stored in or introduced into a retrieval system, or transmitted, in any form, or by any means (electronic, mechanical, photocopying, recording, or otherwise) without the prior written permission of the above author of this book.

This is a work of fiction. Names, characters, places, brands, media, and incidents are either the product of the author's imagination or are used fictitiously. The author acknowledges the trademarked status and trademark owners of various products referenced in this work of fiction, which have been used without permission. The publication/use of these trademarks is not authorized, associated with, or sponsored by the trademark owners.

Dad, I had so much fun talking with you about Scandinavian geography and history. This one is for you.

CHAPTER 1

ELSA

Whenever I am faced with my full name in print, strung out in letters and words like clothes whipping on a line, my visceral reaction is the same had somebody raked rusty nails down a dusty chalkboard. Years of careful practice were cultivated in order to prevent me from physically recoiling at the sight or sound of *Elsa Victoria Evelyn Sofia Marie*.

Most girls are given a first and a middle name—two middle names, perhaps, if the parents are feisty or bound by family tradition. Or even a hyphenated first name, such as Lily-Anne or Ella-Mae. My name, the one my parents bestowed upon me, the one that informs the world who and what I am, is three bloody names too long and hangs around me like a noose rather than the garland surely envisioned. "You are a princess," my mother rationalized when I queried as to why she and my father went vindictively bonkers come naming time.

Fair enough, but my sister (also a princess) has only three names: Isabelle Madeleine Rose. Still lengthy, but far more tolerable. Even my father, the illustrious Prince Gustav IV of Vattenguldia, does not lay claim to so many names; his tops out at four. Indeed, no one in my acquaintance—royal or no—possesses such a lengthy appellation.

Just me.

"You are the Hereditary Princess of Vattenguldia," my mother clarified when pressed further. "Someday, you'll be sovereign over our great land."

Sovereigns apparently have hideously long names, even in tiny principalities like ours that rest in relative, yet fairly wealthy, obscurity in the Northern Baltic Sea. I often wonder if I will be as cruel when I have my own children, if I will saddle them with a name so convoluted and extensive that air must be drawn in between syllables. I like to think not, but the truth is, I'm partial to tradition, especially when it pertains to the throne in Vattenguldia.

Correction: most traditions. Because I am most certainly not in favor of the one my father's private secretary is delivering to me.

By letter from the Secretary of the Monarchs' Council to allow a formal invitation to be extended to Her Royal Highness The Hereditary Princess of Vattenguldia Elsa Victoria Evelyn Sofia Marie.

Sighing, I extract the surprisingly heavy missive from Bittner's age-spotted hands, like a bomb expert under the gun to sever the correct wire or risk the entire building disintegrating around them. Which, considering what waits within, might be a preferable situation. "Gee, thanks."

His smile would be best described as a shit-eating smirk, only that would make me sound uncouth and not very princess-like, or so my parents claim. They've taken it upon themselves to attempt to rein in my so-called foul and inappropriate language as "sovereigns, let alone Hereditary Princesses, do not speak like common sailors." It ought to be mentioned they do not personally know any sailors; the ones I have met working in our shipping industry are quite articulate.

An audible thunk sounds when the envelope hits my writing desk. "Has my father seen this yet?"

"I delivered His Serene Highness's shortly before I came up here."

That's to be expected. "Upon viewing it, did he uncork a bottle of his finest champagne?"

Bittner's exceedingly perfect manners prohibit him from acknowledging this was most likely the case, so he instead says in the crisp, cool, yet distinctive voice of his that would render him perfect to narrate movie trailers, "Prince Gustav was most amenable to receiving his invitation."

I can only imagine. A whole week set aside for hobnobbing with his peers? He's probably frothing at the mouth over the prospect of getting the hell out of the country and away from my mother.

I eye the envelope on my desk, envisioning a baby asp inside, ready to strike the moment I release its apocalyptical contents. "I suppose he will insist upon us attending." Which is inane of me to say, because there is no doubt my father's orders for packing and travel have already been issued. Whether or not we attend has never been up for question, because royals never decline attendance to this particular event.

I wait until Bittner departs before I pick the invitation back up. I have an appointment at a favorite local children's hospital within the hour, so it is now or never. As my silver letter opener hisses quietly through the paper, I remind myself that none of this would be a problem right now if I were already married. Still single at twenty-eight years old, I am considered one of the most eligible women in the world. Being the next in line to a throne, even an insignificant one, will do that to a lady. It's not so much that I despise the thought of marriage, because I do not. Done right, it is an alluring temptation that could provide comfort and companionship in a life such as mine, only none of my experiences so far have led to anything close to persuading me to join my monstrosity of a name and family baggage to another's. Finding the right person to share my life is no easy task; my last few efforts at romantic entanglements all blew up in my face.

Most recently, I made the mistake of fancying decided to sex up a former schoolmate—in public, no less. The press had a field day when Nils and Trinnie were photographed groping one another upon the slopes while I was skiing elsewhere. Much to my chagrin, *Popular Swedish Count Cheats On Vatteng uldian Princess—Will They Weather This Storm?* ran in local newspapers, glossies, and on television for weeks. Pre-Nils, there was Theo and his fervent yet wholly unexpected decision that the church was a better fit for him than a palace. Pre-Theo, there was my teenage crush Casper, who wasn't even an option. None of the other gents in my history are worth a mention.

Why do you have to be so picky? my mother often laments. And that amuses and disheartens all at once, because one would assume Her Serene Highness would wish the Hereditary Princess to marry a man of upstanding character. Personally, I would never term a lady who found her arsehole of a boyfriend *en flagrante* with her so-called friend and summarily dumped their cheating arses from her inner circle picky, though. That was pure practicality.

Although I am sincerely grateful—perhaps relieved is a better word—over extracting myself from such relationships before serious damage could occur, part of me rues not getting engaged (even temporarily) to some nice local before the madhouse of horrors known as the Decennial Summit were to commence. I naively assumed I had time. Time to fall in love. Time to find somebody on my own. Time to grow into my role in the principality.

Yet, time is nearly at an end, because the Royal Marriage Market (or as the unfortunately unattached like myself often refer to it, the RMM) is close at hand.

Irritability skitters down my spine when I finally rip the papers out of the envelope.

Lord Shrewsbury,
on behalf of
the Monarch Council,
requests the pleasure of your company at
the Decennial Summit
at Hearst Castle, beginning 23rd of April

I lean back in my chair, staring at the words in front of me until they fully sink in. Three days? THREE BLOODY DAYS before His Serene Highness and fellow royal cronies go hard-core, full-press in their quest to ensure my ilk and I are popping out sanctioned heirs in the very foreseeable future?

An inner Doomsday clock roars to life, each second a searing reminder of the utter tragedy that lies ahead. A mild panic attack settles into my lungs and chest, and I am gasping like a dying fish as I claw hungrily for air.

Calm down, Elsa. You are a Hereditary Princess. You will act like a Hereditary Princess. You do not let anything touch you. Not even this.

I focus on the details of the missive, ones to bottleneck my fears escaping in wide berths down to a manageable load. I breathe in and out. Fine-tune my focus until it is honed laser sharp upon the silver words clutched within my hands. Deep breath in. *Twenty-third of April.* Deep breath out. *Hearst Castle.* Deep breath—

Hearst Castle?

I mentally flip through the names of palaces and castles inhabited by fellow royals throughout Europe. Maybe it's . . . no. Maybe . . . not that one, either. I move on to various seats of nobility, combing through name after name, but none match. In a fit of annoyance, I relent and open my laptop.

The results come in fast. Hearst Castle *is not a real castle.* At least, not a European one and certainly never inhabited by royalty. Technically, it is a mansion in California, surrounded by several guesthouses.

Sonofabitch.

I click on one of the links and read up on the location. It was previously owned by someone in the newspaper business, a rich and influential man, which I suppose makes him the equivalent of American royalty. Currently, the building is a United States Historical Landmark and open to the public on a daily basis.

I nearly shred the invitation as I grapple to take all this in. The Monarch Council wishes to send the entirety of the world's reigning sovereigns and many of their heirs to a popular tourist destination in California?

Has the MC gone insane?

I storm out of my suite in a righteous fit of indignation, gripping the linen in my fist. Propriety dictates I call ahead, or knock at the very least, but as there are precious few days between the Decennial Summit and my freedom, I bypass manners and decorum and wrench the door to my father's office open. Bittner is in there with His Serene Highness, but that matters little. He has worked for the House of Vasa long enough to know just about everything there is to our quirks, including my occasional warm-to-the-touch temperament that flares to life during the most inconvenient times. Like right now, when I am so upset I can barely unfurl my fingers from the invitation to shake it properly in my father's face.

"My word, Elsa. You appear quite vexed." My father is smooth as butter as he smiles faintly up at me. "Bittner, I wonder what in the world could inspire Her Highness to lose sight of her manners."

Before Bittner can respond (not that I think he would), I slap the paper down onto the antique desk that dominates the room. "Is this a joke?"

Although I guarantee he already knows what I have brought to him, His Serene Highness slides on his reading spectacles and peers downward. "I hoped you'd finally gotten over your . . ." His lips purse as he most likely attempts to assign the most diplomatic phrasing he can to what he considers my ravings. "*Hesitancy* over the Summit. You knew that it was coming at some point this year."

Not only The Prince of Vattenguldia, but the Prince of Tact—because I'll admit to offering (behind closed doors, of course) my sincere feelings concerning the Decennial Summit on more than one occasion. I must clarify that it is not the Summit that has me in fits, it is the infamous RMM. Because, for nearly five hundred years now, alliances forged through arranged marriages concocted at a Summit hosted every decade have often overshadowed legitimate diplomatic work achieved. In essence, single heirs older than twenty-five rarely depart the Summit unattached. Both male and female are lambs to the slaughter.

It is a tradition I desire no part of, one I cannot find it in my heart to embrace.

But that terrifying, archaic possibility is neither here nor there at the moment. The Prince knows my view on this, and, as he sharply pointed out the last time I attempted a debate, I've had my say. Currently, I have other battles to fight. Calming oxygen floods my lungs while I slip on a cool smile. "Not that." I tap on the paper. *"This."*

Dark blue eyes, so much like my own, squint behind his reading spectacles. "I'm afraid I'm not—"

"Do you know where Hearst Castle is?"

His bushy eyebrows rise ever so slightly, aging caterpillars whose micro-movements illustrate volumes of emotion.

Shite. I barked at him; father or no, he is still my sovereign and deserves my respect. Another deep breath is required for me to continue. "My apologies." I assume a more respective, ladylike stance, one hand folded over the other in front of me. "I simply wish to know if you are aware of pertinent details of the location?"

As he leans back, the creaking of a chair sounds in the surprisingly modest yet elegant personal office.

"It's a bloody tourist destination in the United States!"

At this, a small, choking cough escapes Bittner. I quickly apologize again. If I don't get myself under control, Hereditary Princess or no, I'll find myself on the other side of the door in no time.

My father's fingers form a steeple in front of his face, long fingers once elegant and now marked by time and arthritis. "I am well aware of what Hearst Castle is and where it is located, Elsa."

Ah. Of course he is. After all, he serves upon the Monarch Council, although in a much reduced capacity nowadays, what with two heart attacks in three years. Still, I never would have thought my father this naïve about sending so many monarchs and their heirs to such a public location. "What about terrorists?"

When I was younger and lost control of my emotions, my father reminded me that such passion does no monarch any favors. *The key to being an effective sovereign is to remain calm and clear-headed. Never make crucial decisions or arguments when your emotions get the better of you. Productivity and goodness cannot stem organically through heightened feelings, even if crafted under the best of intentions.*

It is a lesson I fail to prove mastered, for another lift of eyebrow is meant to remind me continued outbursts will not be tolerated. "Terrorists?"

"I am concerned about safety logistics that might arise during the Summit. While most of our kingdoms and principalities are constitutional monarchies, it would still be devastating if something were to happen to any of the royals present. What if someone were to catch wind of the Summit? Target us?"

A tiny smile bends one half of his thin lips. "Someone like a terrorist?"

"I cannot possibly be the only one to believe it is a monumentally terrible idea to convene every monarch in the world, alongside their heirs, in a single location, let alone such a public one."

"And yet, we have convened every decade for centuries without incident, Elsa. Nary a terrorist attack, let alone a single act of crime, has ever touched us during a Decennial Summit."

He's right. For all our romantic failings in the press, royals are exceedingly excellent at keeping their shite locked down tight. Even still, I cannot let this go. "Respectfully, my point stands in consideration of twenty-first century politics. There are many countries whose citizens wish to abolish monarchies, viewing them as archaic and unnecessary in light of democracy and socialism. The Summit is an excellent opportunity for the disgruntled to—"

"Are you sure your true concern hinges on our safety?" His tongue clicks quietly in reproach. "Or, is it more likely you are fretting over the RMM?"

Well, yes, but . . . "I am simply saying—"

"Must I remind you that your mother and I were betrothed at the RMM?"

It is a far cry from a selling point. My parents, brought together by politics, are no love match. Other than myself, Isabelle, and Vattenguldia, they have little to nothing in common and do not speak unless in public or necessity dictates more than a written note or a message sent via their private secretaries. As much as it disgusts me to contemplate, I am fairly confident words were not even spoken during the conception of their children. A note was most likely written and delivered: *Let's make an heir. Eight o'clock tonight, my room. Best to be drunk beforehand.*

So, yes. Maybe my mother has a valid point. Perhaps I am picky, because I desire that, if and when I attach my life to another's, it will be to someone I can at least talk to. And like as well as respect. Is it so wrong that I would not mind a storybook tale? Not the horrible bits—no poisoned apples or sleeping spells. I do not even require a prince, let alone a charming one. My life is one of service. Responsibility. Importance. When the day comes and I assume the throne, I simply wish somebody I love to be in my corner. And if I cannot find that, I would rather not marry.

I tell my father, "I am well aware of that, sir."

He slips off his reading spectacles and sets them on the desk. "Let me assure you every precaution will be taken to secure the location. At this very moment, Hearst Castle is closed to the public for renovations and restorations, and is not scheduled to reopen to the public for another two months. While the location is news to you today, the MC has worked closely with the American government for nearly two years to ensure the Summit goes off without a hitch."

His words, so crisp and no-nonsense, leave no door open for dissention.

"I am sure you are curious as to why Hearst Castle was chosen," he continues. "Of that, I will indulge you. After much discussion, the MC decided it best to meet on neutral ground. The United States is a good choice. While we could have easily taken over a hotel, many feel an event such as the Decennial Summit deserves something special. Hearst Castle and its history fit the bill."

I am beating my head against a wall. "It is no longer in use as a residence!"

"Another fact I am also aware of, Elsa."

It is a soft jab; he is informing me that none of my arguments carry any weight in his mind.

I want to argue: It's a tourist trap.

He would counter: I've already addressed that issue.

I want to argue: From what I saw on the website, it is not a very big venue for such a large party.

He would argue: That's part of its allure.

I want to argue: Where will everyone sleep? We have employees to think of, too. Will we all be in tents?

He would argue: You worry too much. It will be taken care of.

I want to argue: Please do not force me to be part of the RMM.

He would argue: The House of Vasa lives and dies by tradition.

But none of this is said. There is no need, not when the outcome is so easily predicted. Instead, I remain silent in my defeat as he reclaims his pen. "You'd best hurry if you are to make your appointment this afternoon. I know the children would be sorely disappointed if you missed story time."

Translation: You are dismissed.

I am at the door when he adds, "Please let your sister know she will be expected to accompany us. There is vital business I must attend to at the Summit, and I will need my girls with me."

At first I am stunned, but that is foolish of me. Of course Isabelle is to come. She is an attractive bargaining chip, after all.

Three days. There are three days until we journey to California. Three days until the Royal Marriage Market opens its doors after being shuttered for ten years.

Three days until life as I know it will change, whether I wish it so or not.

CHAPTER 2

♛
CHRISTIAN

My mother, non-affectionately known to my brother and myself as the She-Wolf, pats my shoulder like I'm once again four years old as she shrewdly eyes what I've just thrown onto my desk. "You ought to be happy about this, Christian. Yet, you look as if you're off to the gallows. Are you terribly sure you aren't a homosexual? Or perhaps asexual? Most men of my acquaintance would be pleased at the prospect of so many potential conquests in such a small location."

She's got a tulip glass in her hand as she invades my personal space, lipstick ringing the rim. It's, what, three bloody o'clock in the afternoon? I make a mental note to inform Parker he needs to do a better job arranging my schedule around my mother's, so meetings like this are never a possibility.

I remold my features and posture until I'm positive I do not appear as I feel. Because, hell yeah, do the gallows feel close at hand. For one, the She-Wolf entered my inner sanctuary with no prior warning. She's a stealthy beast, stalking her prey and pouncing when least expected. Two, she's waving a matching invitation to mine, so she's here to gloat or threaten. And three . . . I refuse to glance at either piece of paper and give her the satisfaction of confirming how I'm truly feeling, even if she already guesses.

She drops into a nearby chair, dress swishing softly against the hideous nylon stockings she insists on wearing every single day of her life. Then she motions to the chair directly across from her. "Think about all the pretty girls that will be present. Why, I can only imagine how eager they'd be to open their legs for you."

Fire ants invade my skin as I struggle to repress the muscles within my body from shuddering. Hearing such a proclamation come from my so-called venerable mother's mouth is revoltingly disturbing. Not that it's rare, as she delights in torturing my brother Lukas and myself with crude humor meant only for our ears. To the rest of the country and the world at large, she's gracious and composed, the epitome of a respectable modern Grand Duchess whose speeches are quoted by millions of admirers. It's why she's the She-Wolf: she's cunning, devious, able to hide in plain sight, and devours those who are weaker than her.

If she weren't Her Royal Highness The Grand Duchess Britta of Aiboland, my mother would have excelled as a movie star or stage actress.

Most of my life, I've managed to escape her daily influence. Shipped off to boarding school when I was just a lad and then away to America for university, followed by several tours of duty within our military, I've lived more years in England, the US, and the Middle East than Aiboland, a Grand Duchy comprising of a series of tiny islands between Estonia, Sweden, and Finland. But a Hereditary Grand Duke can only run away from his duties for so long. I recently returned home and now reside under the same roof as my brother and parents for the first time since I was eight.

"I am most grateful for the opportunity to represent our country during the summit's weeklong meetings," is what I tell the She-Wolf. I'll be damned if I allow her to pull me into yet another futile round where I basically plead for my life as she cackles over how I'll do what she says or else.

At thirty, I'm considered to be one of the most desirable catches in the world, even though, despite our vast wealth, Aiboland more often than not remains hidden amongst much larger powerhouses within the European Union. I received high marks in all my courses for both my undergraduate and graduate degrees at prestigious universities in the United States. I am a patron of multiple charities in Aiboland, America, and various countries in Africa. I served two tours of duty in war-torn countries in the Middle East, eschewing my title and privilege for service. While other princes publically sow their wild oats, I managed to keep my head down, maintaining an impeccable reputation. *Prince Boring*, the American rags that even knew who I was dubbed me—and I'm fine with the title. Better boring than some of the other colorful descriptions peers my age are on the receiving end of. I know how to keep my business mine, unlike those sad sacks. Unlike my own brother who, just a few months ago, discovered pictures in the national newspaper of him buck naked and passed out with tequila bottles clutched in his fists. Barely a year younger than myself, Lukas spends most of his time drunk or screwing royal groupies. He gets to live it up while I pretend to be a perfect fucking robot of a prince for a country that most people in the world don't even know exists.

And now, my iron-willed mother demands her perfect heir to be perfectly amenable toward her plans for me to marry some royal girl and knock her up as quickly as possible. I get that I ought to be thinking about settling down, and it isn't like I'm out there shagging every available woman I can find. The thing is, I'm *thirty years old*.

My choices ought to be mine.

A conversation was attempted with the Grand Duchess about just this a month prior. Fresh off an inspirational speech about the importance of quality health care, my mother's voice turned bitingly acidic when she informed me what she thought of such logic. *Wasn't that what all that time in America was for? Right now, your focus is to find yourself a breeder. Once your heir is born, go ahead and privately play the field all you want. Do your duty first, though.*

Classy, typical fare from the She-Wolf.

Despite what she says and thinks, I'll be damned if I walk into the Summit like a sacrificial goat—or worse yet, a man ready to be auctioned off to the highest, most convenient bidder. There has to be a way out of this.

"Mark my words, Christian." Her nails click against the crystal in her hand. "You will represent us at the Decennial Summit well."

I attempt another tactic, one much more subtle. "It's in California, Your Highness."

One of the allures of living abroad was knowing my mother loathes travelling to any country outside of the European Union. Or, hell, outside our little Nordic corner of the globe. She's a xenophobe of the worst kind. Allowing my Spanish Duke of a father to remain in the country is a struggle.

Her pale eyes wander to the sheer white curtains framing a large window. "I wonder if it's sunny there."

It most certainly isn't sunny in Norsløe at the moment. Stark, diagonal slashes tear the sky apart, leaving nothing but gloom and misery.

"You know, I have it on good authority that the youngest Vattenguldian princess will attend."

Oh, for the love of God.

For years, my mother has been obsessed with the idea of me marrying the younger of the princesses from Vattenguldia, as she covets the prosperous coffers in their treasury, or at least a piece of them, since principality plays the ship registries game to perfection. I've always found it baffling, because, thanks to our alluring offshore banking strategies offerings, Aiboland is far wealthier. No matter. She's willing to sell her son off to . . . bloody hell, I don't know what that girl's name is. Idina? Irina? Inga? Whoever the hell she is, the She-Wolf wants her all in the name of securing a piece of the profits.

I haven't met this girl yet, or her sister who is to inherit the throne. Any information about the Vasa heirs comes either from my mother or the press. They're close to my age and also hail from a tiny principality in the northern Baltic Sea that gets about as much visibility on the global stage as Aiboland. And still, no matter how gorgeous these girls may or may not be, or smart, or funny, or whatever else, I sure as hell am not the least bit eager to bind myself to someone my mother sells me off to.

Someone shouts, and glasses rise, clinking mine in sloshy succession. I shouldn't be drinking so much tonight, let alone in a pub, but after the hour-long lecture my mother tortured me with this afternoon, detailing reasons why I must bag myself the Vattenguldian princess, I made it my mission to ensure the rest of the day was a blur. It was either drown myself in stout or throw myself off the bridge downtown.

"Stop while you're ahead." Lukas' warning is quiet. "There are a number of cell phones angled this way. You don't want to give Her Highness any leverage, do you?"

Arsehole.

I don't bother looking at my brother when I tell him to sod off. I do, however, glance at my personal secretary—only to find him subtly nodding in agreement. But, as annoyed as I am at him for saying that, Lukas is nearly always right. The one time I'd legitimately slipped up in America, when I had been at a fraternity party and was so bloody plastered I became, for lack of a better word, *friendly* with several ladies who had no qualms about selling videos to the press, I was summoned home to endure a diatribe and a slew of threats from the Grand Duchess. According to my mother, I was no better than one of those island boys (which I took to refer to the United Kingdom, despite also having the right to be called an island boy myself) and besmirching of the family's reputation would not be tolerated.

Not bothered in the least by what I've just muttered to my brother, Parker discretely pushes my half-finished stout, the fifth of the night, off to the side. It's then I spy Lady Autumn Horn af Björksund sauntering over to our table just as my secretary discreetly suggests we ought to leave, all five inch heels and long, blonde hair, a canary eating smile gracing her overly plump lips.

"Well, well," Lukas drawls as she closes in on our location. "Look at what just crawled out of her coffin. Here to suck the life out of us, Autumn?"

My brother and the lady aren't exactly on the best of terms after a disastrous short-term relationship that went nowhere, fast. Autumn angled to become a princess and failed after she discovered Lukas was not ready to settle down, let alone participate in a monogamous relationship. The glossies had a field day with the fallout until the Grand Duchess found a way to shut down such unflattering talk about her youngest son.

I am not necessarily Autumn's biggest fan, but duty and propriety dictates I rise up to greet her, whether or not I wish for her company. Air kisses are given on my end, real ones on hers. I murmur, "You look gorgeous tonight, Autumn."

I can practically hear Lukas' eyeballs rolling toward the back of his head behind me.

"Don't you look a bit like you're halfway to three sheets to the wind, Your Highness?"

There's no coquettishness on her behalf or false modesty, which I appreciate. I motion her to join us; Lukas grudgingly shifts further down the white leather couch to make room. Across from me, Parker's eyebrows creep toward his hairline, signaling his readiness toward extracting me from an undesirable situation. Friends since childhood, I could not ask for a more trusted confidant or employee.

A buzz fills the pub; cell phones turn from me to Lukas and Autumn.

The server is flagged to return. "What brings you out and about tonight?" I ask politely.

She scrunches her nose up. "A date."

The server leans down to take her order; appreciation shines in his eyes as he ogles her curves. Lukas asks smoothly, "Did you show him your true face, love?"

She ignores the jab, crossing her long legs and leaning back into the couch. "You're lucky, you know," she says to me. "To have your pick of who you want and not be like the rest of us, slogging through bad dates."

A meaningful glance is thrown Lukas' way. He merely toasts her in return.

As for me, I laugh in her face. Just . . . laugh. And then laugh some bloody more. Lukas is muttering something about getting it under control and Parker's signaling the server once more, and Autumn's regarding me as if maybe I've lost those sheets to the hurricane my laughter is brewing, but I cannot help it.

The bill quickly paid, Parker rises, brushing imaginary lint off his jeans. "Your Highness, I am to remind you of your early meeting in the morning."

Lukas also rises, clapping our mutual friend on the back. "Duty calls, brother."

"Stay," Autumn purrs. "I can promise you a much better time than any old meeting."

I am on my feet immediately. Shite, five drinks really were too many.

"You're unreal, you know that?" Lukas hisses at his ex. Before she can answer, he and Parker steer me toward the door. Whispers surround us, cell phones angle toward us, no doubt catching our every movement. My brother says quietly, "You know Autumn is basically the second coming of the Grand Duchess Britta, right?"

I'm close to puking my guts out at the thought.

"Get it together." Lukas' face is smooth as silk as cameras and phones go off around us. "You're weaving. The She-Wolf is going to have a field day with this. What in the bloody bollocks were you thinking, Chris?"

That I'm tired of being *Prince Perfect*.

CHAPTER 3

ELSA

"Absolutely not."

At least, that's what I think Charlotte is saying, but as her infant is screeching directly into the receiver, I cannot be positive. I remove the phone from my ear, but even a buffer of several inches of air does not decrease the ringing.

"Lottie, I mean this in the nicest way possible, but shove a soother in Dickie's mouth before I go deaf."

I think she shouts, "What?" but the tot is now wailing at banshee levels.

"Give him the soother!" My own voice is dangerously shrill. Thank goodness I am alone in my office, because I must sound like a lunatic, bellowing into the telephone.

"I will not give my baby a smoothie!" is what I think she shouts back. "He drinks milk!"

Oh for the love of— "THE DUMMY, LOTTIE! SHOVE IT IN ITS MOUTH!"

"MY BABY ISN'T STUPID!"

She is clearly sleep deprived if she can't even remember that pacifiers are called dummies. "Where is Josef?"

Dickie's fuss rises a whole decibel. "WHO?"

"YOUR HUSBAND."

"WHO?"

I hang up and ring to have my car brought round. As there are two days left until I depart for California, shouting over a phone is not a productive way to spend my time. I might as well go and shout in person.

When I am shown in, I find Charlotte in a frazzled heap of exhaustion, her hair less than impeccable, her clothes rumpled and stained with what I can only assume to be bodily fluids from the baby sleeping on her shoulder. He hiccups softly as she taps an unsteady rhythm against his back.

I open my mouth, but she hisses at me. So I take a seat and wait until little Lord Dickie is passed off to the nanny I forced upon my best friend. She and her husband believed they could manage their pride and joy all by themselves, but with his job in Parliament and hers as my personal assistant slash private secretary, they quickly realized doing it all themselves was easier said than done.

Even still, Charlotte Nordgren is giving it her best. Normally, she manages my existence with the ease and grace of a military general. I can count on one hand the times she lost her legendary cool with anyone in my presence. Yet, there is a small human who appears to have sucked her soul straight out of her and left a zombie in its wake, because the Charlotte I know would never hush me so blatantly.

"Now," she says as soon as the room clears, "I believe you were asking me to obtain you a one-way plane ticket to Switzerland? Feeling nostalgic?"

I snort. "Hardly."

Charlotte and I met at boarding school in Switzerland. If there is nostalgia there, it's because of her and very little else.

I pour her a cup of tea from the tray the housekeeper delivered whilst mid-trade-off. "Their Serene Highnesses know I am familiar with that country, so it is the first place they'd look. I am willing to go wherever, as long as I can leave within the next twelve hours."

She collapses into an overstuffed chair, arms and legs sprawling in all directions. Judging by the bags under her eyes, I hazard a guess she hasn't slept in far too many hours. "Why do you want me to get you out of the country, Elsa? Have you murdered somebody? Embezzled the country's coffers?" Even her smile is weary as she regards my joke. "That would be so like you, to wait until I was on maternity leave to wreak havoc."

"Worse." I pass her the cup I've prepared. "I am to attend the Decennial Summit in forty-eight hours."

Her eyes widen behind the porcelain. Royals do not speak of the Summit with those outside of their innermost circles; it's how we have managed to keep the gatherings secret in the past. But as my closest, most trusted advisor, Charlotte knows everything there is to know about the Decennial Summit and the RMM.

"Bloody hell, Elsa."

Ah, now she gets it.

She sits up straight, honeyed hair swishing softly around her shoulders. "I'll—I need to call Josef, tell him that I'll be—"

"Don't be daft. You are not coming. Summit or no, you are still on maternity leave."

"Elsa." Her exhaustion beats a path out of the room as steely resolve surges to the forefront. "Where is it being held?"

"California."

"California, as in the United States?"

"Are there other Californias in the world?" I muse.

"This is no time for jesting!"

"I am quite aware of that, despite my pathetic pleas to smuggle me out of the country. Perhaps I ought to have asked you to find me a rent-a-husband instead. Do you happen to know of any reputable escort services?"

Her teacup discarded onto a nearby table, Charlotte locates one of the hundreds of notepads littering her house. "What has His Highness said? Are there any targets for us to know about?"

"Targets?"

"Future husbands," she says grimly. "Whom is Prince Gustav leaning toward? I cannot imagine he's dragging you to California without several goals in mind."

She makes an alarming yet valid point. "Nothing was said to me yet."

"I need to call Josef, see if there are any countries that Parliament has been angling to bolster trade agreements with. Or buffer alliances with, especially within EU voting blocs." She scribbles like an enflamed madwoman. "Last I heard, there was a call toward agricultural outsourcing, considering recent shoddy crops due to global warming. Who right now has good export prices on—" She is out of her chair, rooting around the room for her cell phone. "Dammit. I think there was talk of iron, too. And then there's Her Serene Highness' most fervent desire to become the Monaco of the north, which would require loads of capital."

I would not put it past my mother to whisper names of ludicrously wealthy suitors in my father's ear, all in the name of securing her glory and dreams. "I have received no marching orders yet."

"His Serene Highness never goes into these situations blind." Her cell is extracted from underneath a stack of baby books. "I'll bet everything I own your parents already have somebody selected for you. And then a pair of back-ups if their first choice proves unfeasible."

This is yet another reason why Charlotte is worth her weight in gold. "You realize that Vattenguldia has precious little political pull in the world, right? I highly doubt that any marriage of mine would be able to change that."

I'm impressed my words are steady as this falsehood slides out. My mother has long insisted to anyone in our family that, if I choose right, our principality's visibility could expand exponentially. And as Her Serene Highness has her sights set on tourists from the Americas and Asia and their deep pocketbooks, there is little doubt she looks to cash in on this belief.

After all, the world loves a good royal fairy story.

Charlotte is already dialing her husband. "You are splitting hairs."

"Outside of me fleeing the country right now, I highly doubt that, even if we knew who the Prince is eying as a future son-in-law, I have any other say over what is to happen."

The phone is ripped away from her ear as she stares at me incredulously. "Who are you, and what have you done with Elsa?"

I stir my tea, even though the sugar has long melted. Confident Elsa is currently in crisis mode, thank you very much.

"Many royals marry exactly who they want," she says. "Look at all the commoners and trainers who are now happily married into royalty. Why couldn't you fall in love with your trainer, Elsa?"

"Hedda is an amazing woman, and attractive to boot, but she is already happily married with a whole slew of children," I say dryly.

"My point stands. There are plenty of people of your ilk who are married as a result of their own free will."

"Not if they were single during the Decennial Summit."

She slaps her notepad down upon a table and comes to sit next to me on the couch. "Would Their Serene Highnesses really go through with making you marry someone you don't know? Or love?"

I set my teacup down. "Yes. I neglected to mention that Isabelle is to come, too. It will be a two-fer: the Vattenguldian princesses for two new political gains."

The pity on my best friend's face makes me want to claw my own in rabid frustration.

CHAPTER 4

♛
CHRISTIAN

The rock my father kicks skitters down into the pond at the edge of the palace grounds; ripples barely form as it rolls to hidden depths. He stuffs his hands into his pockets and glances up to the angry sky. "It'll rain today, I think."

It rains a lot in Norsloe, so that's basically like him saying, "Grass is green," or other stupid shite people say when they're trying to make irreverent small talk. But that's Andres de la Warren's *modus operandi*, especially in difficult situations.

Lukas' pack of dogs yip and rush past us, scattering ducks into the pond. My brother shouts their names, but as they are the only truly willful, disobedient creatures on the palace grounds, they pay him no mind. "Fuck the rain," he says. "Let's talk about how Chris and I are lambs off to slaughter tomorrow. Can't you talk to the She-Wolf about this?"

Once upon a time, I believe my father was a confident man. He was popular, funny, and charismatic, a favorite of Spanish society and media. He had girlfriends and money and even played a year on a professional Spanish football team. Within a blink of an eye, his uncle, the King, sold him off to my mother for banking perks during one of the RMMs and shipped him north. Isolated from the Mediterranean, and trapped in what he rapidly realized was an antagonistic, loveless marriage with a She-Wolf, my father initially rebelled until my mother somehow smashed him into submission. None of us know how she did it, but whispers in the palace tell me that all of his *joie de vivre* disappeared until he was nothing but a puppet the She-Wolf trots out when necessary.

He is no true Grand Duke. Instead, he is the Grand Duchess Britta of Aiboland's silent Prince Consort. So for Lukas to even ask him of this is absurd. Still, my father says, his lingering accent more noticeable in the fresh air than inside, *"Mis hijos,* she is resolute about finding you proper matches at the Decennial Summit."

He bends down and digs a smooth rock out of the mud below our Wellies. With a flick of the wrist, it sails toward the pond and skips one, two, three times across the surface.

"I am resolute about telling her she can go to hell," Lukas mutters.

For hours after we got home from the pub, my brother and I brainstormed over ways for me to escape the She-Wolf's machinations. No solutions were found, except for Parker to call the local newspapers and cash in favors to have the photographs from the outing not published.

"I hear," my father says, "that the Vattenguldian girl is lovely, Christian."

"Well, shite. That makes it all okay, right?" Lukas tugs a stick out of one of his dog's mouths and throws it into the distance. "Chris! Did you hear that? As long as the lady is pretty, nothing else matters. She could be an inbred idiot or a raving bitch like the She-Wolf, but as long as her face is good to look at and the babies she pumps out are lovely, you're golden." He pretends to step into line like one of the ceremonial guards outside the palace. "Long live Aiboland, an island of beautiful, unimportant royals in a world that finds monarchies obsolete."

Our father sighs. "Lukas . . ."

Light raindrops splatter against my cheek as I gaze upward. "I wonder what it would take to stage a coup?"

Lukas reclaims the stick from one of the dogs. "Balls of titanium, I imagine." Bitter chuckling escapes him. "Not so doable for emotional eunuchs like ourselves, right?"

"Did you know your uncle planned to arrange your marriage?" I ask our father.

He squats down to pet one of the less obnoxious dogs. As there are five of them, and I've been gone for years, I haven't yet put effort into learning all their names. "I'd heard rumors of the RMM from my cousins, but I certainly never thought I'd be worth any leverage in such matters." The dog leans its head against my father's leg. "But *mi madre* always warned that, as nephew to the King of Spain, my future was not always mine to make."

It's pointless to argue with him, especially as I know he has no pull with the She-Wolf at all. And still I find myself saying, like some kind of bloody fool who just doesn't know when to keep his mouth shut, "It's the twenty-first century. Arranged marriages are archaic!"

"There are plenty of places in the world where that is not the case and you know it," my father counters.

"In First World countries, it most certainly *is* the case. If I'm not mistaken," Lukas' glance around us is exaggeratedly sweeping, "despite this island being a shitehole in the Baltic Sea, we're still considered First World—or so people believe, considering our wealth. So, Chris' point stands." He kicks the toe of a Wellie into the mud, suctioning out a hole. "There are a lot of royals out there right now marrying whoever they feel is right."

"Not during the Decennial Summit," our father says softly.

Lukas turns away, stalking toward the pond's edge.

A weathered hand comes to rest against my shoulder. "*Mi hijo*, you must understand that—"

"No," I tell him. "I really don't."

I'm surprised when he doesn't roll over and just let it go like every other time confrontation finds him in this family. "We aren't like other people. We don't have the luxury of doing what we wish, no matter what the rest of the world thinks of us. You have a duty to this country, Christian. Fighting against expectations will only lead you to pain and misery."

The clouds above us rip open. Lukas barks out an order to round the dogs up so we can head back to the palace. My father moves to follow, but I stay him with a hand on his shoulder. "That's rich, coming from you."

"It comes from me," he says quietly, "because I speak from experience."

I feel like punching something. "I don't *want* what you have. I want . . ." I pull at my wet hair. "Shite . . . love, maybe? At least friendship? If I have to marry somebody, I want it to be because I *choose* to, not because my fucking monster of a mother made me."

But then he's gone without another word. Brown fur flies as the dogs circle him on the path back toward our prison.

CHAPTER 5

ELSA

What do they call those final, desperate moments of the condemned, where sweet, soft mercy is pled for, only to have fragile hopes carefully cultivated be stomped upon with unforgiving steel-toed boots? An appeal, maybe?

Whatever it is, that was me an hour before we left Vattenguldia via private jet. I went to my father with my pride tucked into a pocket, petitioning for compassion and understanding.

He was unmoved. "You are taking this too personally."

"How can I not? It *is* personal. This is my life!"

"Yours is a life of service. You have a chance right now to make a difference for our country, as does Isabelle. Two massively beneficial chances. If you are unhappy with your spouse, do as I've done."

I was agog. "You want me to find myself a good old-fashioned paramour?"

He was incensed with me more than he's been in a long time. I was put soundly in my place, reminded that, no matter if I married a butler or a prince, I would do what was best for Vattenguldia. And I would do it because I am from the House of Vasa, and we live and die by tradition.

Tradition, I am learning, is not as rosy as it was once.

After that edict, my arse was ordered onto our private jet and now I am on the third leg of our journey as we travel from Los Angeles up the coastline toward a tiny town named San Simeon. As we begin our descent, my sister settles in the seat across the aisle. She's stiff and silent, her fingers laced tightly across her lap. I don't think Isabelle uttered more than twenty words the entire journey. Shortly before we departed, she gripped my arm and murmured, "Wake me from this nightmare. This cannot be how it all goes down."

I answered, "Only if you wake me first."

After that, her game face fell firmly in place, but I know better. She is just as distressed as I am by this farce, probably even more so. Unlike my single self, my sister is currently embroiled in a messy yet passionate relationship our parents know nothing about.

I murmur, "Tell Father. It's your *Get Out of Jail* card."

A quick, sharp shake of the head is the only response I receive, leaving me puzzled. Why would she continue to hide such a thing, especially now? Isabelle is reserved, nearly to a fault, but she has never been a pushover—or at least not the kind my parents wished for.

Although, until this week, I would have claimed the same for myself. Yet here we are, the Vasa girls on their way to the latest Marriage Market. Beyond the jet's windows are soft, multi-hued, green rolling hills and choppy waters crashing against golden shores. Further in the distance, our destination materializes: high upon a hilltop, surrounded by dense trees, off-white towers peek out at the ocean.

I have been around beautiful architecture my entire life. I grew up in Vattenguldia, spent much time all over Scandinavia. I attended school in Switzerland, vacationed often in France and Italy. I have viewed stunning buildings from all ages. And yet, the first glimpse of Hearst Castle has me questioning if I have actually ever seen such a stunning site before.

It doesn't even look real. Which is fitting, I suppose, considering I still feel as if this whole bloody situation cannot possibly be happening.

Minutes later, our jet lands on a tiny strip at the base of the hill. An SUV is waiting, alongside the Prince of Liechtenstein. "Gustav! Just in time," he calls out as we disembark. "The MC is meeting in an hour, and your expertise is required."

There is no time for idle chitchat on the runway. Aircrafts from Japan, Saudi Arabia, Malaysia, and Swaziland are all arriving within the hour. In fact, the moment our luggage is stowed and the doors to the SUV are shut, the jet we rode in on shoots down the strip.

"Was the flight comfortable?"

It takes a moment to realize the question was angled at me. I turn away from the window and lie to the monarch from Liechtenstein, "Very pleasant, Your Highness," because I've obviously waded into the River Styx and am rapidly approaching Hell.

If Hell is a gorgeous, glamorous hilltop castle in California.

"My daughter sends her love," the Prince continues warmly. "She wishes she could attend the Summit, but alas, commitments at home keep her away."

There is no chance the Princess of Liechtenstein desires to be here. She's already married. She's probably thrilled she never had to be trotted out at any of the Summits.

Lucky lady.

I tell the Prince, "Please convey my love and regards as well, Your Highness."

From that point on, my father and his friend talk shop. I keep one ear on their discussions—apparently, a number of the microstates want to band together to have a larger voice in global politics—but the view outside my window is far more demanding. We climb the emerald hill via a winding path that brings the castle in and out of focus. Fruit trees and succulents line the road, and I must say, for being in Hell, I am enchanted. And then doubly so once we pull up to a wide set of steps leading up to a courtyard with a marble fountain and a cream colored, Mediterranean cathedral-esque castle.

My father and his friend pay the view no mind as they side-skirt the front façade. But Isabelle and I pause, admiring the towers rising above us as well as the lush ocean views nearby.

This is California? The United States, a land so young that buildings from the early twentieth-century are termed historic?

Isabelle neatly sums up what we see by murmuring, "Wow."

Wow, indeed.

"I read up on the location, Your Highnesses." Startled, my sister and I turn to find Bittner a few feet behind us. "The original owner was keen on collecting European art and architecture. Much of the Castle or guesthouses either have such pieces embedded within their structure, such as the medieval façade and gate in front of us, or had facsimiles created to incorporate."

"It lends a very Spanish feeling, does it not?" Isabelle muses.

"Indeed, Your Highness. And yet, there are pieces throughout the grounds that are Roman, British, Italian, or a host of other countries and time periods." He squints at the tall towers looming on the sides of the building. "It's a mish-mash, to be sure. This is Casa Grande." He motions us forward, toward a side door. "While we are granted more freedom around the Castle than most, I am still tasked to inform you there are many parts we must be careful of or stay away from. The front door, for example, leads to an ancient Roman mosaic entryway that is not to be touched."

We enter into a large medieval yet Roman feeling room surrounded with wooden choir stalls. A woman in a sharp navy skirt and jacket bearing a nametag steps forward. "May I be the first to officially welcome you to Hearst Castle," she says to us. "My name is Nicole, and I'm one of the Castle guides. I'm to take you on a brief tour of the grounds, show you to your room, and answer any questions you might have about your stay here at *La Cuesta Encantada* for the coming week."

A ridiculous question mentally surfaces for a princess nearing her third decade of life—does she perhaps know whom I am to be set up with?

"Thank you, Nicole." I tuck my bitterness away until a later time. "We are most pleased at the opportunity to visit such a beautiful, historic location in California."

Bittner excuses himself to meet up with our father, informing us to contact him immediately if there is anything we need.

Despite yearning to go to whatever bedroom we have been assigned and hide from the inevitable, Isabelle and I follow Nicole for the next half hour as she tours us through the main house, the three guest cottages, sumptuous coastal gardens, stunning patios that overlook the ocean and mountains, and two magnificent pools that leave both Isabelle and I rather envious they are not our own. By the time we reach our room, a smallish affair with one double-sized bed, a writing desk, several chairs, and a fold-a-bed propped in the corner, I grudgingly admit Hearst Castle has officially charmed me.

It is a terrible omen.

The tour guide ensures our luggage had safely arrived in the room and was unpacked. "As I'm sure you noted on our tour, the dining hall, while spacious, isn't large enough to accommodate a full dinner with everyone here. Breakfast, tea, and lunches will be served buffet style in there, but dinners will be held on various patios throughout the grounds. Tonight's will be hosted at the Neptune Pool." There's pride in her smile. "It's a striking sight at sunset."

"Is that the outdoor pool?" Isabelle is ridiculously dreamy eyed for a woman who's on the verge of having to marry someone who is not her fiancé. "The one that has the Roman temple at the front? Because I think I'd really rather steal it from you all and take it home."

Nicole laughs gently, as if this is something she hears all the time. "Yes, Your Highness."

"Planning on sunbathing while we're here?" I ask wryly after the guide shuts the door behind her exit.

"Perhaps." My sister drops down into one of the stuffed chairs in the room. She motions to a packet Nicole brought to my attention that includes my weekly itinerary. "I did a lot of thinking on the plane ride over." Her head leans back against the cushion, dark curls drifting over one shoulder. "Let us at least attempt to make the best out of a bad situation. We're both pale as death. If we must suffer through the RMM, let us come away with golden, California tans."

I glance out the window. A number of other royals are wandering around with their guides. "I wish I could join you, but I will be at meetings."

"Father is asking for more and more of your input lately. At least there lies a silver lining for you."

A rueful puff of annoyance passes from between my lips. "I was handed a dossier filled with talking points yesterday. His Serene Highness is no more interested in my opinions toward Vattenguldia and the world at large than he is with what we're to wear tonight. I am to parrot his viewpoints the entire week."

"Are you nervous?"

I angle away from the window as she offers this quiet question.

"I am," she offers flatly. Sadly.

I come to perch on the edge of the bed. "If you revealed your relationship with Alfons, this would not be an issue for you."

She pulls in a sharp breath before shaking her head.

"Isabelle, you are already engaged."

Her words are quiet yet firm. "I cannot talk about it."

My eyebrows lift upward. Since when does my sister not want to wax poetic about her fiancé?

She leans forward, her voice lowering even further. "It does not matter anyway. Our parents called me into Father's office before we left and laid down the law. Nothing you or I say would mean anything at this point of time. There is no swaying them from what they believe will be best for the country. So, please . . ." Her fingers curve around mine and squeeze. "I am asking you to respect my privacy while we are here."

I jerk back as if she slapped me. "You think Father finding out you are engaged would have no bearing?"

"Elsa!" My name is shrill and angry from her lips. "Shut it!"

And then she blanches, knowing she crossed the line. I stand up, feeling the blood leech from my own face in quiet fury. "Sister or no, you don't get to bark at me like that."

"I apologize. It's just—"

"There is no need to explain anything to me." I step away before I utter something I might regret. "I'm going to take a walk. Ensure my dress for dinner is hung out and pressed."

She bites her lip but nods. And then I am out the door.

CHAPTER 6

CHRISTIAN

Lukas mutters under his breath, "Fuck this," before stalking away.

The She-Wolf slithers closer to where I stand. "Get your brother under control. I will not tolerate him embarrassing us."

The thought of controlling my brother is laughable. For as much as he respects and looks up to me, there's nothing I can say which would convince Lukas that any part of this trip is acceptable. Shite, his only purpose for attending the Summit is to be a pawn for our mother and look attractive to prospective father-in-laws. Me? I can at least claim that I'm here partially for business. According to Parker, I have a full itinerary of meetings scheduled.

The She-Wolf waves across the gardens, toward the Queen of England and her heir. "Ensure you both are impeccably dressed tonight for dinner."

The words, "Go to hell," are so bloody hard to hold back.

The British monarch makes a beeline toward us. My mother turns to me, her hands coming to my shoulders as she smooths imaginary wrinkles out of my shirt. And then she leans forward, pressing matte pink lips against my cheek. "Be a good boy and go and make yourself desirable. I'll see you and your brother at dinner." Thankfully, her focus leaves me so she can call out her friend's name.

Propriety dictates I stay and pay my respects, but the She-Wolf has basically just told me to get the hell away. For once, I'm more than happy to do as ordered, so I depart without another word.

Once I head up the steps, toward the house, I tug out a handkerchief and wipe the lipstick off my cheek. I'm unsuccessful at repressing the shudder of disgust rolling through me, though. Jesus. She's my mother, and I owe her my life, but any touch of so-called affection from her makes my skin crawl.

Goddamn, do I need a drink. Maybe even several to prepare for the horrors awaiting me tonight. I text Parker and tell him to meet me up in my room. If I'm going to get pissed, I might as well have somebody present to ensure I don't make a giant jackass of myself. And then I climb up a winding, tight staircase until I reach the second floor, hoping I can remember exactly where the duplex suite I'm staying in is.

A message from Parker sounds, telling me he's on his way. Before I shove my phone into my pocket, I smack into a woman in the hallway.

"Watch it!" she snaps in accented English.

I jerk back a step, ready to apologize for not paying better attention to where I was going, but then I get a good look at her.

Holy shite.

CHAPTER 7

ELSA

We're in a stalemate, this man and I, where I'm eyeing him warily and he me in return, both deer caught in crossing headlights after nearly colliding in this narrow hallway.

For Christ's sake, he's too handsome. Too everything, really. His eyes are too hypnotizing—vivid, bright amber ringed in mahogany and speckled with freckles that are too appealing. His hair is too wavy, too beautifully brown, like the espresso beans that gift me morning ecstasy. Despite a mild five o'clock shadow, his skin is too flawless. His clothes are too nice, and his stylish leather shoes too tasteful.

Physically, he's just too much *too*.

I wrack my mind to match the face in front of me to the name. Ah. There it is. This is a fellow heir to yet another tiny country in the European Union. This is the Hereditary Grand Duke of Aioboland, Prince Christian.

It is tacky to be so judgmental, especially without hearing his voice or knowing anything other than what the gossip rags say about him, but I want nothing to do with this man. Which is funny, because when I was younger, I secretly yearned to meet him. Close to my age and a fellow Scandinavian, his country isn't too far away from mine. There was a childish hope he might even be some kind of kindred spirit, that he knew what the weight of a crown and kingdom (or a principality or a Grand Duchy) could do to a young heir. Before we ever stepped foot in a room together, let alone the same country, though, his mother shipped him off to boarding school in some foreign country (maybe the UK?) and I'd been sent to Switzerland, leaving anything and everything I was to learn about Prince Christian from the press. All of the assumptions about us being kindred souls were nothing more than rubbish. This prince isn't a kindred spirit. He and I . . . we are nothing but fellow minor royals in a big world filled with more powerful, influential countries.

It is best not to even speak to him—or any of the princes present, at least voluntarily. The RMM is legendary for the amount of one-night stands which occur between heirs.

For a split moment, hot eyes bore into me, blatantly taking me in like he'd never seen another woman before. The hairs on the back of my neck bristle in indignation, but then he blinks, and the look is gone.

Before I turn on my heel, though, he offers what technically can be called a smile that in actuality is too breathtaking to fully describe, with blindingly too white teeth that leave me wondering if they're capped.

"My apologies," he says to me in English, with a too crisp British lilt bearing no hint of our Scandinavian heritage. It makes me simultaneously want to grind my teeth together and sigh in happiness because his voice and accent are way too sexy and fit perfectly with his appearance. And then, just when I think I can't stand properly any longer, he bows to me too perfectly—sharp, from the waist, with an arm crossing his chest, like he's had a lifetime practicing just such a move so the ladies around him would swoon. "I'm—"

No. He cannot be allowed to sweet talk me. Or look at me in such a way. Does he think I'm one of the spares trolling these tiny hallways for a stud? Or that the moment I arrived, I was on the hunt for someone to take my mind off of the RMM?

I hold up a hand and slash it through the air; unbelievably, he silences immediately. Jesus almighty. He's got too perfect manners. Will he stop it already?

I can't believe I've been here for all of an hour or so, and I'm already having to set men straight. Defense mechanisms I didn't even know I had kick into gear. "Look. I don't want you to take this the wrong way, but no matter what you may think, I'm not some easy get. Save your propositions or proposal for someone else." My back straightens, tight as a rod, as manners beat into me by my mother fight to regain control. "I'm not here for *that*."

No matter what my parents believe or insist upon.

It's a relief to say it, to get it out even though I know I'm swimming against the current. Maybe, just maybe, if behind closed doors I manage to make myself undesirable, these princes will dig their heels in and refuse to even entertain the notion of aligning themselves with The Hereditary Princess of Vattenguldia.

In the heat of my words, Christian's mouth drops open, his eyes widening significantly. His cheeks blaze scarlet, like I slapped him smartly for impertinence. Which maybe I should have. Except, this embarrassment is way too disarming on him.

I must get out of this tiny hallway already.

His words are slow-motion confusion. "I'm sorry?"

"I am here for . . ." He knows why I'm here. It is why he's here, too. But I snap, "*Work* and nothing else. Understand?"

He continues to stare at me as if he cannot believe I cut him down so tidily in public. And perhaps he cannot, since even I admit it's nearly unfathomable that anyone would ever reject such a fine specimen of princehood. Except, I am not just anyone. And I'm sure as hell not up for the highest bidder, even if he's as shiny as this one.

Without another word, I drop into a polite curtsey. Just because I am rebuffing his princely charms, I do have some manners. And then I force myself to push past him in the narrow hallway in order to retreat to my bedroom.

As my shoulder brushes up against his arm, his smell curls around me. It's faint, but damn him. He even smells too delicious.

Once out of his eyesight, I break into a vigorous pace. And then I find myself a nice little corner where I attempt to calm my racing heartbeat.

The horrors of this week have already sunk their claws into me.

CHAPTER 8

♛

CHRISTIAN

What just happened?

All I wanted five minutes ago was to go somewhere, anywhere that didn't include spreadsheets or mothers or fathers desperate to fob their precious heirs off to neighboring kingdoms. Preferably somewhere with alcoholic beverages. As I'm trapped on this hilltop for the next week, I figured the next best thing to Sven's Pig & Roast Pub was my room and the small wet bar my mother insisted upon.

And then the Hereditary Princess Elsa of Vattenguldia appeared.

For a moment, I felt . . . not stunned, because that would make me sound like a fucking idiot, but something like it. There was a Norse Valkyrie in front of me here at Hearst Castle, and she was all fire and righteousness and inhumanly lovely, which made sense since she had to be a figment of my imagination. Except, then she spat out her…refusal of a proposal never uttered—

Holy. SHITE. *She thought I was proposing to her!?*

"Your Highness?"

Parker stands before me, stacks of folders in his hands, regarding me as if he fears I had a stroke in the midst of the hallway. Which, I might have, considering what just happened. Women do not randomly go about yelling refusals of proposals never uttered to strangers. Not even at the RMM.

Do they?

"Chris?"

My feet are forced to uproot. "Yeah. Yes." I shake my head; so many crisscrossing cobwebs block rational thought. And then I run directly into a tassel hanging down from one of the lights. Bloody hell, I'm a right mess.

"Are you all right?"

Some Valkyrie just came along, sheared off my balls, and slung them over her shoulder as she rode away, victorious in her mysterious efforts to confuse the living hell out of me. So, no. I am not all right.

But men do not tell each other this. "I'm fine." Why am I so shaken? This is asinine. She's not a Valkyrie. She's clearly a fucking harpy.

And maybe, just maybe she left my balls somewhere here in the hallway. I have a discreet glance around.

"Are you su—"

"Fine."

He holds out a hand and ushers me toward the hellhole I share with my mother and brother. "Might I inquire why you're out in the wide open rather than in your room?" More quietly, as no one else is around, he murmurs wickedly, "Unless you'd prefer to go back downstairs?"

Is he insane? "God, *no.*" Because there is no way I'm going back to hobnob with my mother. No. Bloody. Way. Before the horror of the gardens, I was stuck for two hours of meetings with the She-Wolf sitting right next to me, reeking of dead roses dipped in the world's worst perfume, all the while shoving notes about girls present. It was worse than hell, leaving me positive that in some former life, I was a truly shitty person to deserve such a fate.

"Then, by all means, let's go get you a cocktail."

"Who says cocktail?"

He motions around us. "Frank Sinatra."

"Sinatra was more 50s and 60s than 30s and 40s, which was"—I mimic him by motioning around us—"this place's heyday."

Parker's chuckles rumble from beneath his breath. "You read what I sent you after all."

"I always read what you send me." His eyebrows shoot up in disbelief, so I add, "Also, I feel like Sinatra would have called it booze."

At this, his humor grows louder. "Fine. Let's go get you some booze, Chris. Are you happy now?"

The corners of my lips tick upward. "I'll be quite happy with some booze, thank you." I'm also pleased he's loosening up a bit, too. After years of friendship, far too much formality has crept between us since he took on the position of my personal secretary. When I offered the job, I thought it was a brilliant idea—I could trust one of my best mates, and it would be fantastic to have him around. But then he went and insisted upon a formal distance between us, as if we were no longer mates but simply prince and employee.

But here he is, sounding much like the Parker I've known the majority of my life.

Back in the dual-level room I share with my family, Parker pours us two glasses of cognac. Personally, I find the liqueur disgusting, but as Her Royal

Highness often reminds Lukas and me, "Cognac is what my sire drank before me, and his sire before him. Our family imbibes in cognac."

If only my mother saw the merit of whiskey. Or, hell, stout. What I wouldn't do for a good, strong stout right now. But I sip the warm piss anyway as I settle upon the portable bed I've been provided. I'll be damned if I'm the weak link in a line of cognac drinkers. "What do you know of Elsa Vasa?"

Parker had just leaned back into one of the chairs in the room, his eyes closing against the syrupy sweet sting of the liqueur, but my question straightens his spine. "The Vattenguldian princess?"

At least this is Parker and not Lukas I'm asking, because then I'd never hear the end of it. "Yes, obviously the Vattenguldian princess, unless there is another Elsa running around the RMM. What do you know about her?"

He tugs his overflowing leather satchel to where he's sitting and digs through it for a few seconds before extracting a slim file. From our debriefing prior to arriving at the Summit, I happen to know that there were numerous similar folders within, all containing dossiers of present fellow royals and their families.

He'd urged both Lukas and I to read the files on the flight over. My brother flat out rejected the suggestion. I'd gotten through half of the alphabetized dossiers before napping; it was the easiest way to escape the She Wolf's incessant and frankly revolting scheming over how best to trap the girls she favors into marriage. (Let's just say seduction was involved, a topic one ought to never have with a parent.) Due to the nap, though, I hadn't gotten to the Vs, so the Valkyrie and her ilk are still a huge question mark in my mind.

So he's right. I don't read everything he gives me.

I'm passed a file labeled VATTENGULDIA. "Elsa Victoria Evelyn Sofia Marie of the ruling House of Vattenguldia, the Vasas—"

"Even my name is not so long," I interject, startled.

Parker pays me no heed, continuing, "—is the eldest daughter of His Royal Highness Gustav and Her Serene Highness Sofia. Her childhood was spent at the elite boarding school Le Rosey in Switzerland, where she earned impeccable grades. A graduate of Oxford University, she is twenty-eight years of age and is fluent in five languages. At Oxford, her studies focused on European history—"

I set my glass down on the floor and lean forward. "Yes, yes, I already know that." Actually, I don't. Nonetheless, it doesn't matter if the Valkyrie likes history. All royals like history; studying illustrious family pasts are vain yet indulged ego boosts. "I mean, what do you *know* about her?"

"I was in the process of telling you." A frown twists his lips.

"She said she wouldn't marry me. Or—I don't know. Have sex with me."

Parker startles in his chair, cognac sloshing over the rim of his glass. "You *proposed* to her? To a hereditary princess?"

Christ almighty. I really need to learn how to broach these topics better. I toss him one of Lukas' stray t-shirts to clean up with, wondering where my brother is. I'd think he'd want to be hiding with the rest of us. "No to all of the above."

"But—"

"What I meant to say is, I most certainly did not propose to this woman. Nor did I proposition her."

He studies me for a long moment before tossing the shirt back. "Have you been imbibing today longer than I'm aware of?"

I stuff the shirt beneath Lukas' pillow on the portable bed next to mine. Neither of us wants to ascend the tiny, steep wooden staircase in the duplex to be near our mother's bed. It's bad enough we're all trapped in this same area together. "We ran into each other in the hallway. Before I could even say anything, she barked out she wouldn't marry me. Or have sex, or . . . I don't know. She mentioned proposals and propositions."

This elicits a rather lengthy, hearty laugh on Parker's behalf.

"I'm glad you find this amusing."

"Oh, believe me. I quite do."

I tell him where he can shove his laughter, which somehow ups the hilarity for him. "What if this gets out, Parker?"

None of this sobers him in the least.

I try again. "What if this gets back to the Grand Duchess?"

That does the trick.

"I would not put it past her to orchestrate an engagement at the first word of me having interest in anyone, especially that girl, since the She-Wolf's had her sister at the top of my so-called"—an involuntary shudder rolls through me—"*To Marry* list for ages. You know she'd do it, no qualms involved."

Parker sobers immediately. Of course he knows this. Nothing the She-Wolf does surprises him, because, as one of my oldest friends, he's known the truth of her character since childhood.

"Why would the Hereditary Princess of Vattenguldia believe you were interested in a match?" He pours us both another glass of the crappy cognac. "What happened in that hallway?"

"Nothing. We looked at each other, I suppose."

Parker's eyebrows lift toward his hairline.

Well, shite. "Not *looked* at each other," I quickly clarify.

The corners of the bastard's mouth twitch.

"I meant, we were both in the hallway. We'd bumped into each other. Well, I ran into her. This place is filled with incredibly narrow corridors." I cross my arms, but then realize how that must make me look defensive, forcing me to relax. "Our eyes gravitated toward one another as polite people are prone to do when they are the only ones present. At a distance no less." I don't bother to let him know we were close enough I was virtually drunk on her perfume, a vanilla mixture which was ten trillion times more fantastic than the She-Wolf's dead roses scent.

Parker runs a finger along the rim of his glass. "And a marriage proposal was determined from this look?" He whistles. "That must have a hell of a look, Chris."

Wanker. "I'm telling you, the look was no *look*, or at least, it was no look that one could determine a lifelong commitment from. It was a polite look. A glance, to be more specific." I snap my fingers. "An acknowledgement of another's existence."

"The lady doth protest too much, I believe."

Friend or no, I still issue a quiet warning.

"My apologies. Now that we have firmly defined what kind of look it was, and made sure we've both said the word a dozen times apiece, maybe I ought to continue with what I know about this princess?"

I run a hand across my face. "Go ahead."

"Rumor has it that Her Royal Highness is a straight shooter. This trait has endeared her to the Vattenguldian citizens. Despite their adoration of Prince Gustav, Princess Elsa is viewed as a breath of fresh air in a country that much of Europe overlooks or considers antiquated. She's serious about her charity work, the environment, and keen on ensuring Vattenguldia finds its footing and thrives in today's economy whilst fiercely celebrating its cultural past." Parker rubs the bridge of his nose. "You know, you two may have more in common than you think."

I at least have some manners. "How so?"

He sips his drink slowly. "Concerning the quest to find a suitable match here this week. I'm assuming that, alongside her rejection, Her Royal Highness indicated she has no interest in playing a willing contestant in the RMM, correct?"

My ego will not allow me to relive such humiliation in vivid detail. "In not so many polite words, yes, that was the gist of it."

"Maybe you ought to befriend her. You could be each other's haven in this brothel."

I end up choking—literally *choking*—on the bloody cognac.

As Parker beats my back, I reluctantly allow that the idea, as hideous as it is, might have merit. But value or no, I also have pride and that pride insists there is no good to come from befriending a woman hell-bent on focusing on her . . . what had she called it—*work?*—at the detriment of common decency. Besides, the Valkyrie is a princess the She-Wolf would sell her husband's soul to have me befriend, as it'd be an in to the sister. So, bollocks to that.

When I can speak, I tell Parker, "It's best to avoid her entirely."

He disapproves. Too bad. "Where the hell is Lukas?" I send my brother a quick text, informing him that Parker and I have the booze out, and that if he wants to survive tonight, he better come and have some already.

CHAPTER 9

ELSA

My father tugs at his bow tie. "Are you girls enjoying yourselves?"

I let Isabelle answer, as he must know how I truly feel. "It is quite nice here," she says, her voice smooth and low. She sounds eerily like our mother. "I met some very nice people today."

I try not to roll my eyes while I finish applying lipstick. Had I used the word *nice* twice in a sentence, a lecture requiring me to express myself in less common language would have followed. Isabelle may have gotten the beautiful voice, but at least I can lay claim to an expanded vocabulary.

"Excellent." Our father slips on his coat; my sister acts as valet, smoothing the shoulders out. "This is cozy, isn't it? Us all in a room like this? I feel as if we're camping."

Only His Serene Highness would consider the three of us residing in one of the United State's most famous historical mansions as the equivalent of camping. After fleeing from Prince Christian this afternoon, I overheard plenty of people who once believed only Europe houses architectural masterpieces oohing and ahhing over the mix-matched styling of the Castle. Nonetheless, it is also fairly tiny for the amount of people packed into it for the week. Royals, so often used to having large, lavish spaces all to themselves, are stacked upon one another like sardines in bedrooms in the four houses. Placements were drawn at random so no one family was favored for a better room over the others. That leaves precious little privacy to be enjoyed. Nobody—not even the most powerful and influential monarchs present—have their own room. Sharing quarters with our father is not ideal, even when he generously ceded the bed for Isabelle and me and is sleeping upon a small portable foldaway off to the side, but Isabelle and I figure it could have been far worse, had our mother also been present. But no—she is at home, overseeing renovations to the palace.

As for any employees who tagged along, they're the ones who could argue to be camping since they are lodging in barracks. This is only further proof the MC has lost their collective minds. To require loyal staff to sleep on undoubtedly uncomfortable cots in the equivalent of dorm rooms and use portable showers and toilets? Unforgiveable.

I texted this insanity to Charlotte, who promptly wrote she was grateful for remaining in Vattenguldia—and that I better keep her updated at least ten times over the course of each day.

I also told her I met the heir to Aiboland.

Her immediate response? Is he as good looking in person as he is in the glossies?

I figured it couldn't hurt to tell her the truth. Ridiculously so.

Was he nice?

I wouldn't know. We didn't talk. Which was a lie. Well, all right. Half a lie. I talked. He listened. And now I cannot help but wonder if I came across like a raving lunatic, like the RMM broke me on day one.

Isabelle's murmuring to our father, something about how nice it is to visit California, when a knock on the door sounds. It's Bittner, already dressed in a pristine suit though he will be dining in one of the large tents I spied down the hill. "Your Highness, you requested to be notified twenty minutes prior to supper."

My father grunts as Isabelle straightens his tie. "Do you know who we're to dine with?"

It surprises me to hear him refer to us as a whole. Family style seating is not something I considered. Or am even used to nowadays.

"Lichtenstein and Norway," Bittner offers.

Ten minutes later, we descend the steps toward the pool. Tables covered in snowy white linen, candles, and fresh flowers adorn the patio surrounding the Roman colonnades that circle back to a Greco-Roman temple facade. The sun glows golden in the sky around us, reflecting against the turquoise waters of the pool, and I quietly muse over how the name our tour guide offered us earlier—*La Cuesta Encantada*, or the Enchanted Hill—is so perfectly apt for what is before me.

My father takes my arm. "Not so bad now, is it?"

Soft music from the early-to-mid twentieth century fills the space around us, and I am loath to admit he's right. But he is. In this moment, in this place, there is too much magic in the air to wallow fully in my resentment.

Thankfully, dinner itself isn't traumatic. There isn't too much chatter about the RMM, as this intro into the Decennial Summit is all about friends and colleagues reacquainting themselves. At least, that is my hope when my father spends most of his time discussing family matters and local politics with his fellow sovereigns at the table.

Right when the main course is placed before me, I spot the prince from the hallway at a table on the other side of the pool. He is with his mother, the Grand Duchess of Aiboland, an elegant woman whose poise and ability to masterfully enrapture crowds with her speeches has often sent my mother into jealous fits. He is also with a man I assume to be his brother, thanks to similar features. They are dining with the Swedish and Luxembourgian contingencies, and while his mother listens in rapt attention to the Grand Duke sitting at her side, Christian and his brother are far more reserved with the heirs and spares at their table.

I try not to stare, but goodness, if he isn't the most striking man present in a room full of handsome people. And I hate myself for allowing such a shallow opinion, because beauty is nothing, not when there are so many other traits for a person to be attracted to.

"What's captured your attention?"

I glance away from the enigmatic prince, back toward my sister. "Just having a look around to see who is here."

She nods knowingly. Her attention flits about meaningfully, too. Who present might be our (un)lucky future spouses? It's a nasty business, curiosity and bitterness mingling so closely together.

Neither the Norwegian or Lichtenstein heirs are present; all are safely married with children too young to yet go through the RMM. Rumor has it there is a Lichtenstein cousin upstairs somewhere, but he supposedly fell prey to the stomach flu on the flight over. There is a relief that it's just Isabelle and I alongside the sovereigns at the table. Small talk is all that is expected of us, which is fine by me.

It's maddening how my attention returns repeatedly to the future Grand Duke of Aiboland, though. Each time I take in his stiff countenance, the ugly words that fell out of my mouth ring in my ears.

He wasn't propositioning me at all. Distracted by his phone, and trapped in the same, slim corridor, he simply failed to take note of my presence until too late.

Articulate. Intelligent. Thoughtful. These are all words used by others to describe me, and hours after arriving, I allowed the RMM to wipe them clean away from my personality.

It just will not do. I must apologize to him.

CHAPTER 10

CHRISTIAN

The mercenary charade known as the RMM officially kicks into high gear shortly after an exquisite, gourmet dinner, as only a macabre event like this can: amidst glamour and ghastly intentions. The stars twinkle in the ombré sky, the sights around us are beyond compare, and light chatter and laughter float through the cool air. To an outsider, the scene I'm ensnared within would appear the event of the century. Nothing could be more glamorous than a gathering consisting entirely of royalty.

How wrong they would be.

We're all still gathered around the admittedly awe-inspiring Neptune pool that seamlessly meshes Hollywood opulence and Greco-Roman architecture and art. Lit up, like it is now, all hints of turquoise, shimmering liquid against the black velvet of the hilltop and the faint roar of waves nearby, it's mesmerizing. I don't consider myself romantic in the least, but I have enough common sense to admit it's a pretty damn perfect sight.

"One of the Brits says we're not allowed in unless some park ranger or the like is present." Lukas passes over a glass of champagne. "I guess California has its knickers in a bunch over that."

It's a pity. I sigh as I peer into the golden bubbles of my glass. "Couldn't you find anything stronger?"

He grimaces. "I'm working on it. For now, it's this or the She-Wolf's cognac."

I'll take champagne any day over the family swill. "Where is she, anyway?"

"Sucking the marrow out of some local children, no doubt," he mutters, and I chuckle, because it's quite within the realm of possibility.

He finishes his own glass within four quick gulps. "Let me correct that. She's most likely signing away our royal sperm."

One of the Jordanian princesses, chatting with a friend nearby, blanches at my brother's words before quickly moving away.

I shake my head, but he's in no way embarrassed at being caught discussing bodily fluids at a party. "It's a shame that matricide is illegal in the United States."

The lopsided grin that's charmed far too many women in Aiboland makes an appearance. "I say we risk it and immediately flee the country. How strong is our extradition treaty with Washington?"

Come to think of it, I can't think of a single instance in which somebody was extradited from Aiboland back to the United States. I'm about to tell him this when he hisses quietly, all humor dissipating without a trace. "Oh, fuck me now."

He doesn't need to explain his one-eighty. There's only one thing that brings this level of disgust out in my brother. And she's currently sashaying her way toward us in a slinky black dress better suited for someone at least forty years her junior.

"Don't you dare," I threaten.

But of course Lukas dares. He bolts in the opposite direction as smoothly as one can, abandoning me to face the one person who can bring us both to our knees.

When my mother reaches my side, she discharges what I can best describe as a happy yet entirely evil sigh. "It's a virtual buffet, isn't it?" And for at least the twentieth time tonight, I wonder why all of the other sexagenarians present managed to dress in modest yet elegant encrusted pieces surely meant to highlight their exalted statuses yet my mother chose something that emphasizes her desperation to hold onto youth.

I'm fully aware of what she's insinuating. Hell, it isn't even insinuation, not when nearly half of the words out of her mouth to Lukas or myself over the course of the day were vulgar comments about the women present. Still, I refuse to let her know just how much my skin is crawling. Why couldn't my mother be a feminist instead of a royal pimp? "Dinner was excellent."

The She-Wolf tut-tuts, reaching up to pat her coronet, as if it had somehow fallen off and sunk to the depths of the azure pool when she wasn't paying attention. As though she hasn't been completely on top of every single detail around her since she was three years old. "I wanted to get a good visual in person on the girl you're set to marry before I made up my mind, but she appears to possess hips large enough for decent birthings and I'm informed her menses are healthy."

I repress the familiar shudder inspired exclusively by her that threatens to emerge over this latest piece of information. It's nearly impossible to keep my fingers from curling into fists, or from howling in fury over how she'd actually gone through with her plans.

Bloody hell. I need more booze, and I need it now. It's obvious she wants me to inquire about whom she'd been talking to, which girl with hips wide enough to pop babies out has earned her seal of approval, no doubt so she can delight over my discomfort, but I refuse to give her that satisfaction. I might as well offer up my own marrow for her to suck up, alongside a straw. Besides, I already know, don't I? It's the damn Vattenguldian woman. So, I glance back out at the pool, pull in a long breath as I think of cheerful things, like sailing and good stout and strangling my mother until she can no longer speak on my behalf, or at least claim she can.

I'm going to kill Lukas for abandoning me to the She-Wolf like this. Has he no sense of filial loyalty? Speaking of . . . where's Parker? Employees have been encouraged to come tonight for the after dinner festivities.

A quick, discreet search shows him over by the dessert table. Lucky bastard.

It takes about two and a half minutes of stony yet polite nonsensical pleasantries that have nothing to do with her taunts before she accepts I won't play her game tonight and saunters away. Well, that and I track Lukas across the pool and promptly give up his location.

I love my brother, but it's every prince for himself right now.

When I'm in the clear, I make my way over to Parker and the dessert table, praying safety can be found amongst savory treats my mother would rather die than put into her body out of fear of a single ounce gained.

"Éclair?" Parker asks, passing over a pastry before I can even answer.

I'm tempted, but I wave it off in favor of more champagne.

"That bad, huh?" he asks sympathetically.

"If by bad, you mean she's already having discussions about my future marriage, then yes."

He lets out a low whistle. And it's then I see her, staring at me like I'm the most disgusting human to ever grace the planet. Or maybe more like she's sucking on lemons.

No, not the She-Wolf. It's the Valkyrie. I mean, the Hereditary Princess of Vattenguldia. Which is bloody ironic, right?

To quote my eloquent brother: "Oh, fuck me."

CHAPTER 11

ELSA

There he is, looking so *too* again.

The Hereditary Grand Duke of Aiboland is also looking right at me, which means I'm going to have to get on with the business at hand.

Truthfully, I would rather gnaw off my toes than go over there. And frankly, he appears as if I do head his way, he might be the one to gnaw his digits off, which I really cannot blame him for. If I could have my way, I would be upstairs working and not down here, dressed up like a Barbie doll princess ready to be swept off my feet by a plastic prince (or, at least, apologizing to one). But nobody asked what I wanted, so here I am, ready to lay myself bare for the sake of propriety.

Surely, my mother must be sacrificing lambs or calves or the whatnot back home on an hourly basis to ensure my proper behavior this week, because nothing else could explain the urge to set things right.

I allow myself a deep breath (or, rather, a tiny inhalation that nearly pops the seams of the beaded silver dress I'm wearing), throw my shoulders back, and stroll purposefully toward Prince Christian of Aiboland.

Heavens, why does he have to be so gorgeous?

Make that gorgeous and alarmed, because the instant he registers I am headed his direction, he is once more a deer trapped before a monster truck's headlights. Only, sweet Mother of God. Just as he gets an eyeful of me, I get one of him, too. Instead of wearing the button down and slacks from earlier, he is now clothed head to toe in one of the most delicious tuxedos I've had the pleasure of viewing, proving some people are simply meant for excellent clothes. It is crisp with clean lines, all dark and beautiful and clearly tailored for every inch of skin it touches. But, as perfect as this tux is, his dark hair isn't excessively stylized like so many of the other royals present. It is a bit mussed, not too long or too short, with a hint of wave curving the strands.

Men should not be allowed to be so lovely.

He hovers close to the dessert table, drinking champagne with a good-looking man I don't recognize. Brown hair, although not as dark as the prince's, brown eyes, tan skin, and a smart but standard tux. Not an heir, then, nor, to my recollection, a spare. Charitable thoughts toward this Prince Christian grudgingly roll in, because it is refreshing to find an influential man mingling with somebody who is not next in line, or even surrounded by a bevy of women ready to faint at every crisply uttered, accented word. All of this is maddening, because I do not desire such benevolent opinions forming. Charitable thoughts equal a weakness for my father to exploit. This prince has a younger brother, and younger brothers mean potential spouses, so no good can come of any of this.

Right after dinner was finished and his friends excused themselves from the table, my father informed my sister and me that he found "quality candidates who are of impeccable bloodlines," both of whom "seem to be healthy and well-endowed," and that I, in particular, ought to be prepared to meet the one he felt best suited to Vattenguldia's needs.

Three, thirteen, or thirty, one is never old enough to hear such words from their sire.

"What will you do?" Isabelle had whispered to me when our father left us to speak to the Saudi Arabian king.

I wished I had a clever or well-thought answer to offer, but I was floundering in panic. My only recourse was to make myself as undesirable a candidate as possible.

The point of all of this being: I am well aware that being overseen conversing with Christian is suicidal. His Serene Highness will view it as me leaving the door to his machinations cracked open. It's just, I also am keenly aware, now I have had a few hours between my actions and this moment, that I behaved abominably toward a fellow RMM-er. Common decency trumps self-preservation.

The fellow the Hereditary Grand Duke is with registers my approach with an amused glint in his eyes, which is unsettling. A step forward is taken alongside a proper bow. "Your Highness, I am Parker Laurant-Sinclair, His Highness' personal secretary. May I make your introduction?"

I nod graciously, as one of my station ought to do, rather than spit out brimstone and fire as I did earlier in the day.

"Princess Elsa, I am pleased to introduce you to His Royal Highness, the Hereditary Grand Duke Christian of Aiboland." I incline my head and Parker turns toward his employer. "Prince Christian, I am most pleased to introduce Her Royal Highness, the Hereditary Princess Elsa of Vattenguldia."

It is Christian's turn to bow; like this morning, it's perfectly executed. I am about to volley back a curtsey of my own when he extends a hand out. He wants to shake hands with me like we are, what, best mates? But my mother's ingrained manners win out again. I reluctantly shove my own hand forward until his fingers curl around mine and bring them up to his warm lips.

Oh. Sweet. Merciful. Heavens *above*. Christian clearly secretes hormones out of his skin, because I fight the good fight to quell the most tantalizing of nearly orgasmic chills threatening to overtake my body.

Kisses on hands should not *do* this. My irritation toward this man doubles.

"Your Highness." His words, murmured over my skin, set me ablaze. My heart beats too strongly, too quickly. He smells like a goddamn dream. "It is my pleasure to formally make your acquaintance."

There is no pleasure in his words, though. He's wary, which makes complete sense considering I went batshit crazy on him in the hallway earlier.

I extract my hand and steal a step backward, away from the sharp, clean smell of soap and man. What is happening right now? I'm not . . . This must cease. I am not a lovelorn little girl, constantly searching for her fairy story. I am not here to swoon, not even over this paragon of manly magnificence who not only secretes pheromones from his skin upon contact but apparently via airborne particles, too. "Look." Tartness colors my tone, but it cannot be helped, not even under burgeoning proper manners and shame over loss of self-control. "There is no need for you to act so bloody charming. Save it for someone whose knickers aren't bolted up for the night. There is no need to flirt, either. I've simply come to atone for my behavior this afternoon. I admit I might have overreacted." My head inclines toward the main house. "In the hallway. When we, uh, ran into each other. For that, I apologize."

For a long moment, amidst the clinking of glasses around us and light chatter and sweet music, Christian is slack-jawed in the face of my bluntness. Even Parker is acting as if two heads protrude from my neck. No matter. The Hereditary Grand Duke may take what I offered as he will. I pivot on a high heel at the same time as Christian blurts, "I wasn't proposing. Or propositioning you. Or whatever else it was you assumed I was doing."

I make the very poor mistake of focusing on his mouth as he says this to me. His lips are too perfect, shaped too much like those statues carved by the masters.

"Bloody hell, I don't even know you," he continues hotly. "Besides, you're to inherit your throne. Why would you ever think I would *propose* to you? Narcissistic much?"

This is enough to tear my focus from his delicious mouth back up to his eyes. He's outraged right now, in the middle of an elegant party, no longer attempting to hide behind required yet feigned civility. And this anger from him only piques my interest tenfold, because what kind of perfect man snarls at a woman in public?

Parker hisses in scandalized horror, "Your Highness!"

Apparently I am not the only royal with a language problem in public. Oddly, the similarity leaves me yearning to chortle.

Christian waves his secretary off as I battle to contain the grin desperate to tug my lips upward. No longer the paragon of perfection, not at least in temperament, I allow a few more charitable thoughts about this prince.

Unable to resist the perverse pleasure stemming from such repartee, I say smoothly, "You gave me a *look*. What else was I to think?"

My jab hits its bull's-eye, because Christian's eyes widen in comical dismay. "There was no look!" he barks.

Chortling, according to my mother, is vulgar and completely unattractive. It simply is not to be tolerated from the heir of the Vattenguldian throne. Nor am I allowed to laugh long and hard. I'm permitted polite, quiet mirth that is minimal at best. But goodness, if I don't want to laugh right now in the face of such exasperation, especially when champagne physically spurts out of Parker's nose.

Taking pity on Mr. Amused, I fetch a napkin from the buffet table. And still, I cannot help but volley another round. "There most definitely was a look."

Christian invades my personal space. "By look, you mean a polite acknowledgement of strangers alone in a hallway. If there was a look, that was it. Nothing more!"

Hot damn, outrage is a delectable look on this man. Unbidden images of him, righteous in his convictions as he talks to the Aibolandian Parliament, taunt me until I curse my newly tingling lady parts.

Stupid lady parts. They never think logically.

I cannot be attracted to him. I *cannot*. Attraction at first sight is a fairy story, not reality. Enjoying banter is one thing, but discovering a physical attraction is entirely different. Therefore, I force the foulest memory I possess to the forefront of my mind, of when I discovered my father mid-coitus with someone other than my mother. His Serene Highness was as nude as the day he was born; worse yet, wiry hair sprouted from his surprisingly tan arse.

Appeased at the burgeoning urge to escape to the loo and vomit out what little bit of dinner I managed to consume without popping seams, I offer Christian a, "You may think that."

But then my lady parts rally anew when a delightful flush steals up his neck. How is it possible that my father's hairy arse cheeks are not enough to overcome this man's charm? "As the looker," Christian says, once more crowding my personal space, "I can verify it was the only intent possible."

Hairy arse. Hairy *dimpled* arse. Hairy dimpled arse that rippled when (SHUDDER) my father shoved himself (SHUDDER) into that woman—from behind, no less. I force the scene to loop in my mind as my shoulders square, allowing myself a tiny, nauseated breath. "As I have no desire toward marrying anyone in this godforsaken place, let alone . . . doing anything else, such information is comforting." And then, wholly unable to resist a bit of cheekiness, "*Capiche?*"

His mouth opens. It is a dangerous mouth that offers far too many promises. "Noted, madam."

My father's arse fails me for the first time.

I must be ill, perhaps even with the flu plaguing the Lichtenstein cousin. I am warm and dizzy and clearly not in the right frame of mind, because sharp delight over how this prince isn't fawning surges through my bloodstream.

"Perhaps I ought to stress I have no desire in marrying anyone at the RMM, either, let alone . . . doing anything else." He mimics my cadences. "Present company included."

My mother would be utterly shamed, because I nearly burst out into genuine laughter. It arrives as a snort, but still. I quickly cover my mouth. Right before dinner, I overheard several ladies discussing what they would do to Prince Christian when, not if, they get him alone, and none of the suggestions were innocent. "Good luck with that."

"Meaning?"

"Meaning, if you escape the Summit with your bachelorhood or virginity intact, it will be a miracle. Besides, protests aside, you know as well as I that none of us have any say in the matter anyway."

He gapes at me once more. My lady parts find his astonishment adorable, which is intolerable. This man is a Hereditary Grand Duke. I am a Hereditary Princess. A match between the two of us is not an option, not even at the RMM. I must do something to shut this inappropriate attraction down once and for all. I inhale deeply and say, mentally cringing as I am patently aware of just how blatantly rude and awful this will sound, "You're not a virgin, are you?"

Gaping transitions to sputtering. Parker quickly excuses himself under the guise of finding more champagne.

Well, at least that makes one less person I must humiliate myself in front of, although I am certain the damage is long done. "It is all right if you are," I continue.

Christian stands so close now we share the same, toasty air from nearby heat lamps. "I am thirty years old."

I clearly overestimated him. Asking such a boorish question would send normal, polite folk running. But here this prince is, closer than ever, forcing me to desperately root around for another awful memory to combat his unwanted effect on me. Maybe that of Nils shagging my ex-BFF? It's a nice, angry memory that serves me well in times of need. Only, every breath is filled with Christian, and stars in the sky are twinkling. and my head is swimming, and my bloody lady parts are dancing and crying all at once.

I need someone to shake some sense into me right now. Charlotte would gladly do so if present; perhaps Isabelle will stand in her stead? Because this prince is not meant to be mine. Ever. Not that I would ever want him and all his *too*-ness, anyway. What a hassle it would be, being with a man far more attractive than one's self. Hell, he probably has a different woman for each day of the week. And that is not what I want or need. I would rather have nothing than something that isn't true.

I despise how judgmental I am being. How much I've allowed an attraction to warp my thoughts. I must be ill. I must.

This is unacceptable.

I swallow hard and, pleased my voice is level, say, "There are plenty of thirty-year old virgins. It is nothing to be ashamed of."

His head dips toward mine; dark, wavy hair falls into his eyes and all I can do is watch in utter fascination as an outraged breath sucks sharply into him. "Not that it is any of your business, but I am not a virgin."

Silence fights for space between us amidst the din of the party for nearly a full, agonizing, hot minute, during which we simply, warily study one another. I think I would gladly pay a million euros to know what he thinks right now.

Finally, his mouth opens. "And you?"

I somehow lost most of the air in my lungs once more. "What about me, sir?"

"Are *you* a virgin?"

I have to give it to him: that was well played and ballsy as all get out. "What an impertinent question. I ought to slap you."

I inappropriately wonder if women spank him often.

Christ, he's got a beautiful smirk. "You're avoiding."

I mimic his accent in a low voice. "I am twenty-eight years old."

"Surely there are plenty of twenty-eight year old virgins running amuck in the world."

Not at this party, they aren't. Despite the matrimonial nooses looming over every singleton's head, the sexual escapades planned for this week are already legion. It will be shag central at *La Cuesta Encantada* tonight—myself excluded, of course. "Would virgins be running amuck, though?"

He chuckles, and it is beautiful and unfair and infectious. I bet his mother doesn't tell him how undesirable it is to be seen and heard laughing.

I itch to take a step back but fear it would illustrate just how affected I am by this prince. Instead, my spine straightens while my chin lifts upward in order to coolly meet his gaze. "A lady never discusses such tawdry things."

"Virginal ones might not."

Oh, oh, I very much like how his amusement so easily manifests in his eyes. I murmur, "Do you know many of these mythical women?"

So much for Parker seeking out champagne—I accept a glass from a passing waiter; Christian does the same. "Mythical twenty-eight year old virgins who run amuck or ones who refuse to discuss sex?"

My shoulders lift and drop as I slowly sip the drink. Bubbles dance their way down my throat and into my stomach, leaving the muscles within to match the foxtrot beat spilling through the speakers.

"I know a lot of women," he tells me.

"I'm terribly shocked by this."

"Meaning?"

"Meaning exactly what I said before. There is no way you will make it through the week a bachelor. Your mother must have a lengthy list of requests for you already."

A loud noise sounds nearby; a tray clatters upon the ground. Christian's attention flits away as he traces the sound to scene, allowing me a few inconspicuous steps back.

On the other side of the pool, a waiter is upon his knees, red faced while sweeping broken glass up with napkins as the royals around him sniff in disdain for him daring to exhibit anything other than unimpeachable behavior in their presences.

"Poor sod," Christian says quietly. "How much do you want to bet he'll get sacked over this?"

There is no need to wager. The unfortunate man will most likely be escorted off the premise within the hour.

Christian's focus is once more on me. "Are you challenging me to a bet?"

I abhor gamblers, so this recent development is comforting to discover. It's utterly vile to make light of a man losing his job over something so trivial.

My scorn must be evident, because he quickly corrects, "No, not over the waiter. I'll have Parker look into that shortly and see what can be done to rectify the situation. I meant your claim concerning whether or not I escape the week as a bachelor. It sounded like you were challenging me to a bet."

Attractive *and* altruistic? Temper notwithstanding, he has returned to being simply too much *too* again in my opinion. Why is he even still here? How has my vulgarity not driven him away yet?

I swallow my pride and purposefully, meaningfully allow my eyes to drift lower. It is the wrong move, because images of this man naked flash throughout my mind. Wonderful. I strain to sound amused. "I am merely stating that men like you do not keep much in their pants."

That might have been a tad overkill, because I must toss my drink onto the nearby table in order to beat upon his back as he chokes on a gulp of champagne.

His secretary rematerializes, snatching the glass out of the prince's hand. "Chris! Are you okay?"

Christian stops coughing and jerks away from me. "I'm fine," he insists, careful to ensure our eyes don't meet. Then he quickly fills Parker in on the waiter situation.

Because I have lost my wits and do not wisely use this opportunity to flee like I ought, I ask, "You go by Chris?"

"It's an acceptable nickname for Christian." The owner of the name snatches his glass of champagne back, chugging the rest of the drink. Naturally, this promptly sets off another round of coughing.

Parker is now the one to smack Christian's back, and I am grateful because I most certainly do not need to be touching him again, even if in a life-saving gesture.

"Maybe so," I murmur as Christian, rapidly turning redder from what surely must be embarrassment more than alcohol down the wrong pipe, shoves his friend's hand away. "But it doesn't fit."

"If I might be so bold to ask, Your Highness, how so?" Parker inquires at the same time Christian wheezes, "What does *that* mean?"

I side skirt the men to claim a chocolate covered strawberry from the dessert table. "Chris is a boring name."

"I believe you've just issued an unforgiveable insult to all the Chrises in the world," Christian says flatly while Parker struggles to hold in his mirth.

"Of course I haven't. I simply said Chris is a boring name. Look at Elsa; it is a hopelessly old-fashioned name you find in old women who bake streusel. My parents aged me the moment I came out of the womb." I point the zebra-striped berry at my sparring partner. "Now that is unforgiveable. You were given a nice name and have elected to make it boring when it doesn't suit you one bit."

Too much silence expands between us; I am tricked into looking up at him once more. One of his dark eyebrows arches upward. "Are you saying you don't find me boring?"

Did I? Oh, bollocks. I *did*, didn't I? I clear my throat and smile winsomely. "Just because I don't wish to marry you doesn't mean I find you boring as a bag of rocks."

Both of his eyebrows shoot up, as if I informed him grass is blue and sky is green. As if he doesn't already know he's interesting. Please. Must I remind him of all the glossies dedicated to his comings and goings?

"When we were children, His Highness was teased quite a bit about his name," Parker tells me.

I toss the strawberry stem back onto the table; it's whisked up by a passing waiter in less than a second. "What! Why?"

"I'm named after a religion," Christian grinds out. "There was Prince Jew. Prince Muslim. Prince Buddhist. Prince Hindu. Prince Zoroastrian. There were lots of choices, you see."

Another moment I want nothing more than to just laugh and laugh. "How delightful. Now, those nicknames aren't boring. Sacrilegious, yes, but definitely not boring."

"You have a seed in your front teeth," is Christian's response.

"You are a veritable Prince Charming, publically pointing out women's flaws. How chivalrous of you."

It is annoying how much I like that he refuses to appear properly chastised.

I slowly, discretely lick across the enamel to search out the seed; and then, my eyes once more meet his amber ones, and I am dizzy and—

"There you are!"

—mortified. His Serene Highness materializes next to me, alongside a man. A man close to my age, to be precise. One I have seen in magazines and on the news. A royal man. A single, royal man, albeit one without a country thanks to his wealthy, powerful family being deposed years ago.

Oh, sweet baby Jesus, *no*. It has been less than twenty-four hours.

"It pleases me greatly to introduce you to Mathieu," my father is saying.

My mother's sacrifices and voodoo spells must truly be powerful, because there is no way I ever would have predicted my parents would select the Chambéry prince as the one to secure our line. It isn't that this man is bad to look at; in fact, he is quite handsome in a hipster sort of way, with his black-rimmed glasses, a skull-covered bowtie, and black Converse shoes accessorizing his unconventional velvet tux. But that is neither here nor there, because I am simply going to kill my father. Kill him and assume the throne at a young age.

Mathieu notices Christian and gives a small nod. His attention returning to me, he says, "Your Highness, I cannot tell you how pleased I am to meet you." A hand extends toward me; I reluctantly stick mine out and wait for him to kiss it, only he doesn't. He pumps it up and down, nearly crushing the bones beneath my skin.

My thoughts are uncharitable. *I wish I could say the same.* And also, *my father has finally lost his mind. Alzheimer's? Dementia, perhaps? The Cambérys?!* Out loud, I say graciously, "The pleasure is mine." Except, it most assuredly is not.

Whilst I envision my all too sudden ascension to the throne due to patricide, not to mention regicide, my father exclaims, "Aiboland! I've been on the hunt for you, as well."

I am impressed that, while offering His Serene Highness a polite bow, Christian shows no signs of panic. Because, surely he must know what just such a statement means here at the RMM.

"You've grown into quite a strapping young man. I don't think I've seen you since . . . hmm. You were probably still in nappies."

Only my father could utter something so disparaging and consider it a compliment. Christian handles it well, though, murmuring how pleased he is to renew their acquaintance.

Parker once more discreetly melts into the crowd.

My father is nowhere close to being done with the Hereditary Grand Duke, though. "I've had a nice talk with your mother just this afternoon—"

Alarm finally materializes in Christian's eyes.

"And I would very much like you to meet my daughter."

Ladies and gentlemen, Prince Gustav goes in for the kill in record time. Also, I have apparently been insulting my future brother-in-law, which is painfully, bitterly hilarious as I acted the fool and now I am to know him the rest of my life as family.

Christian inclines his head toward me. "I have had the pleasure of conversing with your daughter for the last half hour, sir."

Haha. Pleasure. Right.

"Not this one." My father shakes his finger. "My heir's off limits to you, as I'm sure you well know. No crown heirs are allowed to match."

Humiliation. Oh, so very much humiliation. And yet he offers an excellent reminder. Attraction or not, this is not to be.

"I meant Elsa's sister, Isabelle." He gestures into the distance, as if Christian is able to intuit precisely which woman on the other side of the pool is being singled out as a future wife. One who is already secretly engaged to her riding instructor back in Vattenguldia.

As Christian subtly attempts to extract himself from my father's clutches, Mathieu steps into my line of sight. "I've heard quite a bit about the enigmatic Elsa of Vattenguldia today."

"That sounds so sinister." I lower my voice to match his. "*I've heard things about you.* Shall I prepare myself to be blackmailed?"

He flinches in what appears to be genuine shock. But then he laughs, albeit a tad bitterly.

What an odd yet curious response.

His voice is strained. "Are there things you can easily be blackmailed for?"

My father is now steering Christian across the courtyard toward Isabelle. I send silent wishes for luck; the Hereditary Grand Duke is going to need them. "I most certainly would not admit them to you if there were."

"Blackmail is a nasty business, isn't it?"

I can't quite interpret the look in his eyes. They are not so free with emotions as Christian's are. "Prince Mathieu—"

"Please call me Mat." Bitterness fades into wryness. "Any time I hear Mathieu, my governess's voice comes to mind, reminding me of some transgression I'd just committed. And believe me, there were plenty to be reminded of."

"All right. Mat." I smile in return to try and offset what I'm about to say. "Let me be honest with you. I am no fan of the secondary objectives of the Decennial Summit."

Surprise, hesitation, and then amusement crinkle the corners of his eyes. "Is that so?"

"I'm afraid so."

Head tilted to the side, he tsks. "You don't sound so sure, Your Highness. *I'm afraid so?* Own your disdain of the RMM, if that's how you truly feel."

Interesting. Even more interesting—or perhaps, reassuring—is how our banter inspires no fevered feelings within.

"If it's any consolation, I'm not here to sweep you off your feet." He's quiet, though. Hesitant.

And yet I am skeptical. "Is that so?"

"Your father seemed . . ." His attention briefly shoots across the pool at the person in question. "I don't want to say desperate, because that would be disrespectful toward you and he, as in these short minutes we've known one another I highly doubt anyone could ever dub you desperate about anything, but Prince Gustav was most certainly determined I not deny him the pleasure of an introduction."

"Determined is such a kind way of putting it." I trace his line of sight and watch my father repeatedly slapping my chagrined sister and her freshly robotic intended so hard on their backs that it's a miracle they don't topple over onto one another and shag like bunnies right out in the open as he probably wishes.

"His Serene Highness is nothing if not tenacious."

"Another bit of diplomacy," I tell the man next to me.

He tugs at one side of his bow tie. "Don't let the skulls fool you. I can be as much a smooth talker as the next."

"Unfortunately, my sovereign doesn't share my view of the RMM." And hopefully his? I move to get another chocolate covered strawberry, but the fear of seeded teeth ultimately keeps my fingers away. "I imagine it comes from being the head of a constitutional principality that just so happens to be a microstate, too. He wants to be useful. Have some kind of historical impact in a world filled with industrial super powers."

Mat signals one of the waiters for a drink. "He views setting up his children as a way to do that?"

"Don't your parents feel the same way?"

His newly acquired glass rises in a bizarrely grim toast but he doesn't say anything further on the matter. For several awkward seconds, his attention leaves me and settles in the distance. Which is absolutely fine by me.

Right before I excuse myself, he asks, "Do you think your sister will fall for Aiboland's charms?"

Of course she'll fall for his bloody charms. I did, didn't I? He's Prince Charming, after all. "I believe I just got whiplash from the change of subjects."

Another silent toast in my favor.

"To answer you, though, I'm sure Isabelle has already identified escape routes. She's no more interested in being auctioned off than I am."

Mat nods in their direction. "Perhaps she decided otherwise?"

I glance back over to where Isabelle is standing with Christian. Our father is no longer present, which means—

Wait. My sister is actually conversing, and while I can tell she is not exactly what I would dub comfortable, there is genuine determination filling her face as she looks up at the Aibolandian prince. Worse, she breaks decorum and touches his arm while she talks to him.

Oh, hell no. My sister is not going to give into the RMM so easily, not when her happiness resides back in Vattenguldia with a dimwitted riding instructor. "Sonofabitch!"

Mat asks dryly, "Am I to take it you're not one of Christian's groupies?"

"*No.*" Shite. That sounded vicious. I allow, with less vehemence, "Most definitely not." Like that man needs more groupies in his life. With all his too-ness, he probably has more than one could ever count.

"From the way you two were talking when I came over here, I would have guessed you were . . ." A lopsided smile slides my way. "Close."

"We—" There is no *we* between Christian and myself, just like I pray there will never be a we with this man in front of me. "He and I met today, which makes us acquaintances at best."

One of Mat's fingers taps against the rim of his glass. And then, with a very straight face, "Not my groupie then, either?"

"Alas, I am not." I sigh dramatically. "I hope that does not crush your delicate feelings."

He sniffs, a finger pretending to swipe away tears.

A reluctant bubble of amusement escapes me.

"Actually, I'm surprised you and Christian haven't met before. Your countries are in such proximity I'd have assumed you two practically grew up together. In nappies, no less."

Oh, haha. "Boarding school is a fantastic way to hide royals from one another. What about you? Do you know him? I thought I saw one of those bro nods when you came over."

"Bro nod?"

I lift my chin quick and short, and he chuckles.

"We resided in America for awhile at the same time and socialized here and there. He's a good guy, if that's what you're worrying about. Not the kind who'd normally go out of his way to seduce stray princesses into marriage. Or sisters." His glass lifts toward his lips. "Although, I suppose it doesn't really matter what his intentions are or not, does it? Not at the RMM, at least."

Isabelle's tight yet giggly laughter, so often admonished by our mother, floats across the pool and into my ears, all nails on a chalkboard. As she's also been inducted in the *laughter is not the best medicine* frame of mind, my curiosity burns like wildfire. What could my sister and that man possibly be talking about? I say quietly, "I don't think any of our intentions are of concern."

Mat's lips press together as he inclines his head in agreement.

"So you're honestly not willingly here to bag yourself a princess?"

"I think," he says, more gravity in these words than any uttered between us so far, "that the RMM is an antiquated, abhorrent notion that nobody in the twenty-first century even ought to consider to entertain. My affection and loyalties should not be arranged by parents, no matter what they might otherwise believe."

It's my turn to toast him. "Hear, hear. Welcome to the rebel alliance, Mat."

CHAPTER 12

CHRISTIAN

All I want to do is go to bed, even if it's in a room shared with the She-Wolf and Lukas. Instead, I'm trapped in the midst of another monarch's snare, pretending I find Isabelle interesting as she talks about . . . well, hell. I actually don't know what she's talking about. I guess I ought to listen for a moment.

Horses. She's talking about horses. She might as well be talking about topsoil, I'm so fucking disinterested.

It's not as if she's uneasy on the eyes. She's pleasant in a bland, royal way that we're all trained to be. I assume she's accomplished, too, or at least it sounded like she might be from the litany of achievements her father bombarded me with as she stood there like a statue. It's just, there isn't the sharp strike of match to petrol between us, no burning flash of attraction that could ever make me reconsider my stance on willingly leaving the Summit a free man. It makes me sound like an arsehole, but all I feel around her is boredom.

The sound of a throat clearing sharpens my focus, only to find Isabelle waiting expectantly. Bloody hell. She's asked me something, hasn't she? I search her face for some kind of clue, but I've got nothing. Is she still talking about horses? I know next to nothing about equines, nor do I care to know much.

When the silence stretches too far, she prompts tightly, "Do you ride?"

"We have a few Arabians stabled in Norsloe, but as I've been out of the country so often these last few years, I haven't had much time to ride them."

That's being generous. I can't even think of the last time I went to the stables. Those horses are my father's, not mine.

Isabelle's eyes narrow, like she can't imagine a world in which there's a person who doesn't drool over the beasts like she does. "Do you play polo?"

Shite, no. Not if I can help it, at least. The last time I did, back when I lived in England, I was unseated and had a goose egg on my head for weeks. "I enjoy tennis quite a bit."

The lines around her mouth tighten, like I've slaughtered a puppy in front of her. Or perhaps, in her case, a foal. What the hell is wrong with tennis?

So I add, "And sailing."

Somehow, that's an even worse answer. "While I was in the states, I played a bit of hockey—"

The lines ease just a fraction. "Field hockey?"

"Uh, no. Ice."

She holds a hand to her mouth and discreetly gasps (or is it gags?), like some delicate woman prone to the vapors in Victorian England. It's either an act, or Isabelle is nothing like her sister, because I cannot imagine Elsa ever swooning, let alone pretending to do so.

They look a bit alike, with the same dark hair and pale skin, but Isabelle strikes me as much more refined than Elsa. Not that Elsa isn't—despite what I've seen, I'm sure she must be, considering her upbringing. It's just, Elsa is willing to speak her mind, as exasperating as it may be. She had the stones to say things I've never heard another princess say before. I mean, asking me about whether or not I was a virgin? At a party filled with our peers? Oddly refreshing, even if I was taken aback by it.

Yet now I'm stuck listening to horse and weather talk. I'm officially, completely, mind-numbingly bored as all hell. I promptly tune Isabelle out once more during her speech on the horror stories she's heard about ice hockey players.

But then another pointed clearing of the throat forces my attention back. Bollocks. I've missed yet another question of hers. "My apologies. Would you mind repeating that?"

Annoyance flickers across her pale face. "I was asking if you know Prince Mathieu."

My eyes swim across the waters separating us to the dessert table Elsa and Mat are still guarding. For having just been set up, they aren't too close together, but then, that's not Mat's style. *She* isn't Mat's style, so it's a bit surprising my old friend willingly allowed himself to be dragged over by Prince Gustav for an introduction.

Last I'd heard, Mat had been quietly dating the same girl for years now. Their meeting had all the makings of a saccharine movie: the Savoy prince and the American met at a coffee shop when she dropped her wallet and he picked it up. I like her, though. While often quiet, Kim has a good head on her shoulders and, at last report, was in her medical residency at a hospital on the East Coast. Despite their stark differences, the pair always made sense to me.

Elsa isn't Kim. So why is he still talking to the Vattenguldian heir? Could it be that this is one of the RMM's grotesque matches? Could he really be willing to throw over Kim in the name of his parents' whims?

I pity the man. I pity Elsa. Damn, it's embarrassing as all hell, but I pity myself right now.

I tell Isabelle, "Yes."

She clearly expects more, because silence fills the space between us. So I add, "He's a decent bloke."

Christ. She's still waiting. What else does she need to know?

"I hope he doesn't assume my sister will readily fall into his arms," she murmurs, watching the same scene I'm annoyingly unable to tear my eyes away from. "Although, they make a striking couple, don't they?"

No. As a matter of fact, they don't. Not even in the smallest—

Wait.

Why do I even care?

"My apologies," I say again. "But I must excuse myself."

She probably thinks I need to go take a piss. I let her think this, not caring one whit about propriety or decorum. I've got to get the hell away from the RMM as fast as I can. It's messing with my head.

Because I most definitely did not like the thought of Mat and Elsa together. And I have no bloody reason to feel that way. None at all.

The RMM has already begun its mind-fucking.

CHAPTER 13

ELSA

My father is sawing logs like a lumberjack desperate to win a contest; Isabelle comes in a close second in her attempts to keep pace with him. I have descended fully into purgatory as slumber gleefully abandons me.

Sometime around three in the morning, I throw on a sweater and jeans and escape the room I share with my family. I weave my way through the eerily still castle until I locate the kitchen. I'm desperate for alcohol to drown me in sleep but am ready to down a glass of warm milk instead. Not wishing to alert anyone to my late night wanderings, I bypass flipping on the lights in favor of the soft light of my cell phone.

I've just opened one of the old fashioned, wooden refrigerators decorating the kitchen when a voice inquires, "Are you running amuck through the castle in the middle of the night, Princess?"

There is a delectable British accent coming from somewhere behind me.

I slowly turn around in the darkened kitchen to find, in the faint beam of my cell's light, the Hereditary Grand Duke of Aiboland propped against one of the stainless steel islands, a mug and a small plate of éclairs in front of him. He is wearing jeans and a hooded sweatshirt bearing his country's military logo, looking a far cry different than the elegant man who nearly choked to death in front of me earlier tonight.

I like this look on him, though. Nearly as much as the other.

"It appears I am not the only one. What brings you to the kitchen so late at night?" Which is stupid to ask, as it is patently obvious as to what he's doing, but lack of sleep doesn't necessarily make allowances for witty observations.

Christian pushes one of the éclairs around on his plate before sliding his cell phone over from where it sat just inches away. He switches the flashlight on and tilts the screen so the island is illuminated. "I couldn't sleep." And then, with a rueful smirk, "The Grand Duchess snores like you can't believe."

There is no way to hold back the grin tugging at my lips. "I have just escaped my father doing the same." I take pity on Isabelle, though. If he truly is the man she is to be matched to, he'll discover this fun fact on his own soon enough.

"And you thought you'd find solace in the kitchen?"

"Have you not done the same?"

He chuckles. "I denied myself the éclairs earlier and then resolved, as I stared up at the ceiling for a good hour, that life is too short to not indulge in things that bring about small joys."

I wander over to the island, positioning myself on the opposite side. "Éclairs bring you such?"

His grin grows. "Hell yeah, they do. Want one?"

Three éclairs rest upon his plate. "Will it bring *me* joy?"

"Have you ever eaten an éclair in the middle of the night, Els?"

I blink at the nickname he bestows upon me. No one has ever called me Els. Not a single person. It's bizarre, because one would think such a derivative would be natural, but Her Serene Highness was strict about such things during my childhood. My name is Elsa. I ought to be called Elsa. Nicknames are common, and she claimed she wanted more for me.

Whatever that meant.

Despite our earlier conversation concerning his own, though, I happen to like nicknames. "As a matter of fact," I say, absurdly pleased at the bestowment, "I have not."

"Then this shall be a first for you." He shoves the plate my way. "Don't worry. Éclairs eaten in the middle of the night have no calories. If they did, I'd be at least five pounds heavier already."

It is impossible to not grin like a fool. Are we really standing here in the kitchen, in the dead of night, sparring with one another again? And why is it so bloody entertaining? *Small joys, indeed.* "Is that so? Well then. This will be more than just a first for eating an éclair in the middle of the night. It will be my first time consuming a calorie free dessert, too. Who knew such things existed?"

"Shall I make you some warm milk, too?"

I blink again, abruptly unsteady.

"You were rooting around in the fridge for milk to heat up, weren't you?" He motions to his own mug. "As it helps with snoring parents?"

I counter with, "Why were you sitting here in the dark?"

"I'd had my cell's flashlight on, but switched it off when noises sounded outside the door. I suppose I wasn't too keen on being caught rummaging around the kitchen in the middle of the night." He touches the ceramic in front of him once more. "Yes or no?"

I gingerly select one of the éclairs, shivering at its coldness. "Actually, yes. I would very much like that. Do you know how to heat up milk?"

The room may be dim, but there's no mistaking the comical yet wounded look he proffers. "Everyone knows how to do that."

"Not everyone. There are surely milk virgins in the world."

He wanders over to the fridge and extracts a carton of milk. "Rest assured, I am no milk virgin. I'm thirty, remember?"

It is my turn to nearly choke as I swallow a far too large bite of éclair.

"No choking allowed. If four a.m. rolls around, the calories will come back."

I clear my throat. "Is three a.m. a magical hour, then?"

He heads over toward the stovetop, where a small pan rests upon another stainless steel countertop. I angle our phones' flashlights his way; shadows crawl around his body as a blue flame erupts from a burner, allowing me to ogle silently at a well-shaped arse. Goodness. Will his too-ness ever cease?

"As a matter of fact, it is. All the best firsts should be experienced at three a.m." He sets the pan on the stove and adds milk. "But it's a witching hour. The magic only lasts for sixty minutes before turning ordinary once more."

With the next bite of éclair, pleasure bursts across my tongue. Curse him for being spot on about pastry-based joy.

In the dim light of our cells, I watch as Christian heats the milk up, marveling at how, just hours before, I was raving at this man in a hallway. And now here we are, clandestinely taking over an unfamiliar kitchen in the dark hours of a sleepless night, and we are chatting easily, and I'm relishing this moment of reprieve.

Life is funny like that.

Minutes later, he brings me a mug filled with steaming milk. "I wasn't able to find any cocoa, or I would have offered you that."

I curl my fingers around the warmth, glancing up at his countenance in the shadowy, artificial light. "I would not have pegged you as one for hot cocoa."

"When I was a lad, my governess used to make it for me whenever I had nightmares. I don't drink it often nowadays, but it's still a comfort of sorts."

I sip the warm milk, reveling in how the day's tension continues to ease from my muscles. "Did you have a nightmare tonight?"

"I think any child over the age of twenty, forced to sleep in the same room as a snoring parent, is in the midst of a nightmare." His head cocks to the side, his smile fading just a bit. "Or, any sane adult trapped at the bloody RMM."

His scorn is genuine, matching mine in vehemence.

Whether I am ready for them to do so or not, all of my earlier resentments melt away. Fine. He is not what I thought. And I've behaved abominably toward him, when it turns out he is just as resentful about this farce as I am. Maybe it's the milk talking, but I no longer wish to resist this prince. Maybe, just maybe, when I was a little girl, wishing for a kindred spirit, I pegged this fellow correctly. So, I take a deep breath and extend my mug. He's surprised, but doesn't hesitate to pick his up, too. Ceramic clinks ring softly in the darkness of the kitchen.

"Maybe," I say hesitantly, unsure if I ought to be voicing such things, "if we both have nightmares at the same time again, we can hunt down that chocolate and I'll make us some cocoa."

He stares at me for a long moment, his eyes inscrutable for once in the shadows of darkness and poor lighting. "Not a hot cocoa virgin then?"

My staged whisper is mocking. "I am twenty-eight years old!"

An easy grin reappears. "I've never had a princess make me hot cocoa before."

"I've never drank it with a prince before, either."

He chuckles quietly. It is a wonderful sound, one that raises goose bumps along my arms, underneath the cashmere of my sleeves. "Then that will be another series of firsts for us."

I take another sip of milk. "That sounds like a club. The Royal First Club, or the RFC."

The weight of his eyes settle upon me once more, and I feel foolish for uttering such a silly, presumptuous thing. But then he releases that perfect exhale of amusement again. "Let us be the founding members of this RFC. And as such, I issue you a challenge: outside of tonight's milk and éclairs, we each must determine three more firsts to experience during three a.m. over the course of the week before we leave."

If I did not know better, I might admit the muscle in my chest skips a beat at such a thought. "If we are running amuck at three a.m. each night, you and I shall be terribly tired during all of our meetings."

"I've got a confession for you, Els. I'm fairly confident I'll be tired during them anyway. Have you had a look at the itinerary for heirs yet? It's boring as all sod. We'll be keen to nap during those hours anyway."

He called me Els again. Prince Charming has officially charmed me—at least tonight, at least in this kitchen. "I accept your challenge."

Skipped beats transitions to sprinting when the corners of his lips tick upward. "You have until cocktails after dinner tonight to suggest another first. I'll suggest one, too. And then we'll decide, together, which of our firsts to cross off our lists. Or perhaps even do both."

Together.

I have been drinking milk, but there is peanut butter in my throat. What am I doing? I ought to turn around and walk away, but when he sticks out his hand, mine goes out, too. And like before, his lips meet the back of my knuckles for the smallest of orgasmic moments.

"All the best deals are sealed with a kiss," he says lightly.

I am a bloody idiot.

CHAPTER 14

ELSA

I am cranky and in possession of dark bags beneath my eyes that no amount of cream and makeup can conceal the next morning. Or rather, later the same morning. Once I returned to my room, Isabelle and my father were snoring louder than ever. The milk helped, but Christian did not. That sexy accent of his haunted what precious few dreams I had.

"You look terrible," Isabelle helpfully confirms as we make our way to breakfast. Our father ran into a friend in the hallway and sent us ahead. Nothing makes a woman feel more childish than being escorted by a parent. And as such, I am not heartbroken in the least over his absence.

My smile is in no way joyful. "How lucky that I can always count on you for the brutal truth." Perhaps I ought to point out she is exquisite as always right now. Of course, she did not have to listen to the deafening noises she and my father were making last night, either.

"I saw you talking with Mathieu last night."

"We spoke," I confirm.

"And?"

"We snuck out of the party and made rabid, passionate love behind one of the palm trees. I am pregnant, and we decided to name the baby Raffaello, move to Italy, buy a villa, and cultivate an olive grove so we can press our own bottles of oil. Our tagline will have something to do with having the most royal of all olive oils. He and I will rusticate happily in the countryside whilst you assume the throne in Vattenguldia."

Her pink tinged lips thin considerably. "That is not even remotely funny."

For all her royal aspirations, sovereign is most definitely not one of my sister's most cherished wishes. "Honestly, Isabelle. What do you think happened? We spoke. He was surprisingly decent, but if you're asking if it was love at first sight, I am not sorry to disappoint. That aside, I believe I've found myself a new friend to wade through the week's trenches with."

It's not exactly a lie, but I am relieved she does not press me for a name, or realize I am now referring to a different man. How awkward would it be to admit I'm on friendly terms with her future husband? Or, worse yet, making plans to hang out with him in the dead of night?

"I overheard Father on the phone with Mother last night. Mathieu is definitely their target for you, Elsa."

Fantastic. "He seems as enthused by the prospect as I am."

She says quietly, bitterness crisping the edges of each of her words, "As we all are. His Serene Highness introduced me to a virtual Neanderthal last night."

I nearly trip on the stairs at such a description. Prince Charming was anything less than charming? Impossible. His too-ness would never allow it.

Isabelle continues, "He is quite good looking, even if he dresses like a panhandler."

At first, I'm startled. Christian, a panhandler? But then I realize my sister has switched subjects and is once more referring to Mathieu . . . who still does not resemble what she's insinuating. "Have you actually ever seen one? Mat is a far cry from that. If anything, he is a hipster. I wouldn't be surprised if he is secretly a music snob." I bump my shoulder against hers. "Also, he was wearing a tuxedo last night. How many panhandlers do you think dress in couture?"

She counters with, "It was velvet. And he was wearing tennis shoes."

I literally clutch the pearls around my neck. "Let us take him out back and put him down before it's too late."

She is quiet for a long moment. "The Hereditary Grand Duke of Aiboland plays tennis."

I clutch the pearls tighter. "Shite, Isabelle! What is this world coming to?" And then, as her mouth turns down, "Please tell me you did not discuss sports last night."

Or at least any that my highly opinionated sister does not approve of, which are all but those dealing with equines.

Dark, curling hair is smoothed behind her ears. "We also spoke of horses."

I have never been more pleased to not be part of a conversation before. And it delights me to know Christian must like horses, because at least now there's something to disapprove of. Horses smell. I am a failure of a princess to believe that, but it's the truth, nonetheless. "Somehow you got onto tennis after talking about horses?"

Her voice drops to a disapproving whisper, soft yet grating against the staircase we descend. "He mentioned he played ice hockey. It's as I said. That man is a Neanderthal."

And he cooks warm milk and offers unsuspecting princesses éclairs in the dead of night. Is he trying out for Man of the Year? Bloody Prince Charming. How did she not fall prey to his charms? Neanderthal, indeed. "Why are you whispering?"

Her nostrils flare. "What if those aren't his real teeth?"

I don't bother informing her I initially wondered if they were capped, too.

According to the welcome packet received upon arrival, morning meals at the Castle are served buffet style in a large dining room that resembles a medieval monastery that found itself in the middle of an American ranch. A long wooden table and antique padded chairs and benches line the bulk of the richly decorated room, the seats filled with chatting royals. Music from the 1930s discreetly pipes through hidden speakers, and as I take it and all the flags lining the ornate ceiling in, I marvel at how time travel is so perfectly desirable here in this house and utterly mundane in my own. How delightful Hearst Castle must have been in its heyday, filled with glamorous movie stars and America's elite. I can almost feel the ghosts of the past brushing my arms, beguiling me to discover their secrets.

"Look at this." Isabelle motions toward a large sign posted on an easel near the doorway. It reads: *Hearst Castle is a historic site, a museum, and part of California's State Park system. You are financially responsible for any damage you cause.*

She passes me a plate. "A house can be a park?"

"More likely the land it sits upon. Didn't you read up on its history before we came?" I should talk, though. My research was cursory at best.

"I didn't have time." Isabelle allows herself an apple and a cup of coffee. "I find it insulting they would believe we are slovenly enough to trash the furniture. We reside in genuine castles and palaces, most of them with antiques far older and more precious than these."

"Careful, sister," I warn lightly. "You sound like the biggest snob in a room packed to the gills with the world's most prolific elitists."

To prove my point, she issues a condescending sniff of displeasure. But then, all the bitchiness on her face dissipates into stark resignation.

"There's Christian. I suppose we ought to sit with him."

"What a ringing endorsement. You *suppose*."

The lines around her mouth grow more pronounced.

"What would Alfons think?" I tease, following the line of sight my sister motions toward with her elbow. Christian, the man he ate dinner with, and Parker are sitting next to and across from one another at the end of the table, sipping coffee.

Dammit. Even in the morning, Christian and his *too*-ness are impossible to escape. Because he really is alluring, with his sleeves rolled up to his forearms and the sun dancing in streaks of blinding light across his wavy hair as he chats with the fellows he is with. And he's wearing those jeans again.

Neanderthal, indeed.

If only he'd had an ugly personality to go with such a visage.

"I don't want to talk about Alfons." And then, remembering the last time she said—nay, snapped—this, Isabelle adds, "Please, Elsa."

There's that statement again. My sister's smile turns wan, tripping warning signals that urge: *caution ahead; proceed at own risk*. Propriety dictates I ought to respect such a wish, but the sister in me simply cannot ignore the pain in my only sibling's eyes. "Is everything all right between you two?"

Dark hair, so very like my own, whispers from side-to-side in a quick jerk. Wan transitions to wobbly.

When had this happened? Just last week, I endured yet another one of Isabelle's quietly voiced convictions over how certain she was that Alfons was her soul mate. Granted, this was not new, but she had been particularly vehement in her faith of their happy ending together. Naturally, I urged caution—and support, despite her beau being as interesting as a wet paper bag (and, if I am honest, about as smart as one, too). But Alfons appears to possess a good heart and certainly fails to strike me as a gold digger out to snatch himself a free ride for life. Did my normally cautious sister jump the gun by becoming engaged to her riding instructor after knowing one another all of a year? Most definitely. But Isabelle was always so happy with Alfons—and happy is something we desperately chase when so much of our lives are dedicated toward ensuring the emotion for others. How did she go from blissfully in love to willing to refuse standing up against the RMM in such a tiny span of time? Or at least not rock the boat?

I murmur her name, but a sharp shake of head plus another jab in the ribs quickly stops any further comments. Then she is off, striding across the room toward her assumed intended, her features perfectly schooled so there will be no further hidden demons betrayed. I know better, though. She would normally never let her guard down in public, so for her to allow me to witness such a fleeting moment means at least one heart must be bruised and possibly crushed. And that is a hard realization for a sister, knowing all at once something horrible has rocked Isabelle's existence and accepting there is nothing to be done other than simply be a leg of support, if that's even what she requires from me.

I am about to follow when I hear, "Ah, there you are, Elsa."

My father stands behind me, a cup of steaming coffee in his hands.

"Your mother rang a few minutes ago. She was most displeased she was unable to touch base with you this morning."

"I fear I must have left my mobile set to vibrate." It is a lie—I sent the call straight to voicemail. I have had neither enough sleep nor coffee for such a conversation.

He grunts, probably wishing he had done the same. "You're to ring her after your meeting this morning. Have your sister join in—it will be easier that way. She wishes to discuss some important matters with the both of you."

Irritation flares at the same time my stomach sinks.

"I'm off to go chat with the MC before the day kicks off, and then I have a quick meeting with the Nordic Council," he tells me, "but I wanted to catch you up to speed on a few crucial matters." He glances over my shoulder. "Isabelle are Aiboland are a union I'm keen to support, Elsa."

So it is official, whether my sister wants it or not.

"If she asks your opinion on whether or not you think she and Aiboland are a good match, I know I can count on you to do what's best for the family and Vattenguldia, hm? Relations between our countries have been distanced for far too long."

If we were behind closed doors, I might just tell him my actual opinion, but as we are out in the open, surrounded by peers, I simply incline my head. But, yeah. Not going to happen. Nor will it happen when my mother pushes the topic later today.

"You spoke to him last night. Do you think his acquiescence will be a problem?"

My legs feel as if they've turned to wood. "Are you inquiring if I believe the Hereditary Grand Duke of Aiboland is an eager participant of the RMM?"

My father chuckles good-naturedly, as if he knows it matters not one bit whether or not Christian is—or any of us are, for that matter. "I have no doubt that that boy will do what's best for his country." He takes my arm and steers me just outside the door. "The Grand Duchess is just as keen for this match as I am."

Now that we are out of view, I say, "Boy? He is older than me."

This only brings forth an affectionate pat on my shoulder. "If necessary, encourage him to see your sister and Vattenguldia in a positive light. I'm sure that won't be hard for you, not if you wish for what's best for our people."

One does not roll their eyes before their monarch, not even when the sovereign is their parent. But goodness, if it isn't difficult to repress the action.

My father sips his coffee, watching me carefully. "I have arranged for you to have tea with Mathieu after your meeting today. It is best you spend some time each day acquainting yourself with him. Remember, we have only until Friday."

Somebody must have come up behind me and clocked me on the head with one of those enormous Acme hammers, because surely, His Serene Highness did not just say what I fear he did.

Did he?

I have never prayed so hard to be hallucinating. Here I was, feeling sorry for Isabelle and Christian, when my own demons are here to roost.

"Your mother and I had several productive conversations with his parents over the last few weeks, and we feel quite certain that you two will get along smashingly," my father continues, oblivious to how he ripped the ground out from beneath my wooden feet. "Mathieu is an intelligent boy. Full of strong opinions." He playfully clucks me under the chin, only the seriousness lining his face and coating his words betray any lightheartedness of the moment. "Sound familiar?"

Weeks? He's been wrangling a deal for my hand in an archaic arranged marriage for *weeks?*

Somebody calls my father's name. "Inform Isabelle she's to meet Aiboland for tea this afternoon, as well. Do your duty, Elsa."

Once he departs, I want to dig out my phone and check the calendar, just to ensure we're in the twenty-first century and not the Middle Ages.

"May I be of assistance, Your Highness?"

I blink and find a server standing in front of me, his tux impeccable for such an early hour. I offer my royal smile: calm and collected as I will be damned if I show anyone within the next room just how shaken I am. "I am heading in for breakfast."

He props the door open for me; I force my feet to uproot and deliver me back into the dining room. Isabelle has, to my surprise, been detained by one of the Monégasque girls and is just now heading to where Christian is.

The moment they notice her approach, the trio of men stand up. Christian cannot let go of his manners for two seconds, can he? You would assume, in a room filled entirely with royalty, we could all let our hair down and not give into restrictive roles such as standing up simply because a lady arrives at a table.

Christian wasn't so chivalrous last night. Fine, that's a lie. He was. He made me warm milk, for goodness' sake.

At the thought of Prince Charming cooking for me, my idiotic heart stutters within my ribs.

"Mind if we join you?" Isabelle is all cool elegance, one of her patented, coquettish slips of a smile attempting to shine through, only to come across as more of a grimace than the flirting she undoubtedly strove for.

Before I can tug her away to press the issue from before, those too fascinating amber eyes of Christian's leave my sister's face to settle on me. Like some ridiculous stereotype, when our visions meet, the breath in my lungs magically disappears until I do not know if I'm actually even on the planet anymore, because surely all of the oxygen is gone. And it is outrageous, because stuff such as this— reactions to someone simply making eye contact—do not exist in reality, even in one as extraordinary as mine.

I am clearly exhausted from lack of sleep, or actually falling prey to the flu I feared last night, because there is no other rational explanation as to why I'm lightheaded.

Thankfully, he glances back at my awaiting sister. "It would be our pleasure." He offers her a smile in return, yet it is radically different than last night's sunny dazzler that lit up a dark kitchen. This morning's is closed-lipped; worse, it doesn't reach his eyes.

I don't think I like this smile at all. Not on him, not like this. But he proves his Prince Charming moniker is well deserved, because Christian graciously pulls my sister's chair out for her. In return, she promptly slams her plate against the table. Is our mother having a stroke somewhere? She's clearly slacking on her spells to enforce proper behavior in the both of us, that's for certain. Because this is not my sister's normal behavior. She is a tough cookie, but normally polite beyond measure. I know this is a hellish experience, but of the two of us, my money was on her to act decently. First the pathetic attempts at flirting, and now plate slamming? What is happening right now?

Christian weathers her mercurial mood in stride. "May I introduce my brother, His Highness Prince Lukas of Aiboland? Lukas, this is Elsa, the Hereditary Princess of Vattenguldia and her sister, Princess Isabelle."

Lukas bows, but it is nowhere nearly as crisp and lovely as his brother's. His eyes narrow upon my sister. "Enchanted, I'm sure."

His accent is not as lovely, either.

Niceties performed, I round the table and place my plate next to Parker's. But right as the Aibolandian heir attempts to politely follow me to my side, no doubt to pull my chair out, too, I grab my own seat and slide it from beneath the table.

Parker's startled into action. "Allow me," he quickly throws out. I wave him off.

"Despite popular opinion, I am fully capable of pulling out my own chair." My words have no bite in them, though. I'm teasing and they're well aware of it.

Lukas, who made no effort to pull my seat out for me, lifts his coffee cup in a small salute, surprise flickering in his eyes.

A distinct chirping of my sister's phone informs us our mother—or her secretary—has sent a text message. Isabelle stiffens and then flinches, almost as if the rings were slaps rather than signals. She remains standing, waiting for the sounds to cease . . . and even then, the light fading from her eyes, she does not move.

The men who share our company shift uncomfortably, as if they know a darkened cloud has come to rain down upon us during our meal.

"Why don't you have a seat, Isabelle?" When she does not readily answer, I switch tactics and motion to the space in front of us. "These gentlemen were in the midst of eating and cannot resume doing so until you've sat. Do you wish them to starve?"

Her trance broken by my teasing, my sister clearly bites back her response but does as asked. As the men sit down themselves, Christian once more catches my attention—and there. Mission accomplished. He doesn't even appear shocked I would say such a thing. A tiny bit of light has returned to his face, to the slight curve of his lips. A small slice of teeth appears for the teeniest of seconds.

That's much better. A morose Prince Charming does no one any good.

One of Isabelle's slender hands rests against the exposed skin just below the roll of his sleeve. A shuddery sigh slips from between her pink lips, one that smacks of forced yet wholly unwanted determination. "I hope I have not kept you from your food too long. Can you ever forgive me? Perhaps we can find a way for me to make it up to you."

Seriously. What is going on here? Did somebody come and suck my sister's soul out of her? She would normally never say such a thing.

The ease Christian had just shown me is once more gone. "Actually," he says slowly, "this my second plate, so there is no need for worry."

Perhaps I am not remembering him correctly. Perhaps I had too much champagne last night, because the man before me is not the same as the one I ate éclairs with in a darkened kitchen. This one sounds robotic. Robotic and annoyed?

What a pair these two make.

"Did you sleep well last night, Your Highness?" Parker asks me.

I turn toward him, grateful for redirection. "None of this Your Highness nonsense, please. Feel free to call me Elsa. And as a matter of fact, I did not. I hazard to guess none of us did."

"You can say that again," Lukas mutters.

My pulse leaps. Did Christian embellish our time together to his brother?

"Was it shag central down in the barracks, too?" Lukas asks the secretary. "If last night was any indicator of what the week's going to be like, I don't know if I brought enough condoms."

Ah. He's referring to himself, then.

Cheeks flaming, Parker uneasily shifts his eggs from one side of his plate to the other. "I can go to town for you if you like, Your Highness."

Christian merely sighs, shaking his head.

Isabelle says suddenly, woodenly, "Christian, what are your plans for the day?"

His attention flies up from his sausage, startled to be singled out. "Back-to-back meetings, I'm afraid." Only, he sounds relieved to tell her this, which is odd, considering his comment about our itinerary last night.

That said, he did make a point to let me know he had no interest in making a match at the RMM. I claimed the same, but he and I know our opinions mean nothing in the long run, especially in light of teas that are already being scheduled. But here he is, sounding indifferent toward my glamorous sister who routinely shows up in glossies.

As Parker cuts a piece of ham, he says, "Your schedules today must match fairly closely."

Isabelle is blank faced for a split second. "I don't have much of a set schedule today—"

"Ah, the joys of being a spare." Lukas tugs out a flask from his coat, toasting my sister.

"My apologies, my lady," Parker continues. "I was referring to Prince Christian and Princess Elsa. I would think that, as the heirs to their respective thrones, they will sit in on many of the same meetings this week."

"It makes sense," I say. "I left my full schedule back in my room, though." My smile is faint. "I failed to read it all the way through it yet." And then, dryly, "Unlike some people."

Amusement flashes in Christian's eyes. "Why isn't your private secretary here with you?"

He actually appears interested in my answer. "How do you know she's not?"

"I have my sources."

He checked up on me? Interesting. I turn toward Parker. "Hello, source."

Parker merely chuckles.

"To answer your question, Charlotte gave birth a few weeks ago. While she was willing to come, the new man in her life had very different ideas, and rightly so." I set my coffee cup back onto the table. "I'm positive she's afraid I'm quite lost without her."

"You probably are," Isabelle murmurs.

It is good to see glimmers of my sister appearing every now and again.

"Are you?" Christian is once more staring at me like my answer is important.

"Would you be?"

"Actually, I would." There is no hint of embarrassment. "Parker pretty much runs my life for me."

"Your bromance is adorable," I admit. "Much like the sisterhood of the travelling . . . well, I'd say trousers that, but we don't have a pair we share with one another whilst chasing dreams and memories across the globe. So let us just say that Charlotte and I are the equivalent of whatever a bromance is, only lady-style. Imagine how cozy the four of us would be together: helpless heirs reliant upon their personal secretaries. A sitcom is born. Or a reality show."

Christian laughs now, so do Parker and Lukas, but it's the Crown Prince's that seeps through my skin, into my muscles and bones. It's the same infectious, wonderful laughter I heard last night, like . . . like he is unafraid to embrace life rather than simply hold on like the rest of us. Truthfully, it is baffling, because just five minutes ago, I wondered if I imagined that side of him.

But, no. Here he is. Christian and his too infectious, wonderful laughter. Something inside me clenches. Flutters.

Isabelle's knife clatters against her plate. "It really is a shame Charlotte isn't here to rein you in from saying such sordid things."

"Sordid? Did you not hear my clarification? Charlotte and I have long since stopped sharing clothes."

"Have you known her long?" Christian asks.

I tear off a corner of a piece of toast. "We went to the same boarding school when younger, which is most likely why she tolerates me so well. I am an acquired taste, you see."

A tiny choking sound emits from my sister.

Christian leans forward. "I'm shocked to hear this. I assumed all princesses run around inquiring about others' virginities. Is this not normal behavior for future monarchs?"

"Don't you mean running amuck?" I cannot help but tease.

"What's this about virgins?" Lukas asks. "Because I'm pretty sure there are none here at the Summit. Not after what I saw going on last night."

My sister saws at her sausage like her life depends upon it.

"Parker and I went to boarding school, too," Christian tells me, ignoring his brother. He's no longer scandalized in the least, which is refreshing. "I wonder if it's the place du jour to foster relationships with one's trusted personal secretary."

Lukas takes another swig from his flask. "Yes, you two went off and left me at home. No wonder I have no secretary of my own."

For a moment, no one says anything, not in the face of such blatant bitterness. I break the silence with, "I'm sure Charlotte often rues the day she sat down next to me at supper for the first time. She had no idea who I was. She simply thought I was some lonely girl. Which, make no mistake, I was, but . . ." A sly grin fights to show itself upon my face. "She certainly got more than she bargained for." I turn toward Parker. "Is it the same for you? Do you ever wish that you'd found a perfectly acceptable bromance to cultivate with a non-royal?"

Parker is thoroughly flustered. "Um . . ."

Christian laughs again. "I can answer for him. Of course it's yes."

We grin at each other then, big fat smirks that stretch the corners of our lips upward in a shared sense of conspiratorial glee. And I am struck by just how much I admire such a smile on this man.

"Elsa," Isabelle says flatly, "Isn't that Mathieu in line for breakfast? You ought to invite him to sit with you, considering . . ." Her pause is meaningful. And irritating.

Because I could almost swear she was telling me to not rock the boat, either, and there is no way that could be right.

CHAPTER 15

CHRISTIAN

The She-Wolf's gloating this morning was nauseating. What a striking pair Princess Isabelle of Vattenguldia and I made last night. How beautiful our babies would be (because "ugly babies are unacceptable"). How lovely Isabelle would be as a consort. How wonderful trade treaties between Aiboland and Vattenguldia would be. I'd say she'd gone as far as picking out china patterns for us, except those already exist and are in a cabinet back at the palace. And then she wrapped all this up with the neat bow over how I was required to sweet talk Isabelle at a private little tea being set up for us after my meetings. Or even engage in a little *afternoon delight* if the both of us were willing.

All in all, the noose around my neck tightened significantly as my mother reveled in her role as royal pimp.

Lukas said nothing during the speech the She-Wolf forced upon us where she dictated our actions over the next few days. My role, in summation: I am not to fuck up what she views as an advantageous match. I am to shower Isabelle with attention and woo her to the best of my abilities, even if I must seduce her. I am to pay attention to what she says, likes, and does. It mattered not one bit when I informed my mother I wasn't attracted to Isabelle, nor interested in the slightest in getting to know her, let alone marrying her.

"Do you think I'm attracted to your father?" was her response. "Or that it was even a consideration?"

She silently challenged me then, and for all the outrage and words simmering within, nothing further came out of my mouth until she'd closed the door behind her.

It was then Lukas said, "You're lucky to have spent most of your life away," as he poured himself a far too early glass of cognac.

I rejected the offer of one myself, and instead of stewing in bubbling anger, I allowed my mind wander back to a certain princess drinking warm milk and eating éclairs in the middle of the night with me. I'd felt not so much as a prisoner of the gallows there. Talking to Elsa was easy.

Unexpected.

Sitting at breakfast, I'd been half-minded to beg Parker to book me a flight to anywhere that wasn't filled with Isabelles and She-Wolves. As if on cue, just as the words were ready to slide out, the princess in question materialized at the table and all my ideas of travel transitioned to curse words.

But then Elsa came over, too. Elsa and all her brash honesty that pales her sister in comparison.

For ten fleeting minutes, I forgot about my mother's demands and simply allowed myself the surprising ease of once more volleying words back and forth with the heir to the Vattenguldian throne. She isn't afraid to poke fun at herself, or me, or hell, even her sister. It shocked and yet pleased me how she continued to pull Parker into the conversation even though most peers would have considered him nothing more than a ghost haunting our perimeter.

As her wit curls around me, I foolishly wish I could turn the clock forward to three a.m., to when I get to see the real her again. Because when she smiles, everything else around us disappears and all I see are mesmerizing little lines that trace the corners of her mouth and crinkles that decorate the corners of her eyes.

It's a bloody gorgeous, addictive smile.

"Elsa," Isabelle says. "Isn't that Mathieu in line for breakfast? You ought to invite him to sit with you, considering . . ."

And now the smile is gone.

Our corner of the table falls silent as Elsa's attention slides away from me toward where Mat is standing in the buffet line with his sister, Margaux. I've never personally spoken to the heir to one of the former royal families of Savoy, but Mat has always spoken favorably about his eldest sibling.

"I believe he already has a dining partner," Elsa murmurs to her sister. She's frowning. Is she jealous he's with somebody else? Does she know that's his sister?

It's on the tip of my tongue to tell her, to ensure the tiny frown lines on her forehead disappear, but then I remind myself that it shouldn't matter whether or not she's frowning. Or if she wants Mat to join us. Or if she's upset he's with another woman.

Isabelle counters her sister's observation with . . . shite, I don't know. Something bitchy sounding. And then she's got that scary as all hell smile plastered on her face again, all gentle and cool and completely forced, like she's either going to inquire politely about the weather or go volcanic here at the table.

All of my mother's instructions and threats come rushing back like a tide I can't escape from for too long. But damn, if I'm not going to keep trying. Come hell or high water, I do not want to marry this girl, no matter what the She-Wolf says.

"I believe our meeting is close to starting," I tell Elsa. "We ought to go."

She pulls her attention away from Mat and stares at me, like she can't believe I just used the word *we*. Lukas' eyebrows shoot up. Parker's staring strangely at me, too; I can't get a good enough read if he thinks I'm being weird or if I totally bungled the time for the meeting. I didn't tell either of them about Elsa and I running into each other last night because . . . I liked the thought that what happened was just ours. Our secrets. Our lists of firsts. Our little club.

And yet, this is another first, too, because I normally tell Parker everything.

He passes me my leather satchel filled with everything I could possibly need in a meeting directed at issues young crown heirs in the twenty-first century are faced with. As if we were children, in desperate need of schooling.

I stand up; I'm oddly relieved when Elsa does, too. "No bag?" I ask as she rounds the table.

"Shite." She blushes and shakes her head. "I mean, crap." A huge sigh escapes her. "I left it behind; I'll have to fetch it."

Parker, who stood up the moment she did, says, "Your Highness, I will be more than happy to ensure that your bag is procured and sent to the meeting right away."

Thank God for Parker.

"You're not my butler." Her grin is wry. "There is no need to fetch anything of mine." She pauses. "Also, no need for such formality, remember?"

"Does your butler fetch much?" I ask.

There. She's smiling at me once more and all seems to be right in the world again. "Actually, no."

"Let Parker get your bag," I tell her. "If I'm not mistaken, he's about to be subjected to a meeting just as boring as ours, only it's like a Personal Secretary Seminar for Dummies. This will give him reason to skip out on at least the first fifteen minutes."

Parker does not argue this in the least.

"Then by all means," she tells him, "please procure my bag. Or, at least inform Bittner I'll need it."

"Bittner?" I ask.

"My father's personal secretary. Who I am fairly certain is quite glad he is not mine. I'm surprised your source didn't fill you in on that, too."

Lukas stays where he is, nursing his flask. He'll be blitzed in no time, no doubt searching for yet another conquest. The She-Wolf will love that. Isabelle stands up, though; I cannot decipher the look in her eyes. It's okay, though. I don't care to anyway.

My stand begins now. I simply nod politely at my mother's choice and inform my brother and Parker I'll meet up with them later. And then I lead Elsa out of the door, relieved that she doesn't flinch when my hand meets the small of her back for the briefest of moments.

"This meeting," she says as we consult a small map Parker packed, "is obscenely asinine. I cannot believe that, while our parents sit in meetings that help shape country policies, we are to be babysat in some kind Crown Heirs' nursery. Why didn't you warn me about this?"

I glance up from the map and take her in. She's wearing a navy blue coat that works well as a dress, and it's sophisticated and simple on her all at once, as if it was tailored exactly for her body—

Wait. What was she just saying? Oh. Right. The dumb as all shite meeting we're off to. As I think she'd rip my head off for complimenting her coat, I say, "My apologies. I thought you might have actually looked in the packet. I'll be sure to keep you updated accordingly from here on out. But you're right. It looks like fucking torture."

She grimaces. "It's bad enough we're here to be . . . ." As we curve up a tight, winding staircase, her voice drops when the Japanese Emperor walks by. "Auctioned off like medieval maidens, but the silver lining was that we were to at least join the adult table, you know? Only, I suppose that's a farce, too."

She's completely spot on. "I find your use of *maiden* terribly sexist, Els."

A startled yet pleased look crosses her face when I call her that, one I definitely like.

Bloody hell. It's day two, and I'm already thinking stupid things.

"Well, you are quite dainty." While humor dances in her eyes, her lips press together hard, like she's fighting to hold something in. It's not the first time she's done it in the small amount of time we've known each other.

It's none of my business, but the question comes out anyway. "Why do you do that?"

"Do what? Insult you?" She leans back, scanning me up and down. "I have the distinct feeling nobody, except your brother, ever finds fault in you. I am just doing my part to keep you humble."

Is she saying she finds me perfect? Or riddled with faults? I'm equally fascinated with both scenarios. She's right, though. Outside of the She-Wolf and Lukas, nobody ever dares to point out my flaws. "Should I be insulted?"

A sly grin traces the corners of her mouth. "That is up to you." And then her lips press together once more, keeping whatever she's desperate to hold onto inside.

"That." I motion at her face. "What are you holding in?"

Her eyes, so expressively dark blue, widen significantly. And then she sighs deeply. "My mother insists it is unbecoming to laugh in public. I know this will probably come as an utter shock to you, but I do try to have some manners."

My own laughter escapes me. "You'll ask me if I'm a virgin shortly after we've met, but won't laugh in public?"

To my surprise, pink stains streak her pale cheeks. But that's not the worst; she hushes me as she angles me toward a nook off the staircase. The movement provides me a long whiff of her perfume. Damn, she smells good. "Fine. I behaved beastly yesterday. I already admitted that." Her eyes trace the stairs before settling back on me. And it's strange, because I physically have to fight off a shiver when they do. "It's just, I didn't want you to like me. Not at first, anyway."

Just as my mouth opens, she clarifies, "Or, you know, propose again."

She's teasing me. I give as good as I get. "I never proposed in the first place. Or," I add, when she prepares to argue, "proposition you."

"Fine. You didn't. I'm just saying—"

I'm unable to help the step forward I take in the already small space. "Look, you don't have to explain it to me. Like I said last night, it's not like I'm ecstatic to be auctioned off, either."

One of her eyebrows arches up. I like that it's not one of those skinny scary ones that looks drawn on by a toddler.

"Even to my sister?"

The ground below me turns soft and unstable. We're not in a truce, I suppose, but in a place where we're conversing like normal people. At least, what I assume normal people converse like. I can admit I don't want to lose that. But as much as she and her sister needled one another at breakfast, they are also siblings with inevitable loyalties, just like Lukas and myself. Nonetheless, I tell her firmly, "Not even to your sister."

How could I even think about her sister when a Valkyrie stands right in front of me?

CHAPTER 16

♛

ELSA

An inappropriate, irrational stab of pleasure surfaces at Christian's quietly voiced conviction. He is uninterested in her. He doesn't want to be a pawn in the RMM any more than I do—not that it matters in the long run, but still.

The loaded silence that fills the space around us is so thick, so tight I am helpless to do anything other than break it. "The writing on the wall says you two are to be matched."

"Much like you and Mat."

It is tacky, but my nose automatically scrunches. "Don't lead her on if it isn't what you truly want."

It is his turn to let out a soft exhale of frustration. "Believe me, that isn't even a consideration."

I would like to believe his sincerity. "My sister is in a vulnerable place right now. She doesn't need to believe somebody fancies her when . . ." A rueful ghost of a laugh surfaces. "That sounds quite secondary school-ish, doesn't it?"

"This whole farce feels secondary school-ish," he mutters, running a hand through his dark hair. And then, "Why didn't you want me to like you, Els?"

I open my mouth to correct him, but he cuts me off, smirking. "I mean friendly liking, of course."

"It isn't that I didn't want you to like me, per se." The urge to kick myself is strong. Why do I keep saying ridiculous things around this man? "If that makes sense. Which it most likely doesn't." I am digging a deeper hole for myself, aren't I? "I suppose I am on the defensive." I lamely wave a hand between us. When it grazes his shoulder, I jerk back at the static shock. "As are you, and rightly so." Good lord, I'm raving once more. And my fingers are tingling, all from a simple brush against broadcloth. "To think I assumed you were the egotistical one, thanks to all of your . . ." I motion toward his face, and then his body, careful to keep my distance. "You know. All of your *too*-ness. And yet, perhaps it was me and my ego that ought to have been of concern."

"My *too*-ness?"

He's shocked. Scratch that—he is amused. And I am officially over this conversation, since the opportunity for me to continue to make a complete and utter arse out of myself is nearly guaranteed. So, I refuse to clarify. "Take the apology as it stands, Christian."

"Is that a first, Els?"

My inhale is sharper than I would like.

"Because I have a feeling that you don't apologize very often. Or that you ever lose control enough to be required to do so." The corners of his lips twitch. "Maybe that's another first. Losing control, especially in a situation like the RMM, when one must be in control every single second."

I cannot even manage to properly gasp, my heart is hammering so hard in my chest. I tell him, hating how husky my voice is, "It's not three a.m. Does this first count?"

All of my efforts to keep my hands off him go to naught when he reaches out and gently tucks stray strands of hair behind one of my ears. "I'll allow it. But just because you're a fellow founding member of the RFC."

My legs are shaking. They are physically shaking.

"Also, just to let you know: apology accepted."

Why did I choose this little nook for us to stand in again? There is not enough airflow in here. It's way too hot, even though it's a cool day.

I force myself to ask, "What's your first?"

"I want you to call me Chris. As boring as that name may be."

I hate the rush that surges through me when he says this. "Other people call you Chris. That is not a first."

"It is a first, when it's less than twenty-four hours after meeting someone. It took Parker years before he broke down and called me anything other than Christian. There aren't a lot of people who use Chris, by the way. Less than a handful."

I swallow hard. "But what if I want you to be Christian to me?"

"Then," he says quietly, "I will be Christian to you."

My eyes drift to his mouth. My pulse increases significantly. The air around us completely disappears. "Why Chris?"

"Chris is familiar," he says, voice low and warm and crisp all at once. "And…I think I want to be familiar to you, Els."

It is impossibly foolish to even consider such a thing, but it's exactly what I want too.

CHAPTER 17

CHRISTIAN

"How was the meeting?"

The question comes from my brother, who miraculously managed to pull himself out of bed (his or someone else's, I'm not sure) to join us out on the patio surrounding the pool.

"Torturous."

I'm being kind with my description. The two-hour meeting, which in reality was the world's oldest crown heir spewing his bitterness over how his mother still lives and rules while he continues to age on the sidelines, was nothing short of a trip to the abyss. There were no discussions concerning key political issues in our respective countries, no hints of alliances to be fostered within the Summit. Hell, we didn't even have a chance to mingle with fellow royals we may have never had the pleasure of meeting in person yet. Nobody else spoke during those two hours. Not a single person. I cannot personally vouch for the others present, but I worried the bastard was hellbent on embezzling any and all joy we might have in our lives until we were nothing but dried husks desperate to escape.

"There was nothing redeemable about the meeting?" Parker asks.

Elsa.

Granted, her eyes were just as glazed over as the rest of the groups, and we didn't speak (because God forbid anyone get a word in), but there was a shared sense of solidarity in our misery.

I focused more on her than the so-called speaker. Every move, every shift, every time she crossed her legs, I noticed, even if just out of the corner of my eye. If I'm being honest, I kept hoping she'd tear the arsehole lecturing us a new one if only to break the tension.

When that never happened, I wondered . . . was it me? Was there something about me that encouraged her to ignore the decorum beat into all of us at a young age? Because what kind of princess goes off the rails like that?

A maddeningly intriguing one, that's for sure. And I've gone straight to bedlam, because I'm thrilled she's showing me these true colors. I'll happily take her brand of feistiness in this sea of boredom.

But I tell my brother and best friend, "Not a damn thing."

Lukas slips his flask out of his coat pocket. "The She-Wolf gave me more specific marching orders while you were at your lame meeting."

I don't know what's worse—acknowledging I pinpointed that Elsa smells like Tahitian vanilla or anything to do with the She-Wolf. "Who is she targeting?"

He takes a long swig before recapping the flask. "Can you believe the Hereditary Princess of Vattenguldia is on her list? The one from this morning's breakfast? I swear, she's fucking obsessed with those girls."

Poor bast—*what the hell?*

"I was under the impression that Her Highness was keen on your brother making headway with the younger sister," Parker is saying.

Elsa? And *Lukas?* Jesus. No. No fucking way. Talk about oil and water.

"She says that if my bro here can't bag the sister, I'm to go hardcore after the heir. Says . . ." He runs a hand through his dark hair and glances around the patio we're sitting on. There are a few people about twenty meters away, but they're easily out of earshot. "Says we will obtain an in into their shipping registries, no matter what it takes. Romantic as all shite, right?" A grimace spreads across his face. "But that's the She-Wolf for you. Doesn't care if she fucks over her kids, just as long as the ink on a trade agreement is legit."

Parker gives me a meaningful look. Arsehole. I ask my brother, "Elsa's her top pick?"

"Secondary. But she wants me working,"—he flashes air quotation marks—"*both angles*, just in case." His tone informs me that it'll be a cold day in hell when he follows through with such an order.

Even still, I say flatly, "You better start looking at others on that list the She-Wolf made for you."

"You doubting my prowess?"

I tug his flask away and unscrew it. "Prowess?" I shake my head as I take a sip. It's whiskey; he came through on his promise to find us the good stuff. "Do you even hear the words coming out of your mouth?"

He rips the flask back out of my hand once I'm done. "Do you doubt I could land that Vattenguldian chick if I tried?"

"Actually," I tell him, more annoyed than I ought to be, "I do. And don't be disrespectful. You do not call future monarchs *chicks*, nor do you talk about *landing* them."

He's wearing sunglasses, but I'm pretty sure he just narrowed his eyes at me. And I realize maybe a little too late that I've just offered him some kind of challenge. Well, shite.

Parker gives me yet another meaningful look.

"How convenient," my brother says. "There's the girl in question."

Across the pool, I spy Elsa and her sister talking to some other people on a terrace overlooking the area. And that reminds me, I'm supposed to go have tea with Isabelle in a quarter of an hour. Fantastic.

Lukas stands up, shoving his flask into his pocket. I'll be damned if he goes over there. So I say quietly, "Sit your arse back down unless you are prepared to give the She-Wolf exactly what she wants."

He turns, eyebrows rising over dark plastic.

I keep my voice low and pleasant, lest anyone overhear us. "You've never been the good soldier, following marching orders. What makes today any different? Are you really ready to just roll over? Bloody hell, Luk. I never thought I'd see the day. Might as well cut your balls off and pickle them for her."

Now he's just pissed—and incredulous, because we both know, if anybody follows the She-Wolf's marching orders, it's fucking Prince Perfect.

"Your next meeting is in ten minutes, Chris," Parker says smoothly. "Prince Lukas, I believe you have one at the same time."

Amazingly, Lukas sits back down. "What the fuck? I'm not the heir. Spares aren't supposed to go to meetings."

Mat wanders up to where Elsa and Isabelle are standing. Are they to have tea, too?

"My mistake," Parker is saying, which is a joke, because Parker doesn't get shite wrong. Ever. But then, he was merely handling my brother before; he knows just as well as the rest of us that Lukas' sole purpose this week is to be a stud for sale. "I thought I'd heard during orientation that there was to be a few meetings for . . ."

"Go ahead." Lukas leans against the cushions of his chaise. "You can call me the spare. Damn, Parker, you seriously need to lighten up. The She-Wolf isn't present. We're mates, remember? You don't need to treat Chris and I like we're—"

Parker smiles thinly. "Royalty?"

Mat leads the Vattenguldian sisters back up the stairs. "Who else?" I ask.

They both appear confused, so I add, "On the She-Wolf's list."

Lukas' sigh weighs down in the air. "The true target is some royal cousin who has been dragged here from Spain. The She-Wolf thinks Dad will appreciate it or something. Like it's some kind of warped peace offering." He scoffs. "Like that will matter to Dad. Like he'll ever think anything good can come of this fucking farce."

"Us," I remind him quietly. "He would argue he got us."

Lukas merely grunts, nursing his flask.

"Have you met this Spanish girl?" I ask. "And also, let's not call her *this Spanish girl.* What's her name?"

"Maria-Elena, but she said she prefers just Maria or Mari."

I'm impressed he knows this. My brother isn't always the best at collecting names.

"To answer your questions, though, yeah, we've run into each other a few times now. She's hot." A small smile slips out. "I might have, uh, gotten a little friendly with her before I knew she was my bloody intended. What about the Vattenguldian girl, Chris? The one with an icicle stuck up her arse. Any hope there?"

No. No hope for either girl, unfortunately, even though I think I might wish for it differently otherwise.

Which is a truly irresponsible wish indeed.

CHAPTER 18

♛
ELSA

I fight the urge to yawn, but it is a battle I'm losing. So I attempt a closed-mouth yawn, with my eyes widening alongside an added head nod so it doesn't appear as if I'm as bored as I truly am. And tired. I'm running on all of about two hours of good, solid sleep.

Mat slides the book he showed me back onto the shelf he found it on. "Not so much a fan of the classics?"

The antique book had been about finance. "Is it truly a classic?"

"To some, perhaps." His morose yet easy smile attempts to coax one out of me, but all I feel in return is crabbiness. Forced relationships can do that to a lady, even with a man as decent as this one. *Especially* after one's father has forced her to spend some so-called "quality" time with said man.

"Do your duty," was His Serene Highness' response when I pressed why I couldn't have tea with my sister instead. But no, she's having tea with Christian, and I am here trying to manufacture small talk with Mathieu.

But small talk we must. "Where exactly is it that you call home nowadays?"

"My family is based in France, but I tend to bounce back and forth between Paris, Rome, and New York."

Ah. That's right; he said he'd lived here in the States, hadn't he? "How do you like New York? I've yet to visit, although I hope to someday."

"It's a brilliant city, filled with a lot of life." There's a dulled twinkle in his eye. "Does it make me a traitor to the EU to say I prefer it to any of the grand cities I grew up in?"

"Oh, it's a distinct possibility."

"If I could," he tells me, words brittle yet light, "I'd happily live the rest of my life there."

Is that grief reflecting in his eyes?

When he faces the books, I bite back the impulse to press him about this, or to even remind him that Vattenguldia is a far cry from New York City. To do so, though, would to encourage intimacy when such closeness is definitely undesired. Awkward small talk is promptly abandoned for uncomfortable silence.

Last night, it was easier to converse when there was mere suspicion. Now that I possess confirmation our parents desire a match between us, my words fail me.

I have nothing to say to him.

"Are you having a good time?"

Bloody Charlotte and her optimism. I lean against the railing closest to me and gaze upon lush gardens. "What do you think?"

She chuckles at the same time the baby lets loose a ripping shout of a cry. "How are your meetings so far?"

At least, that's what I think she says. "Boring as sod, that's what."

"They're about flooring?"

Oh for— "Charlotte, I love you and Dickie dearly, but pass the baby off, okay?"

"What?"

"FOR THE LOVE OF GOD, PASS THE BABY OFF TO THE NANNY."

The Malaysian Supreme Head of State and the King of Cambodia both send sharp, startled glances my way. They are at a good enough distance that they cannot overhear my phone call—when I'm speaking normally, at least. I offer a sheepish smile before slipping down the path toward the stairs leading to the drive.

Thankfully, in my escape from humiliation, Charlotte gives our eardrums a break and does as asked. "Now then," she says once the baby's cries fade, "you were telling me about your meetings?"

"They are preposterous." I nod at a passing groundskeeper as I turn on the drive, heading toward the rear castle grounds. "And honestly, an insult. We are being babysat. There is no real work for heirs to do here. I haven't even had a chance to use any of His Serene Highness' so-called talking points yet. The last meeting I was at? Nobody was allowed to speak. How is that for representing Vattenguldia on the global stage?"

"Has your father indicated who he's angling toward yet?"

I peer into the overcast sky; it looks like the clouds will open up and cry shortly. But I don't head back, yet. I'll risk the rain as long as I have room to breathe. Over the course of the next five minutes, I fill Charlotte in on all the gory details that only a day and a half can bring. She listens quietly (I am certain she takes copious notes, though) while gently coaxing the full story out of me, as well as a request.

When I'm done, she says, "I am on the Mathieu angle." And then, less sharply, "Do you at least like him?"

"I suppose he's nice enough."

"That is hardly a glowing recommendation, Elsa."

"What do you want me to say? That I fell madly in love with him the moment we met?" A forced burst of laughter claws its way out of my chest. "Please. That never happens, especially at the RMM."

"I fell in love with Josef the moment I saw him—"

I cut her off. For being so level-headed, Charlotte's memories of how she and her husband first got together are distorted. "You tossed a drink in his face and called him an arse in front of the entire restaurant. Then you bitched non-stop about him for the next two days."

"I most certainly did not!"

I'm undeterred. "It was so bad you had to pay me a euro for every time you said his name or called him *that arse*. I ended up with a tidy profit."

"The point being," she grinds out, "that love at first sight is a true possibility."

"Love at first sight is an urban legend. Lust at first sight? I'll concede it might exist. But neither happened with Mat," I assure her. With Christian? Oh yes. "He is a decent bloke, but there are no sparks. None. He feels very brother-ish—or at least, what I imagine a brother feels like."

"Oh, Elsa," she says quietly. "That makes me so sad."

"Did you believe there was the possibility of me coming to the Royal Marriage Market and finding true love?" I let out a scoff of derision. "Nobody here is so lucky."

"What about your Prince Charming?"

I halt in the middle of the road. "I don't have a Prince Charming."

"The handsome fellow you met yesterday—"

I counter with, "The one His Serene Highness expects Isabelle to marry?"

"Do you really think that will go through, what with Isabelle and Alfons' engagement?"

I turn back toward the main house and stare up at it. "I fear there is no engagement anymore. Isabelle refuses to discuss Alfons, let alone tell me what has her on edge—RMM notwithstanding."

It's just as much as a surprise to Charlotte as it had been to me.

CHAPTER 19

CHRISTIAN

Thank the bloody stars dinner is over.

Isabelle ate with us tonight, as did Maria-Elena. The She-Wolf was in high spirits, regaling the two ladies with grand stories of Aiboland and her witty, charming sons growing up in such an idyllic place. Only, the ladies forced to endure these embellished stories morphed into wooden statues the entire time, and we dutiful sons were no better.

We weren't the only ones in just such a situation. There were miserable heirs and spares seated at similar tables under the dim glow of heat lamps and fairy lights all around us.

Afterward, when Isabelle excused herself to go powder her nose, I made a beeline straight to her sister. The gloom coloring Elsa's face flitted in and out of view every time somebody turned and spoke to her, and I couldn't stand the thought that she was just as miserable as I was. So, while I rationally knew that going over to her was undeniably irrational in itself, all I could fixate on was how the only moments of pleasure I'd had at all in California so far had been in her company.

Even when we were sparring. Even when she was cutting me down in a hallway. Even if we did nothing more than sit next to one another in silence.

Besides. She has a first to tempt me with.

I catch up with her just as the pair of monarchs she'd been talking to move away to another victim. "I'm disappointed in you." Her addictive perfume leaves me dizzy, making my attempts at levity difficult. "Here you are, acting so civilized. I expected you to be running amuck."

The smartest, slyest smile I've ever seen is offered just to me. "I thought we decided only virgins are running amuck this week."

A welcome chuckle falls right out of me. "Are you finally admitting you're not a virgin?"

"You're a cad, and you have the world snowed when it comes to your true personality. You know that right?"

Only, she's smiling just as broadly as I am. "I do. I also feel it's my duty to admit that plenty of people run amuck, virgins or no. It's apparently the thing to do."

I can tell she wants to laugh so much, but all I get is her lips pressing together in a fit to hold in the gasps.

"You can laugh around me. I promise I won't mind."

"You know what I mind?" She steps closer. "How our parents watch us."

My joviality fades as I glance discreetly in the direction she indicates. Although Prince Gustav and the She-Wolf are mingling with a few of the other microstate soveriegns, their attentions are squarely focused on us. Worse, it's obvious my mother isn't pleased that I'm with this Vattenguldian girl instead of the other.

Fuck her. "Care for a stroll?"

The relief shining from Elsa's eyes is worth the blistering lecture I'm sure to receive later. I lead her through the throng of people, away from our parents' disapproving oversight and toward a much quieter, less populated area of the gardens.

A deep sigh of relief slips through her lips. "You are my favorite right now."

My pulse jumps at her statement, as does my dick. Damn, does this woman look gorgeous tonight. She's wearing a shimmery black dress that reminds me of something straight from the past, something that belongs to this place and its history, and her beauty is equally ethereal in the alabaster lamplight around us.

As I drink the sight of her in, I realize, very clearly, just how attracted to her I am. Painfully so, and after such a surprisingly short time—more than any other woman I've ever encountered.

My equilibrium promptly disappears.

I say, hoping that I sound merely amused and not rattled by this revelation, "I bet you tell that to all the fellows who take you away from the RMM."

She digs through her small clutch she's been carrying and extracts a ball of paper. "Speaking of, have you seen this?"

The Valkyrie is angry. Interesting. I pry the crinkled ball out of her hand and lean in toward one of the nearby globe lamps. "Whatever it is, I'm fairly certain it's not my fault."

"Oh, ha ha." She sighs as I unfold the wrinkled mess. "I wasn't assigning blame. I simply yearn for someone to share in my outrage."

In my hands is a recently released itinerary outlining a sunrise hike for crown heirs. *Foster critical relationships and bond with your peers in glorious nature*, it says in bold letters. There is a generic picture of people I don't know, holding hands and grinning like maniacal fools as they wander down a trail. *Be prepared to write a thoughtful essay afterward detailing the benefits of strong relationships between modern royals in the twenty-first century, to be shared at a special luncheon just for heirs.*

I ask, "Is this a joke?"

"Bittner gave it to me; apologetically, too. So I'm thinking, no. He's not the sort to pull pranks. Did Parker not give you yours yet?"

Parker probably took one look at the asinine paper and threw it into the nearest trash receptacle. Which is exactly what I'm going to do with Elsa's missive. I reform it back into the ball I received it in and stuff it into my pocket. "No. And if he's loyal to me at all, he never will."

She leans against a white wall. "When did the Decennial Summit become the equivalent of summer camp for heirs?"

"If that's the case, perhaps we ought to request campfire songs and roasted marshmallows."

She toes one of the painted tiles below our feet. "Have you ever been to summer camp before?"

"Alas, no, but I have watched films depicting it. Marshmallows are frequently involved."

She's amused. "Why, Christian. Are you marshmallow obsessed?"

Clapping and cheering sound; we peer around the bushes we're hiding behind in an effort to find the source of such gaiety. There are champagne glasses lifted in the air and smiles on many a monarch's face.

It's a toe curdling, hideous sight.

"What in the world?" Elsa mutters, her eyes narrowing as she leans forward.

But I don't care about whatever's going on with everyone else. I'm much more focused on the woman in front of me. Because, let's face it, those cheers can come from nothing good. Not here, at least. Not at the RMM.

"What were you asking?" I prompt.

Her attention returns to me. And I've got to admit, I really like it there. Her lips, which are stained in a really delicious looking red tonight, curve into an astute smirk. This small movement hypnotizes me. "We were discussing your apparent obsession with marshmallows."

I'm wondering what it'd be like to taste those red lips. She's thinking about marshmallows. I want to laugh, even if it's damn near impossible to pull my eyes away from her gorgeous mouth. How is this possible? How can I be so attracted to someone two days after an introduction? "Truth be told," I murmur, "I've never had one before. They always seemed questionable to me."

Elsa nearly chokes on the hilarity trying to get out, and I swear, in this moment, I want nothing more than to actually hear it. It's my newest goal: I will hear her laugh before the end of the Summit.

"What's so questionable about a marshmallow?"

I shrug, grinning. "It's difficult to articulate."

"You'll be wretched at your essay then. If you cannot articulate why marshmallows are suspect and unworthy of your affection, how in the world will you be able to argue the importance of royals sticking together?"

"As I highly doubt I'll be writing such a composition, it won't be a problem at all."

She smiles up at me, her lips tugging up on one side just a bit higher than the other, and it feels like somebody came along and hit me on the back of my head. Damn, this woman is sexy. What if I did kiss her? I'm not imagining this spark between us, am I?

I stuff my hands into my pockets.

"That makes two of us," she says to me. "Will those be our firsts? Standing up to the man and refusing ridiculous essays?"

"It depends." It doesn't appear she can tell I'm utterly turned on right now, thank God. "Have you stood up to the man and refused to write a paper before?"

Her head cocks to the side as she pretends to think, long dark hair spilling across a bared, creamy shoulder. Images of me wrapping that gorgeous hair around my fist as I find out if her lips are as delectable as they look fill my mind. I'm forced to slump against the wall to hide my growing attraction to her. Christ. *Get it together, Chris.* I've never been so physically out of control around a woman before. Why her? Why now? Why here, at the bloody RMM of all places? "For all you know," she's saying, "I did horribly at university because I refused the man his essays all the time."

I raise one of my eyebrows meaningfully. Please. Elsa's toed the line just as well as I have over the years, of that I'm sure.

She rolls her eyes and gently kicks the side of my shoe. "Fine. I never refused an assignment. This would be my first time doing so. Are you in or not?"

A feminine fist is proffered. I knock mine against it, marveling how this small instant of skin against skin feels like foreplay that's going to send me to a cold shower in no time. And for a moment, it seems as if she's just as affected by this insignificant touch as I am. But then she clears her throat and says lightly, "I knew I could count on you."

"We still need a witching hour first, though."

She leans in and Tahitian vanilla floods my senses. It's my new favorite smell. "That's on you, Your Highness. I found us a first."

"For tomorrow," I stress.

One of her fingers traces the line of my collar from just below my ear to the pointed tip under my chin. The air in my chest stills until her fingers leave me. "Three a.m. *is* tomorrow."

I'm a fool, because I allow one hand to curve around her waist for the smallest of moments, just long enough to squeeze gently. And now I'm twice as turned on, as if that was even possible. "If we're going to ditch the hike and essay—"

"Oh, we're really standing up to the man now." Her voice is breathy and soft amidst the chatter beyond the bushes, her eyes darkening in the warm glow of lamplight. "We're not hiking, either?"

"We'll be too tired to hike after being up so late. Besides, it starts at five-thirty a.m., Els. How many heirs do you think are actually going to make it? We surely won't be the only two still asleep during all the so-called fun. If I were a betting man, I'd say no one is going to show up."

I watch her take a deep breath before she says, "Point ceded. Continue."

"So my first is . . . let us follow the Pergola trail and have our hike during the witching hour."

It's her turn to lift her eyebrows. She knows I'm referring to what once must have been a magnificent walking trail: a series of formerly grapevine and fruit tree covered pergolas stretching nearly a mile on the grounds around the castle that are now in rustic yet charming abandon. I traced the line of the trail on the drive up to the castle.

"I've never hiked in the middle of the night," I add. "It will be a first for me."

"I highly doubt that's considered hiking. People strolled the Pergola path all the time before it fell apart."

"Now you're just nitpicking."

Somebody calls her name; and by somebody, I mean Mat. How in bloody hell has he found us?

But then I get a quiet, "Bring a bottle of wine."

Done.

CHAPTER 20

ELSA

"I swear," Mat says as he approaches us, two glasses of champagne in his hands, "if I didn't know better, I'd think you two were hiding behind the bushes."

I take a discreet step back from Christian, realizing it might appear as if I were practically climbing all over him. His *too*-ness distracts me so. "Can you blame us?"

"Only because you didn't invite me to join you." He offers me one of the glasses. "Sorry I don't have one for you, too, Christian. But I thought a glass was in order, as the first official match of the RMM was just announced. Hooray fucking huzzah."

I take the drink, desperately trying to repress the insidious shiver threatening to overtake me. We are on our second day, and an announcement has already been made? And then it hits me. All the clapping and cheering earlier represented a grotesque celebration of victims of the RMM losing their respective freedoms when it comes to matters of the heart.

"Who are the unlucky souls?" Christian asks.

Mat takes a long swallow of bubbly. "My sister and some poor sod from the Greek contingency."

I don't know what to say. It is obvious Mat isn't happy in the least with this match.

Christian lets out a low whistle. "How is she dealing with it?"

"The only way she's allowed to: with her chin up and a smile on her face." Mat's grimace is the direct opposite of what he's describing as he holds up his glass. "Gossip claims there's at least one more announcement coming tonight."

Panic flutters within my chest, even though I figure it cannot be mine. While my father indicated his preference for Mat, he hasn't laid down the decree yet. There is still hope, as slim as it may be.

My whisper is barely voiced. "So soon."

"Do you know who?" Christian asks.

"No, mate." Mat sips his champagne. "But what I do know is that the Grand Duchess has requested the presence of both you and your brother."

Christian swears softly beneath his breath. I am startled by his quiet vehemence, even more so by the obvious sympathy tinting Mat's face. Do they fear it is Christian at risk of an announcement?

The man in question pauses only momentarily to square his shoulders. "I best not keep the Grand Duchess waiting, then."

It is pointless resisting the urge to stare as he takes his leave. I am disconcerted by how unsettled he was, and that's an unfamiliar feeling for me, especially when it concerns a person I've only known a couple days.

"I don't envy him," Mat says, also eying Christian's departure.

I sip the bubbly he gave me slowly. Despite the chilly air around us, my drink is semi-warm. "Oh?"

He rakes a hand through his sandy hair. "How well do you know the Grand Duchess of Aiboland?"

"Not at all," I admit. "Why?"

Mat leans against the wall, swirling the champagne in his glass. "Let's just say that Her Highness is formidable."

I reflect on what I know about Christian's mother. She's smart, elegant, well spoken, and admired by much of the world for being the epitome of a modern monarch, even if one of a tiny country. "Could we not say that about most our parents?"

"I suppose so," he muses quietly. "And still, I do not envy my friend his home life, even if . . ." His shoulders sag, a distance filling his eyes.

"Are you all right, Mat?"

The smile he pastes upon his face is no doubt the same his sister showed the others a quarter of an hour before. "I know we're hiding and all, but they've just put out the most delicious looking gelato. Fancy a scoop?"

I would rather take a knitting needle to my eye than rejoin the party, but as curiosity is burning a fresh path through me, I follow him toward the dessert table.

Minutes later, as I'm nibbling on teeny spoonfuls of gelato, I do my best to pretend I am faithfully listening to a story Mat's telling me about him and his sister when they were little, but my attention is anywhere else.

Okay. That's a lie—not the story he recounts, which I am certain is true, but that my attention is anywhere else. Because it's not. It is specifically refocusing upon one place.

Christian and Isabelle are with my father and the Grand Duchess, near the guest house overlooking the mountains. They're drinking champagne and Isabelle is pale and our parents are so pleased with themselves, it's appalling.

And Christian? His smile is tight and forced, all practiced lines that offer the untrained eye quiet politeness. His Serene Highness may believe Christian is pleasantly enjoying whatever they're discussing. Perhaps Isabelle, too. But me, who has known this prince all of two days, can tell how pissed and miserable he is, and those are two emotions he most definitely wasn't feeling while we were hiding behind the bushes.

Would such forced lines tighten his face if it were me standing next to him and not my sister? Wishful thinking at its finest, especially as he made it quite clear to me he's no more interested in a match at the RMM than I am.

Oh, bloody hell.

I may not believe in love at first sight, but like I told Charlotte, lust at first sight is a very real, very valid thing. Because how else can I explain my sudden obsession with all things Christian?

I tune Mat back in, wondering if my smile matches Christian's.

"It was nice," he murmurs. I'm not the only one whose attention has wavered, because he stares at his sister standing with the man who must be her new fiancé. "And Margaux was happy. I was, too. It's funny how we look back and wish for what we once thought was merely commonplace, yet in reality is a rarity."

"We always look back on memories differently, don't we?"

It is his turn to refocus on me. A quiet exhale of a laugh passes from between his lips. "The grass is always greener elsewhere, I suppose. It just becomes unfortunate when your bare toes have felt such grass."

I shove the spoon into my gelato, unsure how to properly respond. And that is part of the problem—I never quite know what to say to Mat.

He hands his bowl to a passing server before stepping closer. "I'm sorry. That was unfair of me, to unload all that on you."

Now I feel even worse.

"I suppose I'm nostalgic," he continues, "knowing my sister and I will be forced to finally let go of hopes and pasts this week. It's a straightjacket feeling, isn't it?"

Something in me softens at the gentle melancholy I am unsure he means for me to see. I hand my bowl to another passing server. "Have you ever wondered what it would be like to have not been born royal? To not have such expectations on your shoulders?"

His smile is genuine, if not dampened. "All the time. As do you, I'm sure."

Dammit. I suppose there is a bit of an urge to share after all. Words I never would have guessed I'd give him slip out. "When I was younger, I talked with classmates about their lives, and of the choices they were afforded. Even those from wealthy, powerful families still had so many choices before them." The secrets I'm giving him are quiet amongst the loud voices around us. "I began to truly realize that, while I am afforded so many things others are denied or covet, I am still beholden to expectations of thousands of people I do not even know. And those expectations are not always the easiest to live up to, especially when the glare of public life is so bright."

There's his soft exhale of a laugh again, only this time, it is filled with a hint of relief. "Exactly." And then something else fills his eyes—not so much camaraderie, but a sense of understanding compassion coupled with newfound respect. "Although, that's unfair of me to even say or think. Because while my family legacy holds me tight, it must be nothing compared to that in which a throne still rules."

I take him in now, all of him. I finally notice the sharp black vest he's wearing over a crisp gray shirt, the faint pinstriped charcoal pants hugging his lean frame, and the sleek, laceless loafers that leave him reminding me of a green crayon in a box of blues. And I cannot help but wonder just who Mathieu really is.

But what I do know is that his words were weighted with sincerity no matter how heavy they fell between us. So when he moves forward, arms hesitantly opening, I take a deep breath and step into them for a brief hug. And it feels nice. Safe. Extremely brotherly.

Which is not exactly what one desires from their future spouse.

CHAPTER 21

♛
CHRISTIAN

Isabelle is waxing poetic about horses again. Only this time, Prince Gustav and the She-Wolf have joined in, so between the three of them, I've filled my quota of horse talk for an entire century.

As they debate . . . shite, I don't know, different kinds of steeds, I can't help but despair that this is how my life will be going forward. Not so much hearing about animals I care little to nothing about, but that my manipulative mother and potential future father-in-law will always be here to vehemently shove a relationship I do not want down my throat. So much of me wants to just shout, "I'm done, fuck the RMM and the rest of you," but I don't. None of us trapped here do. And it makes us the biggest lot of cowards ever.

I rebel, though, the only way I can in such a situation. Every time Isabelle inadvertently moves closer, I shift another step away. Each time she anemically flirts with me (just enough, I suspect, to appease her father), I pay her back in cool yet polite response. I seriously piss off the She-Wolf, but I don't care.

Isabelle's not awful, to be honest. Polite, if not icy. Smart. Refined. A looker. To many imprisoned in the RMM, this would be enough. Hell, this would be enough for many people outside of this farce I'm trapped in. But the assuredness in my bones tells me it's not enough for me.

I want more.

I want that spark, that flame to petrol. And I know I'll never find it with Isabelle.

CHAPTER 22

ELSA

The Pergola path is uneven in spots, especially in the pitch black of night, and I cannot seem to properly stay on my feet. After the third stumble, I grip Christian's arms in an effort to keep from face planting in abject humiliation.

Keeping it classy and real, Elsa.

He stops to steady me. "Are you okay?"

I assure him I'm fine. "I swear I am not normally so uncoordinated."

It is hard to tell, but in the darkness, it appears a smirk tugs at his lips. Maybe it's best I don't see it, though. That mouth, and the way it curves, is dangerous. "Don't worry. Uncoordinated is one thing I've never thought of when it comes to describing the Hereditary Crown Princess of Vattenguldia."

I ache to laugh. Instead, I shift closer as a gust of wind rattles my balance. "Are bossy, rude, and inappropriate on your list?"

He does laugh. "Possibly inappropriate, but meant in the best of ways."

Before I can request clarification, he clears his throat and releases an arm. The beam of his flashlight waves down the path in front of us. "Almost there."

I am pleasantly surprised he does not release me entirely. A strong hand drops to curl around my frozen fingers. "Shall we?"

It's chilly in a way Vattenguldia never is, but his hand in mine renders me warmer than if we were on a beach in Bermuda. "You know an awful lot about this place."

He takes my teasing in stride. "Parker had me read up on it during the flight here."

My toes find a rock and I stumble again, but this time, he is right here to catch me.

Prince Charming strikes again.

"You know what?" Christian says. "Forget about going all the way to the end. Let's stop here."

"Will the first count? We didn't traverse the entire Pergola."

He chuckles. "I don't think that was the first, was it? I merely wanted to hike the path. We've done so, haven't we?"

I hold aloft an imaginary wine glass. "Cheers to your first, then."

"Hold off on that for just a moment." He shrugs off the backpack he's been carrying and unzips it. In the curved beam of my flashlight's glow, I watch him extract a blanket, a bottle of wine, a corkscrew, and two paper cups.

"You brought wine!"

The blanket spreads out below us. "Why do you sound so surprised? You asked for it, didn't you?"

I join him on the blanket, cross-legged as he passes me a glass. "Do you always do everything a woman tells you?"

"God, no. But then, I don't do everything a man tells me, either."

I wonder what he would do if I told him to kiss me. I bet he's a fantastic kisser, the kind that can make a girl forget just about everything.

I am so pathetic, daydreaming about kissing Prince Charming.

Being attracted to a person, and all the chemical reactions that rock your body when you're in their presence, can be so bloody inconvenient, especially when it is with your future brother-in-law.

He uncorks the bottle and fills our cups. "You're awfully quiet. Are you worried about wild animals?"

It is enough to tear me away from vivid images of us hiding away in a quiet room, tearing off one another's clothes. "There are wild animals around here?"

He passes me a cup. "Didn't your Charlotte have you read up on the place, too? The original owner used to have a private zoo here."

I nearly drop my wine. "There are zoo animals running wild on the property?!"

He chuckles again. "Els. Hold on. Just listen." A warm hand rests on my arm. "What I was saying was, there used to be a zoo here, but most of the animals are gone. That said, there are still some breeds that remain, but I imagine there are also other animals in the region, such as coyotes and raccoons. So yes, there are lots of animals around here. There are animals everywhere in the world."

I angle my flashlight into the darkness surrounding us, desperate to ensure no shining eyes reflect back.

"We can go back if you're worried."

I swallow my uncertainty at the worry in *his* voice. "Don't be ridiculous. How often does somebody get to drink wine in the dark, surrounded by . . ." I lamely motion in front of us. "The possibility of wild animals?"

Soft, rueful laughter spills out of him. "It was a terrible first to request, wasn't it?"

I am tempted to say yes, but I turn toward him and finally decipher snatches of his face in the dappled moonlight. All of the air inside of me ceases its flow as it sinks in that we are sitting underneath the moonlight, wine in hand, and it's exquisitely quiet and still and there are no parents or RMMs or anything else to touch us.

Right now, we are simply Elsa and Christian and no one else.

"No." I am surprised at the strength of this sentiment . "It was the perfect one for tonight."

We drink the wine, serenaded by the songs of crickets, while thoughts and feelings and words flow between us. There is no awkwardness, no searching for trivial niceties to fill the space with. I soak up every bit of himself that he gifts me, and I cannot help but think he does the same. Our time together is comfortable and yet charged with something I can't quite put my finger on.

Something lovely and fluttery and comfortable and exciting all at once.

Later, when we're back at the main house, he says, "Give me your phone."

"Why?" I pass it over anyway.

"I just realized," he says quietly, yet lightly, "that we don't have each other's numbers."

I am far more drunk by this request than from the wine. He offers me his cell in return, and we program our numbers in. "Will I get a special ringtone, too?"

He chuckles. "Naturally." And then he surprises me by escorting me back to my bedroom door. Once we're there, he leans down, his lips right up against my ear. "Sweet dreams, Els."

So much inside me clenches and flutters. Maybe it's because of the darkness enveloping us in this tiny hallway, maybe it's due to the wine, but I return the favor, my lips just as close to his ear as his had been to mine. "Sweet dreams, Christian."

His head shifts, and we stand there, our cheeks grazing one another as I struggle to control my breathing. And then, as he squeezes one of my hands, he brushes his lips against my temple.

The kiss is completely innocent in the grand scheme of things, and yet, my knickers practically melt right off my body.

I quietly duck into my room before I do something unwise. To my relief, or maybe my dismay, my father and Isabelle are once more sawing logs with gusto. I quickly change into my pajamas, but right before I slip under the covers, my phone vibrates.

Thanks for running amuck with me tonight.

If I thought there were butterflies before, they were nothing compared to what rages inside my chest as I stare down at Christian's message.

I ought to type something droll, something lighthearted and fun. But my fingers quiver, and my heart thumps hard within my chest. All my wit abandons me in glorious desertion. Perhaps I am truly sleep deprived, delirious even, because all I can type is: I look forward to us running amuck during the next witching hour.

I groan. We joked about sounding secondary school-ish, but goodness, I just sent us right back to those years, haven't I?

Oh, man. I have it bad for this prince.

CHAPTER 23

CHRISTIAN

"It looks as if it might rain."

I squint up at darkened bottoms of gray clouds lining the sky. Elsa's first has come and gone, and it was done separately. We both missed the morning hike, but so did everyone else save one sad heir. And now here I am on the north terrace, spending a mandatory breakfast with Isabelle after enjoying some pretty damn vivid yet frustrating dreams that starred her sister during the slim amount of time I actually did sleep. Frankly, I'd rather be back in my bed, dreaming about Elsa than talking about weather with Isabelle. "Maybe, yeah."

Icy amusement barely lifts the corners of her lips as she smooths her long hair over her shoulder. At least there has been no talk of horses this morning, but I might as well be watching paint dry, I'm so uninterested in what's happening here.

"California is nice," she adds after a long moment.

I scratch the back of my neck and nod. "Yeah, it is."

"This is my first trip to the States." She lifts her teacup, pinky extended. "I wish we could sightsee more."

More? I want to laugh at such optimism. There will be no sightseeing outside of the grounds. None of the locals, save those working for the Monarch Council, are aware the world's sovereigns are even in the region. Our press offices have us dutifully working back in our home countries. Hell, we don't even have our bodyguards here. But I tell Isabelle, "Me, too."

Somebody calls out her name; when she turns to wave in greeting, I'm glad for the temporary reprieve. It allows me more time to daydream about her sister.

CHAPTER 24

ELSA

I hiss beneath my breath, "How many more of these idiotic meetings must we be tortured with?"

Christian's smile is tempered as we weave our way out of one of the guest cottages, even though it is obvious he's as outraged as I am. "Come on," he tells me quietly. "Let's go somewhere that isn't here."

Sweet relief uncurls my fingers from fists that have minds of their own. We sat in yet another awful Crown Heirs meeting during which we listened to yet another pompous jackass explain why we are best seen but not heard until our sovereigns tell us differently. I might resent my father's talking points, but bloody hell. I have not yet had the opportunity to even utter one, and we're on our third day here.

We disappear into one of the stairwells of the main house. It is quiet; most everyone is either in another meeting or heading to a buffet luncheon. As strange as the location is, though, I like it. Filtered sunlight swirls about us, specks of dust glittering in the cool air. I cannot help but feel that, if we were to stay in this hallway, we very well might wander through a portal in time.

Christian presses his back against the rough, textured concrete of the stairwell and says, "It could be worse." More softly, "It could be breakfast. Or tea."

His brutal honesty stings, as I know exactly what he means. Breakfast this morning was a compulsory tête-à-tête with Mat. Last night's share and tell was over. We had so much to say to one another that the two of us were resigned to chatting about different restaurants. And to know that tea is on the horizon, with the same strained attempts at getting to know one another?

I'd rather return to the meeting so recently fled.

"How was breakfast, anyway?" I ask.

"Well, for once, your sister didn't talk about horses. So there's that."

I am initially taken aback, but then practically choke on all the laughter yearning to find a way out. "You're not a horse fan?"

He pretends to shudder. "God, no."

It feels lovely to smile, *really* smile, after a miserable few hours. "Me, either."

His dazzling grin resurfaces. "How was yours?"

"I can verify Mat and I didn't discuss horses, either."

His hands press together and lift upward. "Thank goodness for miracles, right?"

"The RMM is a terrible beast. Small talk at its worst." Then, much more gently, "I think you're growing on my sister."

Isabelle did not refer to him as a Neanderthal this morning, nor did she issue any pointed comments about her required meal with this prince. In their place was a resigned quietness, a sense of duty no longer verbally laced with animosity, which was unnerving, leaving me to stew about an acceptance that may not have not been there before.

My observation wipes the amusement off Christian's face, albeit slowly. And I regret saying anything, because bloody hell, is his laughter addictive. "Ah."

I bite my lip. Watch him, wondering if I misspoke.

"I've done my best not mislead her, but Els, while I believe your sister to be a lovely woman, I . . ." He runs both hands through his hair. "I can't say she is growing on me."

Logic suggests I let this line of conversation go. Duty argues I must elucidate why Isabelle is the perfect choice to be his future Grand Duchess. Tradition begs me to go and make peace with Mathieu, rather than secretly delight in how my sister's intended sounds wretchedly unhappy at the prospect of a relationship with her.

Tradition, I am learning, is not always the easiest road to walk upon.

I discreetly clear my throat. "You must rue not proposing to someone back home prior to this week."

His puff of quiet laughter smacks of just as much bitterness as his last words. "As do you, I suppose."

Has Isabelle mentioned her devotion toward Alfons yet? I cannot break my sister's confidence, but if Christian were to know . . .

No. Some traditions must stand, even if I wish they wouldn't.

I reach out and gingerly touch his arm. Delicious warmth seeps through the pads of my fingers. "I am certain you've been exceedingly clear with Isabelle, but I would still ask of you to be gentle with her."

His attention lingers on my fingers; seriousness colors both face and tone. "You think I ought to be humoring her as well as Prince Gustav?"

"No," I assure him. How odd he did not mention the Grand Duchess. "Because if you were, I would have to knee you soundly in the balls."

Ah. There's his smile again. Good.

It then strikes me how what I've jokingly threatened could potentially be misrepresented as jealousy rather than sisterly loyalty. At this rate, I will soon rank as one of the least articulate royals. So I clarify, "You know, for leading my little sister on and all."

The upward tilt of his lips grows.

"Because, obviously, sisters before . . ." Oh, hell. Proper articulation truly does abandon me. What is the saying? I am unnaturally flustered.

"Is there a female equivalent to *bros before hos?*" he muses.

I snap my fingers. "Sisters before misters!"

One dark eyebrow lifts, amused.

Another snap follows. "Chicks before dicks!"

Rich laughter returns as an entirely insincere shudder wracks his shoulders. "For the love of all that's good in the world, don't ever say that again."

I lean back against the black railing lining the outer wall, mimicking his position. In this tiny stairway, our feet overlap on the steps. "Are you scandalized?"

I ought to be, standing in such close approximation to him.

"Why should I be?" he says. "I'm not the one shouting about dicks, am I?"

My fingers trace the bumpy ridges on the concrete walls as humor wells within my gut. "Honestly, Christian, I promise that, despite how I present myself, I wasn't raised in the wild." The corners of my lips creep upward. "Or a brothel."

He pushes off the wall, chuckling. And then, before I know it, his body leans into mine, one hand bracing against the wall to my right.

Oh my.

Little fairies sprint laps within my chest as his head ducks toward me, dark hair spilling across his forehead.

Time stands still as I stare into his amber eyes. Desperate thoughts and wishes consume me. *Kiss me. For the love of all that's good in the world, kiss me.*

Instead, he tsks. "How very judgmental of you, Els."

Ah. No kissing, then. Why does that disappoint? It's the smart move, after all.

He continues, "Do you know for certain that all . . ." He pauses, no doubt to choose the right word. Or at least, the most respectful version of what I think he is to say.

I offer helpfully. "Ladies of the night?"

He chuckles again, shaking his head. His mouth is a mere five inches away. It is a beautiful mouth, one I dreamed about quite vividly this morning.

"Fine. Prostitutes?"

"My point is," he continues, "do you know for certain that all such ladies would go around shouting about dicks in stairwells?"

My fingers itch to pull him closer, to brush the hair from his eyes. "You make a valid point. They are probably so exhausted by male genitalia that they refuse to discuss such matters outside of business hours."

A pause fills the scant space between us, one so charged bumps sprout across my arms.

He murmurs, "I think if I were to reach my life span's century mark, I would never be able to guess what all goes on in here." One of his fingers taps gently against the side of my head. "Or what you'll say next."

I am unable to repress the delicious shiver that overtakes me at his touch. "Sweet talker. I bet you say that to all the women you find yourself in stairwells with."

"I don't find myself in such situations often." He pauses once more, eyes intent as they bore into me. "Actually, I've never found myself in this situation."

My mouth opens, a snarky comeback on the tip of my tongue, when he traces my lower lip with the same finger that traced my temple. Another shiver ripples through my body, one a thousand times stronger than before.

When Christian says, "Els," my name is softer than the bird songs outside.

His head dips lowers still, attention focused on where his finger rests on my lip, and I think to myself, *could this moment be real?* Because I very much wish it to be.

Tradition be damned.

Our breaths mingle, warm and unsteady in the silence of the stairwell. My hands move forward with a mind of their own, fingers curling around the cotton of his shirt.

His heart hammers just as strongly as my own, and it steels my resolve. I want him. To hell with logistics. *I. Want. This. Man.*

Our mouths are so close I think his lips graze the finger still held against the delicate skin of mine. My grip on his shirt tightens as I urge his body closer. A soft groan spills out of him, one I yearn to eat up. His other hand clasps my waist, and it's my turn to moan.

To hell with my father, his mother, and the RMM.

I'm about to throw caution to the wind when my name is uttered again, louder and from the floor above, and by someone else.

Bloody hell. It's Mat of all people.

Christian's hand drops and he pulls himself away until his back collides with the wall. Wrinkles mar his shirt from where I clutched him, ones I feel rather possessive toward.

I made those. I'd like to make more.

Mat materializes, his retro tennis shoes squeaking on the stone steps. A quick glance at Christian, who is running a hand through his hair, precedes, "What are you two doing here?"

Almost kissing, I think stupidly.

Christian's more tactful than I, as he says, "Hiding again. How about you?"

If Mat notices how tight his friend's voice is, he doesn't show it. He drops to the step right above us, a hand I do not want touching me coming to rest on my shoulder. "They've opened up the outdoor pool for the afternoon, and Prince Gustav . . ." He swallows, obviously uncomfortable. "Suggested I find you so we might enjoy a swim together."

As he says this, the prospect of doing so sounds as welcome as bashing his skull into the roughened walls around us.

"It's sixty degrees outside," Christian scoffs. "And both pools are unheated."

We nearly kissed. Worse, I wanted it, which is colossally suicidal. He made it crystal clear he is completely uninterested in giving his mother the satisfaction of sweeping any girl off her feet at the RMM—not my beautiful sister, not any of the others girls on the Grand Duchess' list (if there is such), and most certainly not myself.

He and I are friends. Allies.

I hate that I am so utterly attracted to my friendly ally.

"They brought heat lamps out after several monarchs complained," Mat says. If he is trying to sweep me off my feet with charm, he fails miserably.

Which is fine by me. "I'm afraid I must decline my father's suggestion as I did not bring my swimsuit."

Predictably, Mat is not heartbroken in the least by my refusal. To Christian, he says, "Did Lukas let you know there are plans for the heirs and spares to skinny-dip at midnight?" His attention reverts to me. "No bathing suits needed for that extracurricular activity."

Uh . . .

"There you all are."

And now, Isabelle is in the stairwell with us, ascending from the floor below. Fantastic. Perhaps we ought to invite all our parents, too.

When she reaches the step below us, she says, more than a bit irritably, "Elsa, I thought we were to meet for luncheon."

Well, shite. That clearly slipped my mind whilst nearly kissing her intended, didn't it?

Rather than waiting for an answer, Isabelle asks, "What are all you doing in a stairwell?" A sweeping glance precedes, "It's cramped in here."

Mat is the one to answer. "I was informing them about the midnight plans for skinny dipping in the Neptune pool currently making the rounds."

"Uh—" I say at the same time Christian mutters, "We—"

Isabelle overrides us both. "How delightful. A whole horde of naked, royal bums all in one place. Wouldn't the paps have a field day with that?"

Princess Isabelle of Vattenguldia, staying true to form.

"That said," she adds in an oddly determined yet steely voice, "I'm in. Because heaven knows we need some entertainment around here."

Now I have heard everything. My reserved sister wants skinny-dip with strangers and acquaintances? What in the hell?

"One of the Danes sent their man to fetch some decent liquor for the gathering. Oh, and any cell phones or cameras brought are promised to be promptly sunk into the deep end." Mat leans his hand against the wall, right where Christian's was just minutes before, leaning next me as if we are officially a couple.

I attempt to picture Mat naked. While there is no doubt he is beautiful, all lean, sculpted muscles, no tingles accompany such a vision.

The heat emanating from his body even feels different than Christian's.

"Who came up with this idea?" Christian asks.

I am a masochist, because once more, images of *this* man naked flit throughout my mind, prompting far too many tingles to account for. I fear I am blushing, but it cannot be helped. Witnessing a naked Christian must be a religious experience. Pun intended.

Jesus, I am going to hell for that one.

Mat rattles off names of the instigators, and it solidifies my resolve that there is no possible way my naked self will join any of them in that pool at midnight.

I assume my sister's typical role as I visualize the headlines covering such a soirée: *Naked Royals From Across The Globe Drown In Famous Neptune Pool*. Followed by the subheading: *Toxicology reports indicate extreme inebriation*.

Isabelle edges up a step near Christian. I watch how discomfort tightens his muscles, but he is much too polite to move away from her as I know he wishes to. Much like how I yearn to with Mat leaning in to me. And then she startles me, as she grimly reaches up to brush the dark hair out of his eyes I'd wished minutes before to touch.

I have never wanted to slap at my sister's hand before like I do now.

While Mat and Isabelle hash out the known details for the skinny dipping expedition, I force myself to remember my sister is clearly still reeling from whatever happened with Alfons. She normally would never partake in such an activity like skinny-dipping or even willingly stand so close to a man chosen by our parents rather than her heart.

That's the thing, though. This isn't just some man. This is someone our father wants her to marry. A very handsome, funny, lovely man I would really rather she didn't put her hands on because I am selfish enough to be the one who wishes to do all the groping. I mean touching. No—hell, who am I kidding? I mean full-on *groping*.

I surreptitiously glance at Christian; his eyes are unfocused as he stares off at one of the walls. He is listening to them as much as I am.

I attempt to imagine what life would be like with Christian as my brother-in-law. And then I imagine where to find whatever Dane located those good, stiff drinks to ask for some, because it is a terrible thing to envision Christian and Isabelle together.

Before I glance away, his attention shifts to me. Our eyes meet in this tiny stairwell, as we're trapped between our supposed intendeds, and . . . he is *looking* at me again, as if we are the only two people in the entire castle, a pinpoint focus of time and place that charges the molecules and atoms within my body.

It is a look I cannot deny I crave. And that is a shame, because he is not mine to love.

CHAPTER 25

CHRISTIAN

I almost kissed her. Just moments before Mat found us, I almost caved in to my rapidly growing, nearly insatiable desire, and kissed Elsa. And now, these interlopers are discussing skinny-dipping in the middle of the night, and I'm trying to keep my dick from growing any larger, because shite. Elsa naked?

Like far too often lately when I'm around her, I stuff my hands in my pockets. Try to think about less pleasant things, like the meeting we're to go to in a few minutes, the one we'll share with our parents. I'll be sitting next to the She-Wolf for nearly two hours; if that's not able to kill a hard-on, then I don't know what could.

But then, like a moth to flame, I refocus on Els, and I have to subtly shift to hide just how fucking attracted to her I am.

And I am. Almost obsessively so.

I push off the concrete wall and pray that none present will notice the bulge in my trousers. "We'll be late to our meeting if we don't go now."

I don't need to tell Elsa twice. She slips away from Mat's arm so swiftly he nearly trips on the stairs.

"See you at tea?" Isabelle says to me. At least, I think it's to me, as there's no enthusiasm at all in her voice.

I've never been more grateful for assigned seating at dinner in my life.

CHAPTER 26

ELSA

The meeting for Nordic countries held in the library is fairly productive, especially in light that there were no discussions relating to the RMM, so that right there makes it the best meeting I'd been to in California. Furthermore, we heirs are finally allowed to speak, and it does my ego good to be able to bring to light my causes.

While the King of Sweden discusses key economic issues facing Scandinavia, as well as the influx of migrants crossing our borders, my attention drifts back to the stairwell. His Majesty encourages us to locate land and housing to offer to the migrants, and a heated debate arises. I am heated, too, but for entirely different reasons. I know what I want tonight's first to be. I simply must work up the courage to admit it to Christian.

CHAPTER 27

♛
CHRISTIAN

The stairwell is blessedly empty, so Elsa drops down onto one of the steps. "I refuse to go skinny-dipping with the others."

I ease myself down on the step right below her, trying not to remember that, just a little over two hours ago, we were nearly kissing in this same spot. "Then we won't."

She looks astonished, then relieved, then guilty that she's so terribly pleased I say this. "You are free to go, of course."

Has she lost her senses? Isabelle will be there. A naked Isabelle. So, hell no. Unless there is a direct order alongside a sincere threat issued from the Grand Duchess, there is no way I will be at that pool tonight. "Why, thank you. I'm delighted to know I've been a good enough lad to earn such an outing."

I wish she'd gift me with her laughter already. It's dancing in her eyes, seducing me in ways I never would have imaged. "No offense," she says, "but I don't fancy the idea of getting buck naked in front of a bunch of virtual strangers."

I can't help but tease, "We're Europeans, Els. We're famous for our topless beaches," even though the thought of her stripping down in front of the others makes me want to smash my fist into the concrete wall next to us.

"Not in Scandinavia, we aren't. And it sounds as if tonight requires more than just a top coming off."

"You could keep your knickers on, you know."

She groans. "Oh yes, I will be the one lady who refuses to let go of her knickers. I can see how easily the others will let that slide." She shakes her head, grinning. "No thank you."

Her reluctance is fine by me. I'd rather spend my time with just her, anyway. "In any case, midnight is three hours short of our witching hour. It would probably go horribly. There's no magic to skinny-dipping at midnight."

She ducks her head, biting her lip as she studies me through obscenely long lashes. "What about at three a.m.?"

I stretch one of my legs out until it brushes up against hers. It's as if I'm woefully addicted to Elsa. "Everything's magical during the witching hour. I thought we already established that."

She doesn't say anything for a long moment, but I can practically see the wheels in her mind churning. And it's reckless and foolish, but my heart beats a new, uneven melody a bit too forcefully within my chest.

I hold my breath. I wait.

And she says, "The Roman Pool feels magical, does it not?"

I clear my throat. Pray I don't squeak like some kind of lad going through puberty. "Oh, most certainly."

The Valkyrie I'm with leans forward. Says, "If there is to be skinny dipping on the menu, I want it there."

Holy. *Hell.*

"That's my first for tonight, Christian. I want us to go skinny-dipping in the Roman Pool during our witching hour."

Us. Our. Two words I have no right to feel possessive over when it comes to this princess. I strain to sound amused. "Will you be wearing your knickers?"

"I shan't if you don't."

I pretend not to notice her voice shook saying that, but then, I'm pretty sure mine wasn't the steadiest, either.

CHAPTER 28

ELSA

"You cannot be serious."

"And yet," I tell Isabelle, "I am."

She sets her hairbrush down. "You know how this will look once word reaches His Serene Highness. He was most insistent on you spending time in the pool with Mathieu."

Our father is downstairs in the Assembly room, discussing important matters, and I am in our room with my sister, explaining myself for not wanting to skinny-dip. Correction, skinny-dip with the masses. But I will not—cannot—let Isabelle know I am more than fine swimming in my birthday suit with Christian—or at least, I hope I will be. Just the thought of him naked and me naked in the same room has my legs crossing.

"You say that like it's a selling point."

She removes the tasteful dress she wore for dinner and cocktails and tosses it onto a nearby chair. "It ought to be."

For all her demureness in public, my sister has been anything but shy around me, because her bra and panties are off and join the dress in her hunt for something new to wear. "There will be nothing to worry about if His Serene Highness remains ignorant of the entire situation."

She digs out a matching, lacy black pair of panties and bra from her suitcase and slips them on. "You would be surprised at how fast word travels around this place."

"I rather doubt the others will be crowing to the elders about their naked, intoxicated adventures in a pool they've been banned from using, let alone tattling like small children on those who did not take part. Speaking of," I say, lightly yet meaningfully, "I am rather surprised *you* are so eager to join in."

"It is expected." She adjusts the bra. "You really ought to be going, Elsa. Now that I've had time to think about it, Mathieu is quite easy on the eyes. Think how . . . helpful it might be to get sneak peek of what's to come."

I nearly choke on her thinly veiled meaning, even though I have not taken a drink. Outside of her indicating that a naked Mat might tempt me more than a clothed one, I can admit that, while good looking, I am not attracted to Mat at all—and seeing him in all his naked glory will not change that. No, I am instead attracted to the one person I *can't* have.

And yet, contemplating our late night rendezvous, a tiny bit of rebellious fierceness argues I *do* have Christian.

Just not in the way I think I want.

A sweater and skintight jeans are pulled on. "This would be the perfect opportunity for you two to spend more time together," Isabelle continues. "Get to know one another, before the inevitable axe drops."

Have I not been forced to do that everyday already? "Ah, yes. What was I thinking?" I muse, tapping thoughtfully on my chin. "Group skinny-dipping is the perfect time to really get to *know* one another. Please do not take offense when I tell you that efforts toward fulfilling our parents' wishes to encourage me into a farce of a relationship are less than stellar. And honestly, Isabelle. Why the fancy lingerie? You are just going to take it off anyway. Nobody will sort through your pile of clothes if you're all in the pool."

"Christian will be there," she says flatly, "and I cannot have him think I don't always look my best. Or that I am not . . ." Her swallow is audible, her face pinched. "Trying."

I am an utter wench, because I fail to tell her Christian will be just as absent as I. His first, us finally having those cups of hot cocoa together, will be shifted to an earlier time to accommodate my daft request. At midnight, we two will be in the kitchen rather than streaking with the rest of the singletons.

My sister makes a good point, though. Am I wearing cute lingerie right now? Scratch that. I do not desire cute. I want sexy. Do my panties and bra even match? When Isabelle turns away, I sneak a peek down my dress. Pink silk and lace numbers that thankfully match one another stare back up at me.

Thank God.

CHAPTER 29

CHRISTIAN

"The She-Wolf will either be shagging somebody or be too blitzed out of her mind to notice," Lukas says as he pops the tops of the beers he smuggled into our room. "So you don't need to worry about *Prince Perfect* tonight."

"Believe me," I say dryly, "that's the last thing on my mind. But it doesn't matter, anyway. I won't be at the pool with the rest of you."

He passes over one of the beers; it's weak and pale, but better than the piss the She-Wolf has provided us. "Which means you'll be somewhere else, right?"

Hell yeah, I will.

"With Parker?"

"There was that event for private secretaries tonight, remember? Chances are, he's probably on his cot, passed out from the amount of booze consumed."

But Lukas is a dog with a bone. "Okay, bro. It's just us right now. Where in the hell are you sneaking off to in the dark of night?"

I take a long drag from the bottle. "I'm surprised you notice. Most of the time you're not even here."

He grins, dropping into one of the chairs across from me. "I'm not *Prince Perfect*." Then he tsks, the grin widening. "No avoiding the question, Chris. Have you at least hooked up with some of the girls?"

I take another sip and lean forward, dangling the bottle between my legs. "Is that what you're doing, Luk? Hooking up?"

"If I've got to be part of this farce, I might as well enjoy myself." He angles his drink in my direction. "You're avoiding again."

Part of me doesn't want to tell him anything, because it's none of his business. But there's also no way it'll ever get back to the She-Wolf, as Lukas has just as many heart-to-hearts with her as I do. "Fine. I've been spending time with someone."

He slaps his knee. Looks pissed. "It's that Vattenguldian girl, isn't it?"

Am I really so transparent? "Actually," I say slowly, "it is."

"Are you fucking kidding me? Have you lost your mind? Why in the world would you hook up with her?"

I'm taken aback by the level of disgust in his voice. I'm also not down with how he makes it sound like I'm making a horrible choice when I already know just how messy the situation is. But it's my mistake to make. And now I'm pissed at my brother, because nobody is going to malign Elsa in my presence. *Nobody.* "Excuse me?"

He shakes his head. "I can't believe you caved so quickly to the She-Wolf's demands. Weren't you just the one who insisted I take a stand?"

Before I can say anything, he continues, "I admit the Vattenguldian spare is a looker, but Jesus, Chris. I could have sworn you wanted nothing to do with her. When you're together, you act as if she has a contagious disease. And now you're hooking up with her? What gives?"

He's talking about Isabelle. Thankfully, I don't have to knock some sense into him. "You're talking out of your arse. When have I ever given any indication I'm interested in that woman?"

He blinks in confusion.

"I am not hooking up with Isabelle, and if I have my way, I never will be. To be honest, I'm not hooking up with anybody, at least not in the way you're thinking."

He waves a hand in front of him. "Wait. Are you hooking up with her sister? The heir?"

That reminds me. I'm going to see Elsa naked soon. My pants grow way too tight, forcing me to shift in my seat. Being turned on all the time is not a very comfortable state to be in. "Did you not just hear me? No, I'm not *hooking* up with her."

Although, I wish I was. And just the thought makes me shift in my seat once more.

"Let me get this straight. You're sneaking out in the middle of the night to *spend time* with this woman?"

I'm annoyed at how disturbingly confused he is by this. "She has a name, Luk. It's Elsa."

Now his eyes widen. "What does *spending time* together even mean, if not shagging one another?"

I go to answer him, but it hits me. Really hits me. It means more than just me obsessively lusting after her. I think . . . no I know . . . oh, bloody hell. I'm falling for her, aren't I?

Shite.

"Because, if you guys were simply shagging, I'd get it. Okay, yes. She's sexy as all hell. But she's also your equivalent and the heir to another throne. *And* your future sister-in-law. Are you purposely trying to piss the She-Wolf off? Is this some kind of game to see just how far you can push her before she backs down? Because there is no way she's ever going to approve of you two"—he flashes air quotes—"hanging out. Not when it could mess up her plans."

Maybe I ought to knock that sense into him after all. "First of all, anything that happens between me and Elsa has nothing—and I repeat, nothing—to do with the She-Wolf. And secondly, I don't give a flying shite if she approves of whom I'm friends with or not—let alone if it screws with her master plan."

He scoffs. "You've been sneaking out in the middle of the night like a bloody teenager to hang out with your *friend?*"

"I'm not sneaking out. And we haven't hidden the fact that we know one another or spend time together."

"Sitting in your boring meetings is one thing," he argues. "But doing whatever you're doing in the middle of the night is another. Just what the fuck are you two doing, Chris?"

It's enough to lend pause.

"I don't know," I tell my brother quietly. "I really don't. But whatever it is, I don't want to stop."

He nurses his beer for a long moment before taking a sip. "You like this woman. I mean, Elsa."

My forced laughter is quiet. Bitter. "Something like that."

"Do you know if she feels the same?"

"Does it matter? Considering, as you pointed out, I'm most likely going to be forced into marrying her sister?"

"Hell yeah, it does," he says softly.

It surprises me he says this. And I feel like a lousy brother that I misjudge him far too often.

I take another long drag of my warming beer. "I haven't kissed her." Another bitter laugh. "I'm falling for her and I haven't even really kissed her. How's that for fucked up, Luk? I feel like some kind of goddamn teenager right now. I don't know what is up and what is down anymore."

He doesn't know what else there is to say. It's okay. I don't either.

CHAPTER 30

♛
ELSA

The reflection from the alabaster lamps glows warm gold against the cool sapphire water, and with genuine gilded tiles scattered throughout the room, the effect is magical. Most of our peers are enamored with the pool outside, and rightfully so. It is truly magnificent. But this one here, beneath the tennis courts?

This is the one that lures me in like a siren.

The entire room is covered in cobalt and golden mosaics alongside marble statues, leaving me debating whether I am in California or ancient Rome. There is a liquid effect, one fragile and tentative, as if words alone might splatter it away in a dream.

On quiet toes, I wander to where Christian leans against the black tourist railings surrounding the edge of the pool.

"This place," he murmurs, "is truly a portal in time."

I focus on a diving platform before us, resplendent in golden mermaid mosaics. It is funny for him to say such a thing, considering this pool is an infant compared to the palaces he and I both reside within. And yet, he is absolutely right.

My words are just as hushed as his. "It's perfectly enchanting."

He nudges my shoulder. "Too bad we didn't think about bringing the cocoa down here with us."

We drank two cups apiece, so every word uttered to one another now is sweet and chocolaty. I have never, ever enjoyed hot cocoa as much as I did tonight.

"For RFCers," I say, "we have poor planning skills."

He rocks back on his heels. "Speaking of, are you ready for your first, Els?"

No, I think, because now that I had the time to think about what we are to do, I realize it's possibly the worst idea I have ever had. But I refuse to tell him that. "Of course."

He grabs the towels looped around the railing and meanders to the far side of the pool where a white diving board protrudes across the deep water. A small black gate is unlatched, allowing us access denied to so many. I trail after him, straight to the edge of the pool, where marble steps lead into glassy blue. My shoes shucked off, I dip my toes in.

The water is cold. Frigid, to be more exact.

"Verdict?"

I glance up at Christian, loving how his navy sweater makes him appear as if he belongs in this room. "Perfect."

He smirks, pretending to shudder. I nearly shudder, too, at the thought of what we're about to do. Only, not so much shudder, but shiver in anticipation.

We loop behind decorated walls, where statues guard the pool, to discover a much more shallow alcove and twin stairs ascending to the diving platform. He points to one of the sides. "There are dressing rooms in the back."

One of my hands sweeps before us. "The pool is icy. The night is chilly. Are you truly desiring to enter a cold dressing room and prolong the torture?"

He feigns shock. "You said the water was perfect!"

My hands settle upon my hips.

"We don't have to do this, you know."

I arch an eyebrow up.

The towels are dropped near one of the stairs. "You have nothing to prove to me."

"I did not believe this was about proving anything. I thought this was about firsts."

"My point stands."

"Do you find me a prude?"

He laughs, and I swear the waters around us ripple in response. "That's one of the last things I could ever call you."

I ought to be horrified. Embarrassed at the very least. But from him, this sounds like a beautiful compliment.

"I was simply mentioning that you have nothing to prove to anybody, let alone me. If you don't feel comfortable jumping stark naked into a frigid pool, then you most certainly don't have to. We'll still have our cocoa experience to qualify the night as a success."

"That was only one first—yours. Doesn't the RFC allow each member a new first during the witching hour?" I tap my chin. "Perhaps it's *you* who has doubts, and to save face, it is easier to place blame on me."

Although, truthfully, I've never been more nervous in my entire life. I've stood in front of cameras and crowds and know the weight of expectations and crowns. Yet here I am, in the black of night, with cricket songs the only noises to be heard outside of our voices, and my knees are perilously close to quaking.

"I don't think it's chlorinated."

I tear my eyes away from the mosaics glinting up from the bottom of the shallow waters in the alcove next to us, back to meet his. And now, another golden treasure in the room appears —his amber eyes glow just as stunningly as the lights and gilt around us. "I suppose that means we best not pee in the pool."

"Do you tend to pee in pools often, Els?"

I shuck off a sandal and chuck it at him. He dodges easily.

"Okay." He claps his hands together. "No peeing. No swallowing, either."

I wrinkle my nose. "Do you tend to drink pool water often, Chris?"

He stills, wide-eyed, and it occurs to me this is the first time I have referred to him as anything other than his full name, despite his request days ago. And yet, doing so feels intimate and natural and familiar all at the same time.

Chris to his Els.

But then he recovers and tugs off one of his shoes to lob at me. I dodge just in time to watch it sink into the water.

"Well, now you've done it," I say as it settles on the bottom. "We must go in, even if it is only to save your shoe." The corner of my mouth crooks upward.

He chuckles again. "No shallow end. We go in big or go home losers."

I bet he goes in big.

Thank goodness the light is dim in here. I clear my throat and motion toward the diving platform above us. "If we are to do so, it must be from up there."

He cocks his head and studies it. "Ten feet up, maybe?"

I nod. "And the pool is ten feet deep. Toes touch the bottom before we get out."

Amusement is such an appealing look on him.

"I feel like we are sixteen, defying our parents."

His amusement grows. "We've forgone our adulthood this week, remember?"

I smack my forehead. "Right. Of course." And then, because I cannot help myself, "Did you skinny-dip at sixteen?"

He bites his lip. It's another delicious look. "Fifteen, actually. At Lake Como. Lukas and I met some local girls and decided it'd be fun."

"Was it?"

"Bodyguards found us nearly immediately. The She—" It's his turn to clear his throat. His following grin is rueful. "My mother was not pleased. Thankfully there are no pictures, and it stayed out of the press." He kicks off his other shoe. "What about you?"

I follow suit. "Ah, now here's the moment you find out I am actually a prude: a true skinny-dipping virgin."

He tugs his sweater over his head, revealing a white t-shirt clinging to well-defined muscles. "So, what you're saying is that you're a twenty-eight-year-old virgin running amuck?"

I tear my eyes away from his chest and focus on unbuttoning my jacket. "Alas, at least in this instance, I am."

"And what we're really doing is popping your cherry tonight?"

Oh, goodness. We are in a refrigerator, and I am sweating up a storm, I'm overheating so badly. "Put out or shut up already, won't you?"

He grabs the hem of his t-shirt with one hand and tugs upward. I blurt out, terrified of losing what little propriety I possess, "No peeking, though."

He pauses, shirt halfway up. Attempting to not ogle what appears to be the most perfect abs I've seen on a man is a difficult feat, indeed. "How do you expect us to get up to the top of the platform?"

"Not like keeping your eyes closed up the stairs or—" Holy hell, am I feeling like our proverbial virgin running amuck right now. "Oh, forget it. Please proceed."

And he does.

And I wonder why I believed it cold tonight.

He tosses me one of the towels; I catch it before it hits the water. Christian is uncharacteristically quiet, serious even. I cannot determine if this is good or bad—our banter, as cutting or flirty as it has grown to be, always leaves me feeling as if we've been friends for ages rather than mere days.

Just before I make a total arse of myself by staring lusty holes through him, Christian wanders to the stairs leading up to the right side of the diving platform. "See you below?"

I snap out of my reverie long enough to nod and head toward the stairs on the left.

For all of his protestations, Christian is the gentleman I pegged him for that very first day. On the other side of the stairs, he's turned away so I know he cannot see me stripping. And I return the favor, as I am certainly not going to be able to go through with anything tonight if all I do is gawk at his too perfect body. Once cold air kisses my bare skin, I wrap the towel around me.

"Ladies first?" he calls from the other side.

I take his dare. I climb up the stairs slowly, debating with each press of foot against mosaic if I am actually dreaming.

When I reach the top, I find Christian's bare back facing me as he sits at the base of his side of the stairs. A hint of the curve of his buttocks is visible, and the sight of it overheats me. He might as well be one of the statues in this room, he's too picturesque.

Christian and his damn too-ness.

What would he think of me if I climbed down his side and took my time as I traced the magnificent planes of such muscles?

"You okay?" he asks, head tilting just enough to the side that I jerk further into the diving platform area. "Would you prefer I go first?"

I assure him I am fine. I toss the towel back down below; it lands mere inches from the water's edge. And then I jump.

CHAPTER 31

CHRISTIAN

I train my attention on a nearby statue as the sound of her feet climbing the stairs fills my ears, trying desperately not to fixate on how Elsa is naked. Thank goodness the water is ice cold, because I'm truly concerned she'll notice how aroused I already am.

A splash sounds, and then a muffled scream followed by the start of soft giggling. I wish she'd just let go and allow herself to laugh. I mean, hell, we broke into a pool in the dead of night and there's no one around. I paid off the security guard and his dog for the next hour or so. If she wants to laugh, there's no reason she shouldn't.

It's a first I'm dying to experience: the first time she fully laughs in my presence. Although, to be honest, I worry the day she does so is the day I'm no longer able to control myself around her. Elsa laughing is probably one of the most erotic sounds in the entire universe.

Like I need another reason to find this woman desirable.

"Are you coming?" she calls out. It sounds as if her teeth are clattering together, making me anxious to get into there as fast as possible so I can warm her with my body.

I'm clearly a masochist.

I climb the stairs, willing my dick to calm down already. Because Els is in that pool, naked, and I'm going to be in there soon, too, and even though there will be thousands of gallons of water in between us, she and I will be naked together for the first time.

I reach the top of the diving platform and locate her across the pool, hanging onto the edge. Glimpses of her bare arse shimmer through the lamp-lit water as she faces the opposite direction, and bloody hell, if I thought I was hard before, it's nothing compared to now.

When I jump, I marvel at how ironic it is that I'm literally falling.

She wasn't kidding about the water. It's fucking freezing, thank God. All the air is iced straight out of my chest when I surface, alongside my raging hormones. There could be an entire pool of naked lingerie models and I'd still be limp, because this is just as brutal as a polar plunge.

But then Els turns away from the wall and hits me with her smile. And miraculously, my dick twitches back to life, because now I have a brilliant glimpse of her breasts just below the water line.

"Cold, right?"

Not cold enough, apparently.

I swim over toward her, my teeth grinding together so I don't say or do something unwise. I ensure to keep a proper amount of space between us when I grab the ledge.

She's amused. And so bloody gorgeous I can barely handle it.

"How does it feel, having your cherry popped?" Please, God, let her assume the shakiness in my voice is due to the frigid water rather than how the sight of her is affecting me. It's a dumb question I've just asked, asinine even, but I need to keep things the same between us, even if I've turned a corner I don't know I can return from once we leave California.

"Cold." There's that laugh starter again that dies in the hush of the pool. "And like I am in a bath. A frightfully frigid, stinging bath."

"Skinny-dipping not living up to the hype?"

The water around her swirls as she kicks below the surface. "Au contraire." Her eyes meet mine, and in the lamplight, they're the same blue as the water and glass tiles.

I'm lost to her, one hundred percent lost, and gladly so.

"And you?" she asks. "How does this compare to Lake Como?"

I have never, ever craved to kiss a woman more than in this moment. I'm freezing my arse off, we've broken into a historic landmark, and there's a chance we could get caught, and all I want to do is just haul her in my arms and press my mouth against hers until we both forget our titles, followed by countless hours learning every centimeter of her body.

Better, I ought to tell her. So much better. Best skinny-dipping experience of my life. But what I say is, "Eh. It was Lake Como, you know?"

She splashes water at me. I splash it right back, earning myself an erotic gasp.

Bloody hell. I'm way over my head right now.

I dip below the surface, allowing the icy water to knock some sense into me. And then I push off against the wall and glide toward the other side, keeping my horny self underwater until I reach my destination.

I'd give almost everything I have to be able to turn back the clock and meet this woman anywhere but here. But I can't. Our introduction came at the start of the bloody RMM, which is an automatic death knell for any relationship. Plus the

She-Wolf appears dead set on me marrying her sister, and Elsa's supposed to end up with Mat, even though that makes me want to rage uncontrollably.

I shove wet hair off my forehead and stare up at the ceiling. There is no way I can marry Isabelle. I'll go insane. Family get-togethers would be torture. There has to be a way out of this. I cannot meet this woman and marry her damn sister!

Soft splashing sounds behind me. Elsa joins me on this side of the pool. And she leaves precious little space between our bodies, because when she kicks out in her efforts to tread, her toes connect with my leg.

She talks. Talks about . . . I have no idea. Things I want to hear, because they're from her and everything little damn thing about Elsa is fascinating to me. Like how she's got a pair of freckles just below her clavicle that resemble a bite mark. They're so endearing I want to lightly graze them with my teeth, just enough to make her squirm.

I do my best to keep my eyes on hers, even as our bodies gravitate closer and closer until we're mere millimeters away. A brush here, a nudge there, arms pressed together more often than not, and I'm dying a thousand and two deaths because I'm desperate to keep myself shifted just enough away from her that she doesn't discover I've got the worst literal and figurative case of blue balls a man could ever have. But every so often, she glances away or closes her eyes as she talks, and my focus drifts down the smooth column of her neck to the hint of her breasts and deeper still.

I'm supposed to marry her sister.

"How are we going to do this?" she asks me.

My voice turns raspy. "Do what?"

"Get out of this pool. We're going to catch hypothermia, you know."

I can think of a very good way for the two of us to stay warm.

I jerk my head to the right, toward a set of marble steps leading out of the pool. "Or you can just swim into the shallow end and pull yourself out."

I offer my back when she chooses the shallow end route. I close my eyes and tread water, forcing myself to think about the She-Wolf and paperwork and other unsavory things like marrying Isabelle or hell, even just touching Elsa's sister. My teeth chatter uncontrollably; I fear my lips are blue. But I'm worried the woman behind me is worse off, because the sound of her teeth snapping together echoes throughout the room.

Hugging is proper, right? Friends hug. Hell, I saw her and Mat hug once (and for the love of all that's good in the world, just let it be that once), and I'm pretty certain she doesn't feel a damn thing for him. I could hug her. Get her warm before we head back into the main house. Find out what her body feels like in my arms.

I wait until she tells me it's my turn. I dive down, reclaiming my shoe before doubling back to take the exit closest to where I left my towel and clothes. Elsa is off to one side, examining a statue as if it's the most fascinating thing in the world.

Is it possible I'm the only one who feels this way?

I towel off and dress quickly before joining her, clutching the soggy shoe in my hand. Clothes stick to my body. All I want to do is touch her. Hold her.

"You okay?" My voice is hoarse.

She nods, stringy, wet hair slipping across her shoulders until it falls against her back. "Just cold."

She looks more than cold. She looks heartbroken.

Fuck it. I give into my urge. I drop the shoe and towel and pull her into my arms. There's a split second in which her limbs remain folded across her chest before they loosen to loop around me. And then she sighs. It's not a sad sigh, or a resigned one. It's one of relief, I think. Of bliss.

"Thank you," she whispers into my sweater.

God, she feels amazing, like she was meant for me to hold and I for her. All of my self-control is required in order to not bend my head down and kiss her until she's no longer cold.

"I know you have Lake Como," she murmurs, "but as short as this was, I do believe it was the best introduction to skinny-dipping a lady could have."

I close my eyes, my cheek pressing against her temple. If I could speak, I'd tell her I doubt I could ever skinny dip again without wishing it was here, with her.

CHAPTER 32

ELSA

"No."

"Pardon?"

I suck in a steadying breath and repeat, as clearly as one can while terrified they're shooting themselves in the foot, "No."

My father shifts in his chair, his fingers forming a steeple in front of his mouth as he studies me. From the phone sitting in his lap, set to speaker, my mother barks, "What did she just say?"

My hands lace tightly together in my lap to hide the burgeoning trembling threatening to wrack my entire body. "You're asking me to marry somebody I—"

"Ah," my father interrupts softly. "Herein lies the misunderstanding. I'm not asking, Elsa. I'm decreeing."

And so he did, here on the morning of our last full day in California. *You will marry Mathieu. It will be done posthaste.*

I dig deeper within my well to amass courage. "I do not love him."

My mother's voice hisses across the distance. "*Love him?*" she scoffs. "Are you a child or the future sovereign of Vattenguldia? What does love have to do with your duty to throne and family?"

My father is even blunter. "Your mother and I are not in love, and Vattenguldia is far more influential today than it has been in centuries. It is our duty to ensure this remains the case."

My mother doesn't even take offense with his assessment of their relationship.

"And yet, there is still work to be done to help Vattenguldia tap further into today's world markets. Part of that is gaining a share of the Chambéry finances. You of all people know how we need more capital to expand our role in the shipping registry markets."

"And increase our visibility in the world's tourist market," my mother quickly adds.

Normally, my mouth would be shut by now. Arguing is pointless, especially since my father has stiffened significantly, his eyes narrowing as the tendons in his neck strain. He is utterly serious about what's been said, and from experience, I know that once he reaches this place in an argument, there is no more room for discussion.

His mind is made up, as is my mother's.

So is mine. "Arranged marriages are an antiquated notion. Plenty of other royals marry whom they want without destroying their countries."

"You give too much heed to the media." His Serene Highness' fingers lower to tap against the wooden arm of his chair as my mother says this. "Most of those marriages were arranged through bargaining behind closed doors. Politics and necessity have always been the driving forces in royal relationships, whether you want to acknowledge it or not."

Anger and despair seer through my veins. "Mat doesn't even have a country—"

"The Chambérys are four times wealthier than we are. They are influential throughout the EU. A union between you and Mathieu will allow Vattenguldia access to funds and relationships not seen before."

My father adds to my mother's rationalizations, "Ones that will also help establish premier technological infrastructures in our shipping fleets, ensuring our registries are the most sought after in the world."

"Surely we are not in need of their money. Vattenguldia's coffers are—"

My mother interjects, "Politically, we are on a much more miniscule scale than our Nordic counterparts. I would have us be a sought after destination on many fronts—shipping registries is just the beginning."

I throw down my cards. "And if I refuse?"

My father immediately calls my bluff. "Then I will regrettably ensure you never wear the crown."

Rage spikes through my bloodstream. I cannot believe he is even willing to entertain such a thing. "Vattenguldia is a constitutional principality! My removal from the chain of inheritance would take a parliamentary act."

"Just whom do you think I discussed this with prior to the Summit, Elsa? The Prime Minister and the ruling factions in Parliament all agree. Vattenguldia must take steps forward to grow alongside the rest of the world. After perusing candidates, we concluded that Prince Mathieu and the Chambéry family's means would suit best."

I am horrified. I foolishly had no idea that it ever went this far.

"You two seem to get along well. Mathieu is . . ." My father's head cocks to the side. "Unique and a bit rough around the edges, but I have faith he will fall into line and do what is necessary."

I force out the next words. "And Isabelle?"

"The terms of her engagement have already been decided."

I am sick to my stomach. Last night, I went skinny-dipping with Christian, and our time together was one of the most magical, beautiful experiences of my entire life. Afterward, I floated back to my room, my hand in his after a long hug in the poolroom that left me wishing for the kiss we'd nearly indulged in earlier that day. I laid in bed, next to my sister, aching for hours as I imagined all the *what ifs* and *could have beens*, desperate to relieve the pain that wanting him brought on, yet knowing there was no way I could do so in a room shared that openly with my family.

And now today, I summarily learn that there are to be no more *ifs*, *ands*, or *buts*, let alone the elusive *maybes*. Christian and Isabelle will marry.

And I will wed Mat.

Shite. Fuck. Bloody hell. Crap. Bollocks. There are not enough curse words to describe what I feel.

"Don't think I haven't noticed that you and Isabelle's intended have spent much time together this week." The room's temperature lowers at the sound of his voice. "I expect you to utilize that relationship to solidify his acceptance of a match with your sister."

The hell I will.

"Plans have been scheduled for you and Mathieu to rendezvous in Paris in several weeks to stage several public trysts to whet the press' whistles. Afterward, he'll journey to Vattenguldia in order to officially pursue you during the following month." To my ears, my mother's voice mimics bells of yore heralding the arrival of Black Death. "The Chambéry press secretary is already in contact with our office; you not need concern yourself with the details. Simply be your delightful self for the photographers and remember you like this fellow."

I like Mat, yes. *Like*.

And my sister will marry the man I am falling for, and somehow I must talk him into it.

I head down to breakfast after my father departs. I am garbed in a yellow coatdress, nylons I abhor, and sensible heels. My hair is in a sleek ponytail. My makeup is subtle yet flawless. I am the picture perfect example of a modern princess when in reality I am nothing more than a controlled piece of chattel.

When I enter the dining room, I spot Isabelle sitting with Christian, Lukas, Maria-Elena, Mat, and his sister. Parker is nowhere to be seen. Due to the crowded room, there is precious little space between my sister and her intended, and I flash back to mere hours before, when my body was pressed up against his, and it was one of the best goddamn feelings in the entire world.

Soon, when we hug, it will be as brother and sister. And all my late night hugs, if they ever do miraculously happen, will be reserved for the man sitting on the opposite side of the table from Christian, the one with his back to me.

I don't know why I am so disappointed. So crushed. Christian and I could never be anything, anyway, considering our roles to our countries. Not that he would want to, despite an attraction to me; he made it blatantly clear that he had no interest in picking up anyone at the RMM. Besides, I was the one who drew the line in the sand first. *Save your proposals and propositions for someone else*, I told him.

And yet, he is all I can think about. All I think I could ever want.

I ask a server for scrambled eggs, even though the thought of putting them into my mouth churns my stomach. And then I load up on dry toast in hopes that it will settle my nausea, because dutiful princesses do not vomit all over dining rooms.

I close my eyes and suck in a deep breath. I can do this. I will do what I must. I will do what I am told. My life is one of service. Tradition trumps emotions.

I have officially lost my love for tradition.

A hand settles upon my shoulder; my eyes fly open to find Christian beside me, a half-filled plate in his hand.

Undoubtedly like mine, many tangled emotions cloud his eyes. "I wasn't sure you were going to come down for breakfast or not."

I have twenty-four hours left in California. What I ought to do is smile kindly yet distantly. Unravel whatever cords we've fashioned between us and walk directly over to Mat. And yet, as I stare up into amber eyes that hypnotized me on more than one occasion, I realize all I want to do is spend every minute of my last hours here with His Royal Highness, the Hereditary Grand Duke Christian of Aiboland. Even if it is pure torment to do so.

Even if done as mere friends.

Even if we will never be anything more.

"His Serene Highness requested a meeting," I murmur. Over his shoulder I spy my sister, her brows knit as she studies us. Lukas is watching us, too, but more thoughtfully. Thankfully, it doesn't appear as if Mat or his sister have noticed my arrival. "Thus my delay."

Upon request, a server slides a slice of ham on Christian's plate when there is already still half a piece remaining. "Is everything okay?"

My pathetic attempt at a laugh is more akin to a gurgle. "It was crown business."

He sets his plate down slowly. Exhales quietly. "I had just such a meeting this morning myself."

I want to throw the china in my hand against the wall and watch as it smashes into thousands of satisfying pieces.

Christian fails to glance back at the table he deserted when he says, "We have an hour or so before our next meeting. Let's take a walk. Get some fresh air. Unless you'd prefer to sit and eat?"

There is no hesitation; I pass my plate to a nearby busboy. And then we exit through the gated doorway without another word.

Minutes later, we wander onto a tiled patio behind the largest of the guesthouses, one featuring two fountains. The air, cool and crisp, is hushed; whispers of wind through palm and oak trees and bird songs are the only sounds to dare challenge the delicate silence.

I stare up at the first fountain as we pass by. There is a golden girl atop the marble, smelling a rose. The second fountain is a bit different—the girl there leans forward to kiss a frog in her palm.

I know this story. Unfortunately, my ending will not be as happy as hers.

Christian motions toward a seat carved into the wall facing the princess and her frog prince. The space he puts between us as we sit is miniscule compared to that between him and my sister just ten minutes before.

"So."

My word is just as quiet as his. "So."

But he is as reluctant to discuss his meeting with his mother as I am about my parents' edict. Instead, he asks, a hint of a naughty smile curving his lips, "Have you recovered?"

Oh. Perhaps I was wrong? "Um . . ."

"From the cold," he clarifies. "You were in a chilly pool in the dead of night. I worried about you afterward."

Gratitude over how his efforts to make this as normal as possible loosens the lines around my mouth. "I might have inched a bit closer to my sister for warmth, but I was soundly kicked back to my side of the bed and informed my feet were ice blocks."

He laughs, all rich and warm and honeyed, prompting an image of him, in my sister's bed, going through the same motions.

It is a terrible thing to imagine.

"I'm lucky I don't share one with Lukas. One or the both of us would most likely end up with a black eye and a sore back from sleeping on the floor."

"I was surprised to see him this morning," I admit. "He is more elusive than not, it seems."

A sly grin is thrown my way. "Luk got in even later than I did, looking like he'd been at the party of the century."

"Ah. How very interesting. Who do you think he was cavorting with at such a late hour?"

"I think the better question is, who *wasn't* he cavorting around with?"

"Me." I smile brightly. "And you. Our cavorting was limited to a very exclusive party of two."

"Is that what we were doing? Were we cavorting?"

We were falling in love, I think. Wonderfully, miserably, tragically, beautifully falling in love. Or at least, I was. But I say, "Of course. You and I are natural cavorters."

Bittersweet amusement sparkles in his eyes. "I thought our thing was to run amuck."

"That, too." I gently touch the back of his hand. "We run amuck and cavort."

The smile on his face softens. "Only with each other, though. We cavort best when it's with the other."

"Shall we make a deal then? Shall we swear to the other that, when it comes time to cavort, we must only do it together?" My words are light, so is my tone, but part of me crumbles within, knowing what I jokingly request will never come to be.

Gravity invades his face as he shifts on the seat toward me, knees brushing up against one another. I am trapped by his gaze, motionless with his leg pressed against mine. "That's a promise I can easily make."

I am still as the golden princess before us when he slowly, gently pushes stray hairs freshly escaped from my ponytail behind my ears. The feel of his fingers, light as breezes against my cheeks, leaves me hot and desperate.

"Shall we shake on it?" I whisper.

The muscle within my chest ceases its rhythm when he shakes his head. He stares at me then, as if he is unraveling all my atoms, rendering me exposed and vulnerable.

But then he leans forward, lips caressing one corner of my mouth and then the other. "All the best agreements," he murmurs, words just as soft as mine, "are sealed with a kiss."

I consist only of nothing but exposed nerve endings when I replicate his promise. My lips tingle, my heart hammers, and tears swarm my closed eyes. "You have my promise in return."

He tilts his head up, mouth pressing against my temple before resting his forehead against mine. "I'm going to hold you to that, Els."

CHAPTER 33

CHRISTIAN

I ought to be focusing on what's being discussed, but it's impossible. It's about . . . shite, I think the roles of modern monarchs in constitutional governments, which is actually something I'm quite keen on. I've got loads of opinions on the matter, but my attention is shot. It's been shot all week.

Fifteen minutes before I came down to breakfast, the She-Wolf took me aside. Said, "It's been officially decided, Christian. You're to marry the Vattenguldian girl."

For one small, idiotic, yet bloody fantastic moment, I thought she referred to the woman I've spent all my nights this week with. But then reality sunk in. Not Elsa. Never Elsa.

She meant Isabelle.

I was so pissed I told her there was no fucking way I would marry that woman. In return, the She-Wolf informed me in the iciest tone I've yet heard that, in no uncertain terms, I most certainly would. Terms that included Parker's future, Lukas', even my father's. How they would be rendered penniless or exiled, in my secretary's case.

In the end, I was immobilized, because there wasn't a bloody thing I could say that would change the She-Wolf's mind. So I cussed her out, only to have her laugh in my face.

"I am to meet with Prince Gustav today," she continued, like she hadn't just blackmailed the living hell out of me. "We've already hammered out most of the details, but for now, you must begin a public wooing of the girl which will culminate in an engagement within the year." A victorious grin overtook her pinched face. "There's your concession, Christian. You have until Christmas to grow a pair of balls and do what's needed for Aiboland."

I told her, "Fuck you."

Her eyes widened.

So I clarified, "Fuck you, Your Highness."

In response, she slapped the shite out of me. Just hauled her bony hand back and slapped me so hard my teeth rattled and I saw stars. And then she pulled her hand back once more, but I grabbed it before it touched my face. "Hit me again," I told her, "and I might forget I'm your son."

So here I am, in yet another meeting, wondering if my cheek is going to bruise. Seriously, how fucking humiliating would that be? Because men of my age and station don't typically get slapped by their mothers. But worse yet, I'm wondering how I'm going to marry the sister of the only woman who has ever consumed my thoughts, and how I'm going to be able to stand back and watch her marry a man I call friend.

I've known her all of four days. It took only four days to fall after years of not even coming close.

After the meeting, Parker tracks me down. He methodically goes over my itinerary for the rest of the day, and then of the following pair of days once we depart California, but my attention is shot just as easily with him as it was with the Grand Duke of Luxemburg an hour before.

He's discussing the hospital renovation I'm to tour in Norsloe when I say, "The She-Wolf laid down her official decree today."

Parker immediately quiets. Opens and shuts his mouth a few times before he says, "Will the new Hereditary Grand Duchess of Aioboland be Princess Isabelle of Vattenguldia?"

I can't admit it. Won't.

I inform him I need to take a walk. He moves to follow, but I assure him I'm in no need of a minder.

I need to get the bloody hell out of here already.

CHAPTER 34

ELSA

"You're quieter than usual this afternoon."

It is windy—not hurricane gales, but enough of a breeze that my ponytail is not as sleek as it was this morning. I brush back the strands tangling in my eyelashes before facing Mat. "My apologies."

His eyes are undecipherable behind the dark plastic of his sunglasses. "Am I to take it you spoke with your father?"

I glance away, back toward a statue of the Three Graces we have studied for the past several minutes, wondering if they'll favor me with the right words to tactfully address this situation.

"I hope we can find a way to make this work," he says, not waiting for my answer.

Annoyance flashes beneath my skin, reddening my cheeks and neck. His words, his tone are all resigned, bitterly so, even. Why is he not raging?

"I thought you weren't a fan of the RMM."

"Believe me, I'm not. But it appears neither you nor I have any say in the matter."

I turn to face him, anger surging up my throat and out of my mouth. "Do you wish to marry me? Is this what *you* want?"

He takes a long time to answer. "What I want doesn't matter." Even still, he reaches out a tentative hand meant to land safely on my arm or shoulder, but I step away.

"What are you not telling me, Mat? I know you cannot want this. Every time we speak, it is clear that you are as appalled by the situation as I am."

His jaw clenches, but he says nothing.

"It is bad enough that we're in this godawful situation," I continue, "but to know you are keeping something is maddening!"

Heat now fills his words. "Funny, I can't claim that you've opened up, either."

"I am not hiding a damn thing. *I don't want to marry you.* There. It has been said. Can you do the same?"

His body vibrates with frustration, but once more, he holds the bitterness and secrets within. We are in a standoff for a good minute before I realize he will not back down.

I am chewing on glass when I say, "It's really very beautiful here, is it not? The coastlines, I mean."

He is wary. "Yes, it rather is."

"Vattenguldia is scenic, too—only quite differently than this." I scuff the tip of one shoe against the painted tiles sandwiched in between terra cotta ones beneath our feet. "We are more starkly beautiful." I turn briefly back toward him; his hands are stuffed in his pockets as he rocks back and forth on his heels. "Have you ever been that far north before?"

Tension laces his answer. "I have not had that pleasure yet."

"Winters are cold. Days are long." My smile is paper-thin. "The people are stubborn."

"Much like their princess. Stubborn, I mean."

Not stubborn enough, apparently. "It is a tiny country." I am all business now. "One of the smallest microstates in the world. We are practically non-existent in the grand scheme of the planet."

"A tiny country is better than no country, correct?"

The hostility in his words sends me back a step. And then, like one slowly awakening, I realize why Mat's family is so keen to connect their line with mine.

Land is land, a throne is a throne. These are things the Chambérys have been denied for hundreds of years, ever since their small country was swallowed whole by two larger ones and they were deposed.

They have money, we have land.

How romantic.

How traditional.

CHAPTER 35

ELSA

Our last dinner in California was nightmarish. Seating was carefully arranged to reflect new alliances between families, and the entire patio surrounding the Neptune pool was packed with gloomy, stricken heirs whose lives are now nothing more than bargaining chips.

Our long stretch of table featured three families: mine, Mat's, and Christian's. Isabelle was quiet and tense as she picked at her food. Mat was as passive aggressive as myself. Lukas was forced to dine with the Spanish contingency at a nearby table; both he and the girl he was seated with looked as if they were to face the firing squad. Christian turned robotic again, all manners and politeness while none of his natural warmth filled a single syllable uttered.

Our parents, though? Animated and in fine spirits. And why wouldn't they be, having secured whatever political gains they desired by signing away the futures of their adult children?

And now here I am, dancing with Mat under the stars, attempting to not cringe as his hand clasps mine. I will myself to feel something for him, anything, but there is nothing. No butterflies. No tingles. No surges or clenches or lady parts dancing.

Nothing but anger and resentment.

"You didn't eat much tonight."

His attempts at civility grate against my raw nerves. "I am afraid I had some biscuits at tea time this afternoon and found myself without much of an appetite this evening."

I feel, rather than see, his sigh. "Until today, I thought we'd been becoming friends—or at least acquaintances. Some here can't claim at least that."

Now I feel lousy because he sounds eerily beaten down over all this. I am not being fair to him; this wasn't his idea, after all. He is as much a pawn as I am. And still, I scoff, "Friends. Right."

"Better that than strangers."

I look him right in the eyes. In a lot of ways, this man who has so much sadness reflecting back at me is still a stranger. While we chatted over the week, I do not feel as if I *know* him. I have no idea what makes Mat tick or even how he drinks his coffee.

"I suppose there is that," I concede reluctantly.

"Believe me, I'm well aware of how you feel about wedding me. After all, it's how we met, remember? We joined the rebel alliance together—"

I cut him off. "Fat lot that did us."

"All I'm trying to say is it could have been worse. We both could have been . . . matched with people that we might not even be able to talk to." He swallows hard.

The irony of this is not lost on me. Had I not lamented numerous times about desiring a partner I could at least talk to?

"I'm not going to lie and claim I'm madly in love with you, Elsa. Believe it or not, I respect you too much for that. I know you're not in love with me, either. But considering the situation we're in, I'd prefer to at least make a go of being civil. Do you think this could be possible for you, too?"

My animosity is too strong. "Have you ever been in love?"

His eyes flit away, but not before I see the change. "Yes."

There is a quiet desperation to him, one colored with melancholy-tinged regret. And I cannot help but wonder whom the person in question is, and why I can practically feel this man's heartbreak.

"Are you still?"

Without a beat, he ignores my question and asks instead, "Have you?"

I maintain my focus on the man before me and not over his shoulder, toward where I know my sister and her soon-to-be intended are dancing.

"Yes."

And that is painful honesty if there ever was such, yet it is equally inane, because I have known the man holding my sister in his arms less than a full week. The same amount of time I've known Mat.

Damn Charlotte for being right.

The song ends; Mat releases me, only to place his hand at the small of my back as he steers me to the side of the pool. But before we get there, Isabelle and Christian meet us, and my stomach spasms at the pink flush on her cheeks.

And then Christian asks if he can have the next dance with me.

And like the masochist I am, I say yes.

CHAPTER 36

CHRISTIAN

Isabelle rattled on about horses again. Is this my future? A life that revolves around equines?

Dinner was hell. Just the absolute lousiest meal I've ever had. The She-Wolf gloated the entire time; every glance purposefully thrown my way was another metaphorical slap to the face.

I refused to provide her a single moment of satisfaction with any sign of reaction, although my hands curled into balls beneath the table. It's an awful thing, wanting to slug one's own mother, but that rage and desperation built within me the entire meal.

And then I was forced to dance with Isabelle afterward. And she babbled on about her fucking horses *again* until I wanted to tell her to sod off. It didn't help that Elsa was a mere twenty feet away, dancing with Mat. And that his damn arms were around her. And that she was miserable, even though I could tell she was doing her best to appear unaffected and in control.

So when the song was over, and I was finally able to get the hell away from Isabelle, I asked her sister to dance even though it was a terrible idea. Because as I look down at Elsa now, our bodies swaying together to the torch singer and the band playing on the deck overlooking the pool, I wonder, how am I going to live my entire life without kissing her once? *Really* kissing her, where I memorize her mouth and she mine. How will I never make love to her? Not fucking, not sex . . . but something more meaningful. Or never wake up next to her in the morning? Or experience any of the things, mundane or extraordinary, I want to do with her? To her?

"Do you think it's possible we can stroll right out of this party, straight down the drive, and disappear before anyone knows what's going on?" she asks me. But there's humor there, too.

I groan quietly. "Don't tempt me."

"What time do you fly out tomorrow?"

Not soon enough and yet too soon all at once. "Eight A.M. You?"

"Five-thirty in the morning. My father is clearly insane. We are to fly to LAX with Lichtenstein, and apparently he's an early riser."

Tiny bits of ugly panic grip the muscle in my chest. That's only eight hours away. Eight hours before Elsa boards a plane and flies away from me.

"I have it on good authority," she continues, "that there is pie in the kitchen, a kind specific to the region, sent over by a local town but deemed too countrified for tonight's gala."

"Are you part of a secretive pie information network, Els?"

She smiles, and it hits me way harder than my mother's hand from earlier this morning. "Naturally. Here is the first I want tonight: we ought to try some before we leave. After all, isn't pie a quintessential American experience?"

"I believe it's specifically apple pie that's the true slice of Americana."

She mutters, "Har-har."

I continue, undeterred, "I doubt the local pie you've heard about is apple. How delightful. We have a pie mystery on our hands."

She gently presses against me, like she's shoving me. And I chuckle, because the look of amused frustration she lets me see is so adorable. "Are you game?"

"What would this pie mission entail? Should I dress in all black?"

"Sneaking into the kitchen, of course. But that is old hat for you and I. We are to eat as much pie as we can without vomiting afterward." The corners of her lips slyly curve upward. "Unless you're watching out for your girlish—excuse me, *mannish* figure."

I feign outrage. "I bet I can eat you under the table."

Damn, her smile is gorgeous.

"If I join you on this mission, will I be allowed to join PIN?"

She releases a ghost of a laugh, and I feel this tiny breath all the way down to my bones—and pants. "PIN as in Pie Information Network? Certainly. You will receive all benefits entitled to full members, including the opportunity to eat the best pies on the planet."

I'd like to eat her.

"The security guard is making a tidy sum off of me this week, isn't he? I shall have to pay him another visit," I tell her.

She blushes, and just the sight makes my pants all the more uncomfortable. By the time the song finishes, I'm so dangerously turned on that it's a miracle I can even walk.

CHAPTER 37

ELSA

We are alone in the spacious kitchen, leaning against one of the stainless steel islands. Christian located old-fashioned lanterns to illuminate the place where we became more than strangers; the soft glow lends the room a hazy, magical countenance. "What do you call these?" I poke my fork in the berries spilling out of the slice of pie on my plate.

He was right. There was not a single slice of apple pie to be found anywhere.

Christian lifts the flap of the pie box and angles it toward me. "Olallieberries."

"Is that even a real word?"

He laughs, and I resent the sound. It's gorgeous and rich and sexy and unfair to any woman in its vicinity, including me. And that's the rub, because I'm not sure how I will ever be able to resist Christian and all of his lovely, addictive *too*-ness.

"It's here on the box," he's saying, "so I'm thinking yes."

I refocus on the pie below me, because no good can come of lingering on Christian's perfect laugh or how the urge to drift closer to the warmth floating off his lean body is oh so strong right now. Or about how the thought of him and my sister, hanging out in a kitchen at three A.M., gorging themselves on sweets, makes me want to break every dish I can find. "Anybody can make up a word." I shove a large spoonful of pie in my mouth. "Farfleggle."

As sordid images run wild through my mind, I am thankful Christian is too busy cutting himself another slice of pie to notice my flaming cheeks. "Pardon?"

I swallow and take a deep breath, wishing I could just fan myself already. "Farfleggle. I made it up. See? It can be done."

His mouth curves upward at this; it is patently ridiculous how attractive I find him right now, all ease and grace and charm whilst stuffing himself full of pie in the middle of the night in an empty kitchen.

Why did I have to keep on talking to him this week? Why did he have to be so bloody wonderful and easy to be around, my own Prince Charming come to life?

A silver fork points my way, laden with rich berries and flaky pastry. "What does it mean?"

"It doesn't have to mean anything. It is a made-up word. That's my point."

He chews his bite slowly as he considers this, and I suppress an urge to touch his mouth. His lips are stained a tiny bit from the berry juice, and I am too weak in the moment to deny that I would like nothing more than to lick them clean.

I have no doubt the women who have been lucky enough to feel that gorgeous mouth against theirs lose track of time or swoon or feel like they're flying or any of the other banal descriptions people read about in books, because that mouth promises so very, very much.

I think I could hate my sister for all the kisses she'll get from this man.

"But the thing is," he's saying, forcing me to look from his mouth to his eyes, "olallieberry means something. It's a type of berry. Its existence in the lexicon is warranted."

I am daydreaming about kissing. He is thinking about etymology—which is a good thing. One of us must remain focused on the task at hand.

As I take another bite of pie, I search for a proper definition for such a gloriously ludicrous word. And then it comes to me. *Farfleggle: a noun—a princess whose knickers practically drop every time a certain Aibolandian prince looks at her.*

What I tell him is, "Farfleggle: a noun meaning a prince addicted to secretive organizations."

That absurdly attractive smile of his reemerges, and now I am more than just squirmy; I am hot and achy and focused on his sinful mouth again. "So, you're saying *I'm* a farfleggle?"

No. I am. I pray my smile is gracious. "You are most welcome."

At the bemused look on his face, I am unable to hold it in any longer. All the laughter he has sought from me for days now bubbles up and out of me, like fizzy champagne shaken for celebrations.

I laugh. I giggle and laugh and flat-out chuckle. My sides hurt. My mother would be horrified.

Christian's smile slowly fades until he stares at me as if I am nothing more than a stranger who barged into the kitchen and stole his pie.

Was my mother right after all? Is such behavior really so tawdry? All of my frivolity dissipates into awkwardness and another overly large bite of olallieberry pie.

His chest rises and falls slowly, his attention on me in a way that disconcerts. Because he isn't merely looking at me—he is *looking* at me, and I have no idea what it means. It isn't the first time he has done so meaningfully, but even now, even days after immersing myself in all things Christian, I am unable to decode the words behind his eyes.

Which means, naturally, I must shove another bite of pie into my mouth, futilely attempting to ignore how I wish I were shoving something else in my mouth, instead.

After what seems like forever with a fortnight tacked on for good measure, he murmurs, "It's not fair when you laugh like that."

I try not to choke as the glob of pie I just shoved in so quickly fights to slide down my throat. "I am sorry if I offended you, Chris."

He shakes his head, holding out a dismissive hand. "No. Not that."

I try to play it cool. Stifle the hurt his rejection births. "You never told me what you want your first to be tonight."

I am horrified when he stiffens. Even more alarmed when he shoves away from the shiny, metal island, his pie and fork suddenly forgotten. "I should go."

Before I can even form a word, he closes in on the doorway. What just happened? We'd been eating pie and joking and I laughed, which he told me before he wanted to hear, yet now he feels he must leave?

Can he sense how my feelings toward him have shifted in ways I fear I no longer can control?

I do not want him to go. Not yet. Not when our time together is so preciously limited. Two hours from now, I will be on a plane, and the next time I see him might be at his wedding.

Just as he reaches the door, Christian skids to a halt. His palms slap against the wooden doorframe, the sound reverberating throughout the still kitchen.

I want to disappear when my voice trembles as I say his name.

And then Christian strides back across the kitchen, back toward me, his eyes serious and apologetic and hot all at once, and I honestly have no idea what to do. Or say. I haven't the foggiest if he is angry or pulling my leg or any other variation of any emotion, and it's . . . *unnatural*. Because everything else after the first day has been natural, so this is unacceptable.

But then he kisses me.

Finally.

CHAPTER 38

CHRISTIAN

Hearing her laughter was my death knell. Or rather, not necessarily *my* death knell, but that of all of the bloody protections and resistances I've attempted to maintain against Elsa and her charms over the last few days. Her laughter was a gift, all warm and bubbly and wonderful, and it smashed through me, overtaking my very cells until all I felt was joy.

I like this princess. I like her very much. I fear it's more than that, that I'm in love with her. And this absolutely terrifies the hell out of me. We've both been ordered to marry people we don't love. Today, in fact.

But I'm done trying to convince myself I don't feel something for Elsa, or that what I do feel is nothing more than friendship or even lust. I don't want just her friendship. I want *her*. So now here we are, and my lips are touching hers for the first time, and God almighty, she's absurdly delicious, all tangy sweet and sour like the berries. But she's more than that, too. As I deepen the kiss, I have no idea how to explain it other than what I'm tasting is just Elsa, despite never having savored her before this moment. I cup the back of her head, my other hand drifting to her lower back so I can tug her closer, and, thank all that's good in the world, she comes willingly, the strength of her kiss matching my own.

It's the headiest feeling in the entire bloody world.

We're kissing, noses bumping like we're teens experimenting for the first time, but it's more than just my lips on hers. I can't explain it, but my heart's pumping too fast, faster than it ever has when I've kissed a woman.

I'm instantly hard. This woman, no matter what she does, turns me on like no other.

"This is my first," I murmur against her mouth. "This is the first I've wanted all week."

Any restraint I might possess beats a quick retreat out of the kitchen when her fingers dig into my shirt so she can tug me closer. I moan, and so does she, and these sounds have me pressing her up against the island until I fear I'm going to come in my goddamn pants like some arsehole during his first time. I'm on bloody fire, all hard and hot and aching and desiring nothing more than to peel her clothes right off her body, have her do the same to me, and shove the pie off the island so I can climb up there with her and take my time learning every inch of her body.

Things turn frantic, tongues tasting and stroking, hands tugging off shirts and sweaters, mouths seeking out necks and clavicles, and I swear that the ground below us disappears entirely and I'm part of one of those clichés I've always scorned, because I'm fucking floating on air.

I need to be in her. Now.

She unbuckles my belt, tugs at my zipper. I nearly lose control when she cups me.

Just as I'm unclasping her bra, something clatters loudly nearby.

We jerk apart, our feet forced to return to earth. There is a maid staring at us, her mouth opened in shock.

Bloody hell.

Elsa snatches her shirt and turns around, tugging it on.

The woman curtseys, leaving the small tray she'd dropped on the ground where it landed. "Pardon my interruption, Your um . . . Highnesses. I wasn't aware the kitchen was in . . . use. I . . . I can . . . I was just getting some . . . But I can . . . I'll just leave you two . . . to . . . um . . ."

The way she babbles this makes what she'd walked in on sound so seedy, like me finally kissing and touching this gorgeous siren is the equivalent of so many of the other heirs shagging like rabbits upstairs in closets when they don't think others are listening or watching, instead of the life-altering experience it just was.

I've never wanted to bellow at a servant to get the hell out, but I'm pretty damn tempted to right now.

"It is fine." Elsa's smile is indulgent and regal, her voice steady as she steps forward, smoothing her hair as if she isn't affected in the least by what just happened. "We were merely indulging in some late night pie."

If I wasn't so pissed, I might laugh, because it's clear the maid takes *pie* to mean something else, especially when her eyes track down the front of my, well, shite, still open pants. And then I'm incredulous and more than a bit uncomfortable as she continues to stare until I'm forced to clear my throat.

And, you know, tuck myself back in and zip my pants up.

It's enough to snap her out of whatever trance she was in. Her cheeks flush dark pink and she stammers out something incoherent. Elsa flinches at the barrage of words, paling considerably like she's just been caught with her hand in a cookie jar.

Fantastic. Bloody fantastic.

The maid quickly reclaims the tray and slides it onto one of the islands. Before another word is spoken, the door slaps shut from the woman's clipped retreat.

And then Elsa turns to face me, her eyes wide and shiny and worried. And this sight, of all the things I could see, guts me.

I murmur her name when it's quiet again, this single word of two syllables filled with so many emotions that I don't have a bloody clue what else to say. Because what does one say to a person who has consumed both heart and mind so completely in four days? I want her. Desperately. She told me on the first day she wanted nothing to do with me romantically and I'm ordered to marry her sister, but I kissed Elsa anyway. This woman, this princess . . . she's different. Different and lovely and wonderful and witty and desirable. She's a Valkyrie, come to collect my heart. And that kiss? There's nothing to compare it to. It was different, like she is. It was *better*. So I can't help but say her name again, its syllables soft pleas for understanding and an unspoken prayer she feels the same way, because she kissed me back.

Her eyes briefly close; she inhales deeply, fingers resting against her swollen lips. And then she retrieves the pie box from the ground and places it upon the island. "I am departing in a few hours. As are you."

The smile she offers cuts me off at the knees. It isn't the smile I've had the pleasure of witnessing in secret for days now. This is the one she gives everyone else. The one she gives Mat.

This is the smile she hides behind. Dammit. I'm losing her before I even have the chance to win her.

"It was good pie, wasn't it?"

My voice is hoarse. "Yes."

Her eyes are glassy. "You are officially a member of PIN, Christian."

Fuck PIN. PIN is nothing without Elsa. Neither is the RFC.

She blinks and glances away, a soft hint of a laugh coming out of her. Now that I've heard her real laughter, this will never satisfy me. It was beautiful—rich and warm and addictive and exactly like her.

This ghost? This isn't her. She's disappearing right before my very eyes.

"You have been a bad influence," she murmurs, and I swear, my heart drops straight out of my chest. But then she says, "The best kind, actually. I'm glad I got to share so many firsts with you this week."

There's so much I want to say to her. I want to tell her that it was a week of firsts for me, too. The first time I've ever felt this way. That I want to be there for all the rest of the firsts in her life. Or at least have the chance to see if all our firsts should be together.

She steps away from the island, back toward me. A shaky hand comes up to brush the side of my face. "I was wrong, you know."

I can barely get the word out. "About?"

"You." The Valkyrie leans forward, her forehead resting briefly against me before she rises up on her toes to press a lingering kiss on my cheek. And then a softer, sadder one at the corner of my mouth. "What are we going to do, Christian?"

I have no idea. And it is so fucking impossibly unfair to accept that.

I receive another kiss, this time on the lips. But it's too short. It's only a hint of a kiss. I want more.

I want her.

"We should probably get some sleep. We both need to be up in a little bit."

Sleep on the plane, I think. Don't go.

"Thank you for this week," she says, as if I took pity on her and am only here because I am bored or have nothing else to do. "I will always hold these memories close."

A hand is proffered between us; I stare at it in horror. She's going to do this. *She really is going to do this.* She's going to shake my hand, say goodnight, and then she will leave for Vattenguldia, and I will go to Aiboland, and . . . and…we—I'm just to go back to life as it was before?

And marry her sister?

Fuck that. No. *No.* This cannot be how our story ends.

"It was good to finally get to know you, Christian." I flinch at her formality. "I wish you much success. At least now we can be assured that our countries will always have an ally in the other, especially in the MC, once we both assume our respective thrones."

An ally . . . and bloody in-laws. It isn't fair. Goddammit, it simply isn't *fair*.

"What happened to Chris?" I'm not even embarrassed that my voice cracks.

A tear traces a lazy path down her cheek, and it guts me like nothing else. Elsa shakes her head, forcing in a deep breath. And then she extends her hand once more.

When our palms and fingers come together, the sensation is nearly as intimate as our kiss minutes before. Skin on skin, touch to touch. Her fingers curve around mine and mine around hers. Desire once more flares like wildfire through my bloodstream.

I don't want to let go, not yet, but that matters neither here nor there, because if she needs to walk away from whatever it is that compels my lungs to constrict and my heart to thrum in aching beats, then it's her right.

Because no matter what I feel otherwise, I can't have her. She's a Hereditary Princess; I'm a Hereditary Grand Duke. It would never be allowed. We could never have each other, not forever, not without one or the both of us abdicating our rights to our respective thrones. Who would take over? Lukas? Isabelle?

And yet . . .

So much of me wants to say fuck it and take the risk.

"It was good meeting you, too." I lie. It was better than good. It was serendipity during truly shitty circumstances.

She lets go first, dropping into a curtsey before me as if we were strangers rather than people who just ate pie and made out like our lives depended on it. In return, I force my waist to bend forward, one of my hands coming across my chest to cover my heart.

Damn, it physically hurts. Aches like a tin can crushed in a fist.

And then, before I straighten, she's gone.

CHAPTER 39

♛
ELSA

"The week went better than I thought, considering." Isabelle lays her magazine down on her lap, her hands folding primly across the glossy cover. "Don't you agree?"

It requires more than a bit of effort not to shout, poor language and all, "Are you bloody kidding?" in the middle of the small private jet we're currently on. Instead, I say as calmly as one can when they are mentally falling apart, "It had its high and low points."

She glances over at where our father is; he and Bittner are deep in discussion. Voice lowered, she says, "I texted Alfons before we left. Told him we need to talk."

I close the folder I have desperately tried to read in hopes of maintaining some semblance of sanity on this wretchedly long flight and set it to the side. It was not helping. And this conversation isn't, either.

My words are wooden. "I thought you two were on the outs."

Her head dips toward me, a shiny dark curtain of hair swaying my way. "He didn't want me to go this week. We fought terribly about it. He wanted us to elope to Geneva instead."

So now she opens up to me, when all has been said and done. And yet I cannot find myself caring much right now about her personal drama. Not when my heart disintegrated this morning within my chest. "Do you regret not going?"

"To Geneva?" She flips the ends of her hair, brushing the strands back and forth across her chin line. When I nod, she sighs. "I am very conflicted right now, Elsa."

"What will you tell him?"

Isabelle bites her lip, resting her head back against the leather seat. "The truth, I suppose." She drops the chunk of hair in order to pat me on the knee. "How are you holding up? I wished to check in with you last night, but you didn't get in until . . ."

Until it was nearly time to leave.

She and I have always been honest with one another, but our honesty is much like our royal personas: aloof and perfectly presented. Neither of us lied here, but our responses were carefully worded to the point where they straddled the border between fact and fiction.

So I continue our charade. I tell her I am fine. Because technically, I am. Numb, but fine.

She studies me for a long moment, eyes narrowing thoughtfully. "You stayed out late last night. Or rather, this morning."

I reclaim the recently discarded folder. "I suppose I did."

"You disappeared for hours every single day in the dead of night."

I slip out a document. "As did you, I imagine. As did most of the heirs."

"During the late night parties and rendezvous, I never saw Christian, either."

I want to laugh in her face. "How interesting."

I'm practically daring her to press the issue, especially since she has no leg to stand upon. But Isabelle backs down, just as I knew she would. Lines of disappointment pinch her face. And I am left to the documents in my hands, ones discussing parliamentary issues for the upcoming meeting next week, which are far preferable to any kind of heart-to-heart with my sister.

CHAPTER 40

CHRISTIAN

The She-Wolf is reveling in her victory right now; along with numerous glasses of her precious cognac guzzled over the course of the flight home, she's also high as a kite thanks to various pills I don't care to know the name of. Thankfully, she wanders into one of the plane's bedrooms, followed closely behind by one of the flight attendants, so we're in the clear for at least an hour or so.

Most everyone else, including Parker, are sleeping in hopes of staving off jet lag. But my brother and I are too agitated to follow suit.

"Think it'd be bad form if I call for the press to be on the tarmac when we arrive home?" Lukas mutters. His flask is out, mercifully filled with vodka rather than cognac. "Because I'd frame the shite out of a shot of Her Highness hitting the pavement face first, cackling the whole way down. And then I'd send one to every family member as a Christmas gift."

Our fists bump one another. I'd cheerfully go in on those gifts.

"Maybe we could even switch out her official portrait with it. And then Aiboland would really see her for the hag she is."

Most sons have some sort of filial love for their mother, and . . . maybe the two of us do somewhere, but it's nowhere near the surface.

"Honestly, though, this week was a fucking nightmare, Chris." Lukas rolls his head toward me. He's surprisingly sober, considering the amount of booze—correction, cognac—on board the plane and within his flask. "Demeaning as all hell. This is the twenty-first century, not the fifteenth."

My bitterness knows no bounds. "At least you didn't come away with a directive."

"The hell I didn't. It was one of those last minute deals. Last night, when you were doing the fuck knows what with whomever, the She-Wolf tracked me down and told me that I am now officially the future fiancé of that Spanish girl."

"Shite. Sorry, Luk. I thought you liked Maria-Elena."

"That's not the point and you know it. The She-Wolf and I got into it, though. I told her there was no way she could make me marry some girl that I didn't pick, and . . ."

And his cheek is a little swollen today, too.

"She's going to have to physically drag my arse down the aisle," he vows harshly.

"That makes you and me both."

Another fist bump between brothers. "Speaking of, what happened between you and Elsa?"

Everything, I want to tell him—and yet, not enough. "I kissed her this morning. Does that count?"

"It depends. Did it rock your world?"

It did more than that, I admit, surprising even myself. It changed everything.

He leans in, face serious, voice low. "What are you going to do?"

I'm honest. "I wish to hell I knew."

There's no press when we land, just a pair of sleek cars hidden in the dark to take us back to the palace. Lukas and I refuse to ride with the She-Wolf, under the guise of allowing her to return home without any delays. This suits her fine, even though she's come down a little from her high and settled into normal behavior, which has her taunting us at every turn.

"I'll see you in a few hours." Parker grabs his suitcase. Lucky bastard's car is at the airport, so he's able to escape quickly. "I just want to pop home and get showered, check my mail."

I clasp him on the shoulder as my mother's car pulls away. "Take the day off. Everything we need to discuss or do can wait until the inevitable jet lag clears."

To prove my point, he yawns but doesn't argue. I assure him it's my goal to go home and sleep the rest of the day and night so I will be ready for tomorrow morning's meeting with a group of labor union presidents.

Inside the car, while Lukas argues with the driver about music, I pull out my phone and switch it back from airplane mode to read through the lengthy list of texts and notifications waiting for me.

One stands out from the rest: Apple pie—worth tracking down or no?

Yes, goddammit. *Yes.*

I tell her: Good things always are.

Lukas glances over at me, eyebrows raised. I mouth *Elsa*. His thumbs up is surprisingly welcome.

That's what I thought. But I figured it couldn't hurt to get a fellow PIN/RFC member's opinion on the matter.

That will be our next first, I write her. Forget olallieberries. Our mission is to track down an apple pie together.

I hold my breath. Wonder if, on the heels of what's happened between us, what lies before us, she'll balk at my audacity.

In all your years in America, you never ate apple pie?

I've gone from anger and depression straight to flirting. Alas, I did not.

Lukas leans over, intrigued; I shove him back to his side.

"Well, well." A shit-eating smirk twists his lips. "Isn't this interesting. Is pie foreplay I'm unaware of?"

"Sod off," I tell him, but I'm too damn happy to sound forceful enough.

Elsa writes: I'm disappointed in you.

My fingers fly across the touchscreen. We are both apple pie virgins, running amuck in our respective countries. We must pop our cherries at the same time.

Your puns are terrible, Chris. Don't you mean we'll be popping our apples? Or should I say coring our apples? Never mind. I'm wretched at puns, too.

She called me Chris again. Goddamn, I like the sound of that. Nobody's perfect, Els. But she is. To me, she absolutely is.

The tightness in my chest eases when she adds: No eating it without me. Let's cavort with pie again. Promise?

It's a promise I gladly make, without hesitation.

"I think," Lukas muses, "you need to go pop that cherry sooner rather than later."

I slip my phone into my pocket. "Go to hell."

He chuckles. "Is that how you normally interact?"

I pocket the phone. "Spying on others' correspondence is a nasty habit."

"All the good royals do it." His elbow jabs my ribs. "Is it, though?"

"She's . . . not like the others," I admit.

"You mean she doesn't fawn all over Prince Perfect?"

"You really want me to punch you, don't you?"

"Let me ask you this." He leans back against the leather seat. "Do you really think you'll ever be okay with just being her brother-in-law?"

I turn my head and look out the window. Aiboland is cold and clear beyond the frosty glass, the morning sun sharp as it fights its way through the clouds covering our island.

"I'd like to think," he continues, "that if I ever have the pleasure of falling in love with someone, I wouldn't give it up, not even if the She-Wolf orders it so."

Easier for him to say than do, considering our circumstances.

But my brother's words linger long after we get back to the palace and I've taken care of several pressing issues before I can get ready to lose myself in bed until the following morning. It's a romantic notion, giving it all up for another person. But Lukas isn't to inherit the throne. He doesn't have the expectations I have weighing down upon my shoulders. He is ignorant of the She-Wolf's threats toward not only me, but him, our father . . . even Parker.

I'm selfish, but I don't know if I'm *that* selfish.

And still, I don't know if I'm willing to let Elsa go. Not that I have her, not that we're a thing or, hell, even the possibility of a thing, but . . .

I'm addicted. And I'm not ready to lose what she makes me feel.

CHAPTER 41

♛

CHRISTIAN

Lukas mutters under his breath, "Not again."

I glance up from my stout to find Lady Autumn Horn af Björksund sashaying toward us. She's in a tight white bandage dress that screams discothèque rather than pub, especially this one, which is about as low key as one can get in Norsloe.

"If I didn't know you better," I say, "I might interpret your hostility toward Autumn as renewed interest."

"Perhaps you ought to interpret my foot up your arse."

"Well, well," Autumn coos, once she reaches the table we're at. "If it isn't His Royal Highness, the Hereditary Grand Duke of Aiboland, sitting in Sven's Pig and Roast, looking healthy as a horse. And to think the nation feared you might have fallen off the face of the planet, or at least died from tuberculosis or the like."

It's said flippantly, but it's clear she's curious as to why I disappeared. I stand up. "Due to illness, I was forced to cancel all of my engagements. My apologies for any inconvenience."

It's the story that Parker made sure to circulate to explain the trip. I'm not Autumn's true focus, though. She turns to my brother and says, "Look at what the cat dragged in."

He lifts his glass, refusing to follow propriety's insistence that he rise. "Autumn."

I'm not overly keen on the lady in question joining us, but it doesn't appear there's a tasteful way of telling her to shove off. So I motion to one of the chairs at our table; she tosses her beaded handbag down and the two of us sit. "Have you recovered, Your Highness?"

Lukas nudges me from beneath the table, so I cough and pound on my chest a little. "I'm much better, thank you."

She lifts a slim hand, beckoning over a waitress. "It's funny, but I didn't see you around last week, either, Luk." Her eyes narrow in on my brother. "Were you also ill? Or perhaps frolicking naked and drunk once more?"

"We were like dominoes." The lies roll right off his tongue. "The entire family, save the exception of His Royal Highness. One of us got sick, then the next . . . before we knew it, the lot of us at were confined to bed, vomiting like there was no tomorrow coming."

A skinny eyebrow lifts high as she cooly regards him, her mouth twisting in distaste.

It's his turn to fake a cough, clearly overdoing it and thereby drawing attention from those around us. "Still feel it in my lungs."

My phone beeps. I slide it out of my pocket to find: *Hot cocoa doesn't taste the same in Vattenguldia as it does California. Weird, right?*

I push back my chair and tell them, "I need to take a call."

Lukas shoots daggers at me, but I ignore him. I then weave my way to the back of the small pub and head into the kitchen area. Sven, the owner slash cook, issues a greeting. I hold my phone aloft and he quickly wanders out for a break.

I dial Elsa's number. My finger had been itching to do so all day, but I knew she, like me, was probably overwhelmed with meetings and appointments. We'd been gone for a week, so if her schedule was anything like mine, there was a lot of catching up to do.

She answers on the second ring, and I swear, I pretty much melt into a goddamn puddle right in the middle of Sven's tiny kitchen when I hear her voice.

Jesus. I've got it so, so bad for this woman. "You're drinking hot cocoa without me?"

A tiny laugh floats through the receiver, and it's a gift—a really erotic, fucking amazing gift. "Charlotte made some this afternoon while we were debriefing. Who was I to refuse?"

"A member of the RHCDS, that's who."

She's thoughtful for a long moment, which only makes the grin on my face stretch wider. Finally, the soft snap of fingers sounds. "The Royal Hot Cocoa Drinker Society?"

"Drinkers," I correct. "Because societies must have more than one member."

I'm gifted with more of that bloody fantastic laughter, and it leaves me aching to get on a plane just so I can hear it in person.

"I take it you're not drinking hot cocoa?"

"Alas, I'm drinking stout tonight. Lukas and I are at a favorite pub. What are you doing, other than drinking hot cocoa without me?"

"Missing you," is what she says.

Never in my life has my chest felt like it'd been split open, bones and muscles pulled back so the organ that keeps me alive is left so utterly, completely bare. But I feel that way now, hearing the vulnerability in Elsa's voice when she tells me, for the first time ever, what I mean to her.

It'd always been known—assumed, yet never voiced. Because she and I? We clicked immediately. We were on the same page. We're kindred souls.

She misses me.

I lean against the door leading to the back alley, my eyes closing. If only she was standing here in front of me. Or I there, before her. "I miss you, too, Els."

CHAPTER 42

ELSA

The baby chooses the moment Charlotte says, "You're being supremely stupid," to spit up what appears to be cottage cheese all over her silk shirt.

Charming.

Charlotte planned to come to the palace for our briefing this morning, but I was antsy and in need of an excursion, especially after my mother cornered me like a fox in the henhouse during breakfast with a wedding planner. Scratch that. A *pair* of planners, because there are two daughters she's frothing at the mouth to marry off. It has been all of a week since returning to Vattenguldia. One. Hellish. Week. And Her Serene Highness is already in full-blown wedding planning mode.

So here I am, wondering why exactly it was here I fled to, because watching one individual vomit upon another, mother or no, is a very repulsive thing to witness.

"I am talking about you, by the way." Charlotte motions toward me with a questionably wet burp cloth. To a freshly joyful Dickie, in a nauseatingly cute voice, she murmurs, "Not you, precious."

I bat the rag away. "How am I being stupid? I've been here for a mere quarter of an hour, and all we've discussed is the weather and Dickie's sleep schedule."

She rubs her nose against the baby's while simultaneously patting him on the back. "You are moping."

"I most certainly am not moping." Am I?

All right, perhaps I am, just a wee bit. But as I just spent an hour trapped with my mother, an increasingly agitated Isabelle, and a pair of wedding planners, as well as fielded a tense phone call from Mat, Charlotte is lucky I am moping rather than raging.

She is right, though, curse her. I fear I am going through withdrawals, as I miss the Hereditary Grand Duke of Aiboland something fierce.

"You are," she's saying calmly, "and it's stupid."

Just because she's right doesn't mean I must play so easily into her deft yet wily hands. "These sandwiches are delish, Lottie."

The baby lets loose a loud belch. He's a Casanova, all right.

Charlotte ceases her patting. "I know my damn sandwiches are delicious. I am referring to your Prince Charming."

It isn't ladylike in the least, but I shove the rest of one of the cucumber and cream cheese crustless morsels into my mouth. "He ewen't mwhy Pwrin Darwing."

It's clear now that my personal secretary had no intention of going over the upcoming week's itinerary. I am to be interrogated.

Charlotte tosses the filthy burp cloth at me; I do not dodge quickly enough, because miniature white chunks streak down my jeans. I glare meaningfully at my closest friend.

She pays me no heed.

Dickie belches once more, which earns a nuzzle from his meddling mother. "I have known you for a very long time and have weathered being your friend through unfortunate relationship after even more unfortunate relationship."

"Hey now."

"I'm telling you, I have never seen you so taken with a man before. You were so . . . cheerful, I guess, every time I talked to you when you were in California—or cheerful for you. And now you are heartbroken."

"Heartbroken?" An embarrassingly loud snort comes out of me. "Hardly."

It is her turn to offer a meaningful glare.

That's the thing about a true friend. There is no need to offer up secrets for them to intuitively sense something is amiss. Charlotte cultivated the ability to read my emotions like a playbook long ago.

"You are a cow, and I have no idea why I am here, allowing myself to be vomited upon by your squalling infant whilst you spread lies about my person."

Her smile is serene. "Dickie most certainly did so such thing. And it's called spit-up."

I settle further into the overstuffed floral couch, grunting. "The point stands."

"What I am saying is, you like him. And I think that scares the hell out of you, especially as you're set to marry some man you feel nothing toward."

Yet another valid statement. It terrifies me, the strength of the emotions I feel toward Christian. "Fine. I like him. Are you happy?"

"I think it is more than like, though, isn't it?"

"Christ, Lottie. Isn't it bad enough that you got me to admit I like him?"

"It's a proper start." She passes Dickie over so she can pour us fresh cups of tea. The baby and I engage in a staring contest—my eyes narrow, his go wide and, dare I admit it, amused.

"Now," Charlotte continues, "we must work on you admitting you're in love with him."

I sputter out a weak, "I have known him less than a month."

"We covered this, Elsa. Love at first sight is a powerful thing."

"Remember? So is lust at first sight."

She sighs loudly.

I lose the staring contest, glancing away first so I can roll my eyes at my best friend. Dickie celebrates by adding drool to the spit-up on my jeans. No attempt to clean them is made, because I'm positive he'll figure out some other bodily fluid to add to his collection before the visit is over. So I tuck him into the crook of my elbow and rock gently back and forth until he gurgles contentedly. "How many times do I need to say it? Christian was very clear about not wanting a relationship."

"As were you, I believe."

"Exactly."

"He specifically doesn't want a relationship with Isabelle."

I issue another unladylike grunt.

"Just as you specifically don't want a relationship with Mathieu."

I try not to gag. There's enough vomit in the room today, thanks to Dickie.

"And yet, something happened between you two."

I am silent. There is no use denying it. She knows the bulk of the sordid story, anyway. I broke down two days after coming home and told her, unable to keep it all to myself any longer.

"Have you talked with Isabelle yet?"

"As we live in the same palace, we speak every day."

"Smartass. I meant have you discussed with her how you and her soon-to-be-fiancé have . . ." Charlotte waggles her eyebrows meaningfully.

"That's not a conversation I am keen on having. How does one inform their sister of such things?"

"If she is to marry him—"

I wince harder than I'd like, causing the baby within my arms to stir.

"She ought to know what happened between you two. So as holidays will not be awkward."

Discussion or no, awkwardness is assured.

"What of Prince Mathieu?"

"What of him?"

"Have the two of you discussed any of this?"

"I have made my opinion on the matter quite clear."

167

Her lips press together as she chooses her words. "What will you two do, then?"

"Me and Mat?"

"You and Christian," she gently corrects.

I press my head back against the floral couch. "What is there to do? He is to marry my sister." I pause. "More importantly, he is a Hereditary Grand Duke." I ache to surge to my feet and pace, but Dickie's eyes choose this very moment to slowly slide shut. I whisper furiously, "I am a Hereditary Princess."

"These are well known facts."

When I tell her, "It would never be allowed," I must fight the urge to cry.

"Impossible to know unless you try."

I stare up at the chandelier and wooden beams above us for long seconds as the baby in my arms drools contentedly in his sleep. And then I open up my veins and tell her the truth that has been banging at my doors nearly every second since I realized how I truly feel about Christian. "One of us would have to give up our crown to be with the other. It's not as if we can simply merge our two countries together. Being with Christian comes with consequences that are far direr than simply disobeying our sovereigns' edicts. One of us would no longer be what we've always been, what we've been raised to be. How would we chose who gives up that? Which of us is willing to do so? My sister, as you well know, has privately, yet repeatedly, announced how she has no interest in the throne. His brother is a consummate playboy who—well, I admit I do not know him well, but there was no impression he is keen on the job, either." I swallow hard. "And, even if we decided which of us would abdicate, how does one then explain to their monarch and country that another heir must be found because love trumps lifelong duties and commitments?" More softly, "Provided, of course, he feels the same toward me as I do him."

My friend's voice is soft and understanding. "So. You have thought about this, after all."

I am sniffling now. Damn Charlotte and her need to always push for emotional truths until I break. And damn Christian for being . . . well, Christian. Why did he have to be too wonderful? Why couldn't he be boring, or arrogant and insufferable, like so many other privileged men of my acquaintance? But no. He had to reveal himself as my bloody Prince Charming, leaving me to question so much of what I've planned for my life.

The urge to cry pulls at the corners of my eyes and toughens heartstrings in my chest. But rather than let go like I ache to, I press a kiss on the top of Dickie's head and glare at his mother.

I might loathe tradition, but it appears to come out victorious once more.

"All right," Charlotte says gently. "I just want you to be happy, Elsa. That's all."

I press my cheek against the baby's downy head. "If you truly wish for my happiness, then you'll fetch me something to mop up your child's bodily fluids. Good lord, Lottie. He is adorable as all get out, but he sure does make a mess. I'm drenched over here."

CHAPTER 43

♛
CHRISTIAN

My father's mouth is clamped shut. So is Lukas'. For that matter, so is mine. We men languish in absolute, miserable silence as the She-Wolf lays out the agenda for the coming weeks.

I'm to court Isabelle in the most extravagant, obscenely public way possible. Lukas, accompanied by our father, is to head to Spain to do the same, albeit less flagrantly, as the She-Wolf does not want the spotlight off of her so-called "power couple."

"Bed them quickly," she says to my brother and I in an awful business-like tone. "I'll ensure that any birth control issues will be taken care of beforehand. The sooner heirs are made, the better."

It doesn't matter to her that Isabelle or Maria-Elena might not care to be bedded, nor does it occur to the She-Wolf that tampering with one's birth control is vile and a crime.

Every so often, my father catches my eye. Sorrow and apologies line his face, as if his wife's machinations are his fault. And yet, I do blame him—I blame him for not standing up for us.

Hell, I blame myself and my brother, too. We ought to be standing up and telling the She-Wolf no.

We're cowards, and it's pathetic.

My phone vibrates in my pocket. I'm hopeful it's Elsa, but as my mother is explaining in excruciating detail just how my upcoming engagement to Isabelle is going to go down, I don't pull it out.

When the She-Wolf's done, and halfway to the door so she can go and do whatever it is She-Wolves do after devouring their young, I find myself standing up. My limbs are shaking in rage, my hands in fear, but as the noose around my neck has just tightened significantly, I feel like I have little to lose in this moment.

"I wish," I tell her, "that I actually had a mother who gives a damn about her family. Or gave a damn about anything other than herself. You're despicable."

Maybe I'm not a complete coward after all.

She doesn't respond. Not even when Lukas stands up and shows he's got a bit of spine, too.

An hour later, as Parker and I are working in my office, my day goes from shitty to flat-out terrible. Isabelle calls.

I'm tempted to let her go to voicemail, like I have for her last few attempts to ring me over the past couple days. I couldn't bear talking to her, let alone pretending I want anything to do with her, other than her sister. I can't bear it now, but at Parker's urging, I finally answer the phone.

"Maybe, if you two talk . . ." he offers, and all I can think is: *optimistic bastard.*

Once I say hello, I'm greeted with, "It's about bloody time you picked up the phone, Christian."

While her sister may occasionally drop such bombs, I have never heard Isabelle curse before. It's alien sounding. "Um—"

"I do not have time for our typical, bland chit-chat, but there are several things I must bring you up to speed on. I will speak, and you will listen."

She sounds frighteningly similar to Elsa right now—and I'm grudgingly impressed by it. "You've got my attention."

"Just to be clear, I'm not a bloody idiot. I am well aware something occurred between you and my sister in California."

Instinct kicks in. "That's none of your—"

"I may not know the specifics, but I know something must have happened. Elsa . . ." Her sigh is disgruntled. "Allow me to start at the beginning. I'm engaged, Christian."

My answer is sharp. "Not yet, you aren't."

Not ever, if I get my way.

Isabelle releases a rueful, tired laugh. "I am and have been for some time."

"Explain."

"I agreed to marry my equestrian instructor last year. Elsa knew about the relationship, but my parents did not. She urged me to inform Their Serene Highnesses, but . . ." Another soft, irritated puff of a laugh. "Every attempt to broach the subject was stymied by my parents waxing poetic about family history, glory, and of advantageous marriages. Perhaps that makes me a coward, but my lack of action is not important. What is, is that Alfons—my fiancé—and I had a nasty row prior to the Summit. He did not wish me to go, but my parents decreed I must accompany my father and my sister, as some kind of arrangement in the works with Aiboland. To make a long story short, I was blackmailed."

"Is everything okay?" Parker whispers as my arse hits my desk chair.

I hold a finger up as Isabelle continues to blow my mind. "Elsa and our father fought repeatedly about the Summit. I figured since he wouldn't cave to her whims—she, the heir who normally adheres to tradition—any objections I had would be immaterial. And this proved so when I was informed that, if I failed to abide by my parents' wishes and acquire the necessary trade pact and financial backing they coveted from your country, I would be financially cut off. Therefore, I attempted to enter the Royal Marriage Market as gracefully as possible. Only . . ." She sighs. "Christian, it pains me to say this, but . . . we aren't suited. Not at all."

Well, no kidding. "I—"

"You seem like a decent man, but there were no sparks between us. No common ground. Having watched my parents go through the motions of a loveless, hostile marriage, I refuse to have that kind of life. Besides, I'm in love with someone else, and you just won't do, money or no."

Talk about an ego check. *She* was bored with *me*?

"I'm in Geneva right now. Alfons and I have eloped; we're to be married before the night is over. Poverty and love is a future I far prefer to wealth and a tedious husband."

I'm speechless. Radically, fantastically, stupidly speechless. And to think I was bemoaning how my life was absolute pants just minutes before.

"Obviously, my family doesn't know. I left Elsa a letter, but she is at a charity tea. So, she'll know tonight. Here's the thing, Christian. I am certain my sister is in love with you. If I am not mistaken, you're in love with her, too."

I don't hesitate. "I am."

"I watched you two dancing the final night of the Summit. I had never seen Elsa look at anybody the way she does you. It was as if you were her personal Prince Charming come to life. And I spent enough time with you to know that you never looked at anyone the way you did her. The both of you disappeared every night when the rest of us were shagging, drinking ourselves into a stupor, and/or bemoaning our fates. Everyone at the castle knew you two were falling in love. Everyone. I mean, how many times were you two caught *hiding* together?"

For a moment, I fear I might be dreaming, because, for the first time of our acquaintance, I am completely riveted by what this woman is saying.

"Elsa has been miserable since coming home. Secretive. Resentful. Snapping at everyone. A bomb wracked the palace when our mother brought about wedding planners. Elsa is simply nightmarish every time poor Mathieu calls. She's to see him next week, in Paris. Mother insists she's to put on her game face and pretend to fall in love with him in the public light. Thinks that this will bring attention and glamour to Vattenguldia. A crown heir, falling in love with a landless prince in the City of Lights? Her Serene Highness is betting on the glossies having a field day over such a fairy tale. It's her hope that Vattenguldia will linger on the tip of everyone's tongues worldwide."

I'll be damned if I allow anyone but me to give Elsa a fairy tale.

"I'd like to say that I am sorry we are not marrying, Christian, but...as I am deliriously in love with my fiancé, I will not demean what we feel toward one another with this lie. But if you feel anything toward my sister—even in the smallest bit—I advise you to go to Paris next week. Stop Elsa from making the biggest mistake of her life. She will be a fantastic monarch, no doubt, but it should not come at the expense of her personal happiness." She pauses. "I have no doubt our parents have blackmailed her, as well."

Even though I'm dealing with a similar situation, my blood boils at the thought of anyone forcing Elsa's hand. What in the bloody hell is wrong with our parents? The royals in this world? "I'm sorry," I tell Isabelle.

Hushed anger fills her words. "You refuse to go to Paris?"

"Hell yes, I'm going." Fuck the She-Wolf. "I'm apologizing for how wrong I was about you. I was an absolute arsehole. But you're right—we don't suit. Not in the least."

"People misjudge me often. I wish you luck, Christian. I only thought it fair you know all this, because in an hour or so, when their Serene Highnesses comprehend what I've done, the shite is going to hit the fan."

A man in the background on her end murmurs something in German. I think it's: *Time to get moving, my sweet filly.*

Well, aren't they the perfect match?

"Oh, and Christian?"

"Yeah?"

"Alfons did a little digging at the palace for me while I was in California. After our first breakfast together, I promptly had a discreet panic attack and rang him up, begging forgiveness and to look into matters I was too far away to investigate. I am undoubtedly committing treason, but . . . I had to know why my parents were so desperate for Elsa and I to make such advantageous matches. There had to be more to it than simply coveting increased shipping routes and designing tourist traps." An audible breath sounds across the static. "Her Serene Highness has come close to bankrupting the Vasa family's finances. I am unaware of the particulars, but it is clear my father is aware of the issue. We must assume it is why they are so desperate for Mathieu's money—and yours. It has nothing to do with modernizing the technological infrastructures of our shipping registries. A quick call to a friend informed me Parliament already has that covered. This is all about staving off a scandal."

I'm infuriated. As respected as he is in the EU, Gustav is willing to sell out his own children because his wife mismanaged their money? Who does that?

Elsa deserves better. Hell, so does Isabelle.

"Help my sister find the ammunition needed to blow our parents out of the water," Isabelle tells me. "Give her a kiss for me, and let her know I'll call in a few weeks once I'm settled in Germany with Alfons' family."

I hang up the phone and turn to Parker, a low whistle slipping through my lips.

He asks, bewildered, "What was that all about?"

Hope, I think. Bloody, brilliant hope.

I clap him on the shoulder, grinning like a fool. I'm not as down and out as I feared just an hour before. "I hope you're prepared to stay up late tonight, because we've got plans to make."

CHAPTER 44

ELSA

The palace is in an uproar. Isabelle grew a backbone and has left to chase after her fairy story ending.

Dear Elsa,

Life is too short to spend it miserable and trapped in a loveless marriage. Twenty-six years of watching one in motion has proven this to me, as I'm sure it has for you. Thus, Alfons and I have eloped. I love him too much to let him go. It's selfish of me, isn't it? And yet, it's the only truth I'm willing to accept.

I beg you to not be afraid to embrace your truths, either . . . especially those of the heart.

Yours,

Isabelle

My sister thumbed her nose at our parents and resolved to live life the way she wants to, and with whom she chooses to share it with. I am envious, to be honest. And so startled by this turnabout that I do not even know what to say, but I would high five Isabelle if she were standing before me.

Her Serene Highness ignites in fury over the day's events, summoning every member of the staff with any regular contact with my sister in order to personally interrogate them until many depart in tears. *Did Isabelle inform you of her plans? Were you complicit in hiding her scandalous relationship with the stable hand?*

Other than a hapless security guard admitting he saw Alfons' car drive away in the middle of the night, no one had anything of import to add to the discussion.

After several hours of torturing the help, my mother sent everyone away so that only family remains in my father's office. "How could Isabelle do this?" she rages. "Does she not understand the consequences of her actions?"

Only all too well, I muse silently.

My mother continues, words so vehement that spittle unattractively decorates her lips, "She must be found before too much damage can be done. What will the Grand Duchess think—do—when she hears of this? If word were to get out—"

She stops. Turns to my father, her face paling significantly. "We must ensure no one in the palace contacts the press."

"All staff signed a nondisclosure agreement upon employment," I gently remind them.

The note Isabelle left is subsequently dissected until the ink fades from handling. I am also interrogated, although to a lesser degree, finally confessing to my parents that I knew of the relationship between my sister and her riding instructor—and approve of it.

This admission nearly sends Her Serene Highness into seizures.

The palace is placed on lockdown. Cell phones are confiscated from each member of the staff, leaving two-way radios as the sole avenues for communication outside of the heavily monitored general phone line. In an utter fit of paranoia, even my own cell is appropriated, despite my insistence I would never betray my sister to the media.

My arguments now fall upon deaf ears. All my parents can fixate on is how to circumvent the coming media circus.

His Serene Highness orders Bittner to contact a discreet private investigator to track down Isabelle's whereabouts. Come hell or high water, it is my parents' goal to somehow drag my sister back to Vattenguldia and talk some sense into her—or at least find a proper way to spin the situation before word reaches the Grand Duchess of Aiboland's ears.

Well after midnight, as I leave my father's office, I overhear my mother whisper, "What will we do, Gustav? Without Aiboland, we—"

"Hush." His Serene Highness is not gentle when he cuts her off. "There is still the agreement with the Chambérys." His voice lifts. "Elsa? Be sure to close the door behind you."

I do as requested, but their words turn over in my mind for the rest of the night.

I am unnerved at how worried my mother truly sounded.

"I've got an itinerary set up so we can tour all the best sites of Paris."

"It will not be my first visit," I inform Mat. I know I come across as rather bitchy, but the mere thought of playacting the doting, swooning girlfriend makes me want to throw myself out the window, especially on the heels of my sister's bravery.

His words are static-y across the landline call. "But have you been there with an insider before?"

"Funny, I remember quite clearly you telling me you fancy yourself a New Yorker nowadays."

One of my mother's aides is across the room, awkwardly attempting to melt into the wallpaper and paintings rather than eavesdrop as instructed. She's to ensure I do not mention our family's scandal. Furthermore, I am not allowed off the palace grounds without an escort.

They fear I'll run, too—and frankly, it is beyond insulting.

A sound of resigned regret fills my ear. "Elsa, I'm trying here. I know this isn't ideal for either of us, but it's important that we at least *try*. Right?"

Actually, yes—just not in the way he suggests.

I slip into the open doorway to the balcony in my office. It is drizzling outside: cool, soft tears pepper the rocky land and gray, angry sea. I lower my voice, risking my mother's wrath in a desperate Hail Mary attempt. "My sister eloped."

There is a moment of shocked silence between us. "With Christian?"

"With her equestrian instructor." I relate the bare bones of the situation; in the end, I believe him to be just as envious and impressed as I am with Isabelle's gumption.

A discreet glance behind me shows the aide with her nose stuck in a book, appearing wholly unaware that I just did exactly what she was sent to ensure did not occur.

I follow my disobedience with a slice of brutal honesty. "Mat, I appreciate your efforts. I do. But, I simply cannot pretend that I am head over heels for any of this. I like you, I do, but . . ."

"We already established neither of us is in love with the other." He clears his throat. "You're preaching to the choir here."

"If it is not what either of us want, then—"

"It doesn't matter what I want, Elsa. Not anymore."

There's a quiet desperation, an anger that is nearly tangible across the distance. "What does that mean?"

"It means . . ." A hard breath is blown out. "Sometimes, you have to do what's best for others, rather than yourself."

The sadness in his voice unnerves me, as does the resignation that drives each word as if it is a struggle. "Is that what you are doing?"

He counters me with, "Isn't it what we're *both* doing?"

"Then—"

"I'm sorry. I truly am. But I can't back out of this agreement. I wish I could, but my hands are tied."

No amount of questioning from that point on yields any clues as to what he alludes to. I am unsettled by the insinuation behind his words long after our call ends. There is something I am clearly missing, something he's not telling me—which isn't too surprising. He and I are not best friends who share our deepest, darkest hopes and dreams with one another. We are not kindred spirits.

But it appears we are nonetheless in the same boat.

The RMM forced us both into this situation. It just never occurred to me that perhaps some of us may be more forced than others.

I promptly march over to my mother's spy. "I wish to ring my personal secretary."

It is infuriating that I must even issue such a request.

The woman tugs a slip of paper from her briefcase and studies it. A flush steals up her neck, past her crisp collar. "Lady Charlotte is on Her Serene Highness' approved list of callers, Your Highness. Allow me to dial the number for you."

My teeth grind together so forcefully I am positive I've worn away enamel. My parents have lost their damn minds.

When Charlotte answers, I inch toward the balcony again, lowering my voice once more so the stooge cannot hear me properly. "Have you heard back from the P.I. you hired to investigate Mathieu yet?"

"I ought to have a report in a week or so," she says. "I requested it be thorough."

"Get it sooner."

Because maybe my sister has a very good point.

CHAPTER 45

CHRISTIAN

Three days after Isabelle's phone call, I am summoned to the Grand Duchess' office. And once there, it takes all of my self-control not to laugh in her overly Botoxed face. Because the moment I see it, all tight and strained as her fury tries to take root yet remains scarily bland, I know *she* knows.

I owe Isabelle a drink. A whole case of them, even.

She waves her personal secretary out and waits until the door clicks behind him before speaking. "I received a phone call from Prince Gustav this morning that was most . . ." She folds her bony hands in front of her; the knuckles are white in displeasure. "Disappointing."

Mild curiosity is such a difficult emotion to produce when all you want to do is gleefully shout, "Suck it, She-Wolf!" whilst holding up a middle finger to one's mother and sovereign.

This is a bloody fantastic moment.

She chews on lemons as she tells me what I already know. Fumes when she laments the loss of assured connections to Vattenguldia. Seethes when she paints Isabelle as a weak, pathetic excuse for a royal. When she's done frothing at the mouth, I don't give her what she wants, or hell, even expects, from me. I don't exhibit any outrage, nor do I share with her the joy that comes from hearing her plans have gone to hell in a hand basket. I merely nod to acknowledge I've heard her words, and then I wait to be dismissed.

She no longer has anything to blackmail me over. My father, my brother . . . even Parker are currently safe for now. I just need to ensure it stays that way.

Right when I'm to leave the room, she says, "Christian, actions such as Isabelle's will not be tolerated in this household."

I turn back toward her, ensuring my face is blank.

"If you or Lukas ever dare to disobey me, or sully our line by marrying outside of whom I approve, you will regret the day you were born into this illustrious family."

I'm in too good of a mood to be so ungenerous. I'll give her a little parting gift. The door swings open wide. Her personal secretary is at his desk, and there are a few other aides milling about. "Too late, Your Highness. I already regret being in this so-called illustrious family. I think anyone would, when they have a mother like you. No crown is worth this nightmare."

I finally break into the smile that's been chasing me as her indignant howling shadows my departure. It's music to my ears.

CHAPTER 46

ELSA

"Now that your sister has ruined her life," my mother is saying, "we expect you to uphold the Vasa family traditions and do our family proud."

She is overseeing my packing for Paris. Normally this is something Charlotte does, but after Isabelle's departure and my voiced arguments, it appears Her Serene Highness does not trust me to properly pack for the trip. Worse yet, Charlotte is not even to come with. My mother's personal assistant, a meek yet humorless woman named Greta, will have that honor. I suppose it could be worse—my mother could be coming—but there are several local commitments she cannot abandon.

I am officially in medieval, locked-in-a-tower, princess hell.

"Are you kidding me?" I ask from the armchair I've been relegated to. Greta, freshly exiting the closet with an armful of dresses and coats, flinches at my vitriol. "No, really. Are you fucking kidding me?"

My name is a warning from Her Serene Highness' blood red lips.

I am beyond angry, and her disapproval does nothing to stem the foul language she abhors from shooting out of my mouth. For days now, all I have heard from my parents and sovereigns is: *Get to Paris; ensure the press believes the love story is real and magical.* In response, I once more informed Mat that I did not want us to marry. I flat-out asked if he was being blackmailed into this union of ours. All I got was telling silence. Well, silence and a sigh that filled my ear with an alarming amount of distressed resignation.

Anxiety crawls over my skin. *I cannot believe this is happening. This is really happening.*

"Why do you desire me to marry this man so much?" Greta scurries back into the closet as I shout at the woman who gave birth to me. "What kind of mother does this to her own flesh and blood?"

I want answers from someone. *Anyone.*

The woman whose looks I favor stands up, smoothing her slacks. "A desperate one."

It is enough to knock my self-righteousness off balance. Desperate? Desperate for what? The updated technological systems for our shipping fleets? Most of Vattenguldia's commerce comes from corporations based in other lands flying under our flags for a fee usually much less than their home countries. Our personal shipping fleets are miniscule.

Why are they so keen on updating a few dozen ships?

"Why desperate?" I crowd her personal space. Warning bells blare in my ears. "Talk to me, Mother. Perhaps together, we can figure out a solution to whatever problem you're worried about if we simply—"

She turns and exits my apartments before I finish my question, but not before she issues a sharp order for Greta to ensure I receive a proper night's rest before I depart for Paris in the morning.

I march over to my desk and extract a sheet of paper. Then I write a letter to Charlotte, demanding she quiz Josef about shipping technology . . . and to share what dirt she's dug up on Mat's family and situation.

I will get my answers one way or another. I must.

CHAPTER 47

CHRISTIAN

"Are you sure about this?"

Lukas slides a beer my way, his dark eyes uncharacteristically hard to read, but that's okay. I know what my little brother is asking, what the true questions behind the five simple yet weighted words are. More so, I know exactly how he feels about it, even if he won't outright say it.

It's just the two of us right now. Parker is already downstairs, waiting for me, but I needed to ensure I spoke with my brother before I got on the plane.

The beer is stout and foamy, just like I prefer. I let the bitterness twist down my throat before I answer him.

"Yeah, I am."

He nods slowly.

I set the glass down. "Were there any problems?"

My brother's stout remains untouched. "None that I can tell. But, we can trust Gunnar. He's . . . unconventional, but he gets the job done."

It's my turn to nod. "Keep me updated. I want everything in place, just in case . . ."

Just in case the She-Wolf gets wind of familial treachery.

Luk blows out a hard breath. Then he proffers his fist. Mine knocks his, and then I stand up to leave.

CHAPTER 48

ELSA

Greta napped the entire way to Roissy Airport, which was fine by me. It was probably good for her, too, considering the extreme toxicity of my mood. Their Serene Highnesses actually accompanied me to the airport to personally ensure I boarded our private jet. There were a few tense moments in which I feared they would climb the airstairs alongside me. Instead, my father said quietly, "I know you are displeased with the situation—"

"I am more than displeased." It was the frostiest voice I had ever used with him before. At that moment, it did not feel as if I were speaking with my father. In a lot of ways, it did not feel as if I was speaking to my sovereign.

I was communicating with a jailer.

"There are moments in every sovereign's life that are less for the betterment of ourselves and more for the common good, Elsa."

"Your Highness, I say this with all the respect afforded a crown heir to her lord father, but unless you are here to inform me you value my life and choices as an individual and your daughter rather than a piece of chattel you can use to further your personal agenda, I would really rather get on the jet so I might go whore myself to the rich man you have selected for me."

That infuriated him, which was entirely acceptable. I was pretty pissed off myself.

For years, I looked up to my father. He is not perfect, not by a long shot. But he is a mostly good and popular Prince who loves Vattenguldia immensely. I strove to be like him, to also be a beacon of hope and service to our constitutional monarchy. And now . . . now I no longer know what to think, let alone feel toward him or my mother.

The Chambérys reserved me rooms at one of the most luxurious of hotels in all of Paris. My suite is gorgeous and opulent, to be sure, but beauty means nothing if it comes at the expense of a loss of personal freedom.

Thankfully, Greta is to stay in a different room on an entirely different floor. I think the both of us are relieved at such a set-up. She is a nice woman, but she's no nanny. And she shouldn't be, for goodness' sake. She's the personal secretary to the Queen of Vattenguldia. There is no good reason she ought to be hovering over her Hereditary Princess as if, once she looks away, I might drown myself in drugs or dance naked upon bar tops.

"Is there anything else I might get for you tonight, my lady? Perhaps room service?"

My eyes remain on the stunning view of the Eiffel Tower in the distance when I let Greta know I am tired and wish only for sleep.

"Do not hesitate to ring if you change your mind," she tells me. "Oh, and there are some lovely gifts for you on one of the tables in the sitting room."

I wait for the click of the door to signal her departure before I wander over to see what she is referring to.

A huge bouquet of flowers from Mat await me—or rather, from the Chambérys. *Welcome to France*, the card reads. *We look forward to getting to know you.*

It's enough to make me want to shred every single one of the lovely blooms.

Next to the flowers is a welcome basket from the hotel, filled with fruits, chocolates, wine, and various other treats that they foolishly believe will tempt me into believing I have just stepped into heaven.

The bitterness inside me triples.

I am about to head off to take a shower when I spy another item on the table. Unobtrusively tucked between the flowers and the basket is a small box with a blue ribbon around it, no note attached.

I carefully unwrap the ribbon and peek within the box. Inside is a smartphone, with a yellow sticky note on top that instructs me to turn it on.

I am intrigued enough to do so.

The phone is unassuming. There are no apps other than what comes on the base model, nothing to indicate one way or another what it is all about. I turn the slim rectangle over in my hand, but it's unmarked.

I tap open the contacts list—aha. There is a number programmed in, belonging to a C with a number I know all too well. And just seeing it here makes me want to cry and laugh all at once.

Oxygen floods my blood when a shaky finger touches the call button. Then . . . Ringing. Only, the chime in my ear is also somewhere nearby.

And it emanates from just beyond my hotel door.

I lose the ground beneath my kitten-heeled feet, all the air in my lungs dissipating until I am weightless and freefalling toward the door. So it makes sense when his achingly familiar voice, filtering through the plastic and metal in my hand to deep within my ear and soul, leaves me questioning wakefulness.

A sharp pinch to the arm proves lucidity, and then wonderfully, bewitchingly: hope. Because Christian's voice seeps through the painted wood separating me from the hallway.

I rise upon my tiptoes, peeking through a small, golden hole. There, miraculously, wonderfully, is the object of all of my dreams. Christian is standing outside of this godforsaken jail of a suite with a stark five o'clock shadow, dressed in a t-shirt, flannel shirt, jeans, and a baseball hat . . . like . . . like he is anyone other than a prince. As if he is simply Christian, come to see Elsa, and not the Hereditary Grand Duke of Aiboland surreptitiously lingering incognito before the Hereditary Princess of Vattenguldia's suite at the George V at eleven o'clock at night.

"Open the door, Els," he murmurs quietly—not into the phone, but *to* me, like he knows my eyes are already undressing him.

So I do.

The moment the boundaries which separated us are finally gone, all of the practiced words wrangled over for two miserable weeks choose to find better pastures. There is only him and me, and there is really nothing else that matters. Not my parents, not his, not Mat, not anything.

My fingers find their way to his shirt, twisting just barely into the gray, faded cotton, until he falls prey to the undeniable magnetism between us just as strongly as I have. He steps into the room while simultaneously kicking the door closed, sending a thrill shooting up my spine and then lower, transforming my body into a live, hot wire ready to combust. His eyes, so astonishingly, expressively amber tonight, widen and darken all at once. Desire, relief, and an achingly lovely amount of caring reflect back at me, and it humbles and thrills me like no other look could.

His voice is husky and sexy when he murmurs my name. It's pure, unadulterated liquid lust made just for me, so it is impossible, really, to resist gently tracing those delectable lips with one of my fingertips. How can my name, once believed to be stodgily old-fashioned, sound so utterly sensual coming from his mouth?

He's here. I am here. We are here together.

There's so much to talk about right now. Figure out. But the only words I can put together, the only ones that matter are, "Kiss me."

"I thought," he tells me in that lovely, accented voice of his, "you'd never ask."

Oh, oh, does this man know how to kiss, I dreamily muse when Christian's lips meet mine. They're teasing, soft brushes of desire that trigger a massive earthquake in the middle of my chest and a tsunami of wetness in my knickers. Need mingles painfully with ecstasy, and through the fog of bliss that fills the suite we're in, I understand this: *I have never felt this way about another person before.* Never. Not with Nils, or Theo, or any of the other men I have ever been intimate with. I wanted them, yes, but it was like merely sipping a glass of water compared to being a soul lost in the desert, frantic to quench their crushing thirst.

I dig my hands into his rich, dark hair in order to tug him closer, admiring how soft and silky the strands are. Loose ropes of fresh curls twist around my fingers, and I am rewarded with a beautiful, sexy sound that originates deep within his chest.

Speaking of . . .

I let go of his lovely hair, vowing to come back shortly, so I can slowly slide the flannel shirt off his lean shoulders. My fingers lightly trail down his arms until he shudders softly under my touch. *Yes*, I cannot help but greedily think. And then, *more*.

Next comes his T-shirt, and God almighty, his chest—his sculpted, hard, lean chest that would put any Hollywood actor to shame—is here for me to touch. Another thought comes to me, one fierce and strong: *mine*.

I am backed up against the door, the same one he just came through, and as he presses up against me, I delight in knowing he is as turned on by me as I am by him. It is intoxicating, knowing that this man is hard because he's with me. Touching me. Kissing me. A strong leg slips between mine, spreading me wide against the door, and I am panting, I am so desperate to have him. My name is whispered again, and had I not already been wet, I would become so with these sensual, languid syllables from his mouth.

And to think I ever believed rejecting him was a sound idea.

His fingers mimic my action from before, lightly tracing the lines of my arms, raising every hair on my body as goose pimples break out. Past elbows, skirting past my shoulders to trace my clavicle, and then lower until they lightly graze my nipples.

Oh sweet heavens above, I am perilously close to weeping in want and need. *Do it again.*

But I don't need to say it, because he does exactly what I want—little, light brushes and flicks that have me squirming against the door. His mouth, hot and drugging, finds my neck; bolts of lightning are sent straight to the very core of me when he sucks oh-so-gently.

I will not survive this. I fear I will simply dissolve right here and now.

As his teeth graze an earlobe, his fingers shift to untie the fabric belt around my waist. My hand fumbles behind us, toward the lock on the door. He pulls back, curious, and for one, rueful, gorgeous moment, I laugh.

"Have I lost you already?" His head ducks down toward mine, nose brushing the curve of my cheek. "You're distracted and laughing—not that I don't love the sound, it's just . . ."

I cup his cheek, nipping at his bottom lip. "No one is allowed to interrupt us this time. We cannot trust another pan won't be dropped and ruin the moment. Thus, before I lose my mind entirely, the door must be locked."

He reaches higher still, to the deadbolt. A quiet hiss of metal against metal informs me we are good to go.

"Els?"

"Chris?"

His grin is blinding. "I'm ready to help you lose your mind. Kiss me already."

I happily oblige.

After an eternity or an hour or even just a mere minute, Christian has the tiny buttons running the length of my shirtdress unfastened. The sides are spread open, leaving me vulnerable to his hot gaze.

I watch the lines of his throat as he swallows. "No bra?"

I shake my head, dark hair spilling across my shoulders.

"Jesus." His large hands gently cup the side of my breasts. More quietly, "Jesus." Thumbs on both side track across my sensitive nipples, and I bite down on my lip to keep from moaning too loudly.

One hand momentarily leaves a breast to cradle my face, encouraging me to look up at him. "No more hiding."

The confusion that must have reflected in my eyes has him adding, "I don't want you holding back who you are with me. Not here, not now, not ever. Not again. If you want to shout or moan or laugh or do anything like that when I touch you, then do it. Because I promise you, it's something I want to hear."

To prove his point, a moan is coaxed right out of me the moment his mouth closes over my breast. I'm dazed and delirious and yet praying all the same that this is real.

"I've dreamed about it, you know," he murmurs. "My name falling from your gorgeous mouth when I make you come over and over and over again. Fantasized about it for weeks now. When I'm in a meeting . . ." His lips find mine again, licking the seam until I gladly allow his tongue in. "At a charity event . . ." Another kiss, this time hotter and longer than the last, leaving me writhing against his leg. "At dinner . . ." His mouth finds my neck again, sucking harder than before. "Everywhere. All I could think about was you, and how very, very much I want you. How I've desired you like this." More quietly, "I've never wanted anybody the way I want you, Els."

His mouth travels lower still, until it comes back to one of my aching breasts. But his tongue teases, only flicking briefly across the tip of a nipple. "I need to know. . . Am I alone, thinking, wanting these things?"

"God, no." My voice is barely audible. He is a thief who has not only stolen my heart but now my breath.

I have never actually said the three words clamoring inside me to anyone before. Not to Nils, not even to my parents or sister.

He slowly slips the dress off my shoulders and then cups my face. "I know what I'm doing right now is selfish. The first day we met, you were very clear about not wanting—"

My fingers press against his lips. "I didn't know you then. Had I known..." I can't help but laugh again. "I probably would have torn your clothes off right there in the middle of that hallway. Propositioned you myself."

A kiss is pressed against my fingers. "That would have been awkward, don't you think?"

"Awkward and yet an excellent idea."

"I'm glad you said what you said, though. Because it gave me a chance to get to know you." He brushes a strand of hair away from my face, tucking it behind an ear. "And Els, getting to know you was one of the best things to ever happen to me."

The joy I feel right now is world shattering. "Me, too."

"You're probably wondering how I knew you'd be here—"

"Charlotte," I say brightly. I love Charlotte.

"Yes, partially to Charlotte, but also because Isabelle called me the day she eloped and asked me a very important question."

My sister? "What—"

"She asked me if I was in love with you. I told her I was."

Time stops. Just grinds to a brilliant halt, and all there is right now is this moment, here with this man.

"She also told me to get my arse to Paris, because she was pretty sure you're in love with me, too."

When did Isabelle become so wise? "You think?"

"I *hope.*"

All the words filling the atoms that make me, me find themselves stuck in the peanut butter that miraculously appears in the lining of my throat. Because...because opening oneself up to another like this is something you can't take back. Once these words are out there, they are out forever. They can be lost or ignored or forgotten, but never taken back.

But as I stare into those eyes that I do, in fact, love, any question of whether or not I could ever deny what I feel toward this man is answered firmly and soundly. So, instead of tumbling head over feet as I plummet toward uncertainty and yet assuredness all at once, I stretch my arms wide and catch the current. I tell him, "I do, you know. I am utterly, completely in love with you."

I am also utterly in love with the look on his face right now, as Christian, who has always been too much everything else, appears too in love with me.

Damn, do I love his *too*-ness.

"That's good to hear," he says softly. "Or *this* could have been desperately awkward."

I am laughing again, and he's now looking at me as if I am just Elsa, and he is just Christian, and we are simply two people crazy in love and not subject to crowns and countries and duties. A tiny wish is sent off, a silent one, begging all that is good in the world to allow this man to always look at me just so.

Laughter fades away until we are studying one another, silence our friend in the hotel suite. Clocks tick and people around the city sleep, and somewhere around the globe others wake and work and live their lives. But here, in this room, words never spoken out loud before sink quietly into each other's skins, burrowing straight through muscle and bone until they land cleanly in souls. The orderly, regimented lives we've always known and found comfort in are irrevocably altered.

He kisses me again, slowly, carefully, stubble scraping across smooth skin, just enough to remind me that this is real, he is real, and our words and feelings are now officially out there and cannot be recalled. No matter what else happens, no matter what the next day or any of those that follow will bring us, what we feel is finally logged into the census of our lives.

I have never felt more right and sure of anything else in my entire existence.

"I want you, Els." My lips tingle against his whispered words. "Christ, I want you more than anything. But if you want to wait, we can—"

The space between us widens, even if just by mere millimeters. I refuse to allow distance to separate us anymore. "If you don't make love to me tonight," I tell him, voice clear and crisp and regal, "I will never speak to you again."

His hardened length twitches violently against my leg, so I reach down and unbutton his pants. A long, slow hiss tears through him when my hand slides past his briefs (oh merciful heavens, they are red and sexy as all hell) and wraps around the very part I need in me. I had only gotten a brief feel back in the castle's kitchen, but now? Now I'm ready to fully explore Christian. Except . . . I want him in me so bad I can taste it.

I want to taste *him*.

"Els—"

I love how he calls me this. Nobody else in the entire world does so. Nobody else has the right to. Just him. It will only ever be him. "Take your pants off, Christian."

An amused eyebrow lifts up, so I clarify, "Take everything off."

I very nearly drool as I watch him strip bare. A sharp vee and thin trail of hair leads down to one of the most spectacular sights I have ever seen on a man, and the urge to fall to my knees takes hold because Christian naked, as I suspected, is very nearly a religious experience.

He steps toward me, running his hand down my belly until it cups the space between my legs. Fire bolts blaze throughout my body. "Your turn." Unfamiliar, tormented whimpering slips through my lips as he strokes his fingers back and forth. "You're already wet, aren't you? So wet," he adds, smiling as if I have given him the best present in the world, "that you've soaked through your knickers."

Normally, that would embarrass the hell out of me, but not tonight. Not with him. Because I am wet, incredibly so, and it is all because of what I feel toward him and that is nothing—*nothing*—I can be embarrassed about.

He bends down before me, nose perilously close to my belly button. Fingers slowly hook into the sides of my panties and I'm whimpering once more, this time his name, my hands fumbling to clutch at his shoulders.

"Easy, tiger." His fingers trace the rim of skin just under the thin elastic holding my panties up. "As we're not skinny-dipping in a group setting, I don't think you need these, do you?"

God, no.

He chuckles quietly at the look on my face. "Glad to see you agree. But before we go any further, you ought to know that I plan on taking my time tonight. I need to learn every little thing there is to know about your body or I'll go insane."

Amusement pierces the hazy lust surrounding me. "Need?"

A kiss is pressed at the base of the sheer silk, sending another jolt of intensity straight through my core. "Yes. *Need.*"

I gasp with each subsequent kiss. "Seems . . . awfully . . ." The silk dips lower, allowing a kiss to land upon bare skin. "Dramatic."

"Honest is more like it. Damn, Els. You smell like heaven."

I am not embarrassed at this, either. I'm feeling rather dramatic myself at the moment.

Finally, he slides my knickers off, tossing them over his shoulder. For long seconds, he's quiet as he studies my nude body. And then my head hits the door when his slickened fingers find my pleasure point. Silent, fervent prayers are answered because his lips follow his finger, and I am now more than gasping. I am yelling his name. I'm yelling his name and I have not orgasmed yet, although I am perilously close for just a first touch.

He stands, raising my arms above my head. "Trust me," he whispers. I taste myself when he kisses me, an experience I have always refused before, certain it would be disgusting. But I was wrong, because right now, with him? It is an incredible turn-on.

Before I can suck another breath in, he is back on his knees, spreading my legs once more. My hips buck forward against his mouth; I am rewarded with one, then two fingers slipping deftly into me.

I do not know how I am going to keep standing. My knees are perilously close to giving out right now. I will catch fire like a human candle and then melt until there is nothing left of me because surely no person could feel so much and not literally, physically combust.

A noise sounds on the other side of the door, of wheels and plates rattling, and of footsteps. And still, Christian sucks and licks and teases. Not caring if anyone hears me, I cry and yell and do all of those things he wanted to hear—not because he asked for them, but because he knows precisely how to coax them out of me. And when I honestly don't know if I can take it anymore, he gifts me with one, last intense lick.

I shatter into hundreds—no thousands—of little pieces, all carved with his name, and mine, together.

CHAPTER 49

CHRISTIAN

I give Elsa no time to recover from what I hope is the first of several orgasms tonight. She's in my arms and I'm carrying her through the suite, kicking open the bedroom door. And then we're on the bed, which is where she really deserved to be in the first place, and I'm kissing her—not soothingly, like I really ought to, but hotly, reverently, like I don't really have a choice.

In a lot of ways, I suppose I don't. Since the moment I ran into her in a narrow hallway in California, she's possessed my heart and it really only feels like I have it back when she's with me. It's terrifying, this lack of control that threatens to wash me away from my responsibilities every time I even think of her. Responsibilities I was born with, ones that stem from more than family, but from an entire country's worth of people who expect me to assume the throne. Christian, to Aiboland, represents the present and the future. The newspapers often talk about how the country desperately needs to climb headfirst into the twenty-first century. I think about the people I met in grocery stores. Or charity events. Or on the streets. Or anywhere, really.

Nobody ever asks what I need. Not that I expect them to; that's pure hubris. My life is one of service. Aiboland comes before Christian, right? It always comes before my own wants and needs.

But then I met this woman and she made me, for the first time in my life, want something more than I have. So I'm kissing her like I mean it, like I have to because she's my air, my sunlight, my warmth, the very blood in my veins. Like she is the reason the muscle in my chest beats so hard and fast, because she *is*. She makes me feel like I could be more than just what everyone else needs, and that is more intoxicating than any drug or drink in the world. Being here with Elsa, having just tasted her and listened to my name come from between her lips as she fell apart in my hands . . . It's the best goddamn feeling ever.

But I'm getting ahead of myself. I promised to take my time tonight.

I reluctantly break away, staring down at her in the pale lamplight, at how dark hair spreads around her head like chaotic waves across the white, foamy sea of bedspread. At how glazed her eyes are, all liquid desire mixed in her irises. At how swollen her lips are. She truly is a Valkyrie, or at the very least something mercurial and temporary, because surely this can't be real. *She* can't be real. This is just another one of the many fantasies I've built around this woman over the last few weeks, isn't it?

Her hand cups my cheek; her lips brush my own. "Are you okay?"

It's a fist around my heart. Yes, I want to tell her. *Yes*. But, the words are stuck—not because I fear saying them, but because it's just too hard to offer anything coherent right now. So I kiss her instead. Long, and hot, and meaningful. And then I slowly begin to memorize the map of Elsa's body with my hands and mouth. Before I even know what's happening, she slides down over me until I'm deep inside her, so deep all I can do is gasp and then moan. She's tight, so warm, and it's like I've died right here and now and went to heaven, as utterly saccharine as that sounds, because no other time I've been with a woman has ever been so intense.

I had hoped this would happen tonight. It'd been the best of wishful thinking, the blowing of candles on a birthday cake. All I'd expected, though, if I were lucky, was to see her. If the fates aligned, I hoped for a shot to tell her my feelings, as fucking terrifying as that was. But it'd been practically a wet dream wish that I'd ever find myself in her.

But here we are, and it's better than I ever hoped.

She bends over and kisses me, all languid tongue, and I have to will myself not to instantly explode before I even move. But then she lifts up and slides back down and I'm certain my eyes roll right into the back of my head. I grab her arse, hold her tight, and roll us over so I'm the one on top. Her mouth, her wonderfully, tempting mouth opens to—argue, maybe?—about the change in position, but as much as I adore sparring with this woman, I kiss her instead. Kiss her once more like I must, because the need to do so is felt all the way down in my bones and then beyond, straight into the atoms and molecules within. There will be plenty of time to let her ride me later. I'll happily be putty in her hands. But now, for this first time, I want it to last longer than a singular minute.

I pull slowly out of her until I'm nearly out; she cries softly in frustration. I push myself back in, over and over in a steady pace that has her squirming and panting and whispering my name in a voice I pray no man other than myself will ever hear again. It's one of the most brilliant sounds I've ever had the pleasure of listening to, this husky vocalization of two syllables I've resented for so long. But now that they come from her, it's different. As our bodies come together in the best dance I've ever danced, I've never been gladder to bear such a moniker.

I have no idea how long it takes her to come a second time. Too soon, I blurrily think, when her body tightens and then spasms around mine, but then I'm gratefully free falling into what I can only understand to be the most fucking amazing *le petit mort* ever and all of the CinemaScope of my life focuses tightly into just this one woman and what she makes me feel.

CHAPTER 50

ELSA

Bright sunlight filters through the hotel bedroom, disorienting me. A phone is ringing, and I think somebody is knocking on the door, too. I am achy and still oh-so-tired, but then a warm, naked body next to me reminds me of all of the hours I spent having the most mind-blowing sex of my entire life.

Christian is really here.

Silence reclaims the suite, and I spend these soft, hazy moments simply studying him. He is adorable when he sleeps, so boyish, in a way: dark lashes feathering against his cheeks, messy hair dipping across his forehead, and soft, long breaths sighing from his chest.

My own chest tightens in response. For the first time in a long time, I feel not so much free, because such a concept is merely a pipedream to a royal beholden to their duty and country, but relaxed. Happy. No—it's more than that. *Content.*

I brush chocolaty strands away from his eyes, and he stirs—not enough to wake, but enough to shift even closer. His bare chest rising and falling spellbinds me.

Somewhere nearby, a cell phone rings anew; fresh pounding sounds against a door, shattering the blurred stillness of the moment. "Your Highness?" The knocking turns frenzied. "Your Highness!"

Christian jolts awake, groping about as if he overslept and should have already been somewhere, and I fail miserably at not noticing how low the sheets dip against his pelvis.

Yum. And also: *More, please.*

His voice is husky. "What time is it?"

Time to have more sex. "I haven't the slightest."

"Who the hell is pounding at your door so early?"

"Chances are," I tell him wryly, "my mother's spy."

He groans and rolls over so an arm wraps around me. I slide back into the warmth of the bed we share, grinning like an idiot.

"Hi."

He's grinning, too. "Hi."

Our lips come together, soft and quiet, and while most everything falls away, one seductive, glorious thought rises to the surface: *this is real.*

Bam-bam, bam-bam-bam. "Your Highness!"

Christian pulls back, his nose brushing mine. "You should probably answer that." I would never have imagined it possible, but his morning voice is ten times sexier than normal, his accent far more discernible in this sleep-scratched state.

A disgruntled sigh heaves up and out of me. I do not want to deal with any reality other than this.

He kisses my shoulder. "Go find out what this spy wants. The sooner you do, the sooner we can get rid of her."

I hate that he is right. And I hate that I must get out of a warm, cozy bed with a yummy, naked man so I can assure a sixty-year-old woman I haven't fled. I reluctantly slip out of bed and into a robe, all the while keenly aware of Christian's hot eyes upon me. I flip my hair back and say, "If you keep *looking* at me like that, I shan't be able to answer the door."

His smile is deliciously naughty.

It is then the jangle and scrape of keys against metal sounds, forcing me to sprint to the door. It swings open just as I reach for the knob, prompting me to jump back and tighten my robe. Standing in the threshold is not only the hotel concierge and Greta, but Mat with his cell phone glued to his ear.

My mental calendar *ding-dings* with: *brunch with Mat.* And also: *reason why I am in Paris.*

"Are you alright?" he exclaims at the same time the concierge stammers, "Your Highness, please forgive my hasty entry, but when nobody could reach you for some time now, it was advised we check on your welfare," and Greta wrings her hands as she wails, "I was so worried this morning, Your Highness! You weren't answering your phone!"

Brunch was scheduled at eleven. Just how late did we sleep in?

I clutch the robe tighter and offer up an understanding smile to the flustered group. "I thank you for your concern. I simply overslept."

The concierge bows and quickly excuses himself. Neither Mat nor Greta sees fit to follow suit, though. My mother's personal secretary continues wringing her hands, as if she worries I will vanish right before her and Mat is more piqued than I have ever seen him. Stress lines crease his forehead, and a darkish purple color smudges the delicate skin beneath his eyes. He steps forward, past the threshold, shoving his phone into a pocket.

There is no doubt in my mind he is not happy to be here. If I had to pick a more concise description, I would insist he is flat-out miserable.

Greta makes a beeline toward my bedroom, no doubt to get my clothes ready for—wait. *Greta is heading to the bedroom.*

"Wait!" I call out. She freezes, questions filling her eyes.

"Would you mind fetching me coffee?" She opens her mouth, so I add, "Not hotel coffee." Now she's regarding me as if I've lost my mind. And I understand the reasoning; this is an excellent hotel. The coffee is most likely excellent, too.

I lamely add, "Perhaps . . . real coffee? From a café?"

Her dark eyes flit back and forth between Mat and me before easing in ridiculous assumption. Nonetheless, she curtseys and departs the suite, shutting the door behind her.

Mat asks, "Are you feeling ill? You're a bit flushed."

To prove his point, heat crawls up my neck; Mat clearly notices it, because his eyes trace the path too low for comfort. While there isn't anything I'd call interest there—which I am uncertain if I find pleasing or insulting—his focus lingers far too long at the vee of my robe. I pull the pieces together so tightly they turn form fitting.

I wave two fingers in front of my face. "Eyes up here."

He sighs and does as I ask. Even blushes a bit himself. "My apologies."

"Perhaps I ought to be asking *you* how you're feeling."

Something that sounds perilously close to both a sob and a chuckle falls out of the landless prince standing before me. "Honestly? It's been a bitch of a morning. When you didn't show . . ."

Uneasy silence falls between us for long seconds as we warily regard one another. And it's irrational, but a bit of guilt taunts me, considering there is a man in my bedroom, one I'm falling in love with, and instead of being with him, I am out here going through the motions with a man everyone thinks I ought to marry.

I clear my throat. "We need to talk."

He releases another sigh, one born of irritation edged with sadness. And then he covers his eyes with a hand and turns away, shaking his head.

Uneasy silence transitions into excruciating stillness. I am ready to voice my concerns more forcefully when he breathes deeply, straightens his back, and once more faces me.

Frustration reflects back at me. "I'm begging you to let all the arguments go. I can't . . . What's this going to be like, you and I going at this every single time we see one another? Is this our future? One massive row after another? I know you don't want to marry me. You've made that perfectly clear. If you want to argue about it some more . . . do it with those who actually have a say in the matter."

It's enough to draw me closer. "Who would that be?"

He runs a hand through his hair. Says nothing.

"Mat." I touch his shoulder, drawing his focus to me. "Talk to me. Maybe together, we can figure a way out—"

The next words burst out of him. "Stop. Just—I'm trying, all right? I'm doing my bloody best with this incredibly shitty situation. I need you to try, too. Especially when they're watching."

"When *who* is watching? The same people who have a so-called say in this matter?"

He shifts away, his shoulder sliding from my fingers as he clears his throat. "Obviously, brunch is no longer an option. And I think in light of how we're both feeling, we ought to skip lunch as well. Hopefully my parents will understand. Let's try again at dinner tonight. I'll send a car to pick you up at eight."

"Talk to me." I'm begging, but I have no other choice. "I'm blind to something right now. Don't leave me in the dark."

As he steps through the door, a sad little shake of the head precedes, "I'll see you tonight, Elsa."

CHAPTER 51

CHRISTIAN

For one brief, uncharitable moment, I despise my old mate, even as red alerts flash through my mind during the brief conversation between Mat and Elsa. Something isn't right here, and while I now know part of the story behind why Prince Gustav is so keen to ensure Elsa marries into the Chambéry name, it strikes me there must be a pretty soul-sucking reason on Mat's end, too.

Elsa reappears in the doorway, her luminous face reflecting all the concerns brewing inside me. "Did you hear any of that?"

I fold back the covers and pat the empty space next to me. "Yes."

She slips into the bed. "He is hiding something. I'm sure of it."

"You're wearing too many clothes. And yes, I agree about Mat."

When her hands drift to the robe's sash, her head tilts to the side in a way that nearly distracts me from what we need to talk about. "You two are friendly, correct? Do you have any idea what it might be? Why he insists I must try when they—whoever *they* are—are watching?"

"Let me do this." My deft fingers unwrap the knot and slide the silky robe off her shoulders all within two seconds. As shafts of dust-sparkling sunlight filtered by gauzy curtains fall down upon her, I marvel at how my lungs forget how to instinctually work all too often when I'm with this woman.

I force myself to focus on the problem at hand. "What has he told you of his past?"

She takes the initiative to toss the robe across the bed and onto the floor. "Probably as much as I've told him: little to nothing."

I drop a kiss on a pale, smooth shoulder. "Nothing exchanged during those teas you two shared?"

A hand drifts onto my thigh. "What were you and my sister sharing during yours?"

"Not a damn thing." No. That's unfair of me. I clarify, "Actually, she shared an excessive amount about horses and the weather."

Soft laughter curls around us, instantly leaving me wanting much more. "Point made. You were saying? About Mat's past? Something I apparently don't know about?"

My lips trace the sloped curve where neck and shoulders meet. Ah, yes. We were discussing Mat. "When he lived in America, he was involved with a woman named Kim."

She sighs softly, leaning into me, but the moment my words register, I lose her. Elsa leans back, bottom lip pulled once more between her teeth. "When did they break up?"

When I tell her I haven't a clue, she presses, "Is she American?"

I nod. "The last I heard, his family didn't know about her."

She smacks the bed. "He told me he'd been in love before."

"Ah, so you two *were* sharing."

A dismissive hand waves between us. "There were no details other than he'd been in love before. This must be who he was referencing." She glances around. "I asked Charlotte to look into his past, but I've yet to hear from her, thanks to Her Serene Highness' supervision."

"Mat's relationship with Kim wasn't public knowledge," I inject. "He went to great lengths to keep it quiet."

"Yet you knew."

"Well, there were a select number of us who did, yes. It wasn't like I was going to spill his secrets to the press, though. I had a hard enough time ensuring my own business was kept under lock and key. That said, Mat was very protective of Kim. He didn't want the press hounding her movements as they do with so many others that our kind get involved with."

She takes all of this in quietly. "Did you know her?"

I nod. "You'd have liked her, all things considering."

"Why did he never tell his family? Is it because she is American?"

I choose my words carefully; no matter what, this is still not my story to tell. "Partially. It also had a lot to do with the fact that Kim came from an exceedingly violent neighborhood riddled with crime. Two of her siblings are in gangs; one of those is—or was at the time—in jail, the other has been in and out of prison for years. That wasn't the kind of life Kim wanted, though. She worked hard to become a doctor. There was genuine fear on both their behalves, I think, that his family would disapprove. And hers, too."

"They were serious, though?"

I run a hand down her belly, lingering only momentarily at the shallow indentation before heading further south. "That was my impression, yes. He was crazy about her." It's hard to do, but my fingers still. "Els. There's a lot we need to talk about. There are things you need to—"

One hand settles on my lips. The other nudges my fingers to keep moving. "I think," she says slowly, "that perhaps we can talk about this in a bit?"

"But—"

When she kisses me, my hormones refuse to allow me to do anything but what she asks. We come together then, all fierce and soft at the same time, mouths fusing and hands roaming and I'm finally in her once more, moving and feeling and living and dying all at once.

When the next series of knocks sounds, Elsa throws her hands up and lets loose a tiny shriek of frustration.

Assuming it's the secretary who unwillingly tagged along on the trip, I remind her, "To be fair, she took a fantastically long time to find coffee. There must be twenty cafés all within a two-block radius of the hotel." Granted, it was because she thought Elsa and Mat were together, but still.

The woman has promise. I can work with promise.

She presses a kiss against my collarbone before getting out of bed. "What are we going to do, Chris? I can't send her for coffee every time she wants to come in."

Bloody hell, do I like it when she calls me that. That simple nickname, so common, sounds so perfect when it comes from her mouth.

I slide out from beneath the sheets. "Since the day I've met you, I've been paying off one person or another in order to ensure our time together is uninterrupted. What makes this woman any different?"

She simply stares at me for a good few seconds before bursting into that erotic laughter of hers. "You are going to bribe my mother's personal secretary?"

"Might as well. Go let her in. I need to at least put on some pants so she won't run away in terror."

I get a cheeky smile and a firm smack on the arse. "She'd stick around to look. I guarantee that. Don't you remember how long the maid back in California ogled you?"

CHAPTER 52

ELSA

Greta bears three coffees, which is ironically ideal.

"Is His Highness already gone?" She glances around the room, as if she fears Mat may leap out from behind the drapes.

"Yes." I motion to a chair. "Please join me for some of the coffee you must have gone to Nice for."

She blanches. "Oh, Your Highness, please accept my deepest apologies. I—"

I sigh. Poor Greta wouldn't know a joke if it hit her over the head. "No need to apologize. I was merely teasing. I understand why you felt you ought to take your time, even if it was wholly unnecessary. Please have a seat."

Her bottom barely meets fabric when Christian strolls out of the bedroom, looking so delicious in his t-shirt and jeans that I drool right alongside poor Greta.

As he sits down next to me, I think: *mine.*

A hand is extended; she takes it warily, eyes widened and darting back and forth between the two of us first in confusion and then alarm.

I love that this woman speaks volumes with her eyes, and that my mother has not squashed all emotion out of her. "Greta, I would like to introduce you to His Highness, the Hereditary Grand Duke of Aiboland. To make a long story short, this is my boyfriend, Christian."

The poor thing collapses back into her chair, even as she struggles to rise and curtsey before him. "It is a great pleasure to meet you, Your Highness." Only, it doesn't sound like a pleasure at all. She sounds as if she's on the verge of a heart attack.

Christian, for his part, shows no reaction toward the definition I threw out. "The pleasure is all mine, Greta. I've heard wonderful things about you from Elsa."

I think both of our eyes do some talking at that one.

"I know it must come as a surprise to find me here when you were naturally expecting another prince," he continues, words filled with a charming sense of camaraderie that practically undoes Greta, "but I'm going to lay this all out for you. We are all well aware of why you have been sent to Paris instead of Charlotte."

We are? Or rather—he is, too?

"We are quite aware of how my presence places you in a terrible position. Do you rat a grown woman out to her overbearing parents, sovereigns or no, or do you trust your Hereditary Princess to do what is best for herself?" He smiles that too beautiful smile of his. "Greta. You cannot possibly tell me you enjoy assuming the role of a babysitter. Surely this is not what you signed up for when you accepted the position of personal assistant to Her Serene Highness."

The words he utters are, on paper, harsh, and yet they are issued the way a sympathetic friend reaching out for a favor would do. I have not had the pleasure of watching Christian at work before, playing his role. The majority of our so-called meetings in California kept us gagged behind the veil of instruction, and those we were allowed to speak during were opportunities to merely parrot the party line our parents provided us with. But here, in my hotel suite?

Hot damn, I am so attracted to him. Not that I wasn't a mere two minutes before, but his overwhelming charm and diplomacy only ups his *too*-ness factor.

"But . . . but . . ." Greta is stammering.

He continues smoothly, "Obviously, we would ensure it would be worth your while to hold your tongue."

Greta stills, her hands knotting together in her lap. And for a moment, fear raises its ugly head. Will she balk? I can't risk it. "Greta, you've worked for my mother for years. You know she is behaving irrationally in the wake of Princess Isabelle's elopement. I would ask of you for your understanding over how ridiculous it is what they're—"

But she is not listening to me. She's focused on Christian. "How much worth my while?"

He smiles again, practically oozing charisma. "Very worth your while."

Minutes later, Greta departs from the suite, for the ability to spend a very lovely few days in Paris buying whatever it is she desires and going wherever she wants.

Before I can tackle him on the couch, Christian tugs out his phone. "Believe me," he says, eyes hot and dark, "I want nothing more than to kiss you again right now. But Elsa, I need to know . . . are you resolute about not marrying Mat?"

It is a sharp slap of reality right to the face, for sure. Of course I do not want to marry Mat. I have been nothing if not painfully clear about my stance since Day One. But outside of Mat growing a spine and refusing to work with me on a way to dissuade our parents, I have precious few options outside of abdicating in order to get out of the arrangement. And even that is now a long shot, considering Isabelle's elopement and fleeing of the country.

My frustration must surely show, because he sets the phone down and pulls me onto his lap. "Let me tell you a story. One that's far overdue, considering I haven't been able to share it yet, as our ability to converse has been stymied over the last few days. And then you can answer the question, okay?"

For the next few minutes, he reveals the content of Isabelle's surprising phone call. I am stunned, unsure of what to say or do in the face of my sister's accusations and suspicions concerning the agreements made for our hands (especially as they are corroborated by Alfons, a man whose wit and cleverness is more often lacking than not), but when Christian admits Parker and Charlotte looked into the charges, only to find traces of validity behind them, I am at an even larger loss for words.

"Either Parker or myself has been in touch with Charlotte nearly every day since your sister fled," he continues, voice hushed in the large suite. "Her husband is discreetly digging deep into financial matters for us, as he is the closest to the situation." Christian touches my face, fingers brushing softly against my skin. "I'd meant to tell you all of this when I found out, but . . ." His smile is paper-thin. "First, I could not get through to your cell—which Charlotte later told me got confiscated. And then, last night, I got distracted. My apologies."

Anger and sadness war for supremacy within the tight confines of my chest. I want nothing more than to storm the royal palace and force my parents to admit the truth, and yet there's hollowness, too. Who does this to their children?

"I asked you before if you were resolute about not marrying Mat. Els." He gently angles my face until I am looking at him. "Parker is in Paris, armed with everything we've collected so far. Charlotte will be here in . . ." He glances at a nearby clock. "A little shy of an hour. We are willing to pull out all the stops to find the loophole out of this forced marriage, but only if you it is what you want." A small smile is offered, one filled with a sense of sympathetic melancholy. "Of all the people you know, I think you can trust me when I tell you I will understand if you feel you must go through with this. I just want you to be aware that, as of right now, there are options available. You don't have to go quietly, with no say. These aren't the Middle Ages, no matter what the Monarch Council believes. We are not pawns to be moved across a chessboard, all in hopes of bettering future moves for themselves."

It is not fair I have to ask the next question, not when we have known each other a mere month, let alone have yet to discuss if there is even a *we* to consider. But I ask it anyway. "What then? What if we find the loophole out?"

He's quiet.

"I ask, because . . ." I attempt to swallow the growing lump in my throat. "You are still the Hereditary Grand Duke of Aiboland. And I am still the Hereditary Princess of Vattenguldia."

Hands cup my face. "I know. Believe me, I know."

My small burst of a laugh is pitiful. "It is not as if crown sovereigns go about marrying one another. Not even in the twenty-first century."

"I know," he says once more. And then, more gently, "That's a bridge we can cross when we come to it."

So much uneasiness fills me—not about him, not about my feelings for him, but toward the vast reach of empty forever before me that gives no clues about a newly soft future once set so firmly in stone.

My father threatened to remove me from the line of ascension, but with Isabelle the current black sheep of the family, I am the only heir. Hope, as tiny as it is right now, takes hold.

Christian then unspools his own situation. He tells me of his mother, of the plight of his father, and of how his brother and he have been backed into corners all of their lives, too.

I am outraged. Saddened. Jealous and wistful over how those whose family and traditions do not serve as chains about their wrists and ankles like ours do live their lives so freely.

How lovely it would be if we really were just Elsa and Christian.

"Mat doesn't want to marry me. Of that I am certain." I'm firm when I tell Christian this. Composed, when I want to rage. "More importantly, I do not want to marry him." A small smile slips out, a genuine one in the face of so much heat. "He's a nice enough fellow, but he is not the one for me."

I soak up Christian's laughter, reveling in how I can feel it moving through his chest. Appreciating how, after all that's been shared today, such a sincere emotion can still surface. "What a ringing endorsement. *He's a nice enough fellow.* Just what every man wants to hear when a beautiful woman describes him." He reclaims his phone, fingers flying across the touchscreen. I peer down to find Parker's name.

"Notice I didn't say *you're* nice."

He glances up briefly, grinning. "Ah, but I am. Just hopefully in a different way than Mat—at least when it comes to you."

"Digging for compliments, Your Highness?"

The phone beeps in his hand at the same time he chuckles.

"My point is, he feels comfortable rather than exciting, if that makes sense."

Christian's feigned wince is comical. "Nice *and* comfortable?"

"We hugged; it was similar to embracing a brother. Or at least, what I assume that would feel like. Perhaps more like a grandfather or uncle. Or a mere acquaintance."

His fingers tap upon the screen. "Thank God poor Mat isn't here to hear his character maligned so."

"Would you rather me be attracted to him?"

"Certainly not." And then, "I saw that hug. It was a rather unpleasant experience to witness."

I'm amused. "Why, Chris. Are you admitting you were jealous of nice, brotherly, comfortable Mat?"

The phone beeps again. He smiles as he admits, "Only that they were his arms around you, not mine. I was fairly positive you weren't attracted to him in the least."

I gently flick his shoulder. "What an ego you have."

He merely shrugs, grinning.

"You and I hugged, lest you forget. After skinny-dipping."

"I haven't forgotten a thing, especially how it felt anything but brotherly. Or," he says wryly, "in my case, sisterly."

"Speaking of, were Isabelle's hugs sisterly?"

"I wouldn't know. We didn't hug, but I did dance that once with her." His shoulder nudges mine. "Does that count?"

A hand is pressed over my lips to keep my giggle in.

"None of that, Els. If you want to laugh, laugh." He kisses the corner of my mouth. "I'm rather taken with your laughter, you know."

Fragile joy blooms within my chest. "Are you?"

He brushes his lips across my cheek, whispering in my ear, "Very. I think it's my favorite thing to hear."

The phone beeps once more, so I give him a nice bit of side eye.

"Just a minute more. I'm coordinating with Parker right now. He's currently in the suite a floor below us." He types with one hand; the other runs lightly up my bare leg, beneath the silk of my robe. "Ready to help us stop Operation: RMM from fully commencing."

"Thank goodness. I cannot imagine doing anything further with Mat than hugging. Kissing?" A tiny gasp wrenches its way out of me as his fingers trace my inner thigh. "Let alone having sex?" I pretend to shudder to hide my genuine shivers of pleasure surfacing from his light touches. "Any children between he and I would have to be created in a lab, that's for sure."

The phone finally finds its way to a nearby table. "For the love of God, Els. Let's not talk about you and Mat having sex. Brotherly or no, imagining it will only drive me crazy."

I am laughing once more, and it's surreal as anything I have ever experienced, as we are planning on voluntarily blowing apart my orderly life.

I am also leaning in to press my lips against the base of his throat. He smells so lovely this morning, all faint cologne and Christian, mixed with a hint of musk from the lingering residue of hours spent together. "Let us imagine you and I having sex, then," I murmur against his warm skin. "Better yet, perhaps we ought to actually do the deed, and then there will be no need to imagine anything at all."

He grips my hips, fingers digging into the soft silk of my robe. "Parker and Charlotte will be here as soon as he gets her from the airport. There are things we still need to discuss before they arrive."

I find myself smiling at the huskiness in his voice, and of the growing hardness pressing against my thigh. "Surely there will be traffic on the way from the airport."

He groans as I purposefully shift in his lap in order to unbutton his jeans, his words stumbling, his eyes darkening. And then they disappear when my mouth meets his.

CHAPTER 53

CHRISTIAN

Charlotte blows into the room, a hurricane force gale of energy mixed with powdery perfume, followed by a dazed Parker.

"I apologize for the delay," the statuesque blonde says to Elsa, tossing a suitcase, briefcase, coat, and scarf down on the floor. "But this one here"—she hooks a thumb behind her—"drives like he's ninety."

Parker turns a nice shade of Fuck-My-Life red, poor bastard. I clap him on the shoulder as the ladies hug. "Did you bring the documentation?"

He slides the straps of his messenger bag off his shoulder and pats the worn leather.

"As I actually only recently discovered you were coming," Elsa is saying, "there is no need to apologize."

Charlotte's bright eyes swing my way. I'm positive she wants to censure me, but her manners must take hold. A curtsey precedes, "I am honored to finally make your acquaintance, Your Highness."

Elsa says, "None of that Your Highness bit from you, either." She turns to me, practically daring me to disagree with her call for informality.

I don't bother confessing I went several rounds with Charlotte on the phone about this very thing.

"Where is Dickie?" Elsa asks. "Did you leave him behind?"

"Obviously. He's in good hands—between Josef, the nanny, and my mum, he'll be fine. I'm really only here for the duration of your trip, anyway, which is where I should have been in the first place. Speaking of," she glances around the suite, "where is Greta?"

"Christian paid her to go sightseeing and shopping." Elsa ushers Charlotte toward the seating area. "If we're lucky, we won't see her again. My goodness, Lottie. What a novelty this is, not having to shout at one another just to be heard."

Parker clears his throat. "If I'm to make my flight, I need to leave in the next few minutes."

"Do you have everything you need?" I ask.

He nods.

"Wait—where is Parker going?" Elsa pipes up from her place on the couch.

"Good lord, Your Highness," Charlotte says, "did you not tell Elsa anything?"

I asked for informality, didn't I?

"To be fair," Elsa says, "we were distracted. There wasn't always proper time for talk."

"We talked," I stress.

Parker coughs. Charlotte merely rolls her eyes. "Time is of the essence, Elsa. You are only in Paris for three days. If our plan is going to work, we must utilize every last moment available to us."

I love that Els refuses to be chastised, though. "Then by all means, let us talk, starting with where Parker is going."

"New York," I tell her.

Elsa snaps her fingers. "Mat lives part of the year in New York."

"And Kim lives there full time," I supply.

"Parker is traveling all the way to New York in order to talk to Mat's girlfriend? Or, possible ex-girlfriend?" She glances between us. "My time locked away in the tower back home has put me at a disadvantage here over the particulars."

"Somebody must verify a suspicion I have," Charlotte says. "And, as Parker has actually met this Kim, it's best he goes."

"What kind of suspicion?" It's adorable how she sounds utterly suspicious about this herself.

I nod at Parker; he extracts an envelope from his bag. It's passed over to Elsa, who flips through the contents.

Her mouth drops open, photos spilling across her lap. "She's pregnant?"

I glance at the photos, too, a stone sinking in the pit of my stomach. *Mat, what the hell have you gotten yourself into?*

"It certainly appears that way, doesn't it?" Charlotte asks. "Thus, Parker's need to chat with the lady."

Elsa's blue eyes find mine. "I thought you didn't know if they were still together or not."

"Ah, so at least something was discussed," Charlotte muses.

I ignore the jab. "I don't," I assure Els. "As it appears Mat isn't talking about much of anything right now except what his parents are telling him to say, we need to go straight to the source. There aren't any phone numbers associated with a Kimberly Johnson in Brooklyn, but the private investigator Charlotte hired tracked her to a loft which is currently under surveillance by someone other than our man."

"Who else is spying on her?" Elsa asks Charlotte.

"Men who have known ties to an Italian crime family." Charlotte pauses. "Which complicates matters greatly."

Elsa is shocked. "Do these criminals have ties to Kim's siblings?"

"Unfortunately," Charlotte says, "that currently remains a mystery. Our man is looking into it, but obviously, he must move carefully."

Elsa mulls this over. "So you all have been playing spies while I have been under lockdown." A faint smile curves her lips. "Which of you is Holmes, and which of you is Watson?"

"I'm Holmes," Charlotte says firmly. "And most likely Watson, too. These two are the Keystone Cops."

"All right. Parker is going to find Kim." Elsa's fingers find mine. "What is the plan from there? Will he simply ask the woman who the father of her baby is?"

"Pretty much," Parker says quietly. "Although I hope to do so with more tact."

"What if she admits it's Mat's?"

"Then," I tell Elsa, "he is going to put her on the phone with me, and I am going to urge her to get on a plane with Parker and come straight to Paris. If all goes as planned, they will be on a return flight within six hours of landing."

"What then? We bully her to admit this to whom—my parents? Mat's?"

"No bullying," Charlotte assures her. "Consider this logically, Elsa. If your suspicions are right about Prince Mathieu also being forced into this arrangement, it would be terribly hard for him to remain stalwart and abide his parents' wishes when the so-called love of his life, pregnant with his baby, stands before him."

Elsa's off the couch, incensed. "Do you think he knows? Because I cannot wrap my mind around how or why he would marry me if he's expecting a baby with this woman. Granted, I don't know him all too well, but he's never struck me as the sort who would abandon such a commitment!"

I go over to where she is, taking hold of her hands. "We won't know until we ask him."

"Call him." Her voice is shaking. "Get his bloody arse over here right now."

"And say what?" Charlotte asks from the couch. "'*We suspect the woman you may or may not be still dating is pregnant with your baby? What say you?*' What if we are wrong? What if they broke up long ago, and this is someone else's child?" She shakes her head. "What if their split was acrimonious, and neither wants anything to do with the other? The best course of action is to wait until Parker has a conversation with the woman in question first."

"This is my life we're talking about!"

Elsa's hands grip mine, rage and frustration stealing up her neck in flushes. I've never heard her so irate before. "Kim's life, too," I remind her gently. "And Mat's."

Her bright blue eyes swing back to me. "And yours?"

She asks this so bluntly. I return an answer in kind. "And mine."

Her anger abates, just a little. And then she nods, resolute. "Parker, you best be off then. The rest of you, I want to hear and read everything you have on my parents' mismanagement of the family finances. It's far past time."

CHAPTER 54

ELSA

After Parker departs, Charlotte presents everything she and Josef discovered concerning my family's financial crisis.

Vattenguldia is a constitutional monarchy, meaning the royal family is symbolic rather than absolute in power. My father is popular, though, and influential, much like his father before him and his father before that. Parliament listens to the monarchs of Vattenguldia not because it is expected, but rather because their sovereigns tend to have the country's best interests at heart. That said, our family line has always been ridiculously wealthy. Outside of what the taxpayers in our principality pay toward our livelihoods, we also possess vast real estate portfolios, holdings in technological companies, and an immense art collection. Stocks and bonds may be beyond my mother's reach, but the money granted to us by the taxpayers is not. Blinded by her visions for a better Vattenguldia, she directed a secretive investment in what turned out to be a Ponzi scheme, all in her quest to become the Monaco of the North.

Millions of dollars taxpayers trusted us to use wisely are now gone.

Realistically, I can understand why my parents are frantic. Sovereigns or no, it's difficult and shameful to explain to the public why money that comes from their paychecks disappeared and will most likely never be recovered. Short of liquidating the contents of the palace, there is little hope of replacing the money before scandal devastates the principality. In Vattenguldia, no one is immune to audits, not even royals. So what did my parents do, to earn themselves an easy euro (or several millions of them)?

Decide to marry their daughter to a wealthy, deposed royal family in exchange for getting them a foot back into the royal door.

Charlotte is in the other room, on the phone with Josef and Dickie. She's cooing into the receiver, asking the infant if he's having a good time with his daddy. I know this because I fear the entire hotel can hear the conversation just as well as I can.

"The baby isn't deaf, Lottie!" I shout out to her.

Christian gets up off the bed and shuts the door. "Neither is Charlotte."

"She could be." I slip on heirloom emerald teardrop earrings my father gifted me on my sixteenth birthday. Would their value, if sold, be worthy anything toward the debt my parents owe Vattenguldia? "Most likely is. As cute as Dickie is, he has a pair of lungs on him like no other. It is a wonder Charlotte is even coherent."

He wanders over to where Charlotte hung my dress for tonight. It's a timeless yet elegant crepe silk piece, straight off the runways. "I like that this dress. But then, you have an uncanny knack of looking equally beautiful in everything you wear."

My knees weaken. "I can make an excuse, you know. Mat already believes I'm under the weather." Irritation flares at the mere thought of the man.

Christian slips the dress of the hanger. "Mat isn't the villain here, Els, no matter how it might feel in the moment. If our suspicions prove correct, he is just as trapped and manipulated as we have been."

I toss my robe onto the bed and take the dress offered. His eyes are hot as he watches me slide the silk over my head. "See if you can get him to talk to you tonight," Christian says. "Surreptitiously, in case there are those truly watching the two of you."

I turn my back, sweeping my hair over a shoulder. "Zip me up?"

Fingers brush against my spine, first up to the base of my hairline and then down to where back meets arse. A kiss is pressed against a shoulder blade just before the zipper is slowly tugged upward. And I wish, so much, that it was Christian I'd be dining with tonight and not someone else.

"Will you and Charlotte have a pajama party while I'm gone?"

A light kiss finds its way to the skin below my ear before he pulls my hair back. "Oh, most definitely. Followed by a pillow fight."

I turn around. "Careful. She's vicious with pillows. I once had a black eye for half a week when we were children, thanks to her uncannily strong aim."

"Noted." Hands run down my arms. "Despite everything, try to enjoy yourself tonight. Remember, Mat is brotherly and comfortable and nice."

I am up on my tiptoes, a hand curving around the back of his neck. "Pick me up afterward?"

His mouth hovers so closely to mine we breathe the same air. "You sure that's a good idea?"

"No. But I would like you to anyway."

Mat looks, well, like Mat on steroids when I finally reach the restaurant. He is garbed in a crisp plaid shirt and a neat bowtie, along with a deceptively worn looking gray sweater and skinny charcoal trousers that appear painted on. His hair is mussed, his chin scruffy, and his glasses are a bit askew. I cannot deny it—Mat makes for an attractive hipster prince.

Hushed murmurs fill the restaurant as I am led to the table he's already at. Tiny pops of light trail my movements. My bodyguard does a quick scan of the room before melting into the background alongside Mat's. As I approach, he rises, offering me what I am sure he hopes is a welcoming smile. It is more melancholy than warm, though. Strained.

He knows, I cannot help but think. He knows there is a woman out there, one he loves or, at the very least, once loved deeply. And he knows just as well as I that that woman is not me, nor will it ever be.

We hug in greeting, followed by air kisses. As we sit down, a waiter materializes to uncork a bottle of wine already chilling beside us. Mat says to me, "You look lovely tonight, Elsa."

I accept a glass from the server. "I was just musing on how smart *you* look tonight."

Mat chuckles. "Is it the glasses?"

"That, too. It is a nice look—a fitting one for you." For a prince who fell in love with a doctor in America, rebelling against stereotype.

Mat feigns a wince. I lift an eyebrow up in question, so he clarifies, "Nice is such a dagger to the ego."

The urge to chuckle is strong as Christian's words come back to me. "First smart, then nice?" I shake my head, amused. "And to think people come to hear me wax eloquent in speeches."

A chuckle rumbles from his throat, and it's a surprising relief to see a bit of genuine ease line his face. "I've not given many speeches outside of those while in school. I suppose that's a perk to being part of a deposed family."

One, I think to myself, desperate to regain a throne. "Did you enjoy going to university in America?"

Shadowed regret overtakes the smidge of humor he allowed himself to feel. "Immensely so." He glances away, toward the windows facing the streets of Paris. "You went to Oxford in Britain, did you not?"

Nice changing of the subject, Mat. "I did."

He rubs at the scruff on his chin. "I've often thought about going back and getting my doctorate."

I sip my wine slowly, the liquid gold curling through my throat. "In America?"

His sigh is a burst of self-deprecation alongside a quick shake of the head. "I'd hoped so, but . . ."

I trace the lip of my glass until it sings softly. "But you are expected to wed me and move to Vattenguldia."

"Elsa . . ."

I pick up my menu and spread it open. "I've not eaten at this particular restaurant before. I am also in love with another person, desperately so." I smile sunnily over the top of the black leather. "What would you recommend me to order tonight?"

The wineglass at his lips freezes once my words, like air escaping a balloon, hiss between us.

"I'm partial to fish, if you must know. It's a Scandinavian thing, being surrounded by so much water."

The glass finds its way back to the table. He clears his throat before saying softly, "I'm well aware of that."

But I know he does not refer to my dietary preferences. "Are you?"

Eyes close behind his glasses, hands grip the edge of the linen covered table. "Yes." His voice is hoarse. "I'm not blind, you know. I watched it happen. Everyone knew, me included."

"And yet . . .?"

"My hands are tied." So much anger and regret fill his eyes once they fly back open. "You think I like the idea of doing this to a friend?"

"Which friend are you referring to?" I ask lightly. "Me or him?"

"You have to understand—"

I lean forward, incensed. Forget pretending tonight. I don't care one whit if my mother rages back home once she discovers I did not play doting soon-to-be-fiancée during dinner. "I don't understand, because you refuse to inform me as to why you are going along with this farce. Are we currently being watched?"

The waiter reappears, a basket of bread in his hand. Mat quickly orders us both roasted sea bass, sending the man on his way again. "I refuse to discuss this in the middle of a busy restaurant. Not when there are . . . eyes and ears."

"Fine. Where shall we discuss it?"

He shakes his head. "It doesn't matter anyway. Talking isn't going to change the outcome."

"I disagree."

He stares at me, hardness lining the corners of his mouth, frustration surely tickling the tip of his tongue, but just when I think he will continue to argue, he merely sighs.

"I like you," I tell him. "Believe it or not, I *do*. And I think, under different circumstances, we might eventually become fantastic friends. I hope someday we will. But none of that will occur as long as we both keep hiding things from the other."

His lips press together as he kneads his forehead.

"Here, I'll start. I recently found out why I've been ordered to marry you. It is a hopelessly old-fashioned reason, I'm afraid. I'm to marry you for money. Loads of it, from what I can tell." I fold my hands. "Now. Your turn."

For long seconds, I fear he will refuse to answer. I officially called him out—quietly, of course—but I also let him know that I won't back down. No matter what happens between Christian and myself, I cannot go through with marrying a man I do not love.

I'm finishing off my glass of wine when he murmurs, "My reason is less savory. I'm doing it because, if I don't, somebody who means a great deal to me will suffer. And I can't allow that."

He's talking about Kim. He must be. "Mat—"

"If you want to discuss this further, then fine. We will do so." He slides off his glasses and rubs the bridge of his nose. "But not tonight. You're not the only one whose behavior is being reported back, you know. We're supposed to go sightseeing tomorrow, but . . . perhaps you could get food poisoning? Or wake up not feeling your best? I'll come round to check in on you, and we can talk then. Say, during tea?" His lips twist up sadly. "Like old times, if one can consider a week's worth of teas enough history."

I mentally calculate the flight times Charlotte made for Parker and possibly Kim. Afternoon tea is cutting it close—if all goes as planned, the plane from New York will be just touching down in Paris during that time.

A plate filled with artful food is set down before me. I tell Mat, "It's a date."

CHAPTER 55

CHRISTIAN

"May I speak frankly?"

Charlotte has, if anything, only spoken frankly with me since our very first phone call. "Of course. I'm not one to break with tradition," I tell her.

"And yet, you are." Her eyes narrow. "Or at the very least, considering it."

I say nothing. As much as I respect and even like Elsa's personal secretary, reassuring Charlotte of my sincerity of feelings toward her employer is not at the top of my priorities for the evening.

"I believe, even had Elsa never met you, she would balk at marrying somebody she hardly knows, let alone does not love. She and her father went several rounds about this for months leading up to the Decennial Summit. I'm sure you're well aware that she's stubborn—"

"That's putting it mildly," I murmur.

"And wants what is best for her country. Vattenguldia adores her."

"As they should."

Charlotte places the papers she's been reading on the table and turns to fully face me. "It would be a great shame for our country if we were to lose her."

I grab my baseball hat and head toward the door. "It would, wouldn't it?"

Elsa emerges from the restaurant amongst flashes of light and curious faces eager to see not one, but two beautiful, young royals together. She's smiling her regal smile, the one that's patient yet friendly. Mat's right there next to her, his hand on the small of her back.

He leads her to the limousine I'm waiting in, leaning in to whisper something in her ear. Her lips tug up as she places a hand against his cheek, and then they offer each other air kisses. I scoot further down the seat, toward the window separating front and back, ensuring I'm sitting on the passenger side.

The driver opens the car door so Elsa can slide in. Her eyes briefly flick toward me and then back at Mat.

"I'll see you tomorrow," he's saying.

The door shuts, leaving us surrounded by darkened windows. "You are too far away." She pats the seat next to her. "I see no black eyes, so I take it your evening with Charlotte did not end in a pillow fight?"

The car pulls away from the curb as I make my way toward her. "Alas, no. She spent the better part on the phone with her husband."

"And what did you do?"

"I spoke with my brother. My mother is . . . displeased that I am not in the country at the moment."

"Meaning?"

"Meaning I hope you will never forget that the Grand Duchess is nothing like her public persona."

Worry flashes in the cobalt of her eyes.

"It doesn't matter, though. She can rage about it all she wants, but . . . I'm done with her manipulations. I'm right where I want to be."

As I say this, Elsa's regarding me as if I am the only man in the entire world, and it's got me drunk on too many emotions to pinpoint precisely. *I love you*, I want to tell her as I lean in toward her gorgeous face. *I love you. I adore you. I don't want to live without you.*

But I don't say any of these things. Right now, the sentiments are too strong to form coherent sentences, so I kiss her instead. Softly at first, like our first kiss in California, and I'm immediately under her spell, because her mouth is hot and inviting and a black hole I can't navigate away from.

Her hands grip my shoulders, urging me closer. The car slows, no doubt at a light, and somewhere in the back of my mind, I'm reminded how there are only so many lights between here and the hotel. I wish I could say it matters to me, that I'm concerned about propriety or decency or even the risk of us being caught. But the windows surrounding us are dark, as is the one raised in between us and the driver, and the need I feel for Elsa is too powerful to resist.

I pull her onto my lap, easing her legs around my waist on the seat. Our kiss deepens, my tongue tracing hers until she groans into my mouth. Bloody hell, it's a gorgeous sound, and one that makes me hard and hot.

I want her. Here. In this car.

As if she can hear me, Elsa leans back and unbuttons her coatdress. My mouth goes dry, my dick turns to stone.

There's only a lacey bra and barely there panties on underneath.

"You went to dinner in just a coat?" I slide the soft wool off her shoulders before tracing the length of her arms on my path to cup her breasts. "What happened to the dress I helped you into?"

Dazzling, wonderful laughter spills out of her, leaving me even more drunk on happiness. "As you agreed to pick me up, I decided the dress was unnecessary. I changed out of it shortly before I left. Didn't you see it hanging in the bedroom?"

I press a kiss against the base of her throat and suck gently; her head tips back so long hair can spill across the fingers deftly unlatching the clasp of her bra. I gently tug it off, dropping it onto the seat next to me.

Damn, I love her breasts.

I bend down and swirl the tip of my tongue around a nipple; she moans quietly, fingers tightening on my shoulders. I rock her against me, reveling in the feel of my dick against the tiny scrap of silk she's still wearing. My teeth graze the hardened bud before I reclaim her mouth again for a scorching kiss that has me desperate to be inside her.

She tugs my t-shirt up and over my head, tossing it behind her.

I hook my fingers under the sides of her panties. She leans forward and whispers in my ear, "Tear them."

I live to serve this woman.

Her gasp enflames me. I trace the line along the inner leg, from hip to where she's already wet for me. Another gasp falls out of Elsa when my fingers circle the sensitive bundle of nerves between her legs, yet another when I slide a finger deep inside her.

The car slows down again. I don't care the reason why, because she's rocking against my hand, her head thrown back, and I think I'd be okay with the world exploding around us as long as I could see her like this.

She fumbles with the button and zipper to my jeans, words hoarse, a siren's call I can't refuse. "I need you. Now."

I slide my fingers from her as she pulls my rock hard dick out. I fold back the sides of my jeans, shoving them down as far as I can before she drops right on top of me.

And then she rides me, just like she'd wanted to last night. I'm lost to anything but her as the car speeds on, living and dying for every thrust and groan.

CHAPTER 56

ELSA

"That," I tell Christian as I lean down to kiss him, "was another first for me. Car sex, I mean."

A car horn blares outside. I jump and then giggle. *I'm giggling*—and it is utterly delightful to do so.

Hands cup the side of my face. "Me, too," he murmurs.

I look down at his sweaty, gorgeous face. "You've never had sex in a car before? I find that . . . surprising."

He shifts, reminding me he's still snug and warm inside me. "Not a moving car. So yes, this was a first for me, too."

Another horn blares as we slow to a stop. We cannot be far from the hotel now.

I reach over and reclaim my bra. "Is moving car sex far better than parked car sex?"

He brushes my hands away when I attempt to fasten my bra in order to do the job himself. "Oh, most assuredly." One hand curves around my back so he can lean us forward and grab my coat and shirt.

I slowly tug his t-shirt back over his head, smoothing the soft cotton beneath my fingers. "I'm glad."

He doesn't say anything as he gently slides my arms into those of the coat before buttoning it. The car lurches forward; I reluctantly climb off of his lap to allow him to tug up his jeans. I am the one to button and zip him up, though.

He tells me, "I like sharing firsts with you, Els."

I lean forward to kiss him. "Me, too."

"Actually," he whispers against my mouth, "if it were possible, all my firsts from here on out would be with you."

I'm desperate to tell him this is my fervent wish, too, how I have never experienced anything like what I feel for him before, but the moment his tongue touches mine, I am lost once more.

CHAPTER 57

CHRISTIAN

The She-Wolf, according to Lukas, is fuming at her inability to find me. "Shite, bro, if you come home, be prepared to be locked down. Do we even have dungeons? Because I'm sure that's exactly where she'd put you. The She-Wolf is convinced that this is another Isabellegate."

Elsa is asleep in the other room, but a call from Parker shortly after her eyes closed has kept me wide-awake.

Kim was willing to talk to me.

While the actual conversation was short, I laid things out as plainly as I could for her. She cried quietly, but was angry, too.

"I hate Mat's fucking family," she told me, and I flinched in her vehemence. She's a good girl, a nice one (despite my teasing Elsa over what a pitiful word nice is), and it isn't fair that her life, already riddled with upheavals, was even further upended because she had the wherewithal to fall in love with someone of royal blood.

"Are you willing to come to Paris?" I asked her.

She hesitated, unsure about what Mat would think. But then, the steely resolve I'd seen before in her character came to the forefront.

"I'll be there as soon as possible, Christian."

And now, here I am, fielding a phone call from my brother, discussing another royal family worth loathing.

"Did you give her the letter?" I ask. I'd left one, just in case.

"Hell no! Does it make me the worst son on the planet to admit I've withheld it because watching her squirm is a favorite pastime?"

"You're the one who's currently facing the firing squad," I point out. "Not me."

"Only because you're in bloody France instead of Aiboland. The moment your feet touch our rocky soil, you're going to be in front of the firing squad and then the gallows and then you'll probably be dismembered, so the She-Wolf can have you sewn back up into a puppet she can control. It will be Rasputin all over again. How much longer do you think this trip will take? Because I don't know how long I can hold her back before the hounds are set loose."

"Don't you mean wolves? Also, Rasputin never was hung or dismembered."

"Bloody history nerd. My point stands, Chris. The She-Wolf is out for your blood. Now, answer the damn question."

"If I'm lucky, the biggest issue will be resolved by nightfall. Or, at least, be partially resolved."

He scoffs, but wishes me luck. It's appreciated, because I damn well need all the luck I can get.

Charlotte left for the airport to fetch Parker and Kim, leaving Elsa and me to confront Mat. As the woman I love answers the door, I'm reminded of a time the Chambéry prince and I went sailing with friends one late summer afternoon in New England. It was a smashing time, with lots of cold beers drank and precious few prying eyes. We weren't royals on that boat. We were just mates having a good time.

I hope we can make it through this as mates, too.

He isn't too surprised to see me once Elsa leads him to the sitting area of the suite. A hand is extended in greeting; I take it easily. When he says, "Despite everything, it's good to see you," I believe him.

Elsa sits next to me on the couch; Mat chooses a chair across from us. I regret that it comes across so much like an interrogation, but as my brother pointed out, time is of the essence. I ask my old friend, "What's going on?"

Something that sounds too close to a laugh but doesn't have enough humor in it falls out of him. "I know you and Lukas believe you've got the leg up on having the world's worst mother," he tells me, "but let me assure you, I have you beat. My parents . . ." He shakes his head. Releases a hard breath. "Let's just say they didn't take kindly to discovering their only son was keen to spend his life with what they dubbed *ghetto trash*. Nor did they find the idea of their bloodline being eventually sullied by children conceived with a woman who is nothing more than a mutt in their eyes acceptable."

"Jesus." And then, outraged such judgments could be made about a person before even meeting them, I say, "Fuck them. They don't know shite about Kim."

"I said the very same thing, and they followed up with a tidy threat of their own, promising they would make Kim's life and those of her family a living hell if I didn't leave her and marry somebody of their own choosing. Someone who will help regain the Chambéry glory."

The color drains from Elsa's face. For all of Prince Gustav's threats, at least she's never had to hear this one.

"After my family lost power, they became . . . let's say, *friendly* with those whose careers weren't always aboveboard. That relationship has carried over the years and has proved mutually beneficial in ways I won't bore you with, but it's enough to say that, whenever the Chambérys have a problem they need dealt with, these associates are called in."

Puzzle pieces slide in place. Kim is under surveillance because of the Chambérys.

"Does Kim know?" I ask.

He shakes his head. "I simply told her that they disapproved. I didn't want to worry her—she already has too much on her shoulders, thanks to her own family."

I kiss the back of Els' hand before standing up. "I think this calls for some drinks. I'm afraid we're limited here, though. Is scotch okay?"

Mat nods. Elsa urges him to continue.

"See, when my parents discovered I was dating someone they hadn't vetted, they were enraged. I was told to end our relationship immediately; I balked. The enforcers my family utilizes far too often were sent in to rough up one of Kim's brothers."

I nearly drop the heavy glass I'm holding.

To Elsa, he says, "Her family is too closely associated with violence themselves, so for this to happen, on their territory, no less, was intensely frightening."

The woman I love is horrified. I am, too.

"Before I could even wrap my head around what was happening, somebody was sent after Kim, too." He swallows hard. "She spent a few days in the hospital, believing she was targeted by a rival gang rather than the mafia."

I hand Mat the scotch, unsure of what even to say at this point.

"I was assured that the next time my parents' associates were sent out, they would not be so generous." He takes a large swallow of the amber liquid, wincing as it goes down. "I believed them. Although I broke up with her, I gave one of her brothers money to get her somewhere safe." He leans back in the chair, defeat coloring his face. "That was five months ago."

"Have you talked to her?" Elsa asks softly. "Seen her since then?"

"I can't risk it." Bitterness rolls off him in waves. "I didn't even get to see her after the attack, except for photos left in my office. So you see, Elsa, I know this isn't exactly ideal, but I will not be the one to call things off between us. The Chambérys have decreed I'm to marry into the Vasas. If I don't, I can't even bear to consider what could happen to Kim."

Christ. And I thought I had it bad with the She-Wolf.

Just then, a knock sounds on the door. Elsa flashes a meaningful look before going to answer it. I'm suddenly second guessing my decision to bring Kim to Paris. What if she was followed? What if the goons sent to watch her report her actions back to the Chambérys?

But then the woman in question rounds the corner, belly large and beautiful, trailed by Charlotte and a clearly weary Parker. Mat slowly stands up, eyes wide, hands visibly shaking as he takes her in.

It is painfully clear he had no idea she was pregnant.

"What . . ." He swallows, staring at her protruding stomach. "How . . ." And then he's across the room, his arms around her shoulders before anything else can be said. She's weeping, so is he, and if I'm not mistaken, so are Elsa and Charlotte.

Bloody hell, I'm feeling a little misty-eyed myself.

"Why didn't you tell me?" Mat's asking Kim.

"At least now I won't have to knee him in the bollocks," Elsa muses before we give the two some well deserved privacy.

CHAPTER 58

ELSA

"I can't accept these," Mat says.

What utter ridiculousness. Turning to Kim, I take hold of her hand. "It's not nearly enough, but it is a start."

Dark, curly hair swishes around her shoulders as she stares at the emerald earrings in her hand. But she is clearly more intelligent than Mat, because her fingers curl around the gemstones. "Thank you."

For the last hour, we discussed in detail what to do with our incredibly complex situation. The Grand Duchess of Aiboland desires a way to share in the profits of Vattenguldia's shipping registries. My parents require liquid cash—lots of it. The Chambérys covet land and a throne. None have ever asked what it is we, the heirs and children, want. But now that we are all together in an exquisite suite in Paris, the lot of us decide to finally take control of our own destinies.

First up, Christian and I will help Mat and Kim go into hiding. It's not ideal, but they'll be together, which is what they both say they want. Parker claims that, thanks to our private investigator's reports, he was able to find a way into her building that evaded notice—better yet, they were able to depart the same way. Kim placed a call to her family, using Charlotte's cell, begging them to go into hiding immediately. Neither Christian nor I have large amounts of cash on our persons, but I have the emerald earrings to start with. Spiteful as it may be in the moment, I would really rather Mat and Kim have the money than my parents.

Parker and Charlotte fall in strategic mode, arranging flights and accommodations for the parents-to-be. It will not be easy; the Chambérys are still influential in France and Italy, and New York is obviously out as it would be one of the first places combed over in a search for a missing prince.

None of us have all the answers yet—just the determination behind what is right.

"You know," Christian murmurs as alternate destinations are discussed, "perhaps we ought to start a new club. The RRAS."

I tap my chin as I consider this. "The Royal Reluctantly Amorous Society?"

He laughs before he kisses the space just below my ear. "I'm disappointed in you. The Royal Runaway Society."

"Runaway is a singular word, you know. It would be the RRS."

His arms wrap around me, and while they are warm and comfortable and nice, they are a far cry from brotherly, thank goodness. "Semantics."

"First Isabelle, now Mat." I chuckle against his shirt. "Running away has become an epidemic amongst the younger royals of Europe."

Minutes later, Mat meanders over to where we are, hands stuffed in his pockets. "You're going to get your way, Your Highness. We will not be married after all."

My smile challenges the speed of light. "I do so like getting my way."

Kim joins us; their hands clasp together, like magnets that cannot resist one another. He is tender when he urges her to sit down and rest, only to have her remind him women have been having babies since the dawn of mankind, and she'll sit when she's on the plane. Besides, she argues, she's a doctor and would know more than a math geek like him.

Christian was right. I like this Kim.

Mat asks me, faint lines marring his brow, "Will Prince Gustav and Princess Sofia be upset to not get their share of the Chambéry fortune?"

Undoubtedly. But that should not matter in the least to Mat. "They made their bed, and now they must lie on it. The moment you two leave Paris, I will schedule a nice, long talk with Their Serene Highnesses about just such a thing."

"I wish you luck," he tells me. When we hug for the last time, it feels right, because brotherly, warm hugs are perfect for friends.

CHAPTER 59

CHRISTIAN

It goes against every fiber of my being to let Elsa board a jet with Greta, but not myself, yet I know it must be done.

I can't fight Elsa's battles any more than she can fight mine.

Parker and Charlotte snuck Kim out of the hotel, with Mat publicly departing before disappearing in Paris. No note was left—Mat feared that if he even mentioned Kim by name, her family would immediately be targeted. It was best to leave without word, and with as little trace as possible. They flew directly to Scotland to marry, but beyond that, Elsa and I remain in the dark.

"It will be safer that way," Mat reasoned. "Elsa may truthfully claim plausible deniability."

I took him aside, questioning whether or not Elsa would become a target of the Chambérys' wrath. He was adamant she would not—for it she were, and word were to get out, it would ruin any future chances for the family to find their way back to power.

Even still, a conversation between Elsa, Parker, Charlotte, and myself occurred. Bodyguards for the woman I love would be put on alert; precautions would be taken to ensure her continued safety. That night, when the Chambérys realized Mat would not report back, as required, a flurry of calls was made to the police, Interpol, and even Elsa. I was forced to retreat to the suite I'd rented for Parker, uneasy over leaving her behind to face their ire, but for once, the press did us a favor.

Photographs came forth, proving he left the hotel earlier in the afternoon, alive and with a smile upon his face.

Elsa was promptly summoned home, not even an hour after word of Mat's disappearance reached the palace. Greta reappeared, carrying multiple shopping bags from the most exclusive shops from Champs Elysées, and before we could even take a breath, she had Elsa packed and a car summoned.

Our time was over, and I wasn't even able to accompany her to the airfield.

It bloody hurts like hell, knowing she and I are now separated by more than just distance, but by uncertainty and countries, too. Neither of us is required to marry another at the moment, but it does not mean the path before us has cleared. There are conversations that must take place, ones crucial to both of our futures. She must confront her family and then help them find a way out of the mess they've made. I respect the hell out of her for that. The Hereditary Princess of Vattenguldia will do what's best for her country.

As for me . . . I must finish what I've started and ensure the safety and comfort of my brother and father. There are decisions to be made, weighted ones that can't be easily chosen no matter how much we might wish otherwise.

That bridge we hope to cross is not an easy one.

CHAPTER 60

ELSA

Vattenguldia's premier newspaper slaps down before me, rattling my cup of tea at the breakfast table. A picture of Mat and myself, inside the restaurant in Paris, stares balefully up at me. Neither of us appears remotely happy to be there, which makes perfect sense considering we weren't.

Princess Elsa Miserable In Paris, screams the headline. Too bad they didn't see me an hour after that picture was taken, when I was anything but miserable in the back of a limo.

Another newspaper slaps down upon the former. *Prince Mathieu Missing After Cozy Rendezvous With Princess Elsa.* A third is added to the pile: *Distraught Princess Elsa Rushes Home In Wake Of Lover's Disappearance.*

One of my mother's long fingers snaps against the newsprint. "This is a public nightmare!"

"How delightfully ironic, this coming from you of all people." My voice is downright arctic as I coolly look up at my mother.

A sound of startled displeasure rattles out of my father from the other end of the table. His brow is a series of deep valleys as he stares at me from over the edge of his paper.

I fold my hands across my lap. Straighten my back and hold my head up high. I am the Hereditary Crown Princess of Vattenguldia. I can and will do this. I requested both their presences at breakfast just so we could have this talk.

"I know what you did." I motion for my mother to sit down. And then, ensuring eye contact is made with my father, "What you've *both* done. And I am here to tell you today that I refuse to allow you to barter away both my and Isabelle's lives and happiness to cover up your mismanagement of taxpayer funds."

All the color and fire goes right out of my mother as she drops into a chair.

"Ponzi schemes are so tacky, Mother. So is losing roughly five million euros the public expected to be used wisely." From beneath the table, I pluck a folder I brought with me that contains everything Josef, Charlotte, and Parker discovered about my mother's poor investments. "Tell me. How much did the Chambérys promise you in return for my hand? Or even the Grand Duchess? Together, was it enough to ensure no one ever knows about what has been done?"

Her Serene Highness Sofia of Vattenguldia is, for the first time in a long time, rendered completely speechless.

"How dare you speak to your Princess like that!"

My heart skips a terrified beat as I meet my father's eyes. My mother's face may be white, but Prince Gustav's is red with fury.

"I would think that you, of all people, would be equally outraged by what has occurred," I tell my sovereign. "As a member of the ruling Vasa family, I am appalled at how money, earned by our hard-working citizens, was so foolishly thrown away in a time where much of the world is in economic crisis."

"You forget your place," he snaps.

How wrong he is. "I am beholden to this great country, and its welfare is at the forefront of my mind as I consider this situation. As Vattenguldia's future sovereign, I will not allow myself to be used to cover up something so atrocious."

The newspaper in the Prince's hands is folded neatly and placed next to his plate. Lips thinning, there's anger in his eyes, but there's something more than that, too.

I dare to hope it is pride.

Shock gives way to quiet tears from my mother. "You do not understand," she whispers. "The press will crucify us. There may be calls for the dissolution of the crown."

"Almost guaranteed." My tone softens, but only by a bit. "That said, I am willing to work with you to find a solution to replace the funds, but I refuse to become the bargaining chip you hoped for. Consider which is the greater sin to our citizens . . . to those who trust us. The revelations that beloved monarchs sold off their daughters for money, and one fled to escape such a fate? Or that you confess your mistakes, do your best to explain them, and promise to do everything within your power to regain Vattenguldia's trust by rectifying the situation?"

The silence in the room is painful. Part of me wishes to shout at them, to ask why the second option was not considered, why Isabelle and I were so easy to use as their way through this mess.

But I do not. A massive row would not solve anything right now. Neither parent is thinking clearly. I am the Hereditary Princess, and I damn well better act like it.

My country needs me, and I will be here for them, even if their current sovereigns are not.

"There is plenty of art and many antiques in storage that could be discretely auctioned off—or better yet, given to the country's museums in lieu of payment. Perhaps this is the impetus for our family to look at our place in Vattenguldian society, and determine how we may streamline the monarchy's costs."

My father stares at me for several long moments that nearly snap my spine clean in half. But then he nods and reclaims his paper.

The next day, I enter His Highness' office upon request. Bittner is in there, working alongside my father. "You asked to see me, Father?"

Bittner excuses himself. I think, after what went down yesterday at breakfast, he knows better than to stick around for more Elsa bombshells.

"Before we get into it again, Elsa, I wonder if you've heard from your sister?" my father asks.

It is the first time one of my parents have thought to ask this. "In a roundabout way, yes. She is the one who cracked the reason behind why you were so keen for us to attend the Summit this year. Or rather, she and her new husband did."

He's just as taken back as I was by this piece of news. "I was under the impression that fellow wasn't too bright."

"Apparently, he is smarter than any of us gave him credit for."

Isabelle, too.

His Serene Highness is quiet for a long moment. "I am relieved to hear she contacted you."

"Actually, she didn't. She called somebody else who relayed the information to me."

His thick eyebrows go up. "And just who might that be?"

I slide into the antique chair across from his desk. "Prince Christian from Aiboland."

Surprise flickers across his face. "But I thought she wasn't keen on him. She said he was boring as all sod, and begged me not to marry her to somebody who would make her life miserable."

Oh Isabelle. If my sister were here, I'd hug her until she couldn't breathe. "They were not suited for one another, that much is true. And, just to be clear, he is not boring in the least." I gather my courage, even though uncertainty looms before me. "She contacted him, though, as she is aware of the extent of our feelings toward one another, and rightly assumed he would inform me of what she suspected."

Yet another parent is rendered speechless.

"Yesterday, I indicated my willingness to help weather the storm bearing down upon the Vasas. I will even be there at the press conference with you Bittner has scheduled for tomorrow. All I ask is that you are open to what I am about to discuss, and that you might find it within your heart to show me that the prince and father I have long admired is still here."

His wince is painfully visible, as is the regret that lines his face.

"You planned to marry me off to a deposed prince in hopes of earning yourself a pretty euro—"

Regret or no, my name is a warning from his lips.

I continue, nonetheless. "For many, that would be unforgiveable."

He does not apologize, nor did I expect him to.

"And yet," I say, "I am still here, asking for your help."

His lips purse, and many long seconds stretch between us. Finally, he murmurs, "Consider me intrigued."

"The man I have fallen in love with—the one who is in love with me—is a Hereditary Grand Duke, set to inherit his country's throne."

As my statement soaks in, steepled fingers tap thoughtfully against my father's chin. "Is the Grand Duchess of Aiboland aware of this relationship?"

"If she is not yet, she will be shortly." Or so Christian claimed when we departed. As he has never given me any reason to doubt him yet, this will not be the time in which I begin to do so.

My father's chair creaks as he leans forward. "You want to know if such a union is feasible."

"Yes."

He grunts. "And to think you found the Chambéry situation . . . unsavory." His fingers drift back to his desk, lighting tapping out a pattern. "You say you love him?"

"Yes."

A notepad is claimed, alongside a pen. Glasses settle once more across his nose. I wait patiently as ink flows across the parchment, wishing I had the nerve to lean over and read his words.

When he is done, the pen is placed in a neat parallel line to his notes. "I expect you at the conference."

It is as good as I'm going to get right now. We have a long road toward recovery of trust within our family, and there is much to be done to help ensure the Vasa legacy isn't completely destroyed in the annals of Vattenguldian history. But right now, I am content enough to trust—or at least hope—sound advice is forthcoming, and to accept that maybe, just maybe, my parents and I can work through this and rebuild our family's reputation together.

CHAPTER 61

CHRISTIAN

The tarmac in Vattenguldia is cold and slick, the sky dark. It's been three chaotic months since I last saw Elsa in person.

Her principality was in an uproar when Prince Gustav announced the misappropriations of taxpayer funds to the crown. To say things have been going well for them would be entirely dishonest, because calls for the abolition of the monarchy swiftly surfaced in a country typically proud of their heritage. While formal apologies have been offered, and promises for restitutions issued, Gustav never cowered or made excuses so many other sovereigns I know might have been tempted to fall back on, nor were scapegoats utilized. While I still believe what he tried to do to both of his daughters is abominable, I can't help but feel a bit of newly developed admiration toward him, too.

He owned up to his mistakes and is willing to pay the price to rectify the situation.

Elsa stepped up alongside her father, working tirelessly with Parliament and the people to help resolve the situation. And I am bloody proud of her for doing so, because through it all, she has kept her cool and proved to Vattenguldia why, if they decide to keep the monarchy, they are in good hands for the future.

When I returned to Aiboland after my trip to Paris, I discovered that Lukas wasn't joking when he claimed the She-Wolf would lock me down. She and I raged together for days—weeks, even. I'd had it. Once I had word from my brother that all the money I requested be transferred into out-of-country accounts she could never touch, guaranteeing my father and brother financial solubility if push came to shove, I let the Grand Duchess of Aiboland know exactly what I think of her, her lifestyle, how she screwed up both her sons' childhoods, and how she pretty much destroyed my father's life. She threatened to remove me from the line of inheritance and I calmly dared her to.

"If you think I give a flying fuck about what you think of me," I told her one rainy afternoon, "be prepared for a lifetime of disappointment." I picked up a newspaper from her desk, one whose headline screamed about the dwindling importance of monarchies in the world alongside Vattenguldia's scandal. I threw it just off to the side of her. "I'm done being your Prince Perfect."

And then the first call from Gustav came in. And then many more subsequent calls over the following weeks, followed by further calls from his associates in the Monarch Council. I was—and still am—wary as all hell toward their intentions, but it is a start.

So here I am, my heart in my throat as I make my way toward the waiting town car. Gustav's personal secretary waits for me, the door already open. As I slide onto the rich, black leather seats, I receive a text from Charlotte, alongside a picture of Elsa holding Dickie. The lad's mouth is open wide, his fists tight as he bellows silently from my screen. I can't help but laugh at the look on Elsa's face.

"May I inquire as to how your flight was, Your Highness?" Bittner asks from the front seat.

"Uneventful." I send Charlotte a quick text in response, and then one to Parker who stayed behind in order to help Lukas deal with lingering affairs I'm bypassing. "And much shorter than it was to California back in April."

He chuckles politely, and we resume the rest of the drive in silence.

Minutes later, a pink palace trimmed in white comes into view. It's no Hearst Castle, but it's charming in its own regard. The Vasas have ruled over this landmark for nearly four hundred years, and despite current tribulations, I have a sneaky suspicion their lineage will continue to do so for some time. Gustav and Sofia may not be winning any popularity polls, but Elsa sure is.

Once we pull around the drive, I find Prince Gustav waiting by the side entrance. After I exit the car, the embattled prince clasps my shoulder. "It's good to see you, Christian."

"Thank you, Your Highness."

He does not take offense that I declined to offer the same greeting in return. Instead, he says smoothly, "I trust that everything is in order?"

I squelch the urge to laugh bitterly. But that's not fair. I'm here, and that is what counts. "As much as it can be, sir."

Several staff members collect my luggage from the car.

"The Grand Duchess can be difficult at times," Prince Gustav says as we head into the palace. "I would like to say she'll come around, but you and I both know the chances of that are not the kind we ought to be betting on."

And yet, I am at peace with that nowadays. "Change isn't always the easiest," I admit.

But sometimes, it's exactly what's needed.

"What's that?" He motions to the box I hold within my hands.

"A fulfillment of a promise I made your daughter," I tell him.

He doesn't press further. "I had several calls with the Monarch Council this week," he says. "I wish I could give either of you answers and solutions right now, but . . ."

"But tradition wins out."

His smile is tight. "As you just said, change isn't the easiest. In lives such as ours, tradition is often law. That said, many in the MC are not entirely unsympathetic with your plight. Discussions will be had, Christian. Beyond that, I cannot guarantee anything further, at least at this moment." A hand claps my shoulder once more. "Except to assure you that Elsa has my support." Distance crowds his eyes, as he no doubt reflects upon his piss poor choices over the last year when it comes to that daughter—or the other one his actions forced away.

Change is definitely not the easiest.

CHAPTER 62

ELSA

When the smell of burned butter wafts out of the pan, I throw the wooden spoon across the length of the room. Despite Charlotte's insistences, cooking is not a useful tool for relaxation.

"Is that a first, Els?"

I whirl around in the palace's vast kitchen to find the Hereditary Grand Duke of Aiboland lounging against the doorway, holding a square box.

I must be dreaming. Because Christian is supposed to be in Aiboland, attending a groundbreaking ceremony for a new school.

My knees quiver as I stare at him. My hands have no idea what to do. All I am able to voice is his name. Just his name that holds a thousand questions and hopes all at once within two syllables.

Three months. We have not seen one another in person, outside of Skype, in a little over ninety days. Our physical time together has been perilously short, and yet . . . over the past ninety days, the feelings I own for him grew exponentially, even as fears that the future we wish for might not come to pass match in growth.

The love of my life breaks eye contact first, but not before gifting me one of his too divine smiles, all wide and smug and beautiful and delicious, leaving me want to launch myself into his arms and lick the corner of his mouth. "The poor spoon. What did it ever do to you?"

"Burn butter," I say. "And no—it's not a first. I burned the last two attempts at this idiotic recipe."

"I meant throwing it."

"Oh! Well then, yes. I restrained myself until now."

He crosses the kitchen to where I stand. My heart sprints right out of my chest and joins the marathon I know to be coursing through the capitol today. There is a real possibility I am close to passing out, which would be most unfortunate because hope is sparkling through my bloodstream like fireworks in a perfect sky.

"You didn't tell me you'd taken cooking up as a hobby," he says lightly.

"We don't tell each other everything. For example, you failed to inform me that you were coming to Vattenguldia."

"And ruin the surprise?" He tsks. "I think not."

He holds out the box; inside is a pie. I look up at him, my mouth aching from stretching so wide. "Apple?"

"It was past time we finally cavort with pie. PIN has been far too silent lately for my tastes."

I groan at his pun as I slide the pie onto the counter. Then I reach out and press my palms against his warm chest. "Didn't the Grand Duchess have you on lockdown?"

"It was very Rapunzel-ish, to be sure," he teases. "And to think, you didn't come and climb my hair to save me from my tower. I had to escape and find a pie maker all on my little lonesome."

I lift an eyebrow.

"Fine," he says. "Parker went out and bought it for me. He's a handy fellow to have around."

I laugh. Seeing him here, in my kitchen, after so long, though . . . While my feelings for him have never wavered, not even in the tiniest bit, I am also quite aware that, realistically, we are in a stalemate. Neither is forced to marry against our will any longer, but tradition looms in the miles between us. Vattenguldia was—and still is—in crisis, requiring its royals to be ever vigilant in the eyes of the public. Aiboland is nearing the Grand Duchess' Silver Jubilee. There is little time to be selfish and turn our backs on our commitments.

But here he is. In my kitchen. In Vattenguldia.

I love seeing this man in kitchens.

He cups my face. "I missed you, Els. Pie aside, I came here today because I needed to tell you that."

Love, sweet, beautiful love for this man swarms every cell in my body. "I missed you, too." The tiny fairies within my chest begin their dancing. "And I am glad to see you, but I thought you were overseeing a groundbreaking ceremony today?"

He leans forward, his mouth finding mine. I savor this kiss, and how I feel it all the way to my toes. "Lukas is there in my stead. There is a much more important matter to attend to. An RFC matter, to be precise. See, there's a bridge we need to finally cross."

Time grinds to a halt. Nothing moves, nothing but him and me and the hearts in our chests thumping painfully in miraculous unison.

"I thought the bridge was guarded," I say quietly. "Or lost. Or blown apart. Or even no longer in existence, because the MC trolls were guarding the bloody hell out of it."

He shakes his head slowly. "I found the bridge, Els. And I know the way across it. It's simple, really. I don't know why it took so long for me to understand that."

CHAPTER 63

CHRISTIAN

"See, here's the secret: I choose you."

Her blue eyes, so beautifully, fantastically expressive, blink in confusion. They hypnotize me just as easily today as the first night she asked if I was a virgin. And I was, I realize now. Not in the literal sense, but metaphorically, because I'd never truly loved anyone like I love this woman.

"I don't know what the future holds for us." My voice is steady. Calm. Assured. "I don't know if the MC will ever accept a Hereditary Princess and a Hereditary Grand Duke marrying. But I've decided it doesn't matter. I choose you."

"What does that mean?"

"It means, while I have hope that someday the MC and world at large will accept us being together, I'm tired of waiting. Three months is a long time to not see your face in person, Els."

"Yes, fine, I missed your face, too," she says. "But what does it *mean?*"

Our hands twine together. "It means I'm here. We still have a battle within the MC and our respective parliaments, if it comes to that, but good or bad, I'm here. Vattenguldia needs you right now. Let me be someone you lean upon in this time of crisis."

Her words are barely voiced. "Are you abdicating?"

"Officially?" I ask. She nods, so I clarify, "I haven't formally stepped down. Unofficially?" I smile. "Lukas and I had some lengthy discussions about what will happen if the MC doesn't allow us to both retain our titles. He's agreed to take my place if and when it comes to that."

"I cannot allow you do that." She swallows. "You are the Hereditary Grand Duke. Aiboland needs you, especially after the She-Wolf's rule."

I love that she thinks this. Knows about my mother's duplicity. But more importantly, I love that she believes in me. "Aiboland isn't in crisis. Vattenguldia is. And I'm not willing to wait it out to make a decision. I love you, Els. I want to be with you. I hope you want to be with me, too."

"Are you daft?" she asks. But that gorgeous smile of hers returns. "Of *course* I want to be with you."

"Then it's settled. I'm here. It might even be a good distraction for the public, seeing you and I in our star-crossed states. Your parents wanted a fairy tale, right? A public one? Besides. I'm rich, remember? Really, really rich. And I've got all those nice bank accounts the Grand Duchess can't touch with money that has nothing to do with the crown."

An eyebrow quirks up. "You don't even know if I want you to stay."

Good God, do I love her sass. "I hoped my *too*-ness would sway you in person."

She gasps in mock outrage.

"That said, if you want me to leave . . ." I motion behind us, taking a step back.

She tugs me right back. "Damn your *too*-ness," she mutters. "Also, will you ever allow me to live that down?"

"What, admitting you think I have some mystical *too*-ness?"

There's that erotic laughter of hers. "You're not going anywhere, Chris."

"Excellent. Now that we've got that settled—"

"Oh, it is far from settled." Determination fills her eyes. "Come hell or high water, I refuse to allow you abdicate. If we have to be the ones to drag the MC into the twenty-first century kicking or screaming, then that's exactly what we'll do. You and I should not have to choose between love and duty. Tradition be damned. There is room for both. Why couldn't we jointly rule both countries?"

I also love her optimism. Actually, I love everything about this woman.

I love *her*.

I take a deep breath and tell her what I've thought about for weeks now. "Until then, I have a first to put on the table for discussion."

"Oh?"

My hands curl around her waist. "Let's run amuck and cavort together from here on out."

Her eyes widen significantly as she takes in my meaning. "You really are bloody Prince Charming, aren't you?"

"No," I tell her. "I'm just Chris, a guy who happens to be ridiculously in love with a girl named Els." Because that's what it all comes down to, really. Crowns and thrones and obligations matter, yes.

But so does this.

She asks me softly, "All the best agreements are sealed with a kiss, right?"

The corners of my lips tug upward at the memory. "Oh, absolutely."

In a kitchen eight thousand miles away from the one we shared our first kiss in, my mouth touches hers in sweet promise. We meet in the middle of that bridge we've searched for for months, and then we cross to the other side.

And then, after much kissing and the opening of a celebratory bottle of champagne, we finally share a first of apple pie, just like all good PIN members of the RFC should do when they've agreed to spend their lives together.

New traditions, I'm learning, can sometimes be even better than the old.

ACKNOWLEDGEMENTS

As someone who normally thrives in fantasy worlds while writing, I wrote *Royal Marriage Market* as a challenge to myself. I wanted to create a book that had no magic, no fantastical worlds. Only, the deeper I got into the story, the more I realized RMM *does* have a fantastical world (anyone who has been to the immensely gorgeous Hearst Castle will agree), and there is plenty of magic, too—only this time, it's the real kind.

I want to thank my wonderful agent and editor Suzie Townsend for her love and guidance for this story. Gratitude also goes out to Danielle Barthel and Jackie Lindert for their work on the book, my lovely publicist KP Simmon, and Daniela Conde Padrón for the beautiful cover.

Obviously, I must issue a huge shout out to Hearst Castle, as it's virtually its own character in the story. I spent several delightful days there in 2014 doing research, and I could not love the place more. Thanks to all the staff for putting up with my tons of questions!

Vilma Gonzalez, Andrea Johnston, Tricia Santos, Jessica Mangicaro, and Cristina Suárez-Muñoz, please know I deeply appreciative for all the time, feedback, and care you gave Elsa and Christian's story.

To the fab members of my street team, the Lyons Pride, your support means so much. (in alphabetical order) Alexandra, Amy, Ana, Andi, Andrea, Ashley, Ashley, Autumn, Brandi, Bridget, Candy, Carine, Cherisse, Christina Marie, Courtney, Cynthia, Daniela, Ethan, Eunice, Evelyn, Gina, Ivey, Jenn, Jenni, Jennifer, Jennifer, Jessica, Jessica, Jessica, Jessica, JL, JoAnna, Kate, Kathryn, Kelli, Kelly, Keri, Kiersten, Kristina, Lauren, Leigha, Lindsey, Lissa, Maria, Martina, Melissa, Meredith, Natalie, Nicole, Nikki, Peggy, Rachel, Rebecca, Samantha, Sheena, Tina Lynne, Tracy, Tricia, Vilma, Whitney, Yvonne, and all the rest . . . you rock. Hugs to you all.

Jon, you are my true Prince Charming. Thank you for believing in me. Love and gratitude are also sent out to my children and family for all their support, and for sharing me with my computer. You all mean the world to me.

Royal Marriage Market

Also by Heather Lyons

"Each of us here has a story, but it may not be the one you think you know . . ."

"The most unique, fascinating, wondrous book I've read in a very long time! I was glued to every page."
-Shelly Crane, New York Times bestselling author

From the author of the Fate series and The Deep End of the Sea comes a fantastical romantic adventure that has Alice tumbling down the strangest rabbit hole yet.

After years in Wonderland, Alice has returned to England as an adult, desperate to reclaim sanity and control over her life. An enigmatic gentleman with an intriguing job offer too tempting to resist changes her plans for a calm existence, though. Soon, she's whisked to New York and initiated into the Collectors' Society, a secret organization whose members confirm that famous stories are anything but straightforward and that what she knows about the world is only a fraction of the truth.

It's there she discovers villains are afoot—ones who want to shelve the lives of countless beings. Assigned to work with the mysterious and alluring Finn, Alice and the rest of the Collectors' Society race against a doomsday clock in order to prevent further destruction . . . but will they make it before all their endings are erased?

Read on for the first chapter of The Collectors' Society.

THE PLEASANCE ASYLUM

THE CEILING ABOVE ME is a mysterious map of cracks and chipped paint, nearly undecipherable in origins or destinations.

Voids unsettle me, though, so night after night, as I stare up at it, tracing the moonbeams that flit in between hills and valleys, I assign them my own designations. There, that bump? It's Gibraltar. That chunk? The Himalayas. The deep groove near the Southeast corner of the room? The Great Wall of China. The smooth patch nearly dead center is the Pleasance Asylum, which is vastly amusing to me.

I shy away from the splattering of flakes in the Northwest quadrant, though. Those ones, whose ridges grow on nearly a daily basis, are far too easy to decipher. I made the mistake of telling Dr. Featheringstone this during a fit of delirium, and he's not forgotten it. In fact, he's asked me about them again, just now, and he's waiting patiently for my answer.

"They're flakes of paint," I tell him. "Created from age and lack of upkeep."

As he chuckles softly, the thick mustache that hides his lip twitches. "Always the literal one."

I keep my eyes on his face rather than in the area he's quizzing me about. It taunts me though, just over his left shoulder. "Why shouldn't I be? Word games are silly and are best left for children or the elderly who seek to hold onto their wit." The muscle inside my chest works in overtime as I tell him this. He's heard my ravings, and knows my struggles.

"And you are no longer a child?"

I lean back in the still, wooden chair, delighting in how its discomfort bites into my bones. "I hardly think a woman of twenty-five is a child, Doctor."

In direct opposition to his faint yet genuine smile, pudgy fingers stroke his bushy mustache downward. "Many ladies of your standing are long married with family."

He says many when he means *most*. I smooth the stubborn wrinkles on my gray skirt. "It's a little hard to meet prospective suitors in . . ." I glance around the room, eyes careful not to settle too long above his head. "A fine establishment such as yours."

Neither of us mention where I'd been before here, or what I'd seen and done and experienced.

Another chuckle rumbles out of him. "Too true, dear. But you will not be at the Pleasance much longer. What then?"

My fingers knot tightly together in my lap. "I imagine I will be sent to rusticate at our family's summer house near the seaside. Perhaps I will find a nice stableboy to court me, and by the ripe age of twenty-six, we will be living out our bliss amongst seashells, ponies, and hay."

Featheringstone sighs, his face transforming into a look I could sketch from memory, it's given so often to me when I offer up an answer he doesn't like. I call it Disappointed Featheringstone.

My eyes drift to the one window in the room. "I am still not positive my release is the wisest course of action."

"You've been here for over half a year," the doctor says. "Most people in your position would be clamoring to taste freedom."

A thin smile surfaces. That's the problem. I've had a taste of freedom, true freedom, and I'm loathe to accept anything other than such.

"You are in good health," he continues. "Your need for confinement is gone. Your nightmares have decreased significantly." His chair creaks beneath his significant girth as he leans forward. "It is time for you to resume your life, Alice. You cannot do that here at the asylum. You are, as you pointed out, twenty-five years old. You still have many years of experiences ahead of you."

I have many years of experiences behind me, too.

"Perhaps I ought to become a nurse," I muse, keeping the edge of my sarcasm soft enough to not wound. "What a story mine would be: patient to nurse, a grand example of life dedicated to the Pleasance."

"I think nursing school is a grand idea." His ruddy face alights. "There are several reputable ones in London you could attend."

It's my turn to give him a patented look, the one he affectionately calls Unamused Alice.

"Your father has sent word he will come to escort you home at the end of the week."

Unamused Alice transitions to Curmudgeonly Alice.

Featheringstone stands up, glancing up at my past before shuffling over to pat me on my shoulder. He is a nice man, whose intentions for his wards are sincere. It's for this I both appreciate and resent him. An old schoolmate of my father's, he was selected upon my return sorely for this purpose. Too many horror stories about hellish asylums and nefarious doctors rage about England, but my father knew his friend would treat me with kid gloves. While the Pleasance may be physically showing its age, it's amongst the most sought after when it comes to those in the upper class due to its gentle hand and discreet employees.

Sometimes I wish my father hadn't been so kind. It might have been easier had he thrown me into one of the hellholes, where I could have gotten lost amongst the insane.

MANDATORY STROLLS ARE REQUIRED of all patients at the Pleasance, as Dr. Featheringstone believes, "Fresh air is the tonic to many ails." At first, I was resistant to such outings, preferring to stay in my snug room with the door closed, but after several tours with the good doctor and a team of nurses and orderlies, I determined he perhaps had a point. There is a nice pond that is home to a family of ducks, a small grove of trees, and a handful of boring, quiet gardens that house no red roses after the good doctor had requested them removed. Worn dirt paths lined with benches connect the Pleasance's outdoor pleasures, and one can experience everything in as little as a half hour. We patients are never left to our own devices during these Fresh Air Hours, though. Nurses and orderlies mingle amongst the residents, setting up tables for games of checkers, chess, or croquet, although I naturally recuse myself from such frivolity.

Half a year in, and I am still a stranger to most of the folk here. That was by my choice; many of the residents did their best to welcome me into the fold, but I was determined to keep my distance out of early fear of spies.

There is nowhere you could go in which we could not find you, little bird.

"A letter, my lady."

My head snaps up sharply to find one of the orderlies standing over me, an envelope in his hand. I eye the object warily; outside of my parents, whom I requested not to write to me during my stay, no one else of my acquaintance knows I'm here. "There is no need to be so formal with me. We are at an asylum after all."

I think his name is Edward, but it could easily be Edwin, too. Or perhaps even Edmund. A mere incline of the head is given, but I highly doubt my bitterly voiced suggestion means anything to him. The staff here is the epitome of propriety.

I don't want what he has to offer. "Toss it into the fire."

His smile is patient and kind, one borne of tempered familiarity. "Dr. Featheringstone has already previewed its contents." The open flap is jiggled. "Would you like me to open it as well?"

I sigh and set my sketch pad on the bench next to me. The ducklings in the distance scatter across the pond, leaving me without subject to capture. "Go ahead and read it aloud."

A slim piece of paper is extracted. Through the afternoon's golden sunlight, I can determine less than a quarter of the sheet is filled with thin, spidery calligraphy. *"Dear madam,"* E reads, modulating his voice so it sounds very dignified, indeed. *"It is my great hope that I may come and speak to you tomorrow afternoon about a matter of great importance. Yours sincerely, Abraham Van Brunt."*

"That's it?" I ask once the paper is refolded.

"Yes, my lady."

What a curious letter. "I am unacquainted with an Abraham Van Brunt," I tell the orderly. And then, as I reclaim my sketch pad, "I suppose Dr. Featheringstone has already sent off a missive telling him not to bother coming round."

Naturally, he does not know whether or not the doctor did just such a thing. "Would you like the letter, my lady?"

I'm already turning back toward the pond. "No. Please burn it."

The crunch of twigs informs me of his retreat, allowing me to reclaim my solitude. The ducks long gone, I spend my time perfecting the tufts of grass and reeds growing at water's edge on today's landscape.

Alice.

I focus harder, my charcoal furiously scraping across the paper until I remember I don't want to do anything furiously. Not anymore, at least.

Alice.

I close my eyes, focusing on the red and orange kaleidoscopes that dance across my lids.

Alice?

The paper in my hand crumples as easily as my heart. I leave it behind on the bench when I make my way back inside, because I'm positive there was an H etched into it. And to think that Featheringstone is convinced I'm sane.

I haven't been sane in over six years.

The series continues with . . .

"This is not a series for fantasy lovers or new adult lovers.
This is a series for **all book lovers."**
-Book Briefs

Sometimes, the rabbit hole is deeper than expected . . .

Alice Reeve and Finn Van Brunt have tumbled into a life of secrets. Some secrets they share, such as their employment by the clandestine organization known as The Collectors' Society. Other secrets they carry within them, fighting to keep buried the things that could change everything they think they know.

On the hunt for an elusive villain who is hell-bent on destroying legacies, Alice, Finn, and the rest of the Society are desperate to unravel the mysteries surrounding them. But the farther they spiral down this rabbit hole, the deeper they fall into secrets that will test their loyalties and pit them against enemies both new and old.

Secrets, they come to find, can reveal the deadliest of truths.

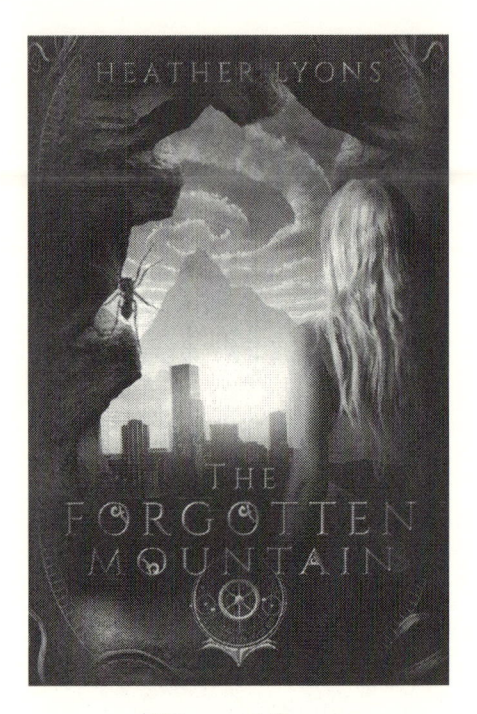

"If I could give a book **a million golden stars**, it would be this one."
-Typical Distractions

After years spent in Wonderland, Alice Reeve learned the impossible was quite possible after all. She thought she left such fantastical realities behind when she finally returned to England.

Now Alice has become a member of the clandestine Collectors' Society, and the impossible has found her again in the form of an elusive villain set on erasing entire worlds. As she and the rest of the Society race to bring this mysterious murderer to justice, the fight becomes painfully personal.

Lives are being lost. Loved ones are shattered or irrevocably altered. Each step closer Alice gets to the shadowy man she hunts, the more secrets she unravels, only to reveal chilling truths. If she wants to win this war and save millions of lives, Alice must once more embrace the impossible and make the unimaginable, imaginable.

Sometimes, the rabbit hole leads to terrifying places.

Be on the outlook for the fourth Collectors' Society book, coming soon!

An enthralling mythological romance two thousand years in the making . . .

"Heather Lyons's *The Deep End of the Sea* is **a radiant, imaginative romance that breathes new life into popular mythology** while successfully tackling the issue of sexual assault. Lyons is a deft storyteller whose engaging prose will surprise readers at every turn. Readers will have no trouble sympathizing with Medusa, who is funny, endearing and courageous all at once. The romance between her and Hermes is passionate, sweet and utterly engrossing. This is a must read!" *–RT Book Reviews*

What if all the legends you've learned were wrong?

Brutally attacked by one god and unfairly cursed by another she faithfully served, Medusa has spent the last two thousand years living out her punishment on an enchanted isle in the Aegean Sea. A far cry from the monster legends depict, she's spent her time educating herself, gardening, and desperately trying to frighten away adventure seekers who occasionally end up, much to her dismay, as statues when they manage to catch her off guard. As time marches on without her, Medusa wishes for nothing more than to be given a second chance at a life stolen away at far too young an age.

But then comes a day when Hermes, one of the few friends she still has and the only deity she trusts, petitions the rest of the gods and goddesses to reverse the curse. Thus begins a journey toward healing and redemption, of reclaiming a life after tragedy, and of just how powerful friendship and love can be—because sometimes, you have to sink in the deep end of the sea before you can rise back up again.

The magical first book of the Fate series . . .

"Love, love, love this book! Such a fun and exciting premise. Full of teenage angst and heartache with a big helping of magic and enchantment. Can't wait to read the rest of this awesome series! Not to mention... TWO hot boys to swoon over."
–Elizabeth Lee, author of Where There's Smoke

Chloe Lilywhite struggles with all the normal problems of a typical seventeen-year-old high school student. Only, Chloe isn't a normal teenage girl. She's a Magical, part of a secret race of beings who influence the universe. More importantly, she's a Creator, which means Fate mapped out her destiny long ago, from her college choice, to where she will live, to even her job. While her friends and relatives relish their future roles, Chloe resents the lack of say in her life, especially when she learns she's to be guarded against a vengeful group of beings bent on wiping out her kind. Their number one target? Chloe, of course.

That's nothing compared to the boy trouble she's gotten herself into. Because a guy she's literally dreamed of and loved her entire life, one she never knew truly existed, shows up in her math class, and with him comes a twin brother she finds herself inexplicably drawn to.

Chloe's once unyielding path now has a lot more choices than she ever thought possible.

Follow Chloe's story in the rest of the Fate series books...

"Heather Lyons' writing is an addiction...and like all addictions. I. Need. More." --*#1 New York Times Best Selling Author Rachel Van Dyken*

"Enthralling fantasy with romance that will leave you breathless, the Fate Series is a must read!" --*Alyssa Rose Ivy, author of the Crescent Chronicles*

ABOUT THE AUTHOR

photo @Regina Wamba of Mae I Design and Photography

Heather Lyons is known for writing epic, heartfelt love stories often with a fantastical twist. From Young Adult to New Adult to Adult novels—one commonality in all her books is the touching, and sometimes heart-wrenching, romance. In addition to writing, she's also been an archaeologist and a teacher. She and her husband and children live in sunny Southern California and are currently working their way through every cupcakery she can find.

Website: www.heatherlyons.net
Facebook: http://www.facebook.com/heatherlyonsbooks
Twitter: http://www.twitter.com/hymheather
Goodreads:
http://www.goodreads.com/author/show/6552446.Heather_Lyons
Stay up to date with Heather by subscribing to her newsletter:
http://eepurl.com/2Lkij

Made in the USA
Middletown, DE
15 May 2018